Copyright © 2022 William Cli

All rights

The characters and events portrayed in this book are fictitious. Any similarity to real persons, living or dead, is coincidental and not intended by the author.

No part of this book may be reproduced, or stored in a retrieval system, or transmitted in any form or by any means, electronic, mechanical, photocopying, recording, or otherwise, without express written permission of the publisher.

Cover design by: William Clifford Armstrong Hemingway

This, my first book, is dedicated to Scrat

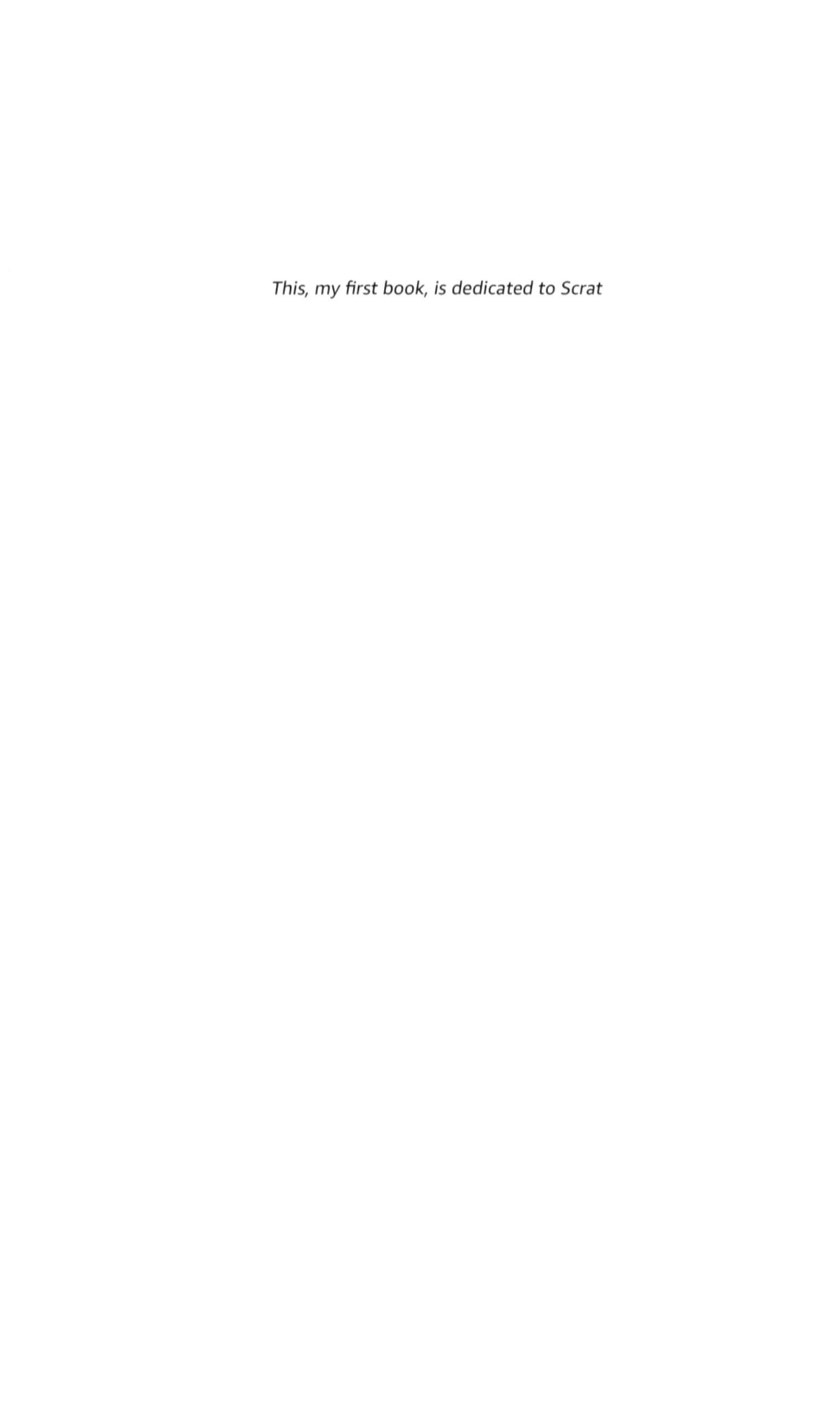

Introduction

This is the first book in my Wonder Island series, discovering a land I created for myself to explore during nights I found it difficult to fall asleep. Now I invite you to come and see it with me, to share its magic with you, and perhaps even inspire you to start your own life changing adventures...

PROLOGUE

"Do you think you could talk to the animals there?" Chloé asked her mother, whilst looking into the eyes of her doudou – a small, stuffed, floppy bunny who was never allowed to be washed - after she'd heard the tale of the Magic Isle for the hundredth time.

"I believe so," Mrs. Duval replied to her daughter, "I'd imagine all kinds of things would be possible on an island like that. Whatever you could dream of my darling," she said softly, as she tucked Chloé into bed and kissed her goodnight.

The story was of a place which Mrs. Duval had heard about, back when she was known as Miss. Manfield and was travelling south through the French-Alps on an escape voyage from her life in England; which at some point had become all too mundane for her. She'd hoped that taking the trip might in some way change her life for the better, which it did by the way of introducing her to her husband, Mr. Giles Duval, but she never could have anticipated quite how much, nor in which ways, it would impact the life of her daughter, Chloé.

Whilst driving alone in her brand-new, sport-blue, rented Renault Clio, she came across an area which she hadn't noticed on her map, named Les-Champs-du-Château-Noir. It was an open fielded area with a small alpine town and some farmland, spreading back towards a valley which snaked away between tall, steep mountains.

A forest of tall evergreens covered the floor and spread all the way to the tops of the hills at the beginning of the valley. As it wound on, the ground between the peaks gradually rose higher, until it reached a great, impressive mountain, blocking off the basin at the end. The mountains towards the end of the valley were much taller than those at the entrance. Their lower halves were covered with forest, whilst the tops were sheer, jagged rock reaching high up into the clouds; some so high that all year-round fresh snow could be found at the very top.

There were also three distinct waterfalls in the valley - one large one towards the end, bringing with it fresh meltwater from the white-capped mountain, which began the main river that flowed between the mountains, and two smaller ones further down, each unique and inspiring to those who sought them.

Mrs. Duval's plan for her journey was that she had no plan at all, and as this place seemed quite beautiful to her, she decided to stay for a few nights so she that might explore this enchanting place. It was on her second night in the town though, whilst chatting to the owners of the local 'Tabac' (Mme. et M. Desplanches), that she enquired about the history of the town and where it got its name from - for as far as she could see, there was no 'Château Noir' in sight.

The owner told her of an old road that leads up into the valley, used now only by people who want to go up the river for white water rafting or for those who want to find some of the many hiking trails, leading to what they were selling as 'world class' climbing routes. "Mais euh, zis road, she goes nowhere," Monsieur Desplanches explained to her.

He did mention, however, that if you follow the road around the first corner of the valley and keep your eyes looking to the right, there's a right turn on to an almost dirt track road. "Follow 'er oll zee way to zee end," he told her, "Zer, you will fine zee Château Noir," Or at least what was left of it as she later discovered. He told her that there wasn't really any history documented regarding the castle itself, nor were there any plans to restore it to how it once may have been.

Yet, one thing that was for sure, was that the people of the town didn't like to have much to do with it, and they most certainly didn't promote it in any way. It seemed to her almost as if they were ashamed, or even slightly unnerved by its very existence.

"Som people, zey say zat euh, a very, very bad... Wot is zee word? Sorcière."

"Sorcerer?" suggested Mrs. Duval.

"Oui, a sorcerer lived zer. A sorcerer 'oo was very, very bad. 'e was a devil."

He divulged to Mrs. Duval that an old diary that was found in a sealed off part of a cellar under one of the original houses in the town, recording days since 'the magic had been taken'; magical creatures, too. "I 'av not 'eard zee Trolls since almost one year, or seen zee fairies," he laughed as he mimicked reading from the diary.

Apparently, so Mrs. Duval was told had been written, the only place now where these things exist is on a strange island, hidden somewhere from the rest of the world, where a magic spring of power flows. Mrs. Duval thought to herself that this is clearly just an extravagant story the townspeople have made up, a story to amuse tourists travelling through, weird enough for them to remember and to speak to others they meet about the place where they heard it - putting Les-Champs-du-Château-Noir on the map. For her at least, the story worked.

Before Mrs. Duval continued south on her drive through the Alps, she thought she'd go and have a look at this Château Noir and see it for herself. She followed the directions as given by Monsieur Desplanches, and sure enough, she found the dirt road leading off from the main road through the valley. She drove for about five minutes through the dense forest, heading slightly uphill as she went, until she came upon a clearing.

Her jaw dropped as she saw it in front of her, the remains of what was clearly a once magnificent castle, with a mixture of traditional French style and Gothic architecture, towered before her in this forest clearing. She parked her little car and began to walk up to the main entrance, treading slowly towards it whilst completely mesmerised by its extravagance.

As she got closer, she noticed that it was partly built from bricks and carved stones, which had been blackened somehow as if covered in soot, but also seemed to be made up from the mountain itself. The side of the castle which nestled into the hill had no visible brick lines and appeared to be completely solid stone, as rugged as the exposed rock of the great alpine peak it sat beneath. Even the base of the castle seemed to blend in with the ground.

Up the walls grew long stretches of vines, some appeared to be dead, but others were still alive with few leaves. The castle had tall spires and towers rising up from within it, with many windows broken and roof tiles missing or hanging off.

One part of the castle built away from the side of the mountain, appeared to have fallen down at some point. There were half crumbled walls on first and second story rooms and huge piles of crumbled up stones and bricks. Before her was a mighty, wooden, double door for the main entrance clasped in wrought iron. Across the doors, to no surprise, hung a chained-up sign which read 'Défense d'entrer'.

Mrs. Duval wouldn't mention the town, the castle or

the supposed evil sorcerer to her young children when telling them the tale of an enchanting, magical island, where a spring of magic flowed. She merely elaborated on the idea of such a place existing, in hope that it would give them both something wonderful to dream about as they drifted off to sleep. Never could she have imagined that this place, this castle, would hold the key to her daughter's life-changing journey.

CHAPTER ONE

Back to the Castle

Chloé Duval sat alone on her bed, clutching her ragged mermaid teddy whose glitter had long since faded. She closed her eyes tight as she tried to imagine the salty sea air rush over her, whilst her own salty tears leaked through and onto her cheeks. Desperately, she willed the image of her and her father racing over the waves of the ocean to bring her happiness and comfort, but since his death, it only ever brought her more pain.

The doorbell rang, the sound echoed inside her for a moment as it brought her out of her head and back into the real world. She knew it would be her boyfriend, Chris, as her mother had invited him round for dinner that evening. Sitting up on the edge of the bed, she wiped her eyes and placed the mermaid back down next to her pillow, then walked over to her mirror to freshen herself up.

Chloé didn't often wear make-up, but on this occasion she opted for a bit of powder to hide the fact she'd been crying alone upstairs. She neatened herself up by quickly plaiting her long, mousey-blonde hair and throwing on a fresh, loose, white t-shirt and a pair of faded pink jeans. The look was completed by putting on her clear-framed glasses, then she headed downstairs to greet Chris, though he was already helping out her mother in the dining room.

Chris (Christopher Inkliff, to use his full name) and Chloé had met when they started 6th form college together, a few years after the death of her father. Chris was a charismatic character who always drew the room's attention, and it was this along with his deep, soothing green eyes (so Chloé thought) that first lifted her out of her gloomy state she'd been stuck in since her father's death. Those eyes along with his warm, tanned looking skin and thick dark hair, made him the perfect specimen in Chloé's eyes; and also in the eyes of most of the other girls at their college, too (and a few of the guys, for that matter).

They weren't a particularly popular couple, as Chris had already been going out with one of the other girls he'd known from secondary school when he first started talking to Chloé, and none of them could work out what he saw in someone who appeared to be so sad and uninteresting. But Chris had been drawn to her story, the Chloé he'd come to learn about who'd existed during the time when her father had been alive, the Chloé who was drawn to excitement and adventure, who had a constant urge to explore the world.

As Chloé neared the bottom of the stairs, she was almost knocked over by her younger brother, Matthéo (Téo), who'd been lured out from his bedroom by the smell of food and the sound of plates clattering downstairs. He was only ten years old when their father died four years ago, and they say everyone grieves in their own way, or perhaps it was because he hadn't shared as many interests with his father as Chloé had, but he seemed to find moving on with his life much easier than she did.

"Hey, Chris," Chloé said as she entered the dining room shortly after Téo, greeting him with a quick kiss (much to her brother's disgust). He and Mrs. Duval had just finished bringing the last of the food out from the kitchen.

"Ah, Chloé, just in time," her mother smiled, "How are you feeling?" she asked, as Chloé slumped down at the table.

Mrs. Duval was a kind, if not overly caring parent, whose shoulder-length, warm-blonde hair sat like a glowing golden aura of goodness around her face. Since the passing of her husband, she'd cut back on her hours at work to spend more time with her two young children, adamant that they would suffer as little as possible from his passing.

"Fine, I guess," replied Chloé, not really making eye

contact with anyone.

"What happened?" asked Chris, concerned.

"Chloé had another nightmare last night, about losing her dad again."

"Oh Cléo," he said (this was just one of the names he called her by). He put down his knife and fork and placed his hand on her shoulder, "You ok?"

"I'm fine, it's just, it takes a while for the feeling too numb again," she said as she stared down at her plate, "Though, it was nice to see him again for a moment." Chloé allowed herself to smile slightly at the thought. After a good cry upstairs and now sitting down to eat with such pleasant company, her mood had begun to lift.

"Actually, mum, in the dream, we were on our way to that place."

"What place?" asked Mrs. Duval

"That place you used to tell me about when I was little, where all the magic is."

"Oh, that place! I haven't thought about that in years. Do you still think about it sometimes?" Mrs. Duval began cutting into her falafel stuffed pita bread.

"Well, not often, really, it's just that, when I was younger I used to dream that dad and I would find it someday, when we were out sailing together."

"Where's this?" asked Chris, with half his mouth full of food and his pita in his hands. He was just hearing about this place for the first time.

"Nowhere, it's just a story my mum made up to make us go to sleep," said Téo, very matter of fact-like. He was going through his 'I'm not a child' teenage years.

"Well, you say that Téo, but actually I didn't make it

up, and the guy I met in the Tabac who told me about it, seemed to think otherwise," Mrs. Duval responded as she smirked and took a sip of her chardonnay.

"My mum used to tell us a story before bed, about an island where magic exists, hidden somewhere out at sea… hence why I used to think that my Dad and I would find it whilst we were out sailing."
"Ahh. And you heard about it in a French Tabac?" Chris asked Mrs. Duval as he took another mouthful of food.
"I heard about it just before I met your father," she said as she looked at Chloé, "From a French man who worked in a Tabac in this little French alpine town I came across, where the black castle was."

"What black castle?" asked Téo.
"*Thee* castle," She looked around at a table of confused faces. "No? Did I not mention the castle to you?" she asked them both, holding back a fork full of salad away from her mouth.
"No," said Chloé.
"You're right, of course, I seem to remember thinking it might scare you."
"Why would it scare them?" asked Chris.

"Well, you see, the rumour around the town was that a very evil sorcerer had once lived in the castle, and no one had been in it since," she said with a jokingly mysterious and eerie tone in her voice.
"Really? I think they were just trying to scare you, mum," said Téo, pushing the salad on his plate to one side before adding tomato sauce to the remains of his pita.
"Why had no one been in it?" continued Chris.
"I'm not really sure, they all acted like it was cursed or

something. I did go up into the valley though, to look at it, but there was a no entry sign on the door. It was a magnificent building though, you should definitely go and see it sometime."

"Where is it exactly?" asked Chris, the only one seemingly interested at this point.
"I think the town was called Les-Champs-Du-Château-Noir, but I couldn't see it on the map I had. I could draw it onto a map for you though if you ever wanted to visit."
"Why wasn't it on the map?" questioned Chloé.
"Absolutely no idea," her mother replied.
"Perhaps it doesn't exist," added Téo, sarcastically.

The conversation moved onto other things over the course of the meal, Téo had plenty to talk about regarding his karate classes and everyone else had to sit and pretend to be interested. Afterward dinner, Chris and Chloé went up to her room to spend some time alone together.

"Hey, I was thinking," began Chris, "Seeing as we'll both be finishing 6th form this year and neither of us have any plans over the summer, why don't we go on a road trip together? We could see that castle place your mum was talking about."
"Drive all the way to the Alps?"
"Yea. We could see the Alps, maybe make it to Italy, and even all the way to the Med if you wanted to try some sailing," he added cautiously, hoping not to upset her.

Chloé remained silent after Chris mentioned sailing, staring aimlessly down at the mermaid and seashell patterned bed spread which she'd had since she was seven that covered her bed where they sat, thinking about when she'd seen her dad on the boat in the dream she'd had. She hadn't been able to bring herself to get back on a boat since her father died, though she missed the thrill of journeying out to sea so terribly.

"You can show me why you and your dad loved it so much," said Chris as he lifted one of her hands gently and drew her attention to him for a moment.
"I guess. It would be nice to get away for a while and back out on the water again," said Chloé as she glanced back down towards the bedspread.
"Exactly, we can have our own little adventure. And best of all, we'll be far away from all the time wasters we've come to know around here."

Chloé thought about it for a moment, wondering if she could handle being away from her mum and brother. She continued to stare down as her thoughts went silent and she felt nothing, just slowly breathing with a blank expression across her face. Until finally she snapped herself out of it, shook her head and told herself that enough was enough, she couldn't go on moping around for the rest of her life and at some point she was just going to have to make the effort to live again; the idea of forever being the victim was not at all her style. So, without another thought about it, she took in a deep breath, closed her eyes and said with certainty "Alright, let's do it."

Over the next few months, they planned their trip with the help of Chloé's mum, whilst the pair of them finished up with 6th form and completed their A-levels. All their hard work led up to one fresh, July morning when, with Chris' metallic-blue Fiat Punto packed full of their luggage, they set off from Chloé's home in Plymouth and caught the ferry across to Roscoff on the north coast of France to begin their journey; blissfully unaware of the kind of adventure which lay ahead of them.

Together they meandered across the country, taking in the sights and experiences it had to offer. From wine tasting in the Loire valley, to taking in the views from the top of the Eiffel tower and sampling fine champagnes in Éperney, whilst tasting as many different cheeses as they could along the way. Eventually they had whittled their way across the country and began heading up into the French-Alps.

As they passed by the stunning, colourful lakes, dramatic mountain scenery and inspiring architecture, the area seemed to be a magical land all in itself. At last, they made it as far as Chamonix-Mont-Blanc, right on the Italian border, before they turned away from the main autoroutes which link France together and followed the directions which Chloé's mother had given to them.

Carefully they snaked along the sharp, windy alpine roads in a southward direction, until they finally arrived in Les-Champs-du-Château-Noir late one evening. Neither of them had been able to look up anywhere to stay in the town before they arrived, so they'd decided to take the risk and look around once they were there; though Chloé grew rather concerned that they'd end up having to spend the night in their little car.

When they arrived, they drove curiously down the dimly lit streets, looking for anything that resembled a hotel or B&B. As they crept through what they assumed to be the centre of the town, they were slightly unnerved by how quiet it was, feeling as though they were in an abandoned ghost town.

Chloé spotted a Tabac which she assumed to be the one her mother had visited, though it appeared to be closed - which seemed strange at only nine o'clock on a Thursday summer evening. They carried on through and out the other side of the town where, to their relief, they spotted a flickering sign that said 'Hôtel'.

Chloé, being the only one out of the pair of them who could speak French (thanks to her French father), was able to converse easily with the old man sat at the reception, whilst Chris stood by in anticipation for Chloé's translation. She got the impression that the mere fact they'd stepped into this place had disrupted the worker from his busy evening of doing nothing, but thankfully, though hardly surprisingly, they had a spare double room available for them which they booked for two nights. After being given directions to the room, Chris grabbed a pizza delivery flyer from the reception desk - noting first that they were still at least within the delivery hours - and they headed up a set of creaky, wooden stairs to their room on the first floor.

Their room wasn't exactly the nicest room they'd had since the start of their journey, very basic and far from cosy, but it was a room non-the less where they were able to enjoy their take-away food and get a good night's sleep.

The next morning, Chloé woke up full of wonder about what it will be like to finally see this mysterious castle, which her mother had discovered all those years ago. She hoped that it would be every bit as enchanting as the stories her mother had told her about the magic island, seeing as the two were linked somehow in the tale she'd been told. As Mrs. Duval had already given them instructions on where to find it, there was no need for them to inquire about it to any of the locals.

After a simple breakfast of French pastries, bread and jams begrudgingly laid out by the same hotel worker who'd greeted them on reception the night before, the pair of them got showered and dressed and headed up the old road towards the valley.

Unbeknown to them, in this particular French town, an English registered car stuck out like a sore thumb. The residents here were not used to foreign visitors, or visitors at all for that matter, since the road up into the valley had been closed off twenty-three years earlier; shortly after Mrs. Duval's visit to the castle

As they drove out of the town towards the valley, it didn't go unnoticed by most of the residents who spotted them; especially one local in particular who was curious to see where they thought they were going. Inevitably, however, whilst driving along the single lane road, sided on either side by fields used by the local farms, they happened upon a road-closed sign just at the beginning of the forest near the mouth of the valley itself.

"Well, that's annoying," said Chris.
"We could just get out and walk?" suggested Chloé, "It's only the road that's closed, it doesn't say we can't go into the woods."
"I suppose so. It looks like a nice spot for a walk anyway," Chris smiled.

With that, he pulled the car into the side of the road and they both go out. They'd made a few sandwiches with the selection of food from the breakfast buffet, which they carried with them in a small, blue rucksack along with some water, which Chris had put together for them before they'd left the hotel that morning.

After locking up the car, they continued on foot into the valley, admiring the majestic, lush, green pine-forest as they entered. Onward they trekked for an hour or so, until they came across what they could just about make out to be an old dirt track, almost unnoticeable through the grass which had grown through it.

"Maybe this is the road?" suggested Chris, "Do you reckon we've come in far enough?" he said as he looked back along the winding road they'd walked along.
"Well, I suppose there's only one way to find out," shrugged Chloé as she turned and began to follow it.

They carried on up the dirt track, following its rough trail through the lofty trees, climbing slightly higher up the side of the hill, just around the first corner of the valley., until at last they reached a clearing in the forest. This secluded spot they had come to was so peacefully still, like it was existing all by itself somewhere unattached to the rest of the world. It sided on one side by the steep, rocky hill of the mountain, where they finally saw the infamous, black castle.

Spires towered up from within its outer walls, gargoyles and other odd-looking creature-statues glared down imposingly at them, spikes and wrought iron spires struck out from the elaborate structure, adding that extra bit of height and majesty to its appearance. It was indeed every bit as impressive as her mother had described it to be and more. Although there was something significantly different about it from what Mrs. Duval had experienced - this time, there was no 'défense d'entrer' sign on the door.

Chloé was the one who spotted the difference, as she pointed it out to Chris.
"Maybe that means we can go in now?" said Chris, "What do you say? Do you want to explore an old sorcerer's castle?" he joked.
Chloé laughed, "Sure, why not."

CHAPTER TWO

It's Not What it Seems

Chloé and Chris walked up to the castle's grand, main entrance, gazing up in awe as they admired its totally magnificent design. Chris was the first one to touch the door, as he pushed his hand against it to see if it would open. With this attempt however, the door didn't move in the slightest, so he tried again only this time forcing his whole body upon it. Even with the extra force though, he only managed to merely scrape the door about an inch along the ground, when it stood stiff again.

The main doors of the castle were two, rather huge

wooden structures, strengthened with strips of iron bars holding the panels of wood together. Over time the doors had become wedged shut with the swelling of the wood and the vines which had grown around the frame. As Chris gave the door another push, Chloé had growing concerns over the creaking noises and gritty pieces of rubble falling from above. "Perhaps there's another way in," she suggested, "Around the side? Or maybe at the back?"

"Just give me a minute," Chris said through a tensed voice as he pushed, "I think I've almost…" The door moved again, about another inch or so, when suddenly a hefty stone came loose from above the doorframe and smashed on the floor right next to his feet, like a fragile glass knocked off a table.

"Right," he said, staring at the rubble left on the stone steps, thankful it hadn't landed just slightly to the left, "Maybe there's a side door that's a little bit less, life-threatening, that we could try."

They walked around to the left of the castle, away from the rocky side of the mountain which the castle merged with, and towards the far side where part of its structure had crumbled. The outer walls of the castle had been built incredibly thick, which left the lower parts still feeling fairly sturdy; sturdy enough for them to climb over, they hoped.

As they walked further round the side of the building, the ground they stood upon began to slope gradually downwards, lowering them away from the ground floor of the castle at the main entrance. When they finally came upon a section of the outer wall which seemed climbable, though fairly diminished it was still almost double the height of the average person. The two of them managed to scramble up however, and before they knew it they were stood within the castle walls; all be it with a few scrapes to the knees and elbows.

Chloé paused for a moment and looked around at the room she could see, imagining what it may have been. The floor was cobbled stone, but with grass and weeds sprouting up from underneath. The dividing wall between this room and the next had partly collapsed and she noticed that there seemed to be something still in there.

She walked over to take a closer look, but what she saw was hard to make out, it was all too overgrown. From the size of it though, and the rough shape she could make out, it looked like it could've been a bed. Was this a bedroom? She wondered. Perhaps a servant's quarters? Or maybe, could it be a prison? She shivered at the thought of being locked away in a small, dark room, cast away to the far side of the stone-cold castle.

Just as she was about to begin searching the room she was standing in for signs of other furniture, or long forgotten objects that might give her a clue as to what it might have been, Chris called to her.

"Cece! Come here! I've found a door," he yelled.

She couldn't see him from where she was stood as he had eagerly wandered further into the ruins, back towards the main body of the castle. She walked carefully towards where his voice was coming from, gently passing over a few crumbled walls until she reached what appeared to be a corridor, where Chris stood at the other end. "I found a door, and it opens!" he said excitedly.

As they stepped through the door, they found themselves in what they could clearly make out to be a large kitchen, which was a complete mess but otherwise very well preserved. On one side of the kitchen was a long wooden table with benches either side; probably where the servants ate, thought Chloé. Stretched along the walls on the other side were wooden cupboards and units, most with their doors open with pots and pans littered about the place. In the centre of them all was an impressive, built-in oven.

Thankfully the kitchen had a few tall windows, letting in enough light through the vines growing over them for Chloé and Chris to see well enough around the room. Neither of them had ever experienced seeing anything like this that hadn't already been 'restored', or made safe for tourists.

"Wow," exhaled Chloé in amazement, "I wonder how long it's been since anyone was last in here?"
"By the looks and overwhelmingly earthy smell of it, a very, very, *very* long time," said Chris.

The pair began to take a closer look at the objects that'd been left behind, it was like being inside a huge time capsule from a few hundred years ago. Fascinated by what they'd found and how it had all been left, they quickly moved through the room full of excitement and wonder as to what else the castle had preserved. They went on through the main kitchen doors which led them to a corridor, with a short, winding, stone staircase at the end.

At the top of these stairs they came out into a grand dining room. Again, quite a mess but otherwise well preserved. Shining light on the dining area was an enormous window, looking out towards the forest, with huge, heavy drapes framing it.

There were beautiful, huge tapestries hanging on the walls, though on a closer inspection they appeared to be depicting scenes of great tragedy rather than beauty. One tapestry, however, at the back of the room, appeared to depict a leader or someone of power. A figure who looked almost human stood in the centre on a rock, making them much higher than the others in the picture. They had what appeared to be spikes or horns coming out from the top of their head; one main horn in the middle and two smaller ones either side.

Around their shoulders hung a long, dark, royal-blue cloak, which reached all the way to the ground. The figure was holding something that looked like a crystal ball or ball of light in their left hand; though they weren't actually holding it, so much as it was hovering above their palm. On top of the ball sat a small, silver-grey dragon.

Their other hand was holding a kind of rope or lead which was tied around the neck of a dark, cherry-red unicorn, stood on the same rock though lower down. This unicorn had huge wings on its back and a tail which seemed to end with a small flame. Finally, at the bottom of the picture was a crowd of heads, all looking up towards the leader on top of the rock, who's soulless eyes were completely black.

The dining table was placed in the centre of the room, which had beautiful, ornate patterns carved along its edges. Some of the chairs around it still stood upright, though most of them now lay on their side on top of the expansive, decadent rug which covered almost the whole of the dining room floor. In the middle of the dining room table, you couldn't miss the bulky, iron chandelier, which had clearly fallen from the ceiling above.

"I wonder what happened here," thought Chloé out loud, "What could've happened causing this place to be just abandoned so suddenly, and in such a mess? Didn't anyone want it?"

"Maybe he scared them off," added Chris, referring to the scary looking figure depicted on the tapestry.
"Perhaps," said Chloé, "But then, what happened to him?" Chris barely gave it much thought and simply shrugged his shoulders, before wandering over to the main entrance to dining room.

He pushed hard and opened the double doors to find a great hall, with two tall, curved, stone staircases built into the back right and left corners. These each lead up to a landing, which wrapped around the hall and met at the other end of the room; each had many other corridors leading off to different parts of the castle.

Between the staircases, right in the centre and higher than the landing, there was an exquisite, round, stained glass window, projecting glistening, coloured light on to the dull, grey, stone floor. Neither of them could work out the patterns or symbols in the window, they couldn't link them to any culture or religion that they had learnt about before.

At the other end of this massive room, there was an archway leading under the landing, towards a set of doors which lead through to the main entrance hall of the castle. The room itself was like something out of a film depicting monarchs of great power, decorated with sculptures, statues and carvings suited to the presence of an imposing royal family.

Chloé had now joined Chris in the grand hall and she too admired the window, "It's incredible," she said, "If we get a house, can we get one with a window like that, please?" she joked.
"Sure, as long as people don't come to the door thinking we're a Church," he replied playfully, reaching his arm around her and clutching her waist.

"So, which way? Shall we try another door or go up the stairs?"
"Stairs," replied Chloé, "If the dining room is anything to go by, imagine how beautiful the bedrooms might be!"

"Which ones?" Chris asked, "Left? Or right?"
"Erm… right?" she shrugged.

So, the two of them stepped carefully up the stairs and onto the balcony-landing above. Standing at the top and looking out across the room, Chloé got a shiver of excitement as she imagined what it must've been like to be the owner of a place like this. Such an impressive castle surely could only have belonged to someone rich and powerful enough to have it built for them in the first place, she thought.

As she stood there taking it all in, she heard a noise come from the dining room. It sounded like something metal falling onto the floor, like a pan or something from the kitchen. "Did you hear that?" she asked Chris as she stopped.

"Hear what?"
"That noise that came from downstairs."
"It was probably a rat or a mouse or something, or a bird maybe?" he guessed, "Come on, let's see what else we can find."

Along the corridor there were small alcoves in the wall where it appeared objects had been displayed, though most of them now were either missing or smashed on the floor. Beautifully framed windows lit up the corridor by day, and from the ceiling hung ornate lanterns to light the corridor by night. As they walked through, Chris made sure to tread carefully, keeping an eye out ahead for signs of crumbling walls or floors that they'd hate to get a nasty surprise from.

"Oh look!" cried Chloé as they went around a bend along the lengthy corridor they'd chosen. She was pointing straight ahead towards a doorway right at the very end. This doorway didn't look like the others along this passageway, for it had a beautiful archway carved into the stone around it. Either side of the door, set into the archway, two pillars had been carved out looking as if they were holding up the arch, which sat atop three stone steps. The doorway as a whole, was set at a slight angle, to the left, continuing the curve of the corridor around the side of the castle.

"That door must lead to somewhere special," Chloé insisted, "Look how much work has been put into the frame. It's beautiful. Plus, it has its own steps!" she said excitedly, "let's check it out."

They walked carefully down the corridor towards it, and then stopped to admire the stone carvings around the frame. Above the door there was a row of ugly looking heads, some more human looking than others, and piercing up between them were three spikes, or horns thought Chloé, resembling those on the head of the figure depicted on the tapestry.

"Do you think this is his room?" asked Chloé, "The guy in that picture?"
"Probably. But I doubt he's here now," said Chris as he reached for the handle.

They opened the door to find a bedroom on the other side, quite a spectacular bedroom, too. There was a tall, well-decorated window on the wall to the right of the door, looking out onto the valley, framed with thick heavy drapes. To the left of the doorway was a large fireplace, big enough to stand in, and the back-left corner of the room was part of one of the tall spires rising up from the castle; where a smaller window faced out into a courtyard.

Pushed against the back wall, raised upon a stone platform was a huge four-poster bed, which still had blankets and pillows on.

Covering the floor space between the fireplace and the stone platform for the bed, lay a beautiful Persian rug which had two armchairs and a small table sat upon it.

This room had also been left in a mess, however, with traces of broken ornaments on the floor and the rug half folded over.

"Now *this* is a bedroom," said Chloé as she admired it.
"Don't tell me," said Chris, "if we get a house, you want one of these, too?" Chloé smiled and tensed up for a moment, unable to contain her excitement.

One of the walls in the bedroom was made of the solid rock from the mountain; there was a long, full-length mirror hanging on this wall, with a wardrobe stood next to it. After having a look at odd objects they could find around the room – trinkets, different coloured bottles, interesting candleholders – Chloé wandered over to admire into the mirror hanging on the rock wall.

Carefully stepping over an old room divider that had been pushed over, she stood very close to the mirror and gazed into it. "If only I could see all the things this mirror has seen," she thought out loud, "All the people who have looked into it." She began to admire the detailed wooden frame as she gently brushed down the side of it with her fingertips.

As her hand got about halfway down the outside of the frame, she felt part of it move slightly as her fingers smoothed over it. She looked at the frame closely as she put her finger back to where she had felt the piece of wood move. When she managed to find the exact piece of detailed carving that appeared to wobble, she grabbed hold of it with her thumb and forefinger and began to pull at it. At first it only wobbled slightly up and down, but as she pulled a bit harder, a long piece of wood extended out from the side of the frame.

As she pulled the piece of wood further outwards, her eyes were curiously fixated on it, until suddenly she heard a sound like a latch opening come from behind the mirror. The noise caused her to look back at the glass, and as she did so, she saw the mirror come free and move outwards slightly from within the frame. Using her fingertips, she pushed against the side of the glass and pulled it as it swung open – it was a door.

As she opened the mirror fully, she saw a hidden passageway leading into the mountain. Chloé stood there, gazing into the darkness of this secret passageway with disbelief, wondering what mysteries might be hidden down there. Could it be just an escape route perhaps? Or might it lead to something enchanting? Something that the owner of the castle wanted to keep just for themselves.

"Chris…" she said, her eyes still fixated on what she'd found.
"What?" he replied, looking through some jewellery he'd found on the floor. Chloé didn't respond. "Hey, Chlo, look at this jewellery I've found. It could be worth a fortune!"
"Chris," Chloé repeated," Look!"

"What?" Chris lifted his head and looked over to Chloé. When he saw the secret passageway she'd just found, his hand suddenly let go of the jewellery, which he was suddenly not so interested in (though he did shove a few gems into his pockets before he got up).

CHAPTER THREE

The Sorcerer's Grimoire

Chris walked over to Chloé and got his phone out of his pocket, using its light to light up the passageway before he stepped inside. Chloé stepped in behind him and they shone the light onto the walls around them. The passage was wide enough for the two to walk side by side, and the ceiling was too high for them to reach. The whole corridor was solid rock, sharp and jagged in places, with wall sconces mounted sporadically that would have once been lit with fire to light the way.

Before deciding to see where the passage would lead,

they inspected the back of the mirror first. There was a handle on it so that you could pull the door shut from the inside, and a latch on the wall which could be triggered via the piece of wood that slides out from the mirror-frame. Knowing that the door shouldn't be able to shut and lock itself (and if it did they could just un-latch it from their side) they decided to follow the passage; into the dark unknown.

Not too far along it, they came to a spiralled staircase, roughly carved out from the rock. At the bottom of the staircase, there stood a stone pillar neatly constructed and displaying decorative features – much unlike the rest of the passageway. The pillar reached about the height of Chris' head, and atop the pillar sat a crown carved in the stone, though more delicate looking like a tiara, which had the three horns incorporated into it – the large one pointing upwards in the middle, and the two smaller ones to either side, pointing slightly back and away from the center.

They stopped and stared at it for a moment, wondering what kind of human-looking being would wear such horns. The devil perhaps? They each wondered.

Then they carried on up the staircase to find another long corridor at the top, unable to see the end with just the light from Chris' phone. Cautiously, they cautiously continued along it. Chris was beginning to feel claustrophobic, as was Chloé, but they were far too excited about what they might find at the other end to let that stop them.

Whilst continuing on down the cold, damp, cave-like corridor, they suddenly heard a noise coming from

behind them. "What was that?" Chris asked, startled.
"I don't know. An echo?" Chloé shrugged.
"Yea. Yea it must've been an echo from us walking," he said, trying to convince himself. The feeling of excitement they had when they'd first stepped into the passageway was beginning to fade, and a feeling of being rather spooked and very much trapped, was setting into them.

As it was summer, neither of them were wearing particularly warm clothes, and they were starting to feel the cooler, damp air of the corridor in the mountain on their skin more than they had earlier. Still they kept on walking, desperate to find out what was at the other end.

Suddenly, like a quick flash of a tiny torch, Chris noticed his light bouncing back off something further along the corridor. As they walked closer they saw that it was a door knob attached to a wooden door. Each of them, hoping that this would be the end to the long, stone tunnel, picked up their pace to reach it. It was Chris who put his hand on the handle first, whilst shining his light directly on it, as he twisted it and pushed and pulled tryingly at the door. It was open.

This door opened out into yet another corridor, though this one was quite short and had windows, and also a set of seven steps at the end leading to another door. They were back inside the castle building itself now, but on a floor leading to part of a tower only accessible via the secret passageway. They walked along the corridor and up the steps to the door, where they both paused for a moment.

Chris placed his hand upon the beautiful azurite doorknob, after taking a moment to admire it. He twisted his hand around and opened the door, where they found the final room; the room that the mirror was keeping people from finding. "Wow…" Chloé said with a large exhale, "What kind of room is this?"

The room had a large circular carpet in the middle, with what looked to be some kind of occult symbol on it, similar the those in the stained-glass window (and equally like none they'd ever seen before), and a point in the centre. Above this, from right in the heart of the ceiling hung a large bronze chandelier, with sharp spikes pointing downwards and some candles still wedged inside the holders.

Against the circular wall of the room was a great fireplace with a huge black pot hanging inside. A row of different sized glass bottles stood along its mantle-piece with a thick, dark blue candle placed in the centre. Tools hung on both sides of the fireplace, though more like things you'd find in a kitchen than next to a fire. In front of the fireplace, on the floor, sat a selection of smaller black pots, and to the right-hand side was a round, wooden table.

The table had a few books on, one open and some stacked, though the pages of the open book were completely blank, they noticed. There was another interesting looking table in the room, more like a workbench, with a book stand and many jars, some of which still had what looked to be remains of dead insects inside. There was a mortar and pestle on the table and scattered about were some small devices which looked like old tools.

Attached to the back of the bench were shelves, some full of plant pots with the dead, shrivelled plants still in them. On the top shelf though there was a small stand, displaying some stick like things, but Chloé and Chris were both unsure as to what they were – wands perhaps? They hoped.

At the other side of the room was a large bookcase, though not all the shelves were full, with a rather lavish, comfortable looking, tall-backed reading chair stood by it. There was a small pile of books that'd been left by the chair, waiting either to be read or put away.

One section of the wall in this circular room was covered in cupboards, some with the door open showing all kinds of strange things that were kept inside.

The room was lit by day through one large, curved window. Looking out of it you could see most of the castle and far down into the valley. Aside from books lying about the room and a few broken bottles, this room didn't appear to have been ravaged like other rooms in the castle.

"I don't know," replied Chris after he'd glanced about the place, "it looks like some kind of Alchemist's room. A dark Alchemist, if I had to guess."

Chloé went over to look at the small tools and glass jars on the workbench, whilst Chris was admiring the sharpness of the spikes hanging from the chandelier. "I wonder what they used to make?" she wondered out loud to herself.

"All kinds of weird stuff probably. God, I know people used to really believe in this stuff, but I've never seen a room like this before, so dedicated to it."

"Maybe the owner of this castle *was* actually a real sorcerer," Chloé mused, "But then, where is he now? Can you kill a sorcerer?"
"I doubt that he was actually a sorcerer. Lots of people believe they have some kind of unholy powers, but usually they're just mad."
"But how could a madman come to own a place like this?" Chris turned to look at Chloé, now with a book in his hand that he had picked up off the floor.
"Mad followers," he replied bluntly.

He then started to look through the book when he noticed that all the pages were completely blank. He didn't think much of it, however, and simply dropped it back down onto the floor as he went over to the bookshelf. Meanwhile, Chloé was still looking at things on the workbench, where there was a hefty book resting on the bookstand.

The book's hard-cover was coated with a soft, thick cloth, dyed a deep indigo blue, and in the centre there was a dark-gold circular piece of metal with the image of the three horns engraved into it. The corners of the cover were protected by a dark metal, speckled slightly with golden flecks in places, which was also used on the spine of the book in strips. She picked up the book and looked inside, where she found pages and pages of listed magical beings, objects, ingredients, potion recipes, spells and curses. Fascinated by what she saw, she stood silently flicking through the pages.

"That's weird," Chris said after flicking through the fourth book he'd picked up from the bookshelf. "All the pages in these books are completely blank. I was hoping they might give us some idea of what was going on here." As he said this he placed the book down and turned to glance out through the window, looking vaguely at the castle. When suddenly, he fixated his eyes on a window in another part of the building, some-way across the courtyard and not quite facing his direction. Did he just see it move? He wondered curiously. As if someone had just closed it? He continued to watch it for a moment, until Chloé, finally responding to what he'd said about the books, disrupted him.

"This one isn't blank, look," she called him over, "It's full of spells and things." Chris walked over to Chloé and thought nothing more of the window; he was too intrigued by what she'd said she found in the book. She passed the book to him, holding it open on a page with a spell and a recipe for a potion that would turn an animal human.

"How weird would that be?" she said as she passed him the book.
"What?" he asked, a bit confused, "The blank page?"
"What? No, the spell, right there," she tapped the page with her finger, pointing at the title, "And this list of ingredients. Look, it even tells you how to make it. I wonder if they'd remember what it'd been like to be an animal?"

Chris had no idea what she was going on about, as far as he could see there was nothing written in the book.

He took the book from her as she held it in front of him, and he turned a few pages to find them all just as blank as the rest, before looking back at Chloé. "Are you trying to wind me up?" he questioned her, not really understanding what was going on – it wasn't really in Chloé's nature to tease in this way.

Chloé insisted that she wasn't fooling around and couldn't understand why Chris was saying that he only saw blank pages. Wondering if he was trying to play some weird joke on her, she went over to the books he'd picked up and had a flick through them. He was right though, all the other books were in fact blank. So why was he saying that the one she had picked up was blank too? When it clearly wasn't. She struggled to make sense of it, but then, she didn't always get his jokes.

"Are you honestly telling me, that you can't see any writing at all on these pages?" she puzzled, now holding the book again and showing different pages to him. He insisted over and over that he saw nothing but blank pages in the book, so Chloé decided to take a picture and send it to her mother so she could confirm that Chris was just playing a lame joke on her.

She got out her phone and opened up the camera app, but as she hovered her phone over the pages to take a picture, what she saw on the screen stunned her. There was no writing there at all.

She couldn't understand it. How was she able to see everything written on the pages, but yet through her phone camera the pages were blank. She tried to convince Chris that she wasn't lying, though she couldn't begin to explain what was going on.

After a while they decided to forget about how or why she could read it and he couldn't, and they sat together on the floor whilst Chloé went through the book, flicking through to random pages, revealing to Chris what was in it. Nothing in the book really told them much about what was going on in the castle however, or who had owned it, nor did it even seem to be specifically light or dark magic – but a mixture of practically anything to do with either.

There were ways to heal a person on one page, then ways to harm someone on the next. Towards the back of the book, Chloé found a folded-up piece of paper wedged inside. She took it out and unfolded it to find that she'd just discovered a map. She showed the map to Chris, but unfortunately, he couldn't see this either.

It was pinpointing a spot in the Atlantic Ocean, somewhere off the coast of northern West Africa. There was an inscription written on the map too, which Chloé read out loud to Chris –

> *Await a moon most full and round,*
> *Only after that, you'll find this ground.*
> *With the rising sun, you'll be sure to find,*
> *But just for a moment, if you look behind.*
> *Time will be short, you must race near,*
> *If you hold back, she will disappear.*

"There's a title as well," she carried on, "On the map. It says 'Île Merveille'…. Wonder Island?" she paused for a moment, until the sudden realisation dawned on her, "This is it! This must be the island my mum used to tell me about!"

"You better not be making this all up," said Chris, "Is there anything else on the map? Like where exactly you have to be to find this island?"

"There're some numbers with little circles and letters, N and W..."

"Perhaps they're coordinates, read them out and I'll type them into my phone."

Chloé read out the coordinates to Chris, "21°27'N, 37°31'W."

"My internet's not strong enough, we'll have to wait until we get back to the hotel to find out where it is."

As Chris was just about to put his phone away, he noticed that it was starting to get late and suggested they think about heading back to town. They decided to take the book and the map with them back to the hotel to study them both further.

Before they set off, they had a quick look around to see if there was anything else worth taking with them. Chloé decided to grab what she was now sure was a wand from the shelf, and Chris took a few interesting looking objects from a cupboard – a magnifying glass that didn't magnify anything, a beautiful looking golden goblet with a blue stained-glass cup, and two pieces of paper that were next to it, that when held together read 'Encore Ensemble' across them in the most elegant handwriting.

They headed back down the secret passageway to the bedroom, though it took them a bit longer whilst carrying their new finds in their hands. They made it back out to the ruined section of the castle, where getting back over the wall proved slightly more difficult. Making sure not to damage any of their new things, they passed them one by one to the top of the wall, and then back down again on the other side.

By the time they had walked back to their car the sun had already left both the valley and the town. Disappearing behind the mountains in the distance, it had turned them into silhouettes against its warm, golden glow. They decided to put their things into the boot of the car for the journey back, and as they did so they noticed tire marks on the road behind them, which clearly weren't theirs.

"Where they there earlier?" Chloé asked.
"I don't know," said Chris, "I didn't notice."

Feeling a little bit creeped out, they drove back to the hotel under the light of the dusky, evening sky, and headed straight up to their room; only to find a note that had been pushed under their door - which read:

>I saw you up in the tower today. I saw you reading the book. How is it that you can you read it? I must know how you do it, and what you know of it. I see you tomorrow, at the castle.

Unnerved by the note, knowing someone had been watching them, they locked themselves inside the bedroom, with absolutely no intention on going back there tomorrow.

Then they began to put it all together - the noises in the castle, the window Chris thought he saw move and the tire tracks behind their car. The whole time they were in the castle, this person hadn't been far behind them.

But who was it, they wondered, and why hadn't they confronted them when they saw Chloé reading from the book? Stranger still, why was he sure there was something to be learnt from it? As much as they were both beginning to feel freaked out by it all, they also wondered if he might be able to answer some of their questions.

As the night drew in, they realised they hadn't eaten much all day and were beginning to feel the emptiness groaning in their stomachs. They hid the things they had brought back from the castle inside one of their bags, a blue and grey hiking rucksack which Chris had packed his things into, and decided to lock that bag in the boot of their car. For dinner, they headed over to eat at the local Tabac; it wasn't too far for them to walk and neither of them really cared much about what they wanted to eat that evening.

Sat in the Tabac, they were trying not to discuss what had happened that day, in case they were overheard by someone who might start asking questions. As they were about halfway through their main meal however, they were approached by the man who'd seen them driving up towards the valley that morning.

He was of average height and quite skinny looking, with bushy, dark brown hair that he had tied back, though some fell forward onto his face as it wasn't long enough for the ponytail. His skin was pale and looked quite dry in places; he also had a rash on his right wrist which he kept scratching. He wore an un-tucked, navy-blue shirt, dark denim jeans and an old pair of black trainers. His age was hard to guess, though they reckoned he was in his mid-thirties.

"Hello," he said to them in a low, calm voice, which had only a hint of a French accent, "do you mind if I join you?" Chris didn't really know what to say, but thought he should say something quickly in case the man just decided to sit down anyway.

"We're kind of in the middle of a conversation, sorry."

"Oh, I am sorry, I did not mean to interrupt," the man said, "I will leave you two alone."

He paused for a moment, looking as if he was going to walk away, then he turned to them again, "unless the conversation you're having is about the book you stole, in which case I think it is best if I join you."

Startled, as they realised that this was the man who'd left the note and who'd been following them all day, they both sat there motionless as they watched him sit down at their table. "So, go on, tell me. How you did it? How did you manage to read what is written on those pages?" he asked Chloé, leaning over the table towards her.

"I'm sorry, who are you?" she asked, "And what right do you have to follow us around and spy on us all day?"

"I was curious," he said, pulling back from her slightly, "How two people from out of town are able to find their way straight to the castle. A castle that's not signposted or advertised anywhere, and which access road is closed off."

"But why would you follow someone driving towards the valley anyway?" Chris said, challenging the man who was making them out to be the suspicious ones. "We could've just been going for a walk in the woods."

"I was merely trying to warn you that the road was closed, and no one was to head up into the valley, but as I tried to catch up to you I saw you head straight for the castle and I started to get suspicious. Now tell me, what did it say?" he urged as he turned back to Chloé.
"Why are you so interested?" she asked.

"Because," he started, then sat back slightly so as not to appear threatening, "I have heard the tales of what this place used to be, and I have also looked through those books myself, trying to find proof that the stories are true."
"And did you find proof?" Chris asked.
"Nothing proving magic exists so far, until I saw you reading from that book."

Chloé grew increasingly more nervous. What if this man was dangerous and began forcing her to reveal what she'd read? She thought it was probably best to cooperate a little. "I think we've all got off to a bad start here," she said, "Let's just go back to the beginning." She paused for a moment and looked at Chris before looking back at the stranger. "Hi, I'm Chloé and this is Chris."

"Very well," he said, "My name is Lancelin."
"Hi, Lancelin. Your English is very good, you don't sound like you're from around here."
"I used to speak it fluently years ago. Now, can we get back to the book?"

Lancelin asked about the island and its whereabouts, whilst Chloé tried to describe to him what she'd seen. He began to come across more curious than threatening, and his interest in the island and wholehearted belief that she'd been able to read the book, soon got them chatting more comfortably. In the end, they all decided to go back to the hotel so that Chloé could get the book out and try to draw a copy of the map. Not knowing exactly how much Lancelin had seen, they kept the other items they had taken from the castle just between the two of them.

Chris waited with him in the bedroom whilst Chloé went to retrieve the book, on her way picking up a pad and pen from the reception desk. Once she got back to the bedroom, she drew a copy of the map as well as she could for Chris and Lancelin to view. She added the writing to it and the coordinates, which Chris then managed to convert to decimal and use on his phone's map.

He typed in the numbers - 21.453069, -37.529297 - and they waited patiently, as his painfully slow internet loaded the area of the map pinpointed by his search. Sure enough, it was the same spot in the Atlantic that Chloé had seen on the map they'd found. Lancelin insisted straight away that they all go to try and find the Island, to which Chloé insisted wasn't even an option.

"Well, we do have that boat booked that we were going to sail from Antibes on," Chris said suggestively.
"You're not seriously suggesting that we steal the boat and head for the Atlantic, are you?" She asked him, shocked by what he was suggesting.
"Why not?"

Lancelin interrupted, "You have a boat? That's perfect!"

"No, no, not perfect," Chloé insisted in a frustrated

manner, "I can't sail all the way to that point on my own, it's too far."

"What if we flew to the Canary Islands and sailed from there? It wou…" Chris was abruptly interrupted by Lancelin.

"No! No flying," he shouted, "I'm, err… I'm too afraid of flying, I couldn't possibly. We'll have to just take your boat, the one in Antibes."

Lancelin's reaction put Chris off wanting to persuade him to take a flight, though his reason for not wanting to fly did raise suspicions in Chris' mind. He turned back to Chloé, "Well we'll help, you can show us the ropes, so to speak," he laughed, trying to lighten her mood. "You can teach us what to do along the way. Look, we already know something incredible and unexplainable is going on, the book is showing you things it's not showing to anyone else. What if for whatever reason it's because you're the one that's supposed to find this island?"

"All right, say we find the island and we get on to it. What if something bad happens there? What if something there tries to kill us?"

"And what if it doesn't?" said Chris, "And we discover something amazing. After all, you said you used to dream that you'd find it someday."

"You already knew about it?" Lancelin interjected.

Chloé went on to explain the story of how her mum had been to this town when she was younger and heard about this place. Then, they carried on discussing what to do about it all well into the night, and by the early hours of the morning, the two guys had persuaded Chloé and she agreed to go with them in search of the island.

◆ ◆ ◆

The next day they packed up everything into their car, along with some of Lancelin's things, and tried to squeeze everyone in.

"Ouch," flinched Lancelin as he tried to crouch into the back seat.
"Are you alright?" asked Chloé.
"Yes, yes, fine. Just a bit of a sore back," he muttered.
"Oh, great," Chris groaned quietly to himself.

Finally, they all managed to get in comfortably amongst their bags and set off for Antibes. They arrived late in the evening and went straight to a hotel which they had booked for the night. Tired and hungry, they ordered more take away pizza, ate and went to bed. The two guys were soon fast asleep; however Chloé couldn't manage to relax.

Her mind was busy going over everything she could remember that her dad had taught her about sailing. She was worried that it had been too long since she had last sailed, and that this journey was way too big for her to tackle without his help. She'd never sailed that far out on the ocean before, and the idea of it was twisting her stomach in knots.

Though her instincts were telling her she couldn't do it and that it would be too dangerous, the more she read through the book she started to imagine what this place might be like, if it really did exist. She sat up in bed flicking through the pages using her phone as a reading light, when suddenly she came across a page that had something written on it, something she couldn't *not* think about from then on. Something that gave her a huge desire to reach this place, and a thought to keep in her mind assuring her it was what she had to do.

CHAPTER FOUR

Stage One: Escaping the Mediterranean

The following day was the day they were to pick up the boat. It was a beautifully dry, hot day down on the coast. The sea sparkled all along the shore, inviting everyone who caught a glimpse of it to jump straight in to refresh themselves from the intense, morning sun. The holidaying French strutted up and down les rues in their latest summer couture searching for their favourite morning coffee, standing out amongst the many tourists of other nationalities trying to act like they belonged.

Chris and Chloé had already booked the boat and prepaid for the duration of their pre-planned trip. Chris gave his credit card details over as their deposit in case they damaged the boat, or if they didn't bring it back on time; something he did very unwillingly, knowing the more realistic length of their journey. It didn't seem to faze Lancelin though - who could care about a huge credit card bill when they were in pursuit of a magical island, he insisted.

The boat was about twelve to thirteen meters in length, with a nice wide cabin big enough for the three of them and their luggage. With only one main cabin however, privacy wasn't really an option for them now that Lancelin had tagged along. As far as Chloé was concerned though, this was already as much as she could bear to manage. Thanks to Chloé's father who had already been saving for their trip, and with the added funds from both Chris and Lancelin, they had managed to rent a relatively new sailing boat, along with the latest navigational system and emergency equipment.

After they'd signed for it and had it shown to them, they popped along to the nearest supermarket to get as much as they could in the way of what they thought they might need – not only food and water, but medical supplies and emergency equipment such as a torch and spare batteries.

Once they were done shopping and had loaded everything onto the boat, Chris and Chloé got to grips with the onboard navigational system. Chris thought it a good idea to download as much as he could on the map on his phone, so they might use it as a backup should they get lost at sea. Finally, Chloé insisted that they each wear their life jackets, at least until she was comfortable sailing again. The guys followed her orders without question, and Lancelin seemed to be taking a bit of care in tightening his up.

"Are you alright with it?" asked Chloé.

"Oh, yes, not a problem," he replied as he hurriedly tightened it into place, leaving no need for her to help him out.

Then they were ready. Chloé carefully navigated them through the harbour and out onto the shimmering, blue water of the Mediterranean Sea.

She didn't find sailing here too stressful, for once she had familiarised herself with the boat she soon began to rediscover her love of sailing. The first section of their voyage was from Antibes to Gibraltar, roughly following the coast to make the navigation easier and allowing easy stops to restock with food and water – as sailing all day under the intense sun proved to be very thirsty work for all of them.

The boat they rented was originally only theirs for two weeks, but thanks to an additional down payment from Lancelin (in cash), they were able to keep it for an extra week longer. This gave them three full weeks before the boat would be reported missing or stolen; unfortunately for them, however, the next full moon was not for another twenty-five days.

Chloé's plan was to reach the Canary Islands within those three weeks for their last stop before heading out into the mid-Atlantic Ocean. She knew that sailing the Atlantic was not going to be as calm and easy as the coastal sailing they were experiencing in the Mediterranean, so she tried to teach the other two as much as she could about how to sail in this first section of their journey. She was also aware of the possibility of storms this time of year, likely to hit as they were nearing their destination.

The sailing boat was equipped with a motor and a full tank of fuel, which they preferred to try and save for the day they might spot the island, in the case that there was not enough wind to carry them towards it in time.

Chloé, being the only one who had sailed before (she assumed), put herself in charge of the boat and the safety of the group whilst at sea. She insisted to the others that if they are to make it to Île Merveille, they were to follow her instruction on the boat at all times; especially if they were to find themselves sailing through rough waters.

After getting herself familiar with the boat on the first day, Chloé spent the next few days of sailing teaching Lancelin how to navigate the boat and teaching Chris about the different sails, ropes and their purposes. For the night time, they came up with a sleeping arrangement to make sure at least two people were awake and manning the boat at all times; they couldn't afford to lose any sailing time they didn't have to.

As their days at sea went by, Chloé switched Chris and Lancelin over to teach them some of the basics of each other's roles. Before too long, everyone aboard the boat had become handy to have around, spotting wind changes before Chloé had pointed it out to them and dealing with small problems whilst Chloé merely supervised.

The weather for the first part of their journey was perfect. Bright blue skies, a calm sea and winds in their favour; a cause of which they were making good progress along the Spanish coast. With the journey ahead and the destination of a lifetime in mind, it was hard for them to notice the stunning scenes around them as they pulled into several different small Spanish harbour towns to restock.

One evening, on the last day before their final stop along the Spanish coast, Chloé went below deck for a nap leaving Lancelin and Chris in charge. Once alone however, she found she had trouble getting off to sleep, so instead she turned to their rucksack and lifted out the Grimoire to have a read through it. As she sat up reading, Chris left Lancelin behind the wheel of the boat and came below deck to get a drink. He saw Chloé awake reading the book and went over to sit with her.

"What's the page about?" he asked as he cosied up to her.
"It's a section on magical plants. This one I'm reading about here, is a small flower, a bit like a daisy I guess, but with a larger centre and smaller grey and dark purple petals. It say's that on their own they're as fragile your average small flower or garden weed, but when linked together in a chain they become almost unbreakable."

"Almost unbreakable? Does it say how you can break them?"
"It might do," she replied, "I haven't read it all yet. But looking through this book it seems that anything in this place is possible, so nothing can be said for sure. It does

say as well though that if you create a chain and link it around the neck of another creature, even a human, you'll have control over them."

"That's a bit worrying," Chris said, thinking what Lancelin might do with this information. Chris had no reason to fear Lancelin, but he somehow couldn't help but feel distrust towards odd strangers that forced themselves into your life so quickly.

"Yea, hopefully I'll find out from this book how to break a chain like that," Chloé continued.

"I'm sure it'll be in there somewhere," said Chris, "But anyway, you should get some rest so you'll be fit to sail with me later on, when Lancelin has his break." Chris then kissed Chloé and headed back up to join Lancelin.

Chloé watched Chris leave and then continued to read the page for a few more minutes before trying again to go to sleep. The page she had been reading though was not the one she told Chris about when he asked, but instead the one she had come across on their night in Antibes, her main interest for making it to the island.

Their last port of call along the Spanish coast was at a town called Estepona, located between Gibraltar and Marbella. Whilst Chris and Chloé both went ashore to get food and water supplies, Lancelin stayed below deck, just as he did so at every other stop before. He had explained to them that he chose not to leave the boat as the items on board were so precious to them and vital for their journey. "This place doesn't seem like a safe place to leave our treasure," he'd point out. "Someone should stay behind to guard it."

Neither of them really objected to having a moment

alone together and agreed that it was best for someone to stay and watch over their precious cargo. Though, Chloé still took the keys to the boat's engine with her, to be sure the boat would still be there in the harbour when they returned.

Chloé and Chris walked into the town with an empty rucksack searching for a supermarket. Before leaving Antibes, they had each withdrawn plenty of cash so that they wouldn't have to use their debit or credit cards to make any payments – making it harder for someone to trace them should they try to. Knowing that the next stretch of sailing would be along the Moroccan coast, they had decided to try and make it all the way to the Canaries without stopping for food or water.

Whilst on land, Chloé went into a sailing shop and asked if they had any books on sailing east to west through the Strait of Gibraltar, that happened to be in English. She knew it could often be tricky with the current of the Atlantic flowing so strongly into the Mediterranean, she and her father had discussed it when planning their trip together. Luckily there was one book they stocked which had some brief English translations in, which had at least a bit information on the topic; though she was still feeling rather uneasy about the whole thing.

After restocking the boat with supplies, they headed back into the town to eat at a café which had free Wi-Fi. Whilst they were there, Chloé searched for information that would be useful and necessary for the next part of their journey, which she downloaded to read properly later that evening.

Once they'd finished up in the café, they went back to the boat and spent the evening around the harbour, as Chloé made their plans for the following section of their voyage.

The next day, due to winds and the strong flow of water that would be pushing against them through this narrow passage, Chloé explained to the other two that they had just two windows of opportunity to make it through. They opted for the first option and so set off from the harbour early, around five in the morning, heading south towards Ceuta on the North African coast. This was the favourable of the two options due to there being less sea traffic at this time, though making the crossing as quickly as they could, meant everyone working on deck.

Without too much hassle, they'd made it south to the north tip of Morocco, where they would then turn west sailing against the current. Everything so far was going well. The wind was on their side and the rising sun behind them was lighting their way. As they were near Tangier however, the wind died down and the strong current began fiercely pushing back against them.

Whilst waiting for some more wind to ride in, they were forced to dip into their motor reserves as they were being dragged away from their crossing opportunity. They started it up and set it to just under its max speed, which didn't do much more than keeping them stationary if not flowing backwards still, only at a much slower speed. They felt helpless as they watched the distance they'd gained that morning begin to rapidly slip away from them. Chloé feared they might have to sail back to Ceuta and wait for a much later time when they could try again with the much busier crossing time - option two.

They'd been sat with the motor running for about half an hour, when Chloé stood up to suggest to the others that they'd have to turn back and wait for their next opportunity to pass through. When as she did so, she noticed large waves ahead travelling in their direction – at last, it was the wind they needed.

She shouted the orders to the others to prepare for sailing into the wind, something they'd practised several times but never into winds this strong and with a current. Luckily the wind was coming from a North Westerly direction meaning that they could use it for heading South West, just skimming the corner at the tip of Morocco and escaping the Strait out into the Atlantic.

As the wind led waves met them, their sales rose up and the ropes violently flapped around. Everyone on deck was in the position and worked hard to reach their goal. Chloé stood steering at the back, shouting strong, precise orders at the others giving them no room for error. Everyone cooperated, and as a team they sailed through their first challenge of the journey, Chris was left feeling ecstatic over performing his newly learned skills so expertly.

After this tough section where the two bodies of water met, it was plain sailing along the coast of Morocco down towards the Canaries. The group effort of getting through the strait had brought them all a bit closer together.

The waters they sailed through along this section were not too difficult for this small crew. With it now being early August, the sun was high in the sky and the temperatures were rising the further south they headed. They even spotted a pod of Dolphins swimming alongside their boat on one of the days, as they neared the Canaries; it was almost as if the magic of the island was enchanting their trip already.

Though the two guys were in high spirits about their sailing achievements to date and felt confident in their sailing knowledge, Chloé remained cautious about the journey ahead. She knew that at this time of year, heading too far south meant that at some point you would reach stormy weather. As much as they had been able to manage sailing into strong winds without too much instruction from her, how would any of them cope getting through a tropical storm? She knew she was going to have to get as much research done on this as she could at their next stop, before the last leg of their journey.

Their only stop in the Canaries was in a place called Arrecife, on the island of Lanzarote. The last day leading up to this stop, the weather had begun to deteriorate and the sea was getting rough. With three to four-meter waves rolling in, crashing against their boat, they were all grateful when they finally spotted their next port of call ahead out of them.

CHAPTER FIVE

Stage Two: Battling the Atlantic

Once moored up in the harbour they decided to rest here for a few days, using the time to repair some minor damages to the sails and for Chloé to plan their next and final stretch of the journey. Time-wise they were doing well, it had taken them fifteen days to sail from Antibes to the Canary Islands, leaving ten days left before the full moon. Also, this meant that they could set sail from Arrecife before their boat was reported missing, giving them time to get out of sight before anyone should start looking for them.

On the second day there, Chloé sat a café to eat lunch and checked the weather for the rest of their trip. It seemed the further away from the Canaries they would be from now on, the worse the weather was going to get. After eating she went back to the boat to find the other two sat eating in silence. She asked them both to meet her below deck to talk about what she'd found.

"Okay," she started, "do you want the good news or the bad news?" After she'd said this, the two guys answered simultaneously – Chris asking for the bad news and Lancelin asking for the good news. Chloé sat staring at them both for a moment before she continued.

"Well anyway, I'll just give you the news as it is. The weather, it seems, won't get much better as we head west/southwest, and there looks to be a storm gathering along our path. The storm, though, shouldn't get to full strength until just after the full moon, and we could see a few days of rough, yet manageable conditions before it."
"When you say… storm," Chris began to ask nervously, "you mean…"
"Wind, rain, waves," replied Chloé, sternly.
"Do you think we'll make it?" asked Chris, wondering if perhaps they'd got a bit over excited about all this and not seen the bigger risks to begin with.

Chloé sat staring at Chris for a moment, until Lancelin broke the silence, "Of course we will, we cannot turn back now. We have to reach Île Merveille." As he said that, Chloé looked towards him and caught him looking at the Grimoire.
"Well if there's a chance we'll die at sea then, to be

honest, I don't think we do *have* to," snapped Chris, getting annoyed at Lancelin for not taking their safety into his consideration.

Seeing Lancelin glance towards the Grimoire, Chloé wondered if there was something Lancelin wasn't telling them. Then she remembered what she'd read in it herself and spoke up. "No, he's right. We have to make it."

Irked that Chloé had seemed to side with Lancelin over himself, and frustrated over the bad weather forecast, Chris got up and left the cabin. Chloé simply sighed then looked down at the floor, then back towards Lancelin.

"Do you know something about the Grimoire, or the island, that you're not telling us?" she asked nervously, not wanting to sound like she was accusing him of anything.

Lancelin responded almost aggressively at first, "What?!" Then took a moment to calm and compose himself so not to arouse any suspicions she may have about him. "No. What I know of the writing on those pages is only what you've told me. Though if the stories about the island are true, I know we'd be fools to give up the chance to find it."

Chloé knew she wasn't getting any more out of him than that, so exited the cabin to find that Chris had left the boat completely and was sat on a bench by the harbour, looking out towards to sea. She went over to him to talk about what had just happened, and to assure him that she wouldn't go onwards with their journey if she thought that it would pose a serious risk to their lives – at least before they were to reach their destination.

Speaking with him, she managed to calm him down and to feel positive again, reminding him of his excitement in the beginning and that it was he who had talked her into this trip in the first place. After that, the two walked along into the town to find a nice bar to sit in and enjoy their last evening on land together, before heading out towards a great unknown the following day.

As they sat together in a bar they'd found along the beachfront, they watched the night creep in from the eastern horizon. They were each very aware that this would be the last night they'd spend in the safety of known civilization for a while. They held each other's hand tightly, both thinking about what events may be lying in wait for them over the days ahead. Once the night sky was above thm and the partygoers were celebrating louder, the two of them slipped away and headed back to the boat to get some rest.

Early the next morning, just before the sun had risen, they set sail from Arrecife, winding through the different islands before leaving the canaries behind, looking ahead to the open ocean. As predicted, the weather grew increasingly worse the further away from land they sailed. Each day saw rough seas, some rain and growing winds.

Putting safety above all else, they'd often have to sail the safest route through the rough patch as opposed to sailing directly towards their destination. After three days of difficult sailing, they were blessed with some calmer weather and a good wind to help them get back on track. Though Chloé knew that at the end of this weather would come the storm she feared.

The calm weather lasted for three days, where the three of them worked with little sleep, ensuring they covered as many nautical miles as possible. As they were nearing their destination, Chloé spotted large storm clouds lurking on the horizon, sending a sickening feeling straight to her stomach as their boat sliced through the deceivingly easy to navigate waters. They had two options now – sail towards it and risk their lives for the chance to reach Île Merveille, or turn back.

"How many days do we have left until the full moon?" asked Chris.
"Two," replied Chloé
"Wasn't the storm supposed to hit after the full moon?" asked Lancelin.
"I guess it's early," said Chloé, hardly moving, keeping her hands firmly on the wheel and her eyes on the horizon as the boat advanced steadily. She took in a deep breath before she continued, "Well this is it. Are we all in?"

Lancelin was the first to respond, speaking loudly over the sound of the water and the air rushing past them, "I'm in." Chris took a moment whilst looking ahead at the storm clouds, before he turned to Chloé and said with confidence, "Let's do it."

Heading towards the storm, Chris went below deck to secure all loose items and to pack everything away back into their bags. Chloé advised him to put their most valuable items, some food and a first aid kit into a single bag within easy reach, just in case.

Before the storm reached them Chloé assigned herself the role of navigator, leaving the other two to take care of the sails, just as they'd done through the Gibraltar Strait. She instructed them both to change the mainsail over to the storm sail, designed to cope better in strong winds and less likely to tear.

Each of them then got into their positions, wearing their life jackets and tying themselves to the boat via a harness which could be quickly detached if needed. Though the storm was growing larger ahead of them, it was heading in a westerly direction just as they were, which luckily for them meant that they wouldn't have to ride all the way through it; they'd merely have to endure the back of it before it moved on.

Never the less, they were all anxious about what awaited them. They all remained silent as they watched the heavy, dark grey clouds speedily roll up in front of them, each of them praying they'd make it through.

The time came when suddenly the wind thrust itself upon them, bringing with it sharp, salty spray from the ocean. The sky was almost black, and the waves were gradually growing higher, bashing against the hull. Chloé turned the engine on to help overpower them.

They could hear the rumbles of thunder getting louder and louder until they started to sound like explosions going off above their heads. The lightning that came with it was brighter and much more violet-tinted than any of them had ever seen before, going off like a strobe light all around them. The waves, now thrashing over the side of the boat, were rocking them from side to side, making it extremely difficult for Chloé to navigate the best course through them. After being knocked so forcefully from one side, the boat had turned so that it's right side was now facing the oncoming waves.

Before they had chance to try and correct themselves another huge wave hit them, tumbling the boat over as they almost capsized before bobbing back upright. Chloé was shouting orders to the others to help correct the boat onto the right path through the waves, but they couldn't act quick enough before the boat was pushed over again almost onto its side.

Chloé shouted to them again, just before yet another wave hit and the boat was rocked over for a third time. This time however, when the boat came back upright, Chris was no longer on it.

The wave had thrust them in a different angle to the times before, as they had just started to turn the boat back to the oncoming waves. A sudden jolt as the boat flung itself back upright had thrown Chris backwards and into the relentless ocean.

Chloé screamed out his name and tried rush over to where he was tied onto the boat. She couldn't make it that far though as she was tied on too, so she screamed to Lancelin to help him. He then moved over to Chris' side of the boat and looked out to spot Chris in the water, where the two of them managed to almost make eye contact for a moment.

During this time, Chloé was clambering to get back to her position at the back of the boat to turn the engine off, worried that it might somehow catch Chris or his rope. Chris then saw Lancelin grab hold of his rope, but before he started to pull Chris back in, it seemed to Chris as though he paused, and just held on to watch him there in distress.

"HELP!" cried Chris as he finally got a moment without water in his mouth.

Chloé turned back and shouted out his name and told him to hold on. Just as she did this, Lancelin finally started to pull him back to the boat. As he was being pulled, yet another wave hit them sideways on and tipped the boat again. Lancelin let go of Chris' rope and held on for himself, as Chloé screamed to Chris to watch out for the boat tipping. Once it flung itself back up again, Chloé continued to Scream at Lancelin to pull Chris back in.

Eventually, Lancelin managed to get Chris back onto the boat, and no sooner was he back on when Chloé shouted to Lancelin to help her get the boat back into the right position. This time they managed it with all three of them still safely aboard, they were now facing into the waves and using the wind to pull them along and keep them upright.

About another hour went by until the waves started to die down, making it easier for them to use the strong wind of the storm to pull them in the right direction for the island.

They sailed on through the cold night until the winds and waves had died down enough for them to untie themselves, then Chris and Chloé went below deck to make sure Chris was all right, and to give him a chance to warm up. Thankfully, all Chris seemed to have was a sprained wrist from where he was holding on as he was thrown from the boat. Although worried he might be in a state of shock, Chloé made sure he was dry and warm and let him sleep whilst she sailed through the night with Lancelin.

The next morning was their last morning before the full moon. The sea had calmed down, the sky was looking slightly clearer and the wind was more manageable. They switched their sail back over from the storm sail, which now had some damage from the strong winds and waves, then sailed back towards their destination.

As it was now Lancelin's turn to rest (though they were all exhausted) he and a now warmed up and dry Chris switched over, giving Chris and Chloé some time alone together on deck.

"How're you feeling?" She asked him.
"Tired, but otherwise just grateful to be alive," he said. "I really hope we find that island tomorrow, you know. And there better be some other way for us to get back home, because there's no way I'm spending another week on this boat. Not to mention another week stuck with *him*."
"I know, I'm so sorry you had to go through that," Chloé said as she clutched Chris' hand. "Wait, what do you mean stuck with *'him'*?"

"Didn't you see him? Sat holding on to the side of the boat watching me beg for my life?"
"What? I saw him let go as the boat rolled over again, but he was in a tough situation."

"No, before that, he was just sat there watching me instead of pulling my rope in."
"I'm sure it just seemed like that, he was probably working out the best moment to start pulling you or something. He saved your life."

"No, he hesitated, I saw him!" Chris insisted, whilst trying not to raise his voice so much that he might be overheard.
"Well, I'm sure it's not what you thought. Why on earth would he want to leave you in the water?"
"I don't know," replied Chris, "But I don't trust him, and neither should you."

Chloé didn't take to well to being told what to do, but she knew she had no argument, as she was rather wary of him already. The two of them ended the conversation there and sailed on for a while in silence.

They made good time on that last day and managed to reach their destined map coordinates by about one o'clock in the morning local time. Once they had lowered their sails, they decided that they should at least get an hour's sleep each before sunrise; making sure that one person would be sat up at all times to keep them from floating too far from where they had to wait.

By now the sky had cleared and the wind had dropped, making it a beautiful night to sit up gazing at the full moon, which seemed to be bigger and brighter than they'd ever seen it before. Whilst in pursuit of something to ease the pain in her life, Chloé thought to herself how she'd forgotten that the world was already such a magical place in itself.

Once they'd all had their sleep, they sat together on the deck waiting patiently for sunrise. Chris and Chloé both shared openly about what they thought the island might be like, and what they'd like to see when they get there. Lancelin on the hand kept quiet about what was going through his mind at this time, instead just telling them he'd rather just wait and see what the dawn would bring.

At last, the moment they'd all been waiting for was finally about to happen, as the colours of the morning sky were painting the horizon and the sun was about to rise up as if from beneath the ocean's surface. Having no idea what was about to happen, Chloé and Chris stood together at the back, right-hand corner of the boat, gripping each other's hand and staring towards the sunrise.

Lancelin was sat further along the boat on the left-hand side. The boat was facing the sun sideways on and this was the side that was facing away from it. Chris and Chloé were both trembling with a mixture of fear and excitement for the unknown that they prayed was about to happen.

The ocean was calm and still. The only sounds were those of the water gently lapping up against the boat, and the ropes and sails clinking as they softly swayed back and forth. They all waited in great anticipation, for the moment that could, quite possibly, be the end of their lives as they'd known them.

CHAPTER SIX

A New Horizon

It started. The tip of the sun burst free above the water on the horizon, shooting its golden rays into the last of the night sky. Chloé and Chris both stood there staring, mesmerised by the bright light and stunning soft colours surrounding it. It was Chloé who first pulled herself out of this hypnotic state as she frantically looked around from right to left, worried that she couldn't see anything appearing and that they were going to miss their chance; or that it was all just too good to be true.

"Chris!" she shouted, pulling at his hand to get a

response out of him whilst she was gazing out at the water, "Do you see it anywhere?"

Chris suddenly came back down to earth with a shudder and then began scanning the surface of the ocean through squinted eyes, hoping to see through the sun's light. "No, I just see water. Where is it?" he pestered, as he tried to remember what Chloé had read to him from the map.

Then they heard Lancelin's voice, as he calmly said out loud, "But just for a moment, if you look behind."

Neither Chloé or Chris had understood what this passage meant, thinking they must somehow look behind the light of the rising sun for land to appear. When they heard this however, they both turned to Lancelin. "Behind what?" asked Chloé.

Just as she said that, Chris grabbed the back of her head with one of his hands and turned her so she was facing the horizon that had been directly behind them, and there it was. An island seemingly growing in the distance, as the light from the rising sun touched upon its shore.

Like a distant mountain range on a hazy day, at first it appeared somewhat fuzzy to them as they squinted and tried and bring it into focus. But the higher the sun rose up from the water, the more clear the island became to them. They all remained quiet and motionless on the boat, gazing out ahead at the new land.

"We're almost there," Lancelin whispered to himself. "What?" Chloé asked him, whilst keeping her eyes on the island.

"We've got to get there," he said hastily, "Now! Let's go!"

They all jumped into action, lifting the sails and firing up the engine. Frustratingly the wind had dropped to a mere gentle breeze by this time, which barely dragged the boat across the flat, calm surface of the water. Chloé instinctively switched the motor up to full speed, and they soon started pushing ahead towards to island.

The three of them were full of excitement, smiling and cheering as they glided across the water as fast as they could, not quite being able to believe that the land truly existed. As they got closer, the size of the island continued to grow with the rising of the sun, until it had risen fully above the ocean.

Only now could they appreciate the grandeur of this magnificent Island ahead of them. The highest mountains were breaking through the clouds above and reaching higher still, almost as if to the heavens. It was so wide that in each direction the ground disappeared off into the distance; this was more than just an island they realised – this was a new land.

Racing ahead, they felt sure they would make it, though they were unsure of exactly how long they had as a time window to make it there in; and also as to how close they had to be to it for it not to disappear again as quickly as it came.

As the bottom tip of the sun had begun to leave the surface of the ocean behind them, the island began to become hazy again, though at first it was just the high mountains. Still racing ahead using the boat's motor, they all began to hold their breath and tense up, hoping and praying that the land would not disappear completely.

Then suddenly, to each of their despair the engine started spluttering through its last drops of fuel, until it finally stopped. Chloé tried restarting it a few times until she remembered, "The gas," she said, shaking, "We forgot to refill the gas on our last stop after we used so much of it passing through the strait." She began to panic.

"Do we not have extra?" Chris asked, hoping that Chloé had just forgotten about any spare they may have had.
"No," she shouted, as she thumped the engine with her fist through frustration. Their only hope was to use what wind there was and pray that it'd be enough, as they helplessly felt themselves slow down almost to a halt.

Ahead of them, they could see the island slowly disappearing as Lancelin started to curse out loud in French, whilst the other two became sick with worry – what would they be greeted with if they were to sail all the way back now, after stealing this boat? And could they make it back without the engine? What if they got stuck in another storm? Did they even have enough food and fresh water to make it back if they were delayed by the weather? As they stood there fearing the worst, they watched as more than half of the island vanished from sight. Each of them stayed quiet, clutching onto the boat and silently pleading that they'd make it in time, as their boat crawled over the water and they helplessly watched the magic island disappearing.

Breaking their silence, completely out of nowhere the water beneath their boat was thrust upwards and they all fell about the place, grabbing on to the boat as it landed back down with a thud and rocked heavily from side to side. They remained clinging on in shock as it swayed, and Chris was the first to speak up when he shouted, "What the hell was that?!"
"I don't know," said Chloé worriedly through her shaken voice, clutching on to the boat for her life.

Before any more could be said, it happened again. This time though it came slightly from one side, frightening them all into believing the boat was going to completely capsize. As it corrected itself, Chloé looked over the rail into the water beneath them, and she was almost certain that she saw something move beneath the boat - something big.

Before she could think any more about it, they all heard the sails rattle as the wind suddenly picked up out of nowhere. Chloé looked towards them, and as she did so she noticed the island once again ahead of them, standing strong above the water, clear in its full glory.

She couldn't believe her eyes as she glanced away from it then back again, making sure it wasn't just a trick of her imagination in this desperate time. When delightedly she could confirm that it was still there, she shouted to the other two to look in the same direction. No sooner than they'd seen it for themselves, they hurried back into their positions and took control of the boat. Using the wind to their full advantage, they tore across the water, rushing towards the land as fast as they could.

Whilst cruising along, they'd stopped worrying about what had just happened to them, until whatever it had been suddenly struck them a third time. This time with far more force, which combined with the speed that the boat was travelling at the time caused it to lift right out of the water; sending them flying through the air before slapping back down against the surface. Having each untied themselves from the boat since the storm, they were all flung from it as it landed back down on its side.

Scattered about floating on the surface, the each panicked as they swam back towards the boat shouting to each other to make sure they were all okay. As the sails had landed in the water, they'd trapped air pockets under them keeping the boat from completely capsizing. They were well aware that their boat would soon sink and so threw together a plan to save what they could from it, before it was too late.

Lancelin and Chris both swam to the tip of the mast to hold on to it, whilst at the same time kicking their legs and pulling it upwards to delay the cabin door for submerging. As they did this, Chloé pulled herself up onto the boat whilst on its side to detach the self-inflating life raft. Unfortunately the boys' attempt was only delaying the inevitable by mere seconds, and they were trying their hardest not to panic about being in the same water as whatever it was that had pushed them over to begin with.

The life raft had inflated rapidly and detached itself from the boat the moment Chloé pulled on its quick release cord. She then shuffled herself around to the cabin entrance, where the water was flowing inside through the open doorway. She manoeuvred herself into the cabin to grab Chris' rucksack, which he'd packed with their valuables and their emergency supplies the day before the storm. He'd chosen his rucksack as it had a waterproof lining, though if the top of it was to be submerged, salt water would inevitably seep inside.

Getting back out of the cabin was not quite as straightforward as getting it. She had to push against the rapid incoming flow of water which was tough to move against. With both her feet and her one spare hand, she used any surface she could find to battle her way back out.

Eventually she made it through and into the open water, where she was forced to aid the rucksack across the surface whilst making sure the top of it remained above the water at all times. The guys had given up on their losing battle with trying to keep the hull from sinking, and they'd swam over to the life raft and pulled it over to greet Chloé. Firstly, they all helped lift the rucksack out of the water and onto the raft, before attempting to get in themselves.

One by one they each pulled themselves up. Lancelin attempted to launch himself up onto it and landed on his side, thrusting himself into the life-raft's squishy, inflated body. "Ahh!" he cried out in pain.
"Are you alright?" Chloé asked, slightly panicked.
"What? Oh, yes, just a sore back, that's all," he replied, as he continued to pull himself on.

Once they were all safely in the raft, Chris and Chloé used the small paddles which came with it to drag themselves away from their sinking vessel. Chris stopped paddling after merely a minute, followed by Chloé as they watched the last part of their boat disappear into the dark, unknown depths of the ocean.

The raft they were now in, was like a small, round, inflatable tent with a zip-up door. It had been well designed to keep them all safe and dry inside, whilst the bottom was weighed down in the water to prevent them from tipping over. The only way to paddle the raft, was for two people to lean out from either side of the door and to drive a paddle each, gradually thrusting themselves forwards.

They continued to stare out at where their boat had been for a short while, before zipping themselves inside, keeping just enough open for ventilation.

"Are you alright?" Chris asked Chloé.
"Yea, I think so. Are you?"
"I think so, just a bit in shock, you know."
"How about you Lancelin?" Chloé asked.
"Yea I'm ok. Did you get the book?" he replied.
"Yea, it's in the bag, isn't it?" she said, turning to Chris.
"Yea, yea I put it in there."
"Phew," sighed Chloé.

They all then sat in silence for a while, drenched in their salty clothes, giving themselves time to calm down and warm up, whilst coming to terms with their current situation.

"What the *hell* was that?" asked Chris, breaking the silence. "I mean, what could make our boat tip over like that?"

"I don't know," said Chloé, "But I think that I might have seen part of it just before it happened. Right after the second hit, I saw a huge, greyish, green looking thing moving beneath us. Almost like the back of a whale, only… bendier," she said as she motioned its movement with her hand.

"Une bête de la mer," Lancelin uttered.
"A what?" asked Chris.
"A sea beast. Some kind of hideous mer-creature. I heard about them in some of the old tales going around my town," Lancelin went on to explain. "Which can only mean that we've reached the waters of Île Merveille. We can no longer be sure what creatures move below us." Chris and Chloé were once again silenced, this time spooked by the eeriness of Lancelin's words.

After waiting half an hour or so to see if the beast would strike again, but having no sign of it, they assumed the coast was clear for now and proceeded to use the paddles to row themselves to the shore. It took quite some time and effort to get there, and they were all exhausted from the sailing trip and the events leading to them being stuck in the raft to begin with. Yet they didn't give up. They took it in turns as they did on the boat, whilst one person rested the other two worked on as hard as they could.

Slowly but surely they neared the shore, rowing faster and harder with excitement as they got closer. Scared as to what might be swimming in the water, they took no chances and rowed the raft right up to the beach; until they felt the weighted water bags beneath them dragging in the sand.

Once they'd stopped, they jumped out one after the other, Chloé being the last one as she passed the bag to Chris before jumping out herself. As she got out, she grabbed the rope from the raft and pulled it from the water and up onto the beach.

All safely on land, they paused for a moment and looked at each other, before Chris and Chloé broke into hysterics as they laughed and jumped about in excitement.

"I can't believe we actually made it!" Chris shouted as he grabbed Chloé's hands.
"It's incredible," exclaimed Chloé, "I can't believe it either!" she laughed, before both their emotions took over them completely and they pulled each other in for a kiss.

After their embrace they smiled at one another, until Chloé turned away to Lancelin to give him a hug. The excitement within her was beaming out through her face, but Lancelin just smiled and flinched however, stepping back within a second of her attempting to hug him. "I'm just so glad to be off that boat," he said, wincing as he pushed his left hand into the lower left side of his back, reminding her of his supposed back pain.

Then they all stood back. With their feet in their soggy, squelchy trainers, stood firmly on the soft, white sand as the hot sun was beaming down on their backs, they looked towards the thick, lush, green jungle greeting them at the back of the beach. They were all so happy to have made it and to be back on dry land, that none of them noticed the different, unusual sounds coming from within the jungle.

They were so happy to be there, that none of them had even thought of the obvious questions yet. Like - where would they sleep? What would they find to eat? *Would* they find anything to eat? They couldn't even care less that they'd been shipwrecked. For all normal worries seemed way behind them, now that they were shipwrecked on a magical island.

CHAPTER SEVEN

The Round King

Before they had reached the shore, it seemed that Lancelin was right – they could no longer be sure what kind of creatures moved below them. As they'd pulled themselves closer to the island, underneath their life raft swam two creatures in particular. Two creatures, who at the time were frolicking together in the warm, crystal-clear water, of la Baie de la Découverte, at the southern tip of Île Merveille.

Being two separate species, the pair had met here to share their somewhat forbidden love, away from the eyes of those who would judge them. Away from the brightly coloured corals and the deep open water where other sea folk were usually found, they swam effortlessly over a seabed of bright white sand, lit up by the sunlight as it glistened through the luminous blue water.

As they saw this strange looking object floating above them, making a splash as it pushed itself towards the beach, the couple stopped playing around and curiously followed it from beneath.

One of these two creatures was a merman. He had thick, roughly cut, dark bluish-green hair, which grew down to just below his chin. His nose was much less prominent than that of a human's, as mer-people didn't have much use for their noses; though like dolphins they still breathed air and were able to hold their breath for long periods of time.

On the upper half of his body he had what appeared to be human skin, but he was in fact covered in tiny fish scales. These scales were similar to the colour of a human's skin who'd been nicely tanned by the summer sun, but without that sun-kissed glow. Around about his hips the scales seamlessly changed, growing larger and switching colours, matching his tail to the colour of his hair.

His tail was almost double the length of his torso and moved much more fluidly, with strong muscles to power him through the water. The end of his tail split off into long strips, which looked like two large, thin sections of webbed skin. His fin was slightly lighter in colour to the tail and almost see-through. Whilst moving effortlessly in the water it stretched about a meter wide and almost two meters in length. Formed in a similar way to this, he had a long thin fin running from the back of his neck all the way down his body; reaching just an inch in height and merging into a dorsal fin between his lower back and the top of his tail. The dorsal fin was also webbed, much the same as his main fin.

His name, like nearly all mer-people's, is impossible to write down, as they communicate with each other underwater using sounds, in much the same way as dolphins and whales do.

The other creature, who was in love with this merman, is known throughout this land as an elementame (meaning element soul). They were merely a human soul without a body, who can use earth, air, fire or water to create their desired image of their missing human form (though something unique to each of them was their face, which they did not have the power to change). By doing this, they are able to be seen and communicate with others around them. Their most commonly chosen form is water - being the easiest to both shape and move about in.

This particular elementame had named themselves Séphorna (Séph for short) and had decided to take on the body form of a female – or at least a mermaid for this moment. When forming their body using water, they create a much denser concentration of liquid, so that to touch it, it is distinguishable from the water around them. They can also choose which colour light to reflect on different parts of their body. Therefore, though still somewhat see-through and shimmery looking,

Séph was still noticeable in the water just as another mermaid, and she'd chosen a mixture of light pink, blue and yellow for her tail and hair colours.

Séph and the merman followed the raft until the water started to get quite shallow, when the merman decided to stay behind in case he was spotted by whatever it was on the surface. Séph then altered her colours to match the clear blue water, making it possible for her to carry on further without being seen.

She followed them right up until she saw the bottom of the raft hit the sand as it stopped. Waiting nervously to see what would happen next, she was startled when Lancelin's feet suddenly punched through the water straight down to the sand beneath. As elementames have no physical body, they can swiftly change their size and shape. So, as she saw Lancelin's feet enter the water, her tail suddenly became her head and vice versa, as she shot off back into the deeper blue; too far away for her to continue watching the newcomers.

When she stopped swimming and looked back in their direction, she thought to herself – were they human feet? Maybe in the moment she'd mistaken them, perhaps it was just a creature with a human-like form? Though any that would be that size, enter the water *and* be out during daylight hours - she knew of none.

Though still rather shaken by the event, she tried to calm herself down and move back in for a second look. As she got closer, she lifted her head out of the water just enough so her eyes were above the surface, so she could see clearly what it was. She could hardly believe her eyes when she looked again, what she saw made her spirit go still - three humans setting foot on Île Merveille.

Panic-stricken, Séph rushed back to the merman and pulled him up to the surface, directing his sight straight ahead towards the humans. The two of them barely moved, stunned in disbelief as they watched the three newcomers drag the raft up onto the beach. Séph then turned to the merman and told him to swim back as fast as he could, and to warn his fellow mer-people and other underwater creatures about the return of human life on Île Merveille, and to advise them all to keep them away from the shore.

After he left her, she remained there alone in the water, frantically trying to think about what she needed to do next. As here in this land, there was an unwritten law to which all creatures had been forced to abide - that no human should again be allowed to set foot upon the soil of Merveille.

She decided that the best thing she could do was to warn the fairy colony, who occupied the area of jungle by this beach. As fairies were one of the few magical creatures with human-like intelligence, they often protected and had control of the area of land which they inhabited.

Séph swam along the shore to the mouth of a slow river, where it entered the sea from within the jungle. The river water wasn't as clear as the sea water, it was mixed with soil and sand it at churned up along its course, but this was the easiest route she knew of to get to the fairies.

She swam up the river until she came to a large, dark turquoise pool at the foot of a gentle waterfall. The pool was a calm oasis hidden in the jungle, surrounded on one side by large boulders and trees, and on the other side a small shore where creatures would come to cool off away from the sea. It was in this pool where Séph rose up out of the water and held her arms out to her sides.

As she did so, her whole being began to spin, getting faster and faster until the water that made up her body sprayed out away from her in all directions. As the water left her, in its place was a small storm of swirling air, looking kind of like a very thin cloud of smoke being blown around in different directions; with a faint outline of a woman's figure within it. Once rid of her watery body, she flew forward in a strong gust of wind, whistling through the trees towards where the fairies lived.

As she reached the outskirts of the area of jungle they inhabited, she flew straight into the ground with a hard thud, over a small space not covered by trees. A moment after she had landed in the ground, the small patch of earth where she had entered started to tremble. Then slowly, it began to rise and break apart, and the body of Séph became clear amongst the dirt and rubble, until she was somewhat fully formed lying face down.

Slowly, the top half of her body rose up from the floor as she pushed herself up to a sitting position. Her body was now made up mainly of earth, with rocks and plants sticking out of her at different parts. Her eyes were now symbolised by two small stones, giving anyone who would be talking to her somewhere to look. When using earth to create their bodies, it was difficult for an elementame to move about very much, as earth was the heaviest of the four elements they could use, and whenever they did, more dirt would fall from them.

Once she had composed herself and looked around only to find no sign of a fairy nearby, she let out a call to the fae - a low, sad sound, signalling that something was wrong. As she cried out, the sound travelled through the jungle far and wide, creating an eerie and unsettled feeling amongst most of the inhabitants who heard it. It was heard all throughout the fairy colony, except by their king – King Tawhio – and others who at the time were inside their sacred, hollow Wharnui tree.

The fairies who inhabited the tropical areas of Île Merveille, looked similar to the indigenous Māori people of New Zealand, except they were about as tall as the length from your wrist to the tip of your middle finger. They didn't wear much in the way of clothes, just enough cloth tied around them to keep their dignity when in the presence of others. Their wings resembled the wings of brightly coloured, shimmering butterflies, each with a unique pattern in the same way our fingerprints are unique to each of us. The wealthier fairies lived in trees, mostly shared by other families though few did have their own, and the poorer fairies lived in the ground.

Fairy colonies throughout the land were referred to by the name of their leader, so, this particular colony was known as the Tawhio fairies. They were not the only fairy colony in this part of Île Merveille, but they were certainly the largest, and the closest to Séph at the time. It was a group of four guardian fairies who were patrolling the borders not far from her as she called, who flew over to find out what creature had made the sound; advising others they saw along the way to stay calm.

The guardians had tattooed armour on their skin, laced with sacred, fairy healing magic to protect them from injuries. As they approached the sound, Séph spotted them and stopped, then began speaking to them instead.

"Are you Tawhio fairies?" she asked.
"That's right, and who…… Séph? Is that you?" asked the fairy leading the search, as they landed on the ground in front of her. Séph was known throughout the Tawhio colony as a good friend of theirs. She'd often visit them for their festivals and concerts, which fairies throughout Île Merveille were known for doing spectacularly well.

"Yes, it's me. Is that you Tai?" Séph responded. She had met Tai several times before as he was often on the patrol closest to the river.
"Oh, Hi! Yea, it's me," he replied, fluttering close to her.
"Was that you making all that noise?"
"It was…"
"What's going on? You've got the whole jungle worried!" he exclaimed.

"Tai, listen, I need to speak with King Tawhio urgently."
"Why? What's wrong?"
"Well," Séph paused for a moment. "I saw humans. Three of them, here this morning, in the bay," she told them cautiously. As she did so, the expressions on their

faces suddenly turned to a combination of worried and confused.

"But, that's not possible. Are you sure they were humans?" asked one of the other guardians, "I thought Alexandra made sure they could never find us again."
"Well, it appears they found a way in, and they're here right now, just on the edge of the jungle."

The fairies stood around, looking at each other and not knowing quite how to react to this news.
"I shall advise the King right away," said Tai, fluttering his wings and flying up so he was now level with Séph's face as he spoke to her. Then he turned to the others, "Let's go," he commanded to the guardians. Then the four fairies flew back towards their colony.

Tai advised his team to warn the other guardian fairies of the possibility of humans, and to stay on high alert, but also not to mention a word about it to anyone else. Then, he flew ahead to the Wharnui tree to find the King.

The Wharnui tree was an enormously wide though fairly short tree, at least compared to others around it, found in the centre of the area of jungle claimed by the Tawhio fairies. From the outside, it looked rather like many different tree trunks blended together, with branches breaking off at different heights and in all directions. At the bottom were thick, strong roots clinging on to the ground and spreading far out away from the tree.

From the branches grew thick green leaves and flowers of every colour imaginable. Upon closer inspection of the tree, you could see, disguised by its bark, little windows and doorways leading inside. On the inside, this tree was almost completely hollowed out, containing an extensive network of rooms and corridors which made up the Royal Palace of the Tawhio fairies.

The interior was every bit as grand and luxurious as a fairy's palace could be, with essence of pure light magic illuminating it, and each room a unique design carved out of the wood. The king who ruled here was a very happy king indeed, having everything he could ever want readily available to him.

Though king Tawhio was known as a happy and kind leader, he was also a rather greedy king. He wasn't the tallest of fairies either, and thanks to the seemingly unlimited amount of delicious food brought to him upon request, he was quite a round shaped fairy. His hair was short, thick and dark, and his wings seemed dwarfed in comparison to most other fairies. They were coloured in many shades of orange with black stripes and swirling patterns. To look at, one would guess his age to be around mid-forty, though the fairies here age at a slightly slower rate than humans.

His people lived in peace, with few problems to complain about. As such, his fairies got on with their lives without having to bother him much – leaving him more time to sit back and enjoy his colony's riches. He was usually found in his day room, lounging on a bed of thick luxurious pillows, having fresh food brought to him and being entertained by all kinds of entertainers.

He had two female fairies, Wae and Aroha, who were

employed to follow him around most of the time. They were slightly younger, full-bodied women, loyal to the kind and who you wouldn't dare try to mess with. They were mainly for him to talk to and to enjoy his entertainment with, but also to provide services such as massages, hand feeding his food to him and making sure things were just to his liking before he entered another room.

This day, for the king, had been playing out much like any other. He was relaxing in his day-room, being fed a mixture of delicious seeds by Wae and Aroha, whilst having his favourite comedian perform for him – blissfully unaware that he'd soon have to get up and actually do something.

After rushing through the jungle, Tai finally reached the entrance to the Wharnui tree. A grand entrance on the lower part of a wide section of tree trunk, with a thick root growing out of the side creating a walkway to the entrance from the earthy ground below. The guards of the palace knew Tai, therefore, after he'd explained the situation to them, they granted him entry to the palace and told him where he could find the king. He proceeded to rush through the many winding corridors, going vertically as well as horizontally, until he reached the doors of King Tawhio's day-room.

He knocked gently but assertively, so as not to disrupt the king too abruptly, and King Tawhio sent Aroha to answer the door by simply flapping his hand in its direction.

"Yes?" she asked, as she saw Tai standing on the other side of the door.

"Hello, my name is Tai, I'm one of the colony guardians. It's necessary that I speak with King Tawhio right away."

"About what?" she said as she looked him up and down. "His Highness is currently indulged in his lunchtime entertai..."

Tai interrupted her by simply barging past and into the room.

"Come back here!" she called after him.

"King Tawhio, your highness, forgive me for the intrusion but I must speak with you urgently," said Tai, "And privately," he continued after noticing the others in the room.

"What? Who? What's going on?" the king said, slightly confused by this sudden interruption. "Tai? Is that you? What brings you barging in here and interrupting me like this?"

"My apologies your majesty, but I..." Tai was interrupted by the king.

"Can't it wait until the end of this skit? Sit down boy and watch, I assure you it'll be worth it," the king said, beginning to chuckle to himself as he relived the comedy over in his head, seeming oblivious to the fact that there was a matter of urgency at hand. He motioned to one of the women to pass him over another plate of food.

"I'm afraid it can't your majesty, it's most important that we act quickly on this," said Tai, trying not to sound too demanding towards the king.

"Act quickly? To what? Oh, very well, leave us, everyone!" The king shuffled around to sit himself up a bit more, "But don't go far," he said, as he winked to one of the females."

The king stayed seated on his bed of pillows, whilst Tai stood neatly next to the bed and began to explain, in a low voice, the news he'd just heard from Séph.

"Humans? But that's impossible," the king chuckled, "Even if they did find the island, they'd have been warned off by the sea beasts before they got anywhere near us."

"Exactly, that's what's got her so worried, how did they manage to make it all the way to our jungle?"

"Quite." The king paused for a moment, trying to make sense of it all. "I'm sure it's probably just some other magic of some kind. Can't really trust these non-fairy folk," the king chuckled again, doing his best to avoid the severity of the situation.

"Right you may be your majesty, however, she has asked to speak with you about what we should do about it. She's waiting for you between here and the river."

"Very well then," the king sighed, realising he'd now have to get up and do something, "I'll go and speak with her if it'll put an end to this nonsense, then I can get back to my entertainment. He really is a good comedian, you should see him sometime Tai," he said, laughing away to himself once again. The king then called the two women back into the room and asked them to get his transport ready, so that he could be taken to see Séph.

King Tawhio spent much of his time sat down and didn't get much exercise. This, together with his particularly small wings for his size, made it rather difficult for him to fly. Therefore, whenever he went anywhere outside of the Wharnui tree that wasn't far enough to be taken by carriage, he had four strong fairies (two male and two female) carry him around on a moderately plush, open-top litter chair.

The chair itself was quite wide so that the king could easily fit into it, and of course, it was extremely comfortable too. It wasn't the usual throne shape, instead, it resembled a wood carving of a wide bowl, tipped to one side and filled with pillows to suit King Tawhio's large, soft body. As the chair was carried, the two female fairies who catered to his needs flew either side of the chair, and two guardian fairies would fly ahead of him, and another two behind.

When everything was ready, the two females aided King Tawhio to an exit from the tree higher up in the branches, so as not to seem to be on any official business by any of his people who happened to spot him leaving.

Tai led the way, straight back to where Séph was sat waiting anxiously for them. The king was carried right up to her, where she greeted him as if he were her own king. She then held out her hand in front of King Tawhio for him to be lowered down onto; giving the chair carriers a much-needed rest. Once stood on her palm he looked up and smiled at her, and began to question her politely about this human nonsense she'd been going on about.

"Your majesty, I'm positive that what I saw earlier were most definitely three humans. The way they all stood and looked at the jungle, the strange clothes they were wearing and the bag they had, neither of which were of this land." There was a moment of silence whilst

Séph waited for King Tawhio to respond. "Do you think that… we must wake Alexa…" Séph was then abruptly interrupted by the king.

"Now, now, let's not jump to doing anything unnecessary. I'll send some guardians to the shore to find these, beings, and we'll decide what to do about them when we know more about what's going on."

Séph agreed with King Tawhio, and she was given permission to use the area of ground within the confines of the fairy colony, which she used when attending their festivals, to wait in safety for the return of the guardian fairies.

Once everyone was back by the Wharnui tree, King Tawhio gave the order for a troop of guardian fairies to search for the supposed three humans. Ten of them were sent towards the shore to look for them, including Tai who led the search. The guardians flew swiftly through the trees without being sensed by anyone, or anything, around them. They had no weapons or shields to carry either, as fairy magic was all they ever used to defend themselves; and being guardian fairies they were skilfully trained to use their magic in battle.

When it came to fairy magic there were several things a fairy could do, one of which was to create illusions. The reality of these illusions depended on how well trained the fairy was at creating them. Most fairies could create an illusion of anything they could imagine, it was as simple as projecting an image from within their mind into the reality around them; and through the light of the magic within them, it would appear.

However, these simple illusions could be destroyed by the mere touch from another being, or you could even walk through them as if it was just a ghost. The illusions created by the guardians, on the other hand, were much stronger, almost real, and difficult to destroy. King Tawhio was lucky enough to have an extremely skilled guardian fairy in his colony who trained the others, which is what helped keep his colony large and strong.

CHAPTER EIGHT

Makin' Magic

During the time that it took Séph to warn the fairies of the presence of the humans on Île Merveille, Chris, Chloé and Lancelin had pulled their raft up the beach and tied one of its ropes to a tree. Exhausted from the journey, they'd decided to re-enter the raft to get some sleep before moving on, unzipping the door and little window on it to create a decent flow of air passing through.

Chloé woke up after about an hour, finding it hard to sleep in such bright daylight, only to find that Lancelin was missing. She also saw that the book had been taken out of the rucksack and began to wonder – could the others read it now that they were here?

As she was staring at the book, she noticed a faint golden glow coming out from between two of the back pages. Was it real? Or was she just tired and dehydrated? She wondered to herself, as she hadn't had any fresh water in a while. She closed her eyes and rubbed them, then looked back at the book. The glow was still there. A soft, warm alluring glow, which mesmerised her as it stole her focus from everything else around her.

She reached out and picked up the book, then opened it to the pages where the glow was coming from. It was the map. She had folded it up and put it at the back of the book after she last looked at it, and now it was glowing, right before her eyes. She opened it up to see the map just as she'd seen it before, when suddenly, to her surprise, the words and pictures on it began to move.

The black markings on the old, yellowish paper, that had once created a picture of a map, were now swirling around on the page. Light began to shine out from between them and the glow from the map grew brighter. The dramatic show upon the page hypnotised her, as she fell into a trance-like state, falling completely unaware of her true surroundings.

To herself, she was now sat holding the map alone, totally enclosed by spinning golden and white light. Dazzled by the brightness, she held her hand up in front of her eyes as the light continued to swirl rapidly around her as if she was sat in the centre of a whirlwind. Then the brightness of the light began to concentrate in front of her, and the light to the sides of her was no longer too bright to look at.

She watched it curiously as it whooshed past her, until she could almost make out images appearing in the mixture of shades within the light. Until suddenly, was that a face she could see? She squinted her eyes and focused her concentration, finding not just any face, but her father's.

The image became stronger as she saw him reach out his hand towards her. Overwhelmed with emotion, she wanted to reach out back to him, but she was paralyzed from the shock of what was happening to her. Then the light began to fade away around her, and the image of her father slowly disappeared with it.

As the light had stopped swirling and rested, concentrated in front of her, she found herself in a new location, completely unknown to her. It seemed to be a huge, light and open cave. The entrance to the cave was behind her, higher up and with a vast pile of rocks and rubble creating a pathway up to it. The sun shone down through the wide entrance way and lit up the cave floor, which was solid rock.

The floor of the cave was so sparse that you could fit a crowd of about twenty people down there, and it sloped down slightly towards the back. The stone was a greyish-yellow colour, giving a soft, warm feel to the whole room when lit up by the rays of sunshine flowing in through the entrance.

Ahead of her now, the bright light had dimmed and Chloé was able to look towards it more easily. From out of the back wall of the cave the light appeared to be flowing, pouring into a pool which covered about a quarter of the base of the cave. Chloé couldn't be sure at this point what it actually was that was flowing. Was it a liquid? Or a heavy gas perhaps? Either way, it was stunningly mesmerising to her, and she picked herself up from sitting on the floor with intent on getting a closer look.

All she could hear at this point, was the tranquil sound of water trickling harmoniously through the rock around her, echoing in the open space inside the cave. As she stood up, she picked up the book from her lap and held it close to her body, as she walked towards the flowing light.

Nearing the pool, she began to hear a voice of someone speaking to her, but who was nowhere to be seen. She thought it sounded like a man's voice, and the sound seemed to be coming from all around her - or maybe even from within her; she couldn't be sure. Either way, it didn't seem to bother her whilst her concentration was transfixed on the light.

"Touch it," whispered the voice to Chloé, in an echo-like, chilling sort of sound. "Take in the light. Touch the light. All the power will…" At the instant the voice was interrupted by another voice, this time speaking her name.
"Cleo," it called.

Chloé stopped walking, this time she recognised the voice, and knew that there was only one person who called her that. Then she heard it again. "Cleo!" It was Chris' voice.

"Chris?" she asked speaking aloud and unsure where his voice was coming from, "Is that you?"

"Cleo!" he said again, "Wakey, wakey!"

As she heard him speak this time, she felt herself being pulled backwards slightly, causing her to lose balance and fall to the floor. As she fell, the cave around her started spinning and turned back into the whirling, spinning bright light. She closed her eyes as the light grew too bright for her, and when she opened them again she found herself back in the life raft.

She tried to explain to Chris what she had seen, though confused by what had just happened, she wasn't quite sure herself. She showed the map to Chris, but still he saw nothing but a blank page. To her the map had gone back to how she'd seen it originally, and it had stopped glowing.

They wondered about the whereabouts of Lancelin too. Chris was sure that he'd abandoned them and that they should watch out for nasty surprises, though Chloé thought he'd simply gone in search of food and water and got lost along the way. At the thought of finding food or water, Chris' stomach began to rumble, so they decided to open up their emergency rations which Chris had packed in the rucksack.

Considering how hungry and thirsty they both were, there wasn't really much to share between them - especially as Chloé insisted they save some for Lancelin. After they'd eaten, they decided to abandon the raft, pack up their bag and head off into the jungle to see what this land had to offer them. Unsure of what they would discover, they strode on with caution in search for food, water, shelter and Lancelin.

As they walked through the jungle, Chris led the way whilst Chloé followed closely behind. Nothing in the vegetation around them seemed recognisable as food of any kind. Growing hungrier and thirstier, Chloé told Chris she needed to sit and rest for a moment.

They sat upon a fallen and overgrown tree trunk, and whilst they were sat down, Chloé thought it would be a good idea to look through the book to see if there was anything written about what they could eat here. So Chris, who was carrying the rucksack, got out the book and handed it to her, trying his hardest not to notice the food and water they were still carrying, which they'd saved for Lancelin. As Chloé took the book, she felt a strange feeling wash over her body, a feeling of strength and certainty. It confused her, as when she'd sat down for a rest she'd started to believe that things were seeming a little hopeless.

She sat the book on her lap and placed her hand on top, with her thumb touching the edges of the pages. She paused for a moment and stared down at the book, feeling almost guided somehow, as if she wasn't in control of her hand or which page she would choose to open it on. As her thumb stroked down over the pages, she decided to close her eyes and go with the feeling inside her, when suddenly she felt compelled to stop.

She pushed her thumb in between the pages and opened the book at this point, still with her eyes closed. Chris wondered what on earth she was doing, and why she hadn't just started from the beginning and looked through. He was becoming increasingly frustrated that he had to rely solely on Chloé to find every little piece of information they needed – what if she accidentally missed something? He thought.

Once Chloé had opened the book, she opened her eyes and looked down on to the page and began to read. Written down on it was what appeared to be a spell, or enchantment of some kind, and some small instruction on how to use such magic. Surrounding the words on the page, were illustrations of decadent chalices and elaborate goblets.

"Well? Any luck?" Chris pestered her, "What does it say?"

Chloé carefully read aloud the inscription she saw written on the page, trying to work out how it would help them as she read it.

> *Enchant this vessel I hold in my hand,*
> *Filled with water found on this land,*
> *And of blood instilled with the light,*
> *May it reveal within, a thirst's most delight.*
>
> *Now fill once again with any liquid you find,*
> *Hold in your hand and reach deep in your mind.*
> *Once poison or bitter shall change with desire,*
> *Satisfying and delicious is the drink you'll acquire.*

"Well that sounds great, but it doesn't really help us *now* does it," said Chris, growing even more frustrated that he couldn't look through the book himself.
"No, I guess not," said Chloé. She continued to stare at the words on the page for a moment, trying to work out how it could help them, to no avail. Then, just as she'd

given up and was about to turn the page, one of the drawings on it caught her eye. She recognised one of the goblets. It looked exactly the same as the one Chris had taken from the castle.

"Chris," she said whilst staring at the picture, "Is that cup thing in the bag? The one you picked up in the castle?"
"It should be."
"Could you hand it to me? With Lancelin's water?" Chris paused for a moment, a little confused, before he gave in and proceeded to search the bag for the items Chloé had asked for.

After handing over the goblet and the water to Chloé, she examined the goblet along with the picture in the book. She was right, this was exactly the same. She re-read the words on the page and thought to herself quietly as Chris watched her, feeling rather useless.

Carefully she opened the water bottle and poured some of the water into the goblet, then passed the bottle back to Chris. She held the goblet tight in her hand and closed her eyes, then began to think of what drink she would like to see most when she opened them again. Something filling she thought, a warm soup drink perhaps or a thick fruit smoothie.

As they were both hot and thirsty, sat in the sticky, humid air of the jungle, she decided to wish for the cold, thick fruit smoothie, made from plump juicy mangos and zesty oranges. Whilst thinking about this her mouth rapidly began to water. She could almost taste the fresh fruits in her mouth.

Lost in her thoughts, she was brought back to earth by the sound of Chris' tone of disbelief whilst muttering the words, "Oh my God." She opened her eyes and asked him what he was talking about, thinking he'd spotted something in the trees. "The drink," he said, "Look!"

Chloé looked down into the goblet and couldn't believe what she saw. The water had turned into the fruit smoothie she had most desired, and she could feel the chill from it reaching through the stained-glass cup of the goblet. Slowly she sipped it, a sip which sent a sensation of relief and satisfaction all through her body, a sensation which made her skin tingle and her hairs stand on end. Neither of them could believe what they had just witnessed. Genuine magic happening right before their eyes.

Chloé handed the goblet to Chris so he could enjoy a taste of the smoothie himself. As it was passed from her hands to his however, the colour drained rapidly from the smoothie and before they knew it, it had turned back into the water it'd started out as. Chris tried to hold back the look of disappointment on his face, as it seemed to confirm a growing suspicion he had - that this journey was much more about Chloé, and that there may be very little in it for him.

"Maybe you need to try it yourself?" Chloé suggested, "The smoothie was *my* desire after all."

Chris held the goblet and looked disheartened down into the water held inside it. Then, closing his eyes, he tried his best to imagine what he'd like to see in the goblet. Annoyingly, however, already unconvinced that this would work for him, the water wouldn't change. Frustrated, he squeezed his eyes shut tightly and pleaded for his wish to be fulfilled.

"Relax," said Chloé, "Try not to just picture it in the cup, but imagine what it would be like to *have* it in the cup." He did as she instructed and he began to relax, drawing on the feelings he had when he thought he would get some of the smoothie that Chloé had created. His mouth began to water as hers had at the thought of the cool, fresh smoothie, and his body relaxed with the joy he envisioned should he at last get to take a sip. He sat with his eyes closed, lost in his imagination, until he heard Chloé speak to him.

"You've done it!" she exclaimed, trying not to startle him, "Look."

He slowly opened one of his eyes and peaked into the goblet. He couldn't believe it, he'd actually managed to change the water. Once he'd seen it, he opened both eyes widely and quickly took a sip, afraid it might disappear. In the excitement, he drank every last drop he could get, afraid it might soon disappear, before looking back at Chloé. There was a moment of stillness between them before they both burst out with laughter through the amazement.

"Thank you, weird, old sorcerer!" shouted Chris as he held the goblet up in front of them both.
"Right then, I guess now we have to find more liquid," Chloé said joyfully. Then they picked up their belongings and headed off in search of any water they could find, now unsure of exactly which direction the sea was in, whether it looked fresh or not.

Unbeknown to them, whilst they'd been sat there discovering the first magical object which they could both use and control, they'd been closely watched by the guardian fairies. When the fairies first spotted them, they'd decided to watch them for a while to see if they revealed their true selves, hoping to find the intruders to be at least something of this land. However, when they heard them complaining of hunger, thirst and not knowing where they were, their fears were confirmed.

CHAPTER NINE

Man Or Witch?

The guardians were about to launch a small, unadvised attack, hoping to scare the humans out of the jungle and back on to the beach. Just as they'd been getting in position, Tai noticed Chris take the book out of the rucksack, and his curiosity caused him to hold back their attempt to scare them off.

He watched by, safely hidden in the trees surrounding them, questioning what information a book in the hands of humans could have on Île Merveille. When he heard Chloé read out the enchantment, something he knew little about, he moved closer to her to get a look at the pages in the book. He could see neither words nor pictures on them, and for a moment he was completely bewildered by what was going on.

The fairies continued to watch in anticipation, to find out what these humans were up to, when to their horror they witnessed this witchcraft for the first time in their lives. These are not mere humans, Tai feared, these are surely witches. But how could they still exist? And what were they up to? His mind questioned frantically. Tai tried to calm himself in order think more clearly.

If, as they believed, the witches had only just arrived, Tai assumed they must've had their powers before reaching Île Merveille – which explained how they got passed the sea beasts, he thought. "We have to get out of here," he whispered to the other guardians, "We must warn the king."

With that, the guardian fairies moved cautiously so as not to be noticed by Chloé and Chris, and they flew back to the Tawhio colony. On the way there, Tai gave orders to the other guardians with him at the time, to warn other fairies to stay in their homes and away from the witches.

Tai entered the Wharnui tree via a side entrance, as agreed upon by himself and the king, where a guard was standing in wait for his return. The guard escorted him straight to King Tawhio, who was once again lounging about in his day room, enjoying delicious food and his favourite comedian. He barged straight into the room before coming to a halt, when he realised he was once again interrupting the king and his entertainment.

"My apologies your highness, but I bring urgent news from my…"

"Ah yes, yes," the king interrupted Tai, before he should arouse any more suspicion for the others in the room that there may be trouble brewing, however, it was a little too late for that.

The king ordered everyone to leave the room, and the two females were whispering to each other on their way out about what they thought might be going on; the king would never normally allow an interruption, let alone two. Once again, the king and Tai were alone in the king's day room, and Tai explained what he'd seen.

"Two witches?" asked the king, "And, you're sure you actually saw them use magic? Magic that say, a vampire couldn't do?"

"Well, a vampire's powers are quite specific your majesty, and this was definitely no vampire magic. Besides, they've been sat out in bright daylight, and they have that glowing skin so is told humans do, when touched by the rays of the strong sun," said Tai. The king paused for a moment, pulling a disgruntled expression as he tried to think about what else they could be.

"Ah!" he began, "What about that, big fairy? You know, the one who travels with the uni…"

"Your Highness, forgive me, but I swear that they are acting like no other natural inhabitants of this land."

"Well," said the king, refusing to accept that any action need be taken, "It still seems there could be a thousand explanations, each much more likely than humans once again possessing the light."

"With all due respect your majesty, if you saw them, I

know you would be sure as I, that these are not beings of this land."

King Tawhio stared silently down at a plate of food he hadn't yet finished eating and sighed, realising that however much he wished to believe that Tai's words were not true, if in fact they were and he did nothing, he would surely be in big trouble. After his pause for thought, going over the news from the day in his mind, the king had noticed an inconsistency between Séph's information and Tai's recollection of what he'd witnessed.

"Tai, did you say you saw *two* witches?" he asked.
"Yes, one male and one female."
"But, didn't Séph say she saw *three* humans?"
"That's correct your majesty."
"Well then," the king smiled, "Are there two or are there three? Or are there five? And are they all witches? Or are they a mixture? We can't very well go up against something when we can't be certain what it is or how many there are."

Tai was beginning to feel frustrated by the king's ignorance to the severity of their situation, and he was trying his hardest not to let this show in case the king would hand over the responsibility to someone else. King Tawhio simply ordered Tai to take his group of guardians back out into the jungle, to search for the third human, and to keep an eye on the two witches to find out just how powerful they were.

However, Tai wasn't satisfied with this outcome, to him there was only one course of action one should take when the presence of a witch was confirmed on

Île Merveille. Under the rule of king Tawhio though, Tai continued to follow orders, and he rounded up the group of guardian fairies to assist him again in surveying the supposed witches; he also got together a smaller group to go in search of the one who was still missing.

Since Tai had left Chloé and Chris, they'd managed to locate the river, and using the enchanted goblet they were replenishing themselves with all the drinks they could think of - which would satisfy both their thirst and their hunger. Once replenished, they relaxed in the shade. Laying down side by side, with their heads both resting on the rucksack, they fell asleep.

Whilst fast asleep out in the open, they had both been too exhausted to worry about just how exposed and vulnerable they were, which made it easy for the guardian fairies to find them again. As soon as they'd been spotted, one guardian suggested that they act quickly, and either capture them and take them back as prisoners, or simply kill them there and then.

Luckily for Chloé and Chris, Tai believed them to be witches, and he couldn't be sure how they would react to being attacked. What if they were sleeping with some kind of protection aura around them, he thought. Or what if they should wake up once back in the colony, get angry, and destroy them all? No, Tai couldn't be sure just how skilled in magic they were and believed it would be a much safer approach to observe them for a while, to find out exactly what they were dealing with.

The couple slept for a long time, so long that the guardian fairies watching them had become restless and were not watching them so carefully. Chris was the first one to wake up, feeling desperate for a pee after all they'd had to drink, and he got up and walked over to a tree to relieve himself. Unknowingly, he had wondered close to where some of the guardians were waiting, though they hadn't yet noticed that Chris had even woken up. As he began to pee, he startled some of the guardians, and as they reacted to the sudden sound of the liquid splashing on the ground, he noticed some leaves rustling close by.

The guardians held themselves still again, however, it was too late, they had already aroused Chris' curiosity as to what was moving between the leaves near to him. After he'd finished, he walked over to them, and carefully he began to part the large, thick heavy foliage of this tropical plant.

The guardians hiding inside were afraid they were about to be discovered, and in their defence, one of them quickly conjured up an illusion of a snake, camouflaged by the leaves. The snake slithered slightly, before tasting the air with its tongue and turning its head to face Chris. With the realisation that he had his hands and head so close to a wild snake, he went cold with fear and his heart began pounding out of his chest. Using all his strength not to jump up and stumble backwards, he slowly started to back away, trying not to startle the snake.

As his hands were gliding slowly back along the leaves, letting them go gently, one guardian fairy hadn't realised he was so close to being touched by him. Facing away from what was going on, the guardian was looking for a way out of the hiding place and a route back to Tai and the others, without being noticed.

Suddenly Chris' hand touched him and almost pushed him off the branch where he was standing. As he was pushed, the guardian gasped and fluttered his wings to steady himself back on to the branch, which Chris heard all too clearly. As he heard the strange sound from within the bush, his attention was drawn to it ever so slightly. The guardian controlling the snake wasn't about to take any chances though, and he caused the snake to hiss and launch its head towards Chris in an attack.

Startled and terrified, Chris shouted and jumped backwards before falling over his own feet. Then, scurrying himself back up, he ran away back to where Chloé was sleeping, waking her up as he got to her. In a shaky voice he apologised to Chloé for waking her up, then explained what had just happened and why waking her had been so necessary. The news of the snake freaked Chloé out too, which confused Tai as he watched all of this play out from his viewpoint. Why would two witches be so afraid of a snake, he thought, perhaps they weren't as powerful as he'd given them credit for. Feeling confident now that he'd be able to capture them both, he gathered the other guardians to discuss a plan of action.

Chris and Chloé moved back to sit by the water, away from anywhere a snake or any other scary jungle creature could suddenly surprise them from. As they huddled together, they worried about how they might have to continue to sleep in shifts, to keep them safe from the creatures lurking in this strange jungle. That thought led Chloé to begin thinking about the last time they'd slept, and how she'd awoken to the map glowing within the book.

She took out the grimoire, hoping that it might once again help them like it did with the goblet, or that it might give her another vision of the glowing pool of light. This time however, she found the book just as she always had before reaching the island, with no guidance to anything specific within it. She looked through the pages anyway, hoping to find something that might explain her vision, or at least something interesting or useful.

As she browsed through the book, Chris noticed some movement amongst the jungle growth ahead of them. At first he said nothing, thinking it might be the same snake or something else that may not attack them if they were to remain still. Then he heard a noise, like a quiet, growling sound, coming from the same direction as the moving bushes. Worriedly he continued to watch and say nothing, Chloé did not appear to have heard anything yet, and he didn't want to scare her any more than she already had been. As he focused his attention on this area, he squinted his eyes thinking that he could almost make out the shape of something, though he wasn't quite sure what.

What he saw first though was enough to cause concern: two glowing yellow eyes appeared from within shadows of the thick, lush, jungle foliage. He carefully nudged Chloé, and without moving more than his mouth, he told her to stay completely still. He watched the eyes advance towards them slowly, noticing more of the creature as it neared the edge of the trees five or so meters ahead of them. It wasn't like a creature he'd seen before, and the more it came into the sunlit patch by the river, the more terrifying it appeared.

It moved on all fours like a stalking panther, with great sharp teeth sticking out from its mouth and two huge heavy horns on its head, curved back like those of a ram. Its fur was short but very scruffy, and coloured a mixture of brown and grey, so it stood out in the bright, tropical colours of the jungle around it. As it slowly edged towards them, growling, Chris and Chloé were frantically trying to come up with a plan to save themselves.

Thinking that they may be able to escape from it by getting to the other side of the river, they calmly picked up the rucksack and attempted to shuffle back slowly into the water. However, just as they were both about to move their feet, vines which burst out of the ground suddenly tightened around their ankles. Inwardly panicking, they both tried to free themselves from the vines without arousing the beast, but as it got closer, Chloé couldn't help but let out a loud scream, to which to beast replied with a great roar.

The sound carried through the jungle, alerting others to the presence of danger here by the river, and both Chris and Chloé felt alone, terrified and doomed. After the beast had let out its roar, it seemed to stand still and glare at them both with its bright yellow eyes, like two small dazzling headlights in the dark. They continued to pull at the vines around their ankles to set themselves free, when to their horror, more appeared from the ground beside them and wrapped around their arms and bodies, strapping them to the ground.

It seemed to them that they were done for as they tried their hardest to wriggle their way out of the vines. Then the beast began to move towards them like a lioness stalking her prey, then opened its mouth to let out streams of drooling saliva.

In the next instant, breaking the tension, another cry was heard coming towards the scene. A loud, angry war cry from a single voice came out of nowhere, making the beast stop deadly still as if someone had just turned it off. It was Lancelin. He was running along the side of the river towards the beast with a long, thin rope of sorts in his hand.

He flung the rope around the neck of the beast and pulled it tight. The rope was in fact that special kind of daisy chain Chloé had read about in the book. Just when Lancelin thought he now had control of this great beast, its body instantly began to disappear in swirls of light, before getting so bright that they all had to shield their eyes from it. When they were finally able to look back, it had gone. The vines that once held Chloé and Chris in place had also vanished, and once again the area by the river seemed calm.

"Lancelin!" shouted Chloé, "Where have you been? Thank god you found us in time!" She stood up and tried to hug him, though it wasn't returned.
"Yea, thanks," said Chris, "Super Lancelin," he joked sheepishly.

"I went to explore a little bit whilst you two were sleeping, but when I got back you'd gone," he explained, "So I rested for a while before setting off again to find you, then when I heard your scream I came running."

"With the magic daisy chain," Chris pointed out, accusingly.

"Yes, I spotted them deeper in the jungle, in a strange area where the trees and plants seem to change to, well, less tropical types."

"However it came to be, I'm just so grateful that you got here and saved us, from whatever that ugly thing was," said Chloé, stepping back from him as he just stood there awkwardly after avoiding yet another embrace. Chris was still not convinced that all this was quite so coincidental, but as Lancelin had just seemed to save his life, he thought it was best not to mention it for now.

Chloé then, realising that Lancelin must still be famished, offered the goblet to him and taught him how to drink from it. Chris noted to himself how Lancelin didn't seem quite as astonished by it as they had, but he couldn't be sure if this was purely down to everything else that had already happened so far – he wasn't the most excitable of characters anyway, he thought. Once Lancelin had quenched his thirst, the three of them decided to follow him back to see the place in the jungle where the trees and plants changed, and to continue on exploring the island together.

As for Tai, after his conjured beast was defeated by a surprise attack, he was now more worried than before about these three. He was convinced that even if these three were not the most powerful of witches, they were still three witches that needed stopping before they had a chance to learn more about their powers; before they became the new age of great sorcerers.

With that in mind, the guardians flew back to the Wharnui tree and gave king Tawhio a detailed account of the events, urging him to take appropriate action. Though he hated to get personally involved in non-fairy matters, king Tawhio could not argue with Tai or the other guardians in this case.

And so, it was done. He gave the order to a pair of messenger fairies, to fly north into the hills of the four seasons, to awaken Alexandra.

CHAPTER TEN

Campfire Magic

The three of them walked through the jungle, with Lancelin leading the way to the area where the trees and plants changed. The flora here consisted of species not usually found in tropical jungles, they were more the kinds which you'd find somewhere warm and mostly dry, like around the coast of the Mediterranean Sea.

Mixed in with the jungle setting, they saw thick-trunked, heavy palm trees and tall stone pines, nestled in with dry shrubs and prickly bushes. Much to their delight, they also spotted some trees baring recognisable fruits such as figs and dates, around others growing bananas and coconuts along the way (at least, they appeared to be just like the ones grown back in the normal world).

The change in flora didn't spread out in an eastern or western direction, but it created a sort a pathway heading north away from the sea, disappearing between two large hills smothered in tropical rainforest, not too far ahead. There was a soft breeze flowing southwards down this path, bringing with it a change in the air – still warm, but fresher and dryer than the humid air in the jungle.

As night was drawing in by the time they reached this place, they decided it would be best to 'camp' here for the night; not that they really had any camping equipment. They found an open, dry patch of ground at the base of a tall, thick, sturdy palm tree, and after gathering together a mixture of fruits to snack on, they decided to make a campfire and settle down to rest.

By the time dusk had fallen they'd managed a decent campfire, and full from their fruity meal - leaving them with a bizarre tingling sensation filling their fingers and toes - they were all relaxed and ready to sleep again. Chloé volunteered to take the first night-watch. Although she was as tired as the others, she was still too fascinated by the experiences she'd had with the book that day, and she was curious about what else it might have in store for them.

Lancelin lay himself down by the fire and used a blanket from the rucksack as a pillow. The heat from the sunbaked floor and the flickering fire was more than enough to keep them warm that night. Across the flames Chris lay down next to where Chloé was sat reading, resting his head on the rucksack and draping one of his arms over her legs as he fell asleep.

Chloé used the light of the fire to read the book as she flicked through the pages, but as the sky grew darker and there was just a hint of light left in the sky above her, she was distracted by the eerie scene of large bats flying overhead; heading down the path of alien flora and on into the jungle. The bats didn't particularly scare her though, as they seemed to show no interest – probably fruit bats she thought – but what did send chills over her skin was the distant sounds of howling and yowling in the hills ahead of them.

Creeped out by the increase of nighttime noises coming from within the jungle, it dawned on her just how defenceless they were to the unknown predators on this island; ones much like they'd already witnessed. With that in mind, she began flicking through the book, swiftly scanning each page for anything that may help them defend themselves. It was hard for her not to get sidetracked, however, when she'd flick past pages about all kinds of different creatures you'd only hear about in fantasy novels - dragons, wood nymphs, unicorns etc. - and many that she'd never even imagined before.

As she continued to turn page after page, all of a sudden the pages of the book began to glow, just as the map had, and before she knew it she was watching the pages speedily flick over all by themselves. She moved her hands away from the pages so they wouldn't get in the way, as she watched this miraculous activity play out before her. Until suddenly, it stopped, even more abruptly than it'd started. The page that the book was left open on was a page showing a magic ash protection circle, a simple form of magic protection used when sitting around an outdoor fire. Chloé was impressed by the convenience of this book, being able to help her out all the time, though she hadn't the slightest idea how – or why.

To create the magical ash protection circle, all Chloé had to do was burn a pile of sticks and leaves that had come straight from a tree or plant, assuring that they still had life running through them. Once burnt, she could use the ash to create a full circle around them. The circle would then offer protection to those inside it, as long as the original flame that incinerated the live ingredients was still burning strong – and the stronger the fire in the middle meant the stronger the protective magic would be.

So Chloé grabbed the torch from the rucksack and wandered around the area where they were camping to gather what she needed. She looked around at the trees thinking this would be the easy part, until she remembered how hard it was to actually burn wood that hadn't yet dried out. She stood with her back to the fire, shining her torch around to get some inspiration for what would burn the quickest and leave behind enough ash; however nothing in the jungle looked particularly dry and/or highly flammable. Stumped by what little choices she had, she turned back to the fire.

As she gazed beyond the flames in thought about how much she might need to even make a circle big enough, she caught sight of a patch of dry shrubbery and thirsty looking bushes amongst the new flora they'd camped by. They'd burn so much quicker, she realised, and with that, she took a sharp knife from the rucksack and began cutting up some fresh kindling.

Once she'd gathered plenty, she created a safe spot on the dry ground to burn the shrubs, and she used some sticks already burning in their campfire to set them alight. The pile she'd put together lit up with ease, though as the branches and leaves were all quite thin and spindly, they were not appearing to leave behind an awful lot of ash. Chloé was determined to try out this circle of ash protection, and so she wondered out further to gather as much as she could find that would burn.

Once she'd gathered all she could, she sat by and watched as it all burned down to create an ash pile sufficient enough to create a circle around them, albeit a small one. As the flames were almost burning out and it was mainly glowing embers that remained, she separated them from the fine ash using a large, thick leaf from the jungle and used it to move them back into the flickering campfire. Then, using the same leaf so not to burn herself, she scooped up the ash bit by bit and created her little ash circle around the three of them, with the campfire burning bright in the centre. Not knowing exactly how this magic would work, she sat awake within the circle, keeping guard with the book in her arms until she inevitably drifted off to sleep.

As she slept there, out in the open and using Chris' body for her pillow, Chloé still had the book gripped tightly in her hands, as it gently began to glow once more. As it lit up with the soft, warm golden glow, Chloé began to dream; but was it a dream from her subconscious? Or another vision from the book? She couldn't be sure.

This time was different than before, however. In fact, she was unable to control her own actions and was merely viewing a scene of herself as the dream played out. She could see herself sitting in the same light, open cave where she'd been before, listening to the tranquil sounds of water trickling through the rock around her.

Ahead of her, she could see the shimmering light still flowing from the wall into the pool it created on the cave floor. She watched herself stand up and pick the book up off the floor, clamping it close to her body. Then just as before, she heard the whispering voice guiding her, telling her to take in the light.

She observed herself as she walked over to the pool, clutching the book to her chest as she cautiously took each step. As she reached it, she stopped for a moment, taking one last look around to view things from a perspective she may never feel again; before delicately submerging her right foot into the light.

Once her foot was submerged it broke up the light, shattering it into beams of bright white light which shone upwards from around her ankle. Then she proceeded to put in her left foot, which resulted in the same reaction, and continued to walk in slowly until she was up to her waist.

The book and the upper half of her body had not yet touched the light, and the rays of bright light were still shooting out from the pool where the surface touched her body. Chloé looked down at the book and took in a deep breath, before plunging the rest of her body backwards into the pool. Leaping beams of light commenced sprouting out from the pool in all directions, shooting at the cave walls in a miraculous display, until suddenly they all dropped, and everything fell calm once again.

Now, Chloé could hear the sound of delicate singing around her, like the kind of voices you'd imagine if someone said they heard angels singing to them. She floated gently on the surface as she listened peacefully, with the light lapping up over her like water; she appeared to be in a state of complete serenity.

After a moment of floating around in the light, Chloé watched as she began to bring herself upright, before walking back out of the pool. Although this seemed like a dream, Chloé could feel herself watching by with anticipation, as if she was watching it on a television show and she was desperate to find out what would happen next.

After exiting the pool, the book was now glowing as she kept it close to her body, and she walked away back to the centre of the cave, then stopped. She lifted her right hand slowly out in front of her and looked down at her palm. She was desperate to find out what she was going to see herself do, when all too suddenly the whole room filled with the brightest of light and she lost sight of everything. She'd been woken up.

She jumped up as she threw her eyes open, confused and wanting to know what had happened. She looked to her side to find Chris was missing, then looked over to Lancelin when she heard him sitting up, after also being suddenly woken by what had happened.

"Chris?" shouted Chloé.
"What the hell's going on?" grumbled Lancelin.
"Chris's gone," she exclaimed worriedly.

As the two of them fell silent wondering where Chris could be, looking around into the darkness beyond the campfire, they heard a groaning noise coming from towards the jungle near to them. They both looked towards it, fearful of what it might be, before Chloé suddenly realised that it might possibly be Chris. "Chris? Is that you?" she shouted in the general direction of where the noise came from.
"Yea, it's me," he responded in a queasy voice.

Once he'd confirmed that it was him, she started to push herself up to go and help. As she stood up however, she was stopped by a dramatic warning from Chris, ordering her not to move.

"Why? What happened? Are you okay?" she asked frantically.
"Well, there seems to be some kind of force field around you two that doesn't want me to come in, so it threw me flying through the air. But other than that, I'm fine."
"Force field?" Chloé said quietly to herself, trying to come up with an explanation. When suddenly it dawned on her, "The ash circle!" she yelled back at Chris, "It worked!" Of course, he had no idea what she was going on about, so she explained to Chris and Lancelin how she'd found this in the book and created it whilst they'd been sleeping. Amazed that it had worked, and just how well it had worked, Chloé stood there smiling to herself and looking at the impressive circle she had

created.

"Well, did it say how you get back in?" asked Chris, bringing her back into the situation. Chloé hadn't read anything about how to get back inside the circle without breaking it, so she tried to come up with an idea quickly. Chris had clearly been able to pass through with no problem on the way out, so she assumed that meant that from inside the circle the magic force field wouldn't affect you. With that in mind, she came up with the idea that if she was to break the circle from inside, perhaps that might just break the protective magic and allow Chris to re-enter.

Carefully, she walked over to the ash circle and crouched down on the floor beside it. With her hand, she nervously reached down and touched the ash to make sure it was safe to do so before trying to move it. After nothing happened to her as she poked her finger into it, she swept a small amount of it to one side causing a gap in the circle, half expecting something to happen as she did so; some kind of sign that the magic had been broken.

"Well?" asked Chris, getting impatient with Chloé's lack of communication since he'd asked if she knew a way for him to get back in.
"Try now," she said.

So, Chris cautiously walked back over to the circle, and warily he reached his hand out in front of him to touch the magic force field. His had was shaking, he really didn't want to go flying backwards through the air again. As it reached the space above the ash on the floor, he closed his eyes tightly and his body tensed up. Without realising, he was still moving his hand forward as the rest of his body was held tightly clenched, and he reached within the circle. "Chris look!" shouted Chloé gleefully, "You're in!"

Once Chris saw that he was able to pass back through to within the circle, he jumped over and breathed a sigh of relief. Chloé then reshuffled the ash on the floor to create a full circle around them once again, hoping that this would reinstate the protective forcefield.

The pair of them both sat back down as they gradually began to laugh over the situation, and about how amazing this protection circle was. Though they'd experienced magic already, each time they witnessed something new they couldn't get over just how incredible it was. Lancelin, however, didn't seem as impressed as the other two by this protective force field Chloé had created. Instead, he shrugged it off as child's play, small tricks to impress people who had no idea what real magic was. The magic he'd read about in the diary was far greater than any of this, he assured them.

After Chloé and Chris had calmed down from the excitement, feeling safe inside the circle, they all went back to sleep around the campfire.

The next morning, both Chris and Lancelin went to gather some more fruit for breakfast, though by this time they were both craving something a bit more substantial. They also they gathered some more coconuts so that they might use their milk in the goblet.

Whilst they all ate, Chloé told them both about the

dream she'd had before realising that she hadn't yet told Lancelin about her original vision back on the beach. As she explained to him what had happened, Chris was wondering why the story wasn't seeming to impress him – does he know more about this place than he's telling us? Chris thought to himself.

"The spring of power," said Lancelin, as Chloé was describing the flowing light from the rock.
"Spring of power?" she asked.
"It's written about in that old diary they found in my town. The island is thought to be the only place on earth where magic flows up from deep underground, nourishing everything that exists here with magical properties."
"You don't have this diary with you by any chance, do you?" Chris asked.
"No, it's kept back in L'Hôtel de Ville."

Chris didn't believe Lancelin on this one, he was sure Lancelin had other sources of information which he wasn't sharing with them.

"So, this spring of power, why am I seeing it?" asked Chloé.
"Who knows," shrugged Lancelin, "It's thought though that when a human enters the spring, they absorb some of its magic into their blood, blessing them with power to command for themselves. Maybe the spring is calling to you. Perhaps you have a destiny it knows about, something it needs you to do."

Chloé had no idea what this adventure had waiting in store for her when they first set off from Antibes, but she had wished that it would be possible for herself to possess such powers; especially after seeing the spells in the book. But why would the spring be calling to her, she wondered, what made her so special?

Chris thought this all sounded a bit too convenient, and he never really trusted much of what came out of Lancelin's mouth. "So this spring is alive, is it? And it's calling out to Chlo, who has no idea what or where it is?" Chris began to question Lancelin's theory with a hint of sarcasm.

"Alive, aware, I'm not sure," said Lancelin, "But I'd certainly like to find it."

"Well if it does want her to find it, why hasn't it shown her how to get there?"

"Don't you get it? This is an enchanted land, we may already be being guided without realising it," said Lancelin, sounding cryptic and mysterious.

"Well if we're being guided, which way do we go now?" argued Chris, pointing out that none of them had any idea where they were. Then the two of them were interrupted by Chloé.

"North," she said, "We follow these new trees, and we head north."

"Huh? what makes you say north?" asked Chris.

"I don't know, it's just a feeling I have," she said, whilst stood holding the book. As she said that she looked at Lancelin and smiled, knowing that he trusted her feeling too and that they both believed they were being guided somehow.

Chris saw this glance, and it frustrated him that they were bonding over this mutual blind belief, something that he just couldn't understand. But not wanting to start an argument with Chloé, and having no better idea on which way to go himself, he gestured to her to lead the way. So, the three of them gathered up their belongings and began heading north, leaving behind the dusty, ash remains of the campfire and their circle.

CHAPTER ELEVEN

The Lonely Cottage

The previous evening, as Lancelin had lead Chris and Chloé to where they'd camped, King Tawhio sent his two messenger fairies off on their mission.
The king's messenger duo was made up of a brother and sister team named Kaitiaki and Karereki (or Kai and Kare for short). Kai, the brother, was the tallest of the two and also the eldest. They were both a slim build, had matching armour tattoos (given for being part of the king's royal defence force), and wore a small piece of a light magic crystal as a pendant around each of their necks.

Both their hair was long, thick, dark and frizzy, and they always wore it in matching styles; mostly with just the front of their hair tied back behind their heads. The pair were well trained for such expeditions, normally having to go between fairy colonies in time of conflict, and together they were both smart and strong. As a team, their success and strength of their magical abilities is part of what had helped the Tawhio fairies become as strong and large a colony as they are now.

After king Tawhio had given the order, Kai and Kare exited the Wharnui tree via a back exit. They flew together to an area of wide open space near the edge of the colony's confines, where they stood silently and held each other's hand.

Whilst they stood there, they stared straight out ahead of them into the empty space, free from trees and rocks, and with the lowering evening sun shining gently over one side. As they gazed out ahead, small beams of light began to appear and swish through the empty airspace just above the ground. More and more light beams continued to appear, overlapping and swirling around each other until a vague shape started to appear in the centre of it all. The area filled with light was much larger than the two fairies themselves, more like the size of a boulder that you could just about see over the top of.

As the two concentrated on the light they were creating together, suddenly two large, fierce, feathered wings of light burst out from either side. Following that, behind the wings light poured out along the ground, in long, windy snake-like trails. Then from the front, a bright beam of light shot up towards the sky, and a piercing squawk came blaring out as it split in two. With that, the whole shape of this creature, a kind of bird which they had created, became clearer, and the light from its body began to fade; revealing its true colours.

The glowing light continued to dim until it had almost

gone from its body, though flashes of light still swished and swirled around as they were finishing creating the creature. Its identity became more defined as the light dimmed, until finally, all the light that was left was the white-yellow light glowing from its eyes.

The messenger fairies had created what they referred to as a Manukah bird. The bird's feathers were a dull bluish grey on the top side, and underneath they replicated the colours shining down from above; making it pretty much invisible when viewed from below.

It had enormous wings, like those of a great white pelican, designed purposefully for helping it fly over long distances without getting too tired. Its head though, was somewhat more like a heron only with a shorter neck, and had a lengthy, pointed beak which was about as strong as diamond; it also doubled up as the sharpest of spears.

Its lengthy tail feathers curled up during flight, but on the ground they could be moved independently from each other, and they acted likes whips should the bird need to fight. The Manukah bird also had powerful, razor-sharp claws, capable of crushing solid rock into dust.

This was not a bird that was found naturally on Île Merveille, instead, it was their own creation that they'd come up with together, helping them get from place to place safely and rapidly. Their Manukah bird had served them well in the past, protecting them whilst flying over various battlegrounds, however, they were still uncertain about what dangers this new threat had brought to their land.

Even though this was a bird which they'd created through magic, to them he was real. Each time they brought him back they were happy to see him, and they spoke to him about the mission they were about to embark on. The messenger fairies fluttered around the Manukah bird and smiled, excited to see him again, before nestling themselves between the feathers on his back and gripping onto them tightly.

Once they were in position, they held on as the Manukah bird began to stretch his wings and tail feathers, then extend out his neck before finally flapping his wings for take-off. The bird began to fly upwards, high into the dusky evening sky above the thick canopy of the jungle, and into the warm glow of the setting sun. Together they headed north, inland over Île Merveille, towards the hills of the four seasons which lay a long way ahead of them (especially for two fairies). Through the night they travelled, soaring above the ground below, both too focused on their mission to even think about getting any sleep; for this was a task no creature had attempted before.

By the time dawn approached, Kai and Kare had reached the hills, soaring gracefully over the uneven ground below them. It was summer here and the sun was rising early, destroying the inky night sky with bright, warming beams of pink, orange and yellow. The rolling hills beneath them were now coming into colour. A mixed, splodgy canvas of fresh, green meadows, rich, emerald forests and teal and azure lakes connected by powder blue rivers, covered the land beneath them.

The higher valleys were cradling the light morning mist, which began to sizzle away as the sunbeams gently began to break through the misty-white vapour. Out ahead of them beyond the hills, they were close enough and high enough now to make out the top of Le Grand Mont de Merveille, Île Merveille's highest mountain peak, twinkling far on the horizon.

They knew that Alexandra's home was here somewhere, but hadn't the faintest idea where to find it. Consequently, they decided to fly lower and search for someone who might be able to help.

As they flew lower and the sun continued to rise over the hills, they saw in more detail what was below them. The great lakes were nestled into steep valleys, their ferocious rivers cut through the rock creating immense gorges, flowing into the lazy rivers further down where the locals would soon come for a morning drink. The fresh, green meadows where in fact speckled with different coloured wildflowers, many blessed with magical properties only known to a skilled Merveille botanist.

The smells of this part of Île Merveille were different to the ones Kai and Kare were used to back in the tropical south. Though, as they had been to this area once long ago, smelling the fresh, morning scent was almost like remembering it from a dream they'd almost forgotten.

They landed in a meadow just on the edge of a dense forest, with a deep, wide, lazy river gently flowing between the two. As they landed, Kai and Kare flew up off the Manukah bird as he disappeared in a swirl of light beneath them. "We'll summon if we need you," said Kare as the bird disappeared.

Then carefully they flew over to the river, whilst scanning the area for signs of anyone, or anything, around them. They landed next to the water where they each began to have a drink, unaware that they weren't the only ones by the river that early in the morning. For hidden within the tall grass of the meadow, a hungry snagon had picked up on their scent and was slithering up behind them.

A snagon was a large snake, only with a head like a dragon, and thick scales that stuck upwards slightly on its back, with piercing spikes on the end. Varieties of snagons were found in most parts of Île Merveille, except for in the ice regions of the high north, and they existed in different colours depending on their surroundings.

This one was as green as the grass, with small yellow points on the tip of its spikes and rusty-red speckles on its face. It had eyes just like a snake, round and yellowy green, with a black slit down the middle and a sideways blink. Atop of its forehead it had a thick horn pointing backwards, with scales reaching halfway along it, leaving a sharp point of bare bone at the tip. On either side of its head sticking out from the temples, it had two more, though these were on a much smaller scale.

The snagon quietly moved closer and closer, as the two, unaware fairies drank from the river. They were fairly smart as far as snake-types go, and it knew that fairies could easily protect themselves unless it struck them from just close enough.

Silently, with its tongue, it tasted the mouth-watering scent lingering in the air from the two warm, healthy bodies. The snagon was almost close enough, just another few centre-meters would do it. When suddenly, as if out of nowhere water came flying at them all from the river, causing the snagon to slither off in fear back into the long grass; the fairies too fell backwards onto the ground.

"Has it gone?" they heard a sweet voice ask worriedly, as they came back to their senses. Wiping the water from their faces, they slowly blinked opened their eyes, only to see the blurry form of a large body stood in the water in front of them. Startled, Kai grabbed Kare's hand and fluttered upwards as fast as his wet wings would take him.

"Oh, no, it's ok," the voice said softly, "I was just trying to scare off the snagon. Nasty creatures they are."
Kai and Kare both fluttered in the air, ready to dart away from where the voice had come from. As they looked down, to their relief they saw a female centaur looking back up at them. Most of her legs were submerged in the river still, as she stood facing the shore where the two

fairies had been sat.

She was a young adult, who had dark-sandy coloured fur with a thick, light blonde tail. Her long, straight, human hair matched the colour of her tail; the ends of it were wet from being in the river. As she stood looking up at the fairies, she held her arm across her breasts to cover them.

"You'll have to excuse me, there isn't normally anyone else down here this early in the morning," she said in her gentle voice as she reached on to the shore to pick up an item of clothing, which she wore only over her top half. It was a dark green t-shirt, made from rough linen type material and tied up at the back with coarse string, and the sleeves sat just below her shoulders.

"You saved us from a snagon?" Kare asked.
"Well, yes! You have to look out for them around here this early in the morning, you know," she said as she was lifting up her long hair, making sure none of it was caught under her t-shirt. "I love coming down here early on summer mornings, between the night creatures going to bed and the day creatures waking up. It's so peaceful."
As she spoke she walked out of the river and sat down in the grass, then began cleaning under her fingernails with a small, sharp twig.

The way she spoke, with her soft, innocent, feminine voice, Kai and Kare weren't sure whether to ask her about Alexandra or to ask where her parents where.

"Well, thank you for saving us," said Kai.
"You're welcome," she replied with a smile and a little giggle, "They don't scare me."

Kai and Kare continued fluttering about in the air above her, as she continued to look down and clean her fingernails. Quietly they muttered to each other, trying to decide whether to ask her about Alexandra or not, or to look for someone else who might take their mission more seriously.

"I'm Chevelle by the way," she said, introducing herself as she smiled and reach out her hand to politely shake theirs. "Oh!" she giggled, when she realised their hands were much smaller. Kai then flew down and stopped close to her back on the horse-like half of her body, followed by Kare.
"Do you mind?" he asked her as he was about to land.
"Oh go ahead," she said smiling, waffling her hands in the air, motioning to them to carry on.

"Thank you. Well, I'm Kai and this is my sister, Kare."
"How do you do? Cute little fairies. Though, you don't look like any of the others I've come across in these woods. Are you from another valley?" Chevelle asked them, going back to checking how she was getting on with her nails.

"We're from the Tonga Jungle, in the far south of Île Merveille," Kare said.
"Oh, I've heard about the far south!" she said before letting out a happy, dreamy sigh "Where it's never cold and you have the warm sea and soft, sandy beaches," she smiled to herself with her eyes closed, imagining what it would feel like. "I'd love to visit there someday. So, are you two on holiday?"
"Not exactly," said Kai.

"We're messenger fairies for our King," said Kare, "And we're here because, we need to get a message to..." she paused before mentioning Alexandra's name, too nervous to say it, not knowing what Chevelle's reaction would be. Chevelle motioned with her head and her hands for Kare to continue and reveal the name.
"To Alexandra," Kai added.

Chevelle looked confused for a moment, then looked upwards with her eyes, her head tilted to one side, whilst she searched in her head. Then, when she realised who the only one she could think of with that name was, she looked at them both with her eyes wide open.

"As in, THEEE Alexandra?" she blurted out, "I didn't realise she was awake these days."

"She's not," Kare said, "We've come to wake her up." Chevelle gasped at the news, knowing there must be a serious reason for wanting to wake her.

"Has something bad happened in southern Merveille? You really should try to solve your fairy squabbles without…" Chevelle was interrupted by Kai.

"We've seen witches."

"Kai!" shouted Kare. The two fairies stood in silence, waiting for Chevelle to react to their news. As with everyone before them, the news was met with disbelief, so Kai and Kare told Chevelle what they knew.

Chevelle knew where Alexandra's house sat in the hills of the four seasons because it's the only place they're warned not to visit, for fear of accidentally waking her up. She asked kindly if they would spare mentioning her name to Alexandra, should she ask, for she wanted to help them but had no proof that what they said was true. The two insisted that the Tawhio fairies would take full responsibility should this be a false alarm, and so she kindly pointed them in the right direction.

"Head in that direction (she pointed roughly north-west) to the flat top hills, sitting just before the last set of mountain tops where the snow still remains. There is a forest in the basin lying beneath the rocky flat tops, with a meadow sat centred and a stream cutting diagonally across it. Follow upstream to where the water exits the trees, and there, just inside the forest, you'll find her little house."

Kai and Kare thanked Chevelle for her help and advised her to warn others to stay on the lookout for these three strangers. After that, they said goodbye to her and left her by the river, flying off up into the sky on the back of their Manukah bird.

They flew on further north to where the mountains rose higher, looking for signs of snow still resting on the tops. At last they saw some white-capped mountains in the distance, even now in the height of summer, the air that high was just cold enough to keep the snow from melting away. Once they'd flown close to them, they turned west and continued to follow the zig-zagged line of hills still with snow on the top, until eventually Kai spotted a few hills that seemed to stick out a little further to the south than the others.

Then, when Kare looked to confirm this, she noted the flat top hills sat lower, just slightly further south still. They flew on the back of the Manukah bird straight overhead until they confirmed the forest, the meadow and the stream below them.

"This must be it," said Kai.
"I hope so. These clothes we're wearing really aren't made for the temperature at this kind of altitude," added Kare, as she created a thick blanket to wrap around them whilst she shivered in the icy-fresh air.

They landed in the meadow, and again the Manukah bird disappeared upon reaching the ground whilst the fairies fluttered above, scoping out the area. There was an eerie sense of desertedness about the place. Besides from the stream babbling over the stones, there was not a sound from another soul nor a gust of wind to be heard. The warm, intense, uninterrupted rays of the morning summer sun were beaming down onto their bare skin, relieving them from the chills of the high-altitude air. The mixture of smells coming from the grass and the wildflowers as they heated up, and the moisture evaporating from the ground beneath them, made the air feel thick and humid.

They flew over to the stream to check its direction, feeling pleasantly refreshed by the chilled air brought with it, cooled down by the bitterly cold meltwater as it trickled away on its journey. As they followed the water upstream towards the edge of the meadow, Kare was on the lookout for any more snagons hoping to catch a lunchtime snack; or anything else that might want a taste of them. But there was nothing. No one at all could be seen or heard up here - not even birds sang amongst the trees.

As they approached the edge of the woods, they took one last look around them. They were closed in by smooth hills at each side, and the flat top rocky peaks beyond the woods they were about to enter. The only entrance into this basin by foot was a large gap in the hills far beyond the trees at the other end of the meadow, where the stream eventually flowed out from. The gap was at the south tip of the area, making an entrance for the winter sunlight to still shine into the basin, keeping life going through the cold months (*if* there had ever been life here at some point).

They searched around and still neither of them had sensed any other living creature up there with them, which was beginning to set their nerves twitching. Kai unknowingly lowered his feet onto a stingingly cold stone, sticking out just above the water in the stream. The second he touched it he quickly pulled his feet up and away from it, whilst letting out a loud shiver which broke the eerie silence and startled Kare. Nervously they pulled themselves together and continued up the stream into woods, where just inside, they found a quiet, little, quirky cottage, stroking the stream as it flowed by.

The stream was wider inside the woods, more like a small river, which was cut off by a cute, make-shift dam just before it exited the trees. It made a slight curve as it flowed alongside the cottage, and the wall of that part of the home came straight out from under the water as if it was part of the riverbank.

From an upstairs room, a Juliet balcony which was sheltered by a whimsically carved archway, poked out slightly over the water, shading two windows on the floor below it, which were closed up with faded, dusty-red, wooden shutters. What they could see of the walls (that weren't covered by plants climbing up them) they were built with, now dirty, white stone.

The roof, which was in need of some attention, was a slightly curved, arched roof, with cute little windows poking out from it, and a crooked chimney peaking over the top. Sticking up from the other side of the cottage, they could see a turret reaching just higher than the rest of the building, with its own circular, pointed roof, finished off with a sharp iron spike on the top.

A bit further up the river there was a quaint little bridge, connecting a path that led into the woods with a path on the other side of the bridge, leading up to the front door of the cottage. The entrance way was sticking out at an angle from the main body of the house, with a curved, wooden door sheltered by a porch, inside which hung an old, rusty lantern.

There wasn't much of a garden here anymore, most of the place was overgrown as if the forest was taking back its land which had once been stolen. The whole place looked as if it was once a friendly, welcoming little home, where passers-by might feel comfortable to come up and visit. But could that have been part of a cunning trick they wondered, a way to pray on the kind-hearted souls, lost up here in these lonesome hills.

Kai and Kare cautiously flew up to the entranceway, then paused for a moment.
"What now?" asked Kare
"Well, I guess we just, ring the bell."
"But how will she hear us if she's sleeping?"
"Well, if there's no answer, we can then just try opening the door."

Kai and Kare spent a few minutes deciding, or more like arguing, over who should ring the bell. Neither of them wanting to take the first step alone. So inevitably, they decided to ring it together. With that in mind, they began looking for a rope to pull which would sound it, or even just a bell on a little shelf they could ring themselves; but they found no such thing.

So, their next idea was to knock. But who would hear the knock of two little fairies on a human-sized door, they thought to themselves. And more to the point, how would it wake anyone? Then Kai came up with an idea.

"I've got it!" he said, "Move back."

With that, they both flew backwards out of the entranceway, and Kai looked towards the door again. Then, using his powers of imagination, his magic created a large replica of his hand, clenched in a fist just in front of the door. This wasn't just large for them as fairies, this fist was about the size of a human head. Being rather nervous, Kai didn't have his full control over his magic at this point, however, he followed through with his idea and motioned with his own hand as the replica copied, and knocked on the door.

Amongst the tranquillity of the woods, the knock seemed to make a loud, booming sound, which rumbled throughout the trees; yet there was no sign of anything scurrying away. The vibrations from the knock caused an unsettling of dust, dead leaves and twigs, triggering them to emerge from their resting places around the whole of the cottage entrance. As quickly as he'd come up with the idea, Kai caused the fist to disappear out of sight, as the two of them fluttered in the air at a safe distance from the door.

They stayed silent for a while, waiting for something to happen, but there was nothing. No sound of anyone moving inside the cottage, and the woods still remained in their serene and peaceful state. Kai and Kare looked at each other and shrugged their shoulders.

This was definitely where the centaur had said Alexandra's house would be, but now they were here, how would they get to her and wake her up, they wondered. They decided to simply try to open the door, which unfortunately turned out to be either locked or jammed shut, and then they flew around the cottage checking each closed-up window.

Whilst checking, an idea suddenly sprung into Kare's mind, "Why don't we just fly down the chimney? It's clearly not in use." They both looked up towards it. "See, there's no smoke coming from it," she pointed out. With no objection from Kai, they both fluttered cautiously down the chimney, arriving safely inside the house.

CHAPTER TWELVE

Les Fruits Rouge

Whilst the king's messenger fairies had been searching for the resting place of Alexandra, Chris, Chloé and Lancelin had set off, continuing along their journey whilst following Chloé's lead; as the only one who had the faintest idea which way they should go.
The walk was long and tiring. With no sign of a river or even a trickling stream, they were glad they'd filled up their empty water bottles with coconut milk, which they used to make refreshing drinks in the goblet along the way. Until eventually, once they had passed between the two jungle smothered hills and others beyond them,

they came to a small lake; appearing like an oasis along their hot, dry trek.

The lake widened the area of non-tropical trees and plants within the jungle region, and at the other end they could see that it was fed by a large waterfall, tumbling down over a tall cliff which the lake was nestled into. The lake, however, didn't appear to be flowing out from any other river. In fact, it seemed as though it was disappearing through an underground exit at the southern tip of the lake.

The water glistened stunningly in the sunlight, shimmering with soft hues of azure and turquoise. Chloé walked straight up to it and began splashing water onto her face, to rinse off her sweat and the dust from the dry the earth they walked upon; though as she opened her eyes again she noticed something strange in the reflection.

Once she'd stopped splashing the water onto her face, the image appeared more clearly to her and she realized that it wasn't her reflection she could see at all, but the cave she had visited in her visions with the spring of power within it. She wondered and stared at the image for a moment, before recalling the sound of trickling water she'd heard when she was inside the cave. Perhaps that water flows to this lake, she thought to herself, which meant that all they had to do was simply follow the flow upstream to find it's source; though how they'd get to the top of the waterfall she had no idea.

She explained her epiphany to the other two and suggested that they needed to find a way up to the top of the cliff, which wasn't met with much enthusiasm from Chris. After examining the landscape, it looked as though the best way up to the top would be to follow the cliff around to the left, back into the jungle, where it appeared to slope somewhat more gently and they'd have a better chance at scrambling up.

First, however, they decided they needed a rest. With the sun high in the sky, it was an exhausting walk in the intense, late summer heat. They found a shaded spot under a collection of trees on the shore of the lake, which looked to be some kind of pine trees, where they sat together and rested for an hour or so. Chris and Chloé even went for a swim to freshen up; after not washing properly for quite some time they were beginning to feel pretty grubby.

Whilst they'd been swimming, Lancelin had wandered off to find fruit for their lunch, of which he returned with just a few ripened bananas and oranges – all he could find that appeared recognisable to them. After their break, they got dressed again and packed up, then headed off into the jungle searching for an easier spot to ascend the cliff.

They walked for a few hours, trying hard not to lose their sense of direction. Luckily for them, the cliff began to smooth off into a long hill which they could easily hike up, although the warm, sticky, humid air of the jungle did make it that much more tiring. As they climbed higher and higher, they were beginning to catch glimpses through the trees of the view out over the top of the lower jungle behind them. They all tried their best to keep track of the direction they needed to head in, so as not to get lost for good in the dense foliage of the enrapturing jungle.

Eventually, the ground seemed to level off, and they walked through the trees roughly in the direction they believed the waterfall to be in. They'd come so far from it however, and without any real point of reference, none of them really could be sure which way they were heading.

Another hour or so went by and the three of them were getting tired and worried, marching along on their blistering feet believing they were completely lost. When thankfully, completely out of the blue Chris spotted a similar tree to the ones they'd sat beneath earlier that day by the lake. Chloé felt so relieved as he pointed it out to them, that she instantly gave him a tight embrace accompanied by a kiss as the feeling rushed over her. They tore over to it, blocking out the aches and pains that they'd gained over the course of the day, only to spot more and more of them from that point on; which assured them they must be heading in the right direction.

As they walked on, the jungle began to fade away and the forest became sparser, with only the non-tropical flora remaining. The ground beneath their feet became dry and dusty again, just like the area of ground they'd camped on. They strode on hoping to find the waterfall, when it occurred to Chris that they couldn't even spot the cliff anymore, nor hear the sound of the roaring water. Chloé was sure though, that if they kept walking they would come to it sooner or later; her sense of direction was still strong, even if she was beginning to doubt it.

As the forest here was not half as dense as the jungle, they could see the sky much more clearly, and the light from the evening sun seemed to stay around for them much longer. Persistently they kept moving forward, growing ever tired and weaker until Chloé stopped for a moment to take look around, as it dawned on her that even though they had more light here than they did in the jungle, their daylight hours would soon be up.

"If we don't find it soon, we're going to have to stop to set up camp again, before the sun goes down," she pointed out to the others. Chris stopped to stretch his back and looked over to Chloé, right before he spotted something not too far away behind her.

"A house," he said slightly confused, unsure if he could really see it or not.
"What? Where?" asked Chloé after taking a moment to register what he'd just said.

Chris pointed as Chloé and Lancelin both looked to where his sight was fixated on. "A big house!" exclaimed Chloé, surprised at the sight of something manmade – or at least something that looked manmade. "Let's go to it. Maybe someone lives there? Or at least it could be somewhere we could rest for the night."

"I don't know," said Lancelin nervously, "We don't know who, or what might live there."

Knowing Lancelin didn't want to go, made Chris even more determined to visit it. So he began walking towards it anyway as he announced to them, "There's only one way to find out!"

As they approached the house, the size of it became much more apparent to them. It was a huge, gothic looking, stone mansion, the centre of it shadowed by the giant east and west wings; the west being the most prominent with a tall brick tower built on to its side. There was a long, gravel pathway leading up to it, broken up in the middle by a large circular pond, with an impressive, perfectly round Versailles fountain in the centre, carved exquisitely out of stone.

Littered about around the grounds in front of the mansion, were more of the beautiful, strong, bulky palm trees, with an abundance of tough, green palm leaves sprouting out from the tops. Other colourful, inviting looking plants, the types you'd expect to see in the grounds of a rich, southern Italian home, had been thoughtfully placed about the area as if someone had hired an exclusive landscape artist to design the whole place.

The house itself was not lacking in detail either, from the iron spires coming off from the high dormer windows, to the border around the foot of the house. Every inch had been built to perfection, to exude the grandeur of its size and status. At the end of the gravel path sat large, cold stone steps, leading up to an imposing doorway; intimidating any who dared come up to it.

Once they'd reached the beginning of the gravel path, the atmosphere surrounding them had changed slightly. For the first time since the storm at sea, they saw clouds in the sky. Contrasting in colour, they were a dark, bluish grey on top, with the sun's setting rays spraying a mist of pink, peach and orange onto the underneath of the heavy, broken clouds.

As they walked down the path, the sound of gravel beneath their feet suddenly seemed so bizarre to them. A sound so familiar and which would be normal in a man-made setting of a human town, felt so abstract in a world which felt so far from their own.

As they neared the mansion, they noticed that the plants and trees close to it didn't seem quite as warm and colourful as they had when they first spotted them. Some almost looked dead, or even frozen in a deathly state. The fountain wasn't running either, and on a closer look they saw it had sunken into the ground on one side, and that it was scarred by several large cracks in its pools. Further along the path as they approached the building, Chloé noticed something odd about the windows – they were all boarded up with broken pieces of dark brown wood, roughly nailed into place.

The sun was now beginning to disappear behind a range of low lying hills to the west of them, and from underneath the clouds gathered above it, it shone through, allowing some of its golden, orange beams to light up now only the top half of the mansion. When the light did this, they all noticed something peculiar - the colour of the mansion changed. From a cold, dark grey which now gloomed in the shadow of the clouds, it became a light, warm, sandy shade of beige in the sunlight.

"Well, if it's all boarded up, I assume that means no one lives here," Chloé suggested, trying to lighten the mood.

"I wouldn't assume anything here," Lancelin added, looking up at the windows.

Lancelin's behaviour towards the mansion made Chris blind to his own feelings towards the place, and all he wanted to do was whatever Lancelin didn't want to do; hoping to uncover any secrets he may be keeping.

"Maybe it's been abandoned like that castle was," added Chris, "It could be perfectly well preserved for us inside. I'd much rather sleep on an old bed or sofa than on the floor again."

"As long as they don't smell," uttered Chloé, turning her nose up at the idea of sleeping on an old, dead person's bed.

They decided to first try knocking to see if anyone would answer, as they stood sheepishly in front of the large, wooden doors, then they'd try again just to be sure. A few minutes passed until Chris tried knocking a second time, then they waited for another few minutes before assuming that no one was home. They all stood there nervously at the top of the curved, cold, stone steps, looking at each other until Chris finally took it upon himself to be the one who'd try and open the doors.

The doors themselves were quite heavy, but thankfully they weren't locked as Chris found when he managed to swing one of them open and get a glimpse inside. The interior of this house bared a similar resemblance to the black castle, it was indeed a home for the rich and powerful; though here there were very few soft furnishings, and no light at all shining in through the windows.

Chris took the torch from the rucksack and slowly entered the house, with Chloé and Lancelin following closely behind. As they cautiously entered the entrance hall, Lancelin left the door open behind them to let in what light was remaining from the setting sun.

Chris shone the torchlight around the room, and above them he saw a big, bulky, wooden chandelier, with about forty or fifty chunky, creamy-white candles wedged onto it. Ahead of them was a wide staircase, with a maroon coloured carpet running down the centre and two black, beaten metal bowls sat either side, upon the beginning of each stone bannister.

To their left was an open archway leading into another room, and to their right were several sets of double doorways, which curved at the top to create a sharp point in the centre. They decided to go through the archway first to find somewhere to rest, somewhere that wasn't too far from the main entrance - having easy access back out of the mansion suddenly became something of an importance to each of them. As they went through, Chris saw that it seemed to be a kind of living space, with a huge, Persian rug, dark in colour, and several ornate wooden benches upon it; all facing a wide, stone fireplace.

In this spooky, shadowed setting, the three of them quickly agreed that this room would be fine to sleep in, providing they got a fire going to shine some light upon it. Together they went back outside to gather wood and anything they could find that would help them light a fire in the fireplace.

Whilst looking outside in the dusky, evening light, Chloé noticed that many of the trees around the house were baring more fruit. She spotted oranges, plums, peaches, cherries and many more, without any concern to which season it was. So, instead of gathering wood, she took it upon herself to gather food. To her fright, however, she noticed that it wasn't only fruit that hung in these trees, but a colony of bats.

Some were just waking up in the last light of the day and beginning to fly about, which was how she spotted them to begin with. Not wanting to disturb them, fearful they might bite or scratch her (or worse, get caught in her hair! As told the tales she'd heard as a young girl), she took as much fruit as she could from the lower branches. Holding her takings cupped in her baggy t-shirt, she hurried off to meet up with the guys.

They all went back inside, leaving the main door still slightly ajar, and created a fire in the fireplace. It was just large enough that it managed to light about half of the room, though as the benches were sat rather close to the fire, they cast long shadows reaching beyond the archway into the entrance hall, and which filled the back corners of the room behind them.

Together they sat and ate the bountiful fruit that Chloé had gathered, which seemed to be the most delicious fruit any of them had ever tasted. Each piece of fruit tasted so sweet, and the juice was so thick and succulent. Whilst busy indulging themselves, none of them took their eyes off the food as they gorged on it. Chris was first to finally feel full enough to sit back and enjoy the moment, as he slouched on the bench and looked over at the mesmerizing flames of the fire whilst savouring the delicious flavours, before breaking his stare and peering over at Chloé. As he did, he noticed a dark stain around her mouth.

"You may want a tissue," he joked, "I think you got a little too personal with those cherries."
"I haven't had any cherries," she said, confused. Then she looked back at him. "Besides, you're one to talk!" she continued as she pointed out the stain around his mouth too.

"What?" he asked, before wiping his mouth with his arm. As he looked down at his arm afterwards, he saw a dark-red smudge on his skin, then he looked at the nectarine he held in his hand which he had just taken a bite out of. The inside was completely red and oozing. As he noticed, he quickly threw it away on the floor.
"Ahh! What's wrong with that nectarine?!" he shouted.

Then Chloé and Lancelin both looked at the fruit they'd bitten into and also saw the thick, red juice oozing out from inside, before throwing them on the floor in disgust. Chloé spat out as much as she could from her mouth, and then they decided to cut open the rest of the fruit with a knife to see if they were all the same.

Upon inspection, the rest of the fruit seemed normal when cut with the knife, but as Chris slowly took a bite from one of the cut open oranges, Chloé and Lancelin both noticed what was happening. The fruit changed when bitten, it changed to a dark-red mush, though Chris still felt the familiar texture of the fruit it had started out as.

Chloé decided to consult the book before they ate anymore, and if in doubt they would simply squeeze the juices from the fruit into the goblet and drink from there - before she did so, she made sure to wipe her hands clean of this mysterious juice. As she held the book on her lap, in her mind she focused on the fruit whilst closing her eyes, hoping that she could gain some control over the book when trying to find what she needed to know.

Slowly, she took in a deep breath, calming herself and trying to connect her energy with the book. Chris and Lancelin watched by, Chris especially trying not to feel uncomfortable watching Chloé acting so weird. Sure enough, as the times before, she felt her hands guided as she gently felt along the pages to find the one she needed. Once she'd opened the book, she carefully opened her eyes and looked down at the page, and she read out what she saw.

"Blood fruit."
"What?" asked Chris.
"Fruit that turns to sweet, tasty, fruit-flavoured blood when bitten into." Chris blurted out a gagging noise after she read this, sickened by the thought of what he'd just eaten. Chloé continued to read on. "Originally

grown from seeds that were enchanted by a witch many years ago, producing fruit which turns to blood with a single bite. The fruit enabled her to feed her newly turned vampire children, allowing them to live without having to kill anything or anyone." Her voice grew quiet as she read the end of the last sentence, "Guys I think we really need to le..." she was abruptly interrupted by Chris.

"Shhh," he went, as he touched her leg with his hand and used his eyes to point her attention to the archway leading into the entrance hall, "There's someone there," he whispered. Chloé and Lancelin both looked towards the archway, which until now they'd had their backs to, and there, standing in the centre, they saw a faint outline of a tall figure.

CHAPTER THIRTEEN

The Countess

The three of them were paralyzed. They all sat silently in fear and stared at the unknown figure. For a moment, the only sound and movement in the room were that of the fire, as it flickered away in the fireplace. The tension built, and it felt like a lifetime to them until the person under the archway finally broke the silence. "I hope that doesn't stain my carpet," they said, in an eerily calm voice.
The voice sounded female, with a slightly eastern European accent, though very precise and clear. It sent a chill through each of their bodies. "Aren't you going to pick them up?" she continued.

Lancelin was the first one to act, as he hurriedly reached down to pick up the fruit which the others had thrown on the floor. "We are so sorry, er… madam, the fruit came as a bit of a shock to them," he said as he squirmed around to grab the discarded array of fruit.

Them? Thought Chris. Was he implying that he wasn't shocked? Or perhaps he was just suggesting that he hadn't joined in with throwing the fruit on the floor, Chris continued to question to himself. After that, the person under the archway moved calmly closer to them, into the light of the fire. They could see her more clearly now, a tall, slim woman wearing a long, black dress.

The dress glistened slightly and hugged her body tight, reaching from around her neck, all the way down to the floor, trailing off in a squirmy, thin train of fabric behind her. The dress was sleeveless and also had a gap sliced out down the chest, exposing her bare cleavage underneath. She also wore a slightly tattered and ripped looking, burgundy, rough-cotton wrap, resting on her shoulder on one side and draped over her elbow on the other, as she rested her left hand on her hip.

Her frizzy, curly hair was pulled back and tied up in a neat mess, which sat just a bit lower than the crown of her head; with a few curly pieces breaking free and hanging down. The colour of her hair was a very ashy, light blonde, which contrasted against her cool, dark skin. Down by her side she had an animal walking next to her, which at first they assumed was a dog, but later realised it appeared to be more like a jet-black fox.

Chloé stutteringly began to apologise for being in the house, as she fumbled about to close the book and reached for the rucksack so that she could slip it back inside. However, as Chloé closed the book, the woman caught a glimpse of its cover. She recognised its design. Its coloured material and the emblem engraved in the dark gold metal on the front cover was very familiar to her.

She stopped and stood to the side of the fire, with its light bouncing off them and back to her so that she could see their faces in more detail. Once she'd stopped, she appeared to sniff their air for a second, a bit like when you pick up the scent of something but you're not quite sure what it is, before she continued to speak to them.

"Please, don't feel you must leave. I think we got off on the wrong foot, didn't we? Allow me to introduce myself," she began. Just as she'd finished that sentence, the whole room was suddenly lit up. Candles set in wall sconces around the room were rapidly lit one by one, followed by five basketball-sized, glass balls, which hung from the ceiling via chains, and somehow had the air inside them set ablaze. This was not done through any magic of her own, however, but by a small, fire-bodied elementame whom she controlled.

As the flames lit up the place, the light revealed four other people standing in the room behind where they were sat, three male and one female. The men were dressed in dark grey, tight fitted trousers, two of the pairs had been ripped below the knees, and they had no shoes on either. The other man's trousers were neat and he wore black pointed shoes. On their upper bodies, they wore very loose-fitted, faded white shirts. The scruffier men's shirts were missing buttons, whereas the other one's shirt was all buttoned up.

The female wore a dull-white dress which reached down to her knees, with a dark grey shawl over her otherwise exposed arms and shoulders, and a pair of tatty, black leather, lace-up boots. They all stared at the three of them sat on the wooden bench, without any trace of emotion showing through their faces. Once the room had been lit, the woman continued to introduce herself, "I, am Countess Veshnica."

There was silence as the three of them grew increasingly nervous in her presence, until Chris broke it by introducing them all. "Nice to meet you, Countess Veshnica. My name's Chris," he said as he held out his hand to shake hers, to which she didn't respond to, "And, this is my girlfriend, Chloé." He put his hand on her shoulder as he introduced her. "And he is our, erm, friend, Lancelin."

The countess smiled kindly at them, until she looked at Lancelin. The look she gave him, just for a few seconds, had a slight sense of confusion about it. After she'd paused for a moment staring at him, she smiled again at Chris and Chloé and invited them all to join her in her dining room, where she assured them that her 'children' would bring them something to eat; which would be a little more to their liking. Not knowing how long the countess had been watching them for, they assumed that she would know if they lied about having to leave. So, fearfully they followed her through the house.

Every room they entered was lit up just seconds before they stepped into it, once again by the small, enslaved elementame. As they walked through the different rooms and corridors of the mansion, they were each trying to spot their best escape route, though the choices were slim to none.

Upon reaching the dining room, they were greeted by more of the countess' 'children', who were dressed similarly to the ones before. Her children were spoken to and treated more like servants, but yet servants who she seemed to care for in some way. They obeyed her every command, and yet some she would greet them with a kiss on either cheek.

The dining room was decorated much the same as the rest of the house, minimalist with dark wooden furniture and cold, grey stone walls and floor. The room was lit by a fire in a fireplace, which stretched along the back wall, and many candles placed about on the table. Her fox, Vulp, curled up on a tattered, red blanket in front of the fire.

After they were seated, the countess ordered some of her children to bring her guests something to eat, something that would, "delight their taste buds and satisfy their stomachs." Whilst they waited for the food to arrive, they sat nervously at the dining table, being questioned by the countess as to how they ended up in her house.

"And, what about that book I saw you reading, it looks like rather an impressive, weighty item to carry around with you," she said.

"Well," began Chloé, "It's kind of how we found this Island to begin with." She looked nervously at Chris and Lancelin as she spoke, unsure of how much information she should give away. "We found it while on holiday in France, and there was a map in the back of it, which… only I could see."

"Only you could see?" queried the countess.

"Yes. To everyone else the pages appear blank, except to me. I can read them."

"Magic?" asked the countess, seeming a little excited.

Chloé shrugged her shoulders, "I guess so."

"Incredible. Truly the greatest."

"Greatest what?" asked Chloé.

"Do you have any idea who that book belonged to?" Chloé shook her head. "The mark on the cover of that book, my dear, is the mark of the greatest sorcerer who ever lived."

As the three of them sat there taking in what the countess had said, their food was served. Each plate had something different on it, which just happened to be each of their favourite foods.

Chloé was served a plate of saucisson brioché – French sausage baked inside a brioche loaf, which is then sliced like bread and served, just as her father would make for her as a child. It came accompanied with steamed potatoes and some green salad leaves.

Chris was given a rustic Italian pizza, with thick, creamy mozzarella, slices of fresh, juicy tomato and topped with basil leaves.

Lancelin was served a bowl of cold beef stew and dumplings, which to Chris and Chloé looked very dull and unappetizing, though Lancelin seemed to love it.

Starving for any food other than fruit, Lancelin and Chris dug into their meal straight away, however, Chloé was reluctant at first to accept food from such a stranger. She questioned the countess, as to how her cooks knew exactly what to serve each of them without asking what they'd like, and how they just happened to have it all in the kitchen ready to make. Though not wanting to offend her, she worded her question more like a compliment, so not to sound ungrateful.

The countess was rather vague with her answer, but assured Chloé she had nothing to fear, and that she herself would eat some from her plate if it pleased her. Still not fully convinced, she reluctantly began eating her meal, her actions overpowered by the rumbling emptiness of her stomach. To her delight, the saucisson brioché was every bit as delicious as she'd imagined it would be, and before she'd thought much more about it, she'd almost devoured everything on her plate.

As the three of them were just finishing their food, one of the countess' children came into the dining room to announce that her husband, Count Raul Báthory, had returned from his hunt.

"My Rue-Rue's back?" she said with excitement, "Please, excuse me whilst I welcome my husband. I will tell him all about you three and I'm sure he'll be very interested to meet you. Then, once he's settled in, I'll send one of my children for you and we can all get together, in the red room perhaps, that's his favourite." After she said this, she smiled at them all then left the room, along with Vulp and her children behind her. Chris, Chloé and

Lancelin all remained sat at the table and waited until the others were out of sight before beginning to speak again.

"Rue-Rue?" said Chris first, causing Chloé to blurt out a quiet laugh.

"And what's with all these slave "children" she has?" Chloé asked lightly. They had both been holding in their emotions of fear, panic and disbelief, ever since they had first spotted the countess, which caused them now to become giddy, helping them to deal with their threatening situation.

"Do you think they're going to drink all our blood?" asked Chris jokingly.

"Probably!" laughed Chloé. After she said that however, their laughter began to deteriorate.

"Shit, they might actually drink our blood!" said Chris, coming to terms with the severity of their situation.

"But wouldn't they have done something to us by now? Aren't vampires supposed to be able to like, hypnotize you or something?" asked Chloé.

She decided to check the book quickly, whilst they were all alone, to see if it had anything to say about vampires. "Even if they could, perhaps they have something else in mind for us," suggested Lancelin, whilst Chloé reached into the rucksack. She opened the book as usual, and just as the times before, she managed to open it on exactly on the right page. She read out loud what she saw:

'Vampires.
A human looking creature found on Île Merveille, seen mostly at night when it is safe for them to come out. Almost immortal, their bodies continue to remain healthy after reaching their peak growing stage. They survive by drinking the blood of another living, non-vampire creature. They are either born to vampire parents or turned through a

possessive bite from another vampire, followed by a ritual. Each time a vampire turns a human being, known after as their child, their physical strength and naturally given powers grow stronger.

A vampire's powers include – switching between bat form and human form, turning humans into vampires, incredible sense of smell, self-healing, screeching at such a high pitch that they can break glass and cause ears to bleed. Note - Advanced vampires can also read other's inner desires.
To protect against a vampire – use sea salt which will burn their skin, or take them into daylight whilst in their human form, which will melt their cold skin to the ground and kill them. Another alternative is to use bright, concentrated magic light, such as from a unicorn's horn, which will also melt their skin.

As vampires cannot live in the presence of strong light, they are unable to take in the light from the spring to become more powerful. Although many witches have turned Merville creatures into creature-human hybrids over the years, none have attempted this with a vampire; for fear it would create an all-powerful, unstoppable, immortal being.'

Fear had set itself into each of them by the time Chloé had finished reading this. They knew that even if the countess had been good to them so far, that her intentions surely weren't to remain kind. As they sat at the table, Chloé put the book back into the bag and they began to think of how they could escape the mansion.

As a protection, Chris came up with an idea to each have a bottle filled with sea water – therefore containing sea salt – by turning the water left out on the dining table using the magical goblet and filling their old empty water bottles. Unfortunately, as water and sea water looked the same in the goblet, much to their disgust they each had to try a sip first to be sure it had changed.

Other than this, which they all knew wouldn't be enough to save them should the vampires attack, they knew they had little chance to escape until the next morning. Unsure they would even last that long in the vampires' company, they decided to make a run for it whilst they had been left alone. So Chloé put the book back in the rucksack and handed it over to Chris, who insisted he carry it most of the time due to its weight. Each armed with their saltwater, they left the dining room in the opposite direction to where the countess had made her exit.

They'd taken a candle from the table to light their way, as they walked down a dark corridor leading away from the dining room. It led them to the entrance of a large kitchen. The kitchen had several huge windows that had been long boarded up, with just a few long cracks allowing the moonlight to shine in. In the back corner of the kitchen they spotted another door, a solid, sturdy looking door, the type that might lead them outside.

Chloé ran over to it to try it out, whilst Chris followed next to Lancelin who was carrying the light. Unfortunately the door was locked, but given that this was their nearest exit, Chris decided to try and force it open somehow; though he wasn't going about it very discreetly.

"Shhhhh!" went Chloé, "They'll hear us," she whispered. Chris stopped for a moment and looked at the door, knowing they weren't going to get it open anytime soon.

"What about the windows?" he suggested, "If we can pull off the boards, we might be able to get them open."

As they turned around to walk away from the door and over to the windows, they spotted two of the Countess' children standing in the entranceway to the kitchen. There was a moment of silence as they all looked at each other, which was soon broken as one of the vampires spoke. "The count and countess are waiting for you now, up in the red room. Please, follow us," They said in a morbid tone.

The three of them stood scared, staring at the two vampires. Chloé was the first to agree to come along, whilst reaching into her pocket for her water bottle. Seeing this, Chris and Lancelin both reached for theirs as they walked towards the kitchen entrance. As Chloé was just about stood next to them, she'd already sneakily unscrewed the lid, but she noticed the vampires had begun to pick up on the sea water scent.

It was now or never, and Chloé quickly threw her water into the face of one of the vampires, followed by Chris throwing his water into the face of the other. Their skin began bubbling and burning as it turned a deep, hot red, and they let out screams so highly pitched that they broke the glass windows in the kitchen. Chris ran over to the windows and pulled at the wooden boards as hard as he could, managing to pry some of them away, leaving a gap just about big enough to squeeze through.

Lancelin was last to throw his water over the vampires, seemingly a little reluctant, which didn't go unnoticed by Chris as he waited for Chloé to exit through the gap he'd made. Chris was next to wriggle his way out after pushing the rucksack through, followed by Lancelin. Together they fled the grounds of the mansion and ran off into the night as fast as they could.

The countess, upon hearing the screams, ran frantically down to the dining room in search the two children she'd sent. But before she'd got there, she picked up on the scent of burning vampire flesh and followed it to the kitchen. When she saw what had happened, she stopped and let out a great cry of sorrow and anger for her two injured children. Shortly after, one of her other children arrived in the entranceway to the kitchen, to find the countess kneeling on the floor, supporting the heads of her two injured vampires.

She turned to them, with tears of blood running down her face, and demanded ferociously, "Find them! Take your brothers and sisters and bring these humans back to me! Go!" and with that, the countess' child ran back to gather their siblings.

Moments later, swarms of bats burst out of the mansion from both the main front and back entrances, surrounding the building entirely, before splitting off in all directions, hunting for those who had escaped.

CHAPTER FOURTEEN

Witch Wake-Up

Earlier that day, Kai and Kare had safely arrived inside the cottage, where it was almost pitch black. Not being a lover of cold, dark places, Kare took it upon herself to use her power to light up the room by scattering about a few, small balls of light around the place. Once lit, they could see that the room they'd arrived in appeared to be the kitchen, though with the cottage being so small, the rooms were merely divided by curved wooden archways without any doors. The furniture in the cottage was quite chunky and wooden, and pretty basic. There were a few bookcases stuffed full with dusty old books, and a nice, cosy looking living area towards the front entrance. Kai and Kare flew around in the dim light, looking around for clues as to where Alexandra might be. As they fumbled about, looking at book titles that had been left out and searching shelves and cupboards for clues, they were unaware of the pair of eyes they had awoken, watching them from one corner of the room.

"Miauooo!" they heard coming suddenly out of nowhere. Kai and Kare rushed to each other and clung together in a tight grasp.

"Hello?" asked Kai to the shadows around them.

"Miauoooo!" yowled the creature again. The strange sound started as a cat meowing and ended more like an owl hooting.

"Is someone there?" asked Kare nervously, still holding onto Kai.

"We're looking for Alexandra."

Then they heard movement coming from a dark corner of the living room. It sounded like a small creature, not too heavy, making slow, tapping footsteps. Then gradually out of the shadows, it emerged. It was a meowl.

The meowl was a creature that was somewhere between a house cat and an owl. This one in particular was a rather dainty meowl, with beige fur/feathers (though white down its front) and brown stripes curving over its back, progressing into a circle then a spot on either side.

It had a cat-shaped head, with small cat-ears and a dainty owl's beak where a cat's nose and mouth would normally be. It stood up like a cat, though its front half was more owl-like with lots of soft feathers and a puffed-out chest. Its front legs also had owl claws on the end in place of paws. The back half had fewer feathers and more fur, with soft little paws at the base of its back legs, and a long slender tail with a black tip. The meowl also had the wings of an owl on its back, which it could fold up neatly and tuck onto its sides.

As the meowl walked up to them, jumping from one item of furniture to the next with the agility of a cat, the two fairies began to back up slowly towards the fireplace. Upon seeing them move, the meowl stopped in its tracks and sat down.

"Miauoo!" it said again, tilting its head in curiosity whilst wondering what they were up to.
"Please," began Kare bravely, "We're looking for Alexandra. We bring news worthy of awakening her from her eternal slumber."
"That's right," added Kai, trying to sound assertive, "About three new witches we've seen."

The meowl looked at them both, tilting its head from one side and then to the other, trying to decide what to make of these two little beings. "Do you think it can understand us?" Kare asked Kai, to which he simply shrugged his shoulders.
"Do-you-know-where-she-is?" asked Kai, in a patronizingly loud and clear voice.

However, as he was finishing his question, the meowl turned away and jumped with a flap of its wings up onto a shelf, where the light was shining just enough for Kai and Kare to see. Up on this shelf, there were a number of items which the meowl agilely manoeuvred itself around, until it came to a picture hanging in a frame, slightly above the shelf at the other end.

The meowl sat down neatly on the shelf, facing sideways towards the picture, though the light wasn't bright enough for them to make out exactly what it was a picture of. At first the meowl simply groomed itself for a moment, using its beak to neaten up its feathers as opposed to a cat licking its fur. Then it turned its attention to the wooden frame, whilst twitching its head around in an inquisitive manner. Next it began pawing at the frame with its front claw, tapping it as cats do, to get some kind of reaction out of it.

With a few bats of the meowls paw, to Kai and Kare's surprise the picture swung away from the wall, revealing a small opening behind it. The meowl then stepped up and inside the wall through this entrance, and pulled the picture back into place with its tail, slamming it shut.

Kai and Kare both stood staring at this little secret door which the meowl had disappeared behind, wondering how long they should wait before deciding if it would come back or not. They waited in silence, not knowing if the meowl would swiftly pop back out from behind or under any other random piece of furniture. After a short while, they decided to carry on snooping around the cottage, looking for clues as to how they might reach Alexandra; or if she'd even ever been here at all.

Kare then looked behind a thick, rug-like curtain which was hung from the ceiling and appeared to be covering a gap in the wall. Sure enough, behind it she found another archway, this time revealing to a narrow, winding staircase which led to the floor above. Creating a glow around herself to light the way, leaving Kai to take control over lighting the downstairs, she fluttered her way up the stairs to see what she could find.

She'd just about made it to the next floor, when abruptly out of nowhere a startling, clashing sound ripped through the sleepy silence in the cottage, jolting them both and sending their hearts racing. The noise was something like the sound of a pile of pots and pans crashing onto the floor. Kare swiftly raced back to Kai to check if he was alright, assuming it was he who'd caused it, unbeknownst that he was also fanatically searching for her, thinking she'd just bumped into something.

Fluttering about in search of one another, Kare crashed

into Kai as she burst through the entrance to the stairwell. They both let out a scream of shock upon the collision, then proceeded to calm themselves down when they realised it was still just the two of them. Once they knew that neither of them had caused the noise, they flew back over to the fireplace and waited, standing close by one other and gripping each other's hand. They were beginning to feel uneasy in this cramped, dimly lit cottage, so much so that sweat was now beading across their foreheads. They waited here together by their escape route eagerly anticipating the next disturbance.

Unbeknown to Kai and Kare, once the meowl had disappeared into the wall behind the painting, it had begun making its way down to a secret area hidden beneath the cottage. It sauntered through a number of narrow tunnels, winding downwards and leading into the rooms beneath the fake home. Conveniently, a meowl's eyes had an extra, magical ability, allowing them to see perfectly clearly whilst in total darkness.

The area beneath spread much wider than the cottage itself and the ceilings were higher, creating much more space; indeed, more suited to someone of normal human height. The room the meowl came out into would be best described as the work-den of a potion master. Walls covered by tall bookshelves and cupboards, empty glass vials lying about on work surfaces and messy wooden tables. There was a curved corner fireplace with countless candles melted into the mantelpiece, and traces of broken glass could be found in the cold soot inside it.

On one of the work surfaces sat items that wouldn't look out of place in a chemistry lab, as well as short, stumpy pencils and scrap pieces of paper with endless notes scribbled upon them. On another workbench rested a round iron pot, held up over wide dish full of ash. Across the room in another corner was a tatty looking olive-green sofa, with a few beige pillows on it and a gold throw draped over the back. The floor and the walls were built of stone, with the odd wooden beam to help hold up the structure.

The meowl flew through this room, passing over one of the workbenches on its way and accidentally knocking a pile of small metal plates over as it skimmed across its surface. Once at the other side of the room, it pushed open a door that had been left slightly ajar, leading into a long hallway.

To the left stood a door made from a metal found only on Île Merveille, named Plufort. It was the strongest substance known on this or any other land, which could only be moulded by magic after being treated with a potion only very few knew how to make. Otherwise, this metal was known to be indestructible.

To the right there were many other doors, though simply made of wood, spaced out down a long corridor crafted with a wooden floor and soft, pickle-green wallpaper splashed with gold flecks; the corridor was so old that the wallpaper was peeling off in places and had many scratched cut into it. The meowl wondered down to one very specific door, not too far along. This door was also left slightly ajar, and it just happened to be the resting place of Alexandra.

The meowl strutted into the room without a bother and walked right up to her large, four poster bed, which had soft, heavy, blonde drapes loosely attached to each poster. The meowl jumped up onto it with such ease, as if it had simply levitated itself up there, and landed gracefully next to Alexandra.

Here upon her bed she lay on her side, peacefully breathing in an ageless deep sleep. Her long, wavy, crimson red hair hugging the curves from her once white pillows to the edge of the bed. A soft, earth-toned blanket had been pulled over her up to her chest, which she appeared to still be holding wrapped tightly around her.

The meowl stepped up onto the side of her body then sat down, looking at her face whilst twitching its head around from side to side again. Then it walked along her and stepped down onto the bed in front of her face, where it sat facing her. It then began to rub its face up against her cheek and purr like a cat, before it rubbed the whole side of its body along her face.

With still no reaction from Alexandra, the meowl sat once more in front of her face, then lifted its front claw up and began tapping her gently on her left cheek and nose, much like a cat when trying to get a reaction from an inanimate object. Yet again, Alexandra remained undisturbed, until the meowl let out one of its cries, "Miauoooo!" it howled.

After that it looked back at Alexandra to see that she was beginning to stir. Her eyelids started to flicker as she half opened her eyes. The meowl then watched by as she closed them again and rolled over to go back to sleep, and it knew its job wasn't yet finished.

So, the meowl then stepped back up onto Alexandra and began clawing at her, the way a cat does before it decides to lie down, only with the owl claws this was not quite as harmless. Abruptly she awoke and sat up in her bed, and as she did her meowl jumped back down to the ground and graciously trotted off back out of the room and up into the cottage.

As Alexandra sat up in bed, she began rubbing her eyes as she came around from her deep slumber. Then gently she opened them, whilst all the candles in the room grew flames as she did so.

Back up inside the cottage, Kai and Kare were still stood by the fireplace when the meowl emerged from behind the picture on the wall, shutting the secret door once again behind it. The meowl leapt from the shelf and spread open its wings, as it swooped down to the floor and grabbed hold of a circular rug with its claws as it passed it. It didn't pick up the rug however, it merely dragged it across the floor and left it placed just in front of the front door.

After that, it flew away to a corner of the room where it landed upon a perch it had, mounted onto a small bookcase. All three were silent. Kai and Kare had no idea what was going on, or if this meowl was even doing anything related to what they'd said to it earlier. For a moment they focused on the rug that had been moved, then on the front door, before turning to stare at each other and shrugging their shoulders. They stood a minute more until deciding to head back out of the cottage via the chimney.

Fortunately for Kai and Kare, they had waited just long enough before deciding to leave, for had they hung around merely seconds less, they may have missed what was to happen next.

Just as Kare took her first step towards the chimney, they heard another strange noise. This time it was more of a clunky noise, a bit like an old heavy lock being turned. She spun around quickly, facing back into the dimly lit room, squinting to see if she could make out what had made the sound; it seemed much closer to them than the last one.

Again they heard it. Together they huddled closely, frightened of the unknown. "What do you suppose it is?" asked Kare.
"I have no idea," Kai replied hopelessly.

As they both stared nervously into the motionless room, they couldn't miss it when the rug began to lift up from one side, as if it had suddenly become stiff and was now hinged to the wooden floor. They were both confused. For a moment ago that was (what appeared to be) solid wooden panels nailed into place, and the rug was just a normal rug. "Witchcraft," muttered Kai, as he held his left hand to his chest.

Now, what they were seeing was not only the rug lift up, but a hole in the floor beneath it; and a hand holding up what was now clearly a door. They were stunned, believing that this would be it, the moment they would meet Alexandra face to face.

Everyone on Île Merveille knew of her, the witch who ended all witches was how she was known. They all knew that as long as she lay sleeping, there was a chance that humans might once again harness the sacred light that flowed from within their land. Of course, some creatures here welcomed this, for as long as humans and magic could mix, the inhabitants of Île Merveille were free to mix with the rest of the world and live as one; though unfortunately, many preferred the idea of exploiting the weaker, non-magical creatures of the world for their own benefit.

However, this was not the ideal as far as Alexandra was concerned. She wanted to keep Île Merveille hidden and protected from human involvement, restricting any other human from ever again coming into contact with the light from the spring again. Thankfully for Alexandra, the Tawhio fairies were in agreement with her, for as long as there was no threat of witches, wizards, sorcerer's or such like, the large Tawhio colony were able to keep their rule over the Tonga jungle.

Slowly Alexandra began to emerge from the secret door in the floor, exiting via a spiral staircase below it. Kai and Kare watched in amazement, in awe at the power which she exuded simply from people knowing the story of her past.

CHAPTER FIFTEEN

Potions & Portals

At last, she had entered the room fully. Her silhouette they could just about make out as she stood in the shadowy doorway, once they'd pulled back their balls of glowing light to exit with them. Calmly she stepped forward, away from where she'd entered the room, before abruptly tapping her right foot once on the floor. Before they had chance to wonder why she'd done it, they were both startled by the sound of the door behind her slamming shut into the floor. With their hearts beating a mile a minute, they clenched each other's hand tightly, as they both swallowed with the loudest gulping sound they'd probably ever made. Alexandra was the first to speak. "Who here claims to have seen a witch?" she asked in a low tone with a hint of a northern English accent.

"Erm...we do," said Kai and Kare in unison.

"Your Excellency," added Kare nervously, bowing her head slightly hoping to please Alexandra.

"Who's we? I can hardly see a thing in here," with that, Alexandra took in a deep breath, then exhaled forcefully.

The moment she exhaled, all the shutters and windows of the cottage burst open, banishing away the dust on them in swirling clouds as they did. What was left of the glowing balls of light which Kai had created were suddenly extinguished, resulting in a nervous sideways glance at each other between Kai and Kare.

Alexandra rubbed her eyes as they adjusted to the light, before continuing to question the room. They could see her clearly now, a woman of average height with a slim but curvy figure. She wore a skirt which reached down to her ankles and had a slit to the knee, made from a dull, burgundy cloth which appeared to be one piece of material folded over, creating a double layer with the top layer ripped to fall to different lengths.

Her top was made of the same material, also ripped looking around the edges, it covered her chest and most of her stomach, and it was tied up in knots holding it together over several places across her back; with just one piece reaching over her left shoulder.

A simple, scuffed, bronze ring was all the jewellery she wore, and her voluminous, tousled, wavy red hair fell about her shoulders, reaching as far down as her lower back. Her intense, stormy coloured eyes glanced around the room as she asked, "So, who was that who spoke?"

Kai and Kare cautiously fluttered timidly over to a table closer to Alexandra, so that she may look upon them more easily as they answered her "We did," they announced together.

"And I presume, as you woke me up, that you're sure of this…"

"Yes. There are three. We though…" Kai was interrupted by a sudden outburst from Alexandra.

"THREE?!" she snapped, "And how long have they been here?"

"Only since yesterday morning… we think," said Kare timidly.

Alexandra stared away from them for a moment whilst she took in the information, "And where are they now?" she asked.

"We, er… we're not sure exactly," said Kai, sheepishly.

She looked back at them with an expression that was in equal parts shocked, frustrated and disappointed at the same time. She tapped her foot on the floor which sprung open the secret door, then she hurried back down the spiral stairs. Kai and Kare heard the clunking noises again, though this time much clearer with the door in the floor left open. Innocently they began to fly over to have a look down the stairs, but their path was obstructed as the meowl flew frantically towards them, screeching, yowling and forcing them back to where they'd been stood.

A short while passed until they heard the clunking noise again, followed by Alexandra as she came back up the stairs. She looked at them, and then to the meowl. "Right," she said, before turning and exiting the cottage through the front door.

Kai and Kare had both noticed that she'd had something in her hand, and they wanted to follow her to see what she was going to do; though they feared being warned off by the meowl again. So, they looked at the meowl, who was now sat back upon its perch with its eyes half shut and slowly blinking.

"Can we…" began Kai, looking at the meowl and pointing towards the door.

"Is it ok if…" added Kare.

"Is he going to sleep?" asked Kai.

"Meowl?" said Kare.

"Let's go," whispered Kai out the corner of his mouth. Then with that, they both flew out the door to follow Alexandra.

They saw that she had gone out into the meadow and was stood facing south, towards the entrance to the basin in the distance. Together they remained at what they felt was a safe distance, sat on a branch of a tree at the edge of the woods, with a good view of what was going on. They watched as she looked at a glass bottle which she held in her hand, a similar shape to a pizza-oil dispenser though not quite so large, before pulling out the cork from the top.

From the bottle, she poured out a thick, purple, creamy liquid, which she smeared over the palms of her hands. Kai and Kare looked at each other and shrugged, then watched on silently wondering what on earth she was about to do.

She proceeded to lift her arms out straight with her palms facing forward, then lifted her arms slightly higher so that her palms faced the sky ahead of her. They saw that she began to speak, though they couldn't hear what she was saying, and as she began to speak, she closed her eyes.

As she spoke with her palms held up facing out ahead of her, they noticed her hair begin to move, as if it was blowing in a breeze which hadn't yet reached them, which then grew noticeably stronger and stronger. Before too long, there was a forceful wind blowing southwards through the once still, sleepy basin which Kai and Kare had arrived in.

They moved closer to each other as they continued to watch Alexandra, when, to their surprise, her legs gave way as she fell to her knees. Kare stood up, concerned and wanting to help, but she was held back as Kai grabbed her hand and looked up at her shaking his head.

After she'd fallen to the ground, Alexandra placed her hands on the floor either side of her, with her palms face down on the grass. She bowed her head and continued to speak words which the fairies couldn't hear. As she spoke to the ground, Kai and Kare began to hear noises around them, noises that weren't coming from animals, but from the earth.

The steady stream which flowed by the cottage began to flow louder and stronger, and distant creaks and sounds of rock-fall from high in the mountains around them echoed across the basin. It seemed like the earth around them was waking up to her words, the flowers in the meadow and the branches of the trees were all now dancing in the wind which she appeared to have summoned.

Alexandra then sat upright and looked at her hands, the purple mixture she had smeared onto them had vanished. She stroked the grass on the floor in front of her before standing up, then turned to head back to the cottage. She walked right past Kai and Kare and went straight inside, where they followed her closely so as not to get left outside alone. Once they were all back indoors, they looked at her, waiting for an explanation of what just happened, to which she calmly responded with, "And now, we wait."

All day the three of them sat together inside the cottage, and Alexandra begrudgingly used her magic to feed them as they waited together. They passed the time engaging in small talk. She explained to them that the purple substance she'd smeared on her hands was an offering to the land, one of rich nutrients and sweet, tasty delight. She told them she had offered this to the earth she stood upon in return for information as to where she might find the three strangers on Île Merveille.

After that, she introduced her pet meowl, named Tuca. This creature was not only extremely wise by nature, but her guardian who had the ability to sense oncoming, immediate danger, should it be heading her way. Alexandra was also interested to hear how things had been on Île Merveille since she'd put herself into her deep sleep, many years earlier. So, Kai and Kare filled her in on just about everything there was to know about their colony, and their view on how things seemed to be on the island these days.

They sat together well into the evening, just after the sun had set, when their chit-chat was interrupted by a bang on the door, which made everyone jump up and brought their conversation to an abrupt end.

A startled Kai instantly grabbed hold of Kare's arm, then they both looked to Alexandra to do something. It took her a moment to realise what this was about, and when she did, she quickly got up from her chair and hurried over to the front door. Cautiously she opened it, and peering out into the softly lit forest, she listened to the all the sounds she could hear. It was clear to all of them that the most dominant was that of the river flowing by.

With that being heard above all else, Alexandra walked over to it and plunged her right hand into the water, without even a flinch from the sharp coldness she must have felt. Upon pulling it back out, she rubbed her fingers against her thumb and gazed out ahead of her, with a look of deep concentration in her eyes. She then lifted her wet hand to her face and sniffed it.

"They're still in the south," she said, moving her hand

away from her face, "But further north from your jungle."

Next came a strong gust of wind, blowing northwards this time, carrying with it some dry, dusty dirt. Alexandra watched the dirt as it was swept across the floor around her feet, until she suddenly looked ahead and grasped out into thin air with her right hand. After that, the wind died out like the last puff of air coming out of a dead balloon, and she turned to the cottage to use the light shining out from the front door to view this which she had caught in her hand.

It was a piece of palm leaf with a red stain on it. She examined the stain closely, sniffed it, then rubbed it with the tip of her finger. Kai and Kare watched curiously until they saw Alexandra begin to delicately taste her finger after rubbing the stain, prompting a look of disgust on their faces.

"Vampires," she said, "A large family of vampires." Alexandra then turned her gaze towards the fairies, "Do you know of a large family of vampires north of your jungle?" she asked.

"Well, I suppose it can only be Raul and Veshnica Báthory," Kai said nervously as he looked to Kare for confirmation.

"Right, well you must take me to them and then you may return to your colony."

"Alexandra I must warn you, the Báthory family is very large, and very strong," warned Kare.

"Well, aren't all vampire families?" Alexandra shrugged off their warning. Then as she thought about it, she realised that it wouldn't hurt to take some extra protection. She again descended into her hideout underneath the cottage, whilst Kai and Kare sat with Tuca in the living room, eagerly awaiting her return.

As she came back up the stairs, they saw that she had

donned a long, dark grey cloak, made of material not too heavy to flow on the breeze behind her as she walked. The cloak was big enough to reach all the way around her, and it was held together across her collar by a dark-bronze coloured, circular clasp, weighing down enough so that the cloak sat evenly across her shoulders from front to back. She had also roughly tied her hair up at the back of her head, revealing a large hood on the cloak. Hidden underneath she wore a small, brown satchel, though the fairies weren't quite sure what she was carrying inside it.

Alexandra didn't want to waste any time in getting to the vampire's home, with fear of losing the trail. She knew that the tropical south of Merveille would be a long flight for the fairies, so she agreed to use magic to get them all to the vampire's home; from where Kai and Kare were free to continue on back to their colony.

Out of the satchel she pulled another glass bottle, though unlike the last one which had had square edges, this one had a curved shape with a very slim neck. The liquid inside was much waterier, and it was pale yellow in colour.

"Right," she said to Kai and Kare, "I'm going to carefully drip this onto the door, turning it into a temporary portal. Once I've applied all the liquid, I'll need one, or both of you," (she said after upon realising the size of them compared to the door) "To open the door. All the while picturing a place in view of the vampire's home… But not too close."

Kai and Kare agreed, then watched as Alexandra began shaking out the liquid, splashing it over the wooden door. Once she'd finished, the two of them decided on a safe place they could arrive at, then held hands and flew towards the door.

Using their powers, they imagined a clasp around the door handle which they turned to open the door. As they let go the door swung outwards (which was odd as before it had only opened inwards) and outside they could see the dry, warm landscape surrounding Raul and Veshnica's home, and the dark, eerie mansion sat ahead of them.

Kai and Kare looked at Alexandra and nodded, confirming that that was the right place, as she then looked over to Tuca signalling her to come with them. Once Tuca was perched on her shoulder, she walked carefully through the doorway, clutching her cloak as she went. Kai and Kare followed close behind.

The door slammed shut once the fairies had flown through, and they all stood outside under the night sky, in the still, warm summer air. Alexandra stood out in the open, staring at the dark mansion. "That's it?" she asked the fairies, just to be sure.
"That's it," they replied.

"Right, well thank you, umm… what were your names again?" Alexandra asked, her mind occupied with more important things when they'd mentioned earlier.
"Kai and Kare," they replied.
"Erm, your excellency," added Kare as she bowed, not knowing what Alexandra expected.

"Of course, Kai and Kare. Thank you for coming to me today, your loyalty will not be forgotten, and you may pass that message onto your king. Now you must go, and I wish you both a safe journey back to your colony." She didn't know exactly what was going to happen once she'd made herself known to the vampires, but she couldn't be thinking about the fairies whilst staying strong, should her little visit take a turn for the worst.

Kai and Kare fluttered off and found a spot to create their Manukah bird, which they rode on off into the night, back to towards the Tonga jungle.

Stood there now with only Tuca as company, she took in a deep breath and pulled her hood up over her head.

Then she looked at Tuca and began to stroke her cheek with her finger, before saying, "Once again, it's down to you and me, Tuca. Let's go." And with that, she walked under the light of the moon towards the vampire's mansion, with one aim on her mind – putting an end to these new witches.

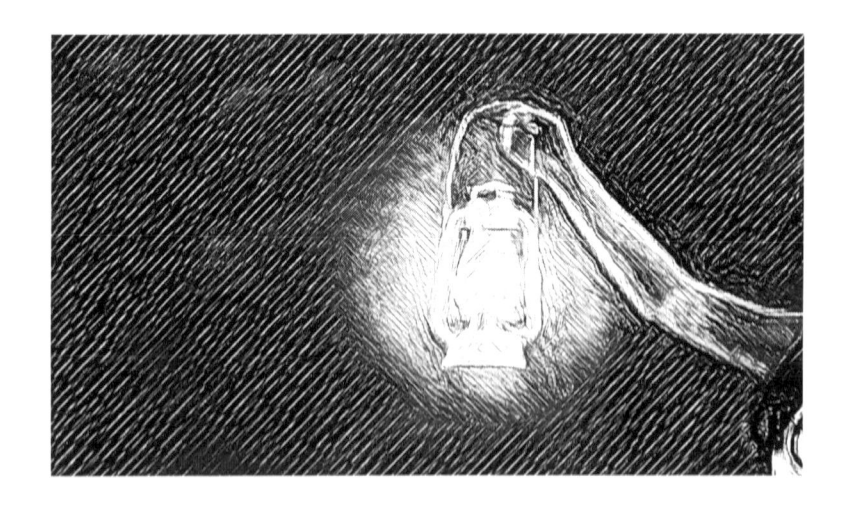

CHAPTER SIXTEEN

Old Magic

As Alexandra walked towards the vampire manor, she got a surprise when suddenly she witnessed the swarms of bats bursting out from the main entrance. She crouched down, huddled under her cloak and hiding Tuca under there with her. The bats flew out across the barren grounds surrounding the manor, straight over Alexandra as she hid, her scent protected from them by the cloak she was under. They headed in all directions, disappearing into the nearby woods, on the hunt for Chloé, Chris and Lancelin.

Once they'd passed, Alexandra stood up again, looking around to confirm that there were no more heading her way. Once she was sure they'd gone, she continued heading towards the manor, wondering if any vampires actually remained inside or not. Either way, she was determined to find answers on this night.

Chloé, Chris and Lancelin, after fleeing from the vampires, had run across the grounds that extended out from behind the manor. It was a large garden, much in need of repair and a touch of life adding to it, which they ran through as fast as they could, desperately searching for a way out.

Upon reaching the other end, they found they were closed in by a tall, stone wall, separating the garden from the dusty pine forest behind it. Due to the wall's dishevelled state however, they each managed to climb over it, passing over the rucksack holding all their belongings as they went, landing themselves within the slight shelter of the trees. Lancelin insisted that they stop here for a moment, complaining that he was out of breath from running. But, as far as Chris saw it, stopping for a rest was just not an option; not at this critical moment in time.

The two of them began arguing, Chris couldn't understand how Lancelin could even think that this was at all a time to rest. Chloé stepped in to stop the commotion, trying to be a voice of understanding between them, though she knew Chris was right. She managed to convince Lancelin to run just a bit further with them, that they might find a safer place to hide within the darkness deeper in the forest. Through his increasingly shadowy ways (as Chris saw them) Lancelin seemed far less reluctant to argue with her like he had done with Chris, and he'd backed down to Chloé straight away; which Chris found extremely frustrating.

He was already sure that Lancelin wanted him out of the way but just couldn't work out why. This wasn't a time for confrontation though, Chris knew he had to simply bite his tongue if he wanted to keep moving away from the vampires - the bigger of two evils as he saw it. So together they ran deeper into the forest, searching for a safe place to rest until sunrise.

Meanwhile, back at the manor, Alexandra had reached the front door, which had been left ajar since the mass exodus of all the bats. Respectfully she stood outside, with Tuca perched upon her shoulder, and listened for any motion coming from within.

The air that night was still, and Alexandra could hear the distant sound of the bats screeching in the woods; she was aware that they may return at any given moment. She knocked solidly on the large, open door three times, then waited for a sign of life coming from inside. But there was nothing. No one came to answer the door in the moments after she'd knocked, so she decided to enter uninvited.

She knew that vampires of such status, living in places as big as this, lived together in large numbers. So, to lessen the risk of a guard or even an ambush hiding on the other side of the door, she first took a step back. Then, as she channelled her powers through her mind, she forced the two doors to swing wide-open causing them to crash loudly as one hit the wall and the other a small table behind it. The disturbance was enough to make even the sleepiest resident jump to their feet.

After peering inside, she gracefully entered into the grand entrance hall, lit up only by the silver light of the moon shining in through the open doors. Finding it difficult to see, she was seconds away from using her magic to light up the room, when Tuca discreetly interrupted her by squeezing Alexandra's shoulder gently with her claws.

This was Tuca's way of warning Alexandra of a nearby threat, without arousing their suspicion. Calmly she looked around to see what danger may have found her.

As before, when Chris, Chloé and Lancelin had entered, some of the children of the count and countess had managed to sneak up on her, lurking in the darkness which engulfed the house. Tuca's ability to see in the dark and to sense upcoming threats, had helped to alert Alexandra, eliminating the element of surprise for the vampires; which was just about their only tool when fighting off a powerful witch.

She squinted as she peered into the dark corners of the room, before her gaze was lost as she tried to focus on the deep blackness of the rooms beyond the entrance hall. Feeling it pointless staring into pitch darkness, she moved her right hand out from under the cloak and lifted it up to almost head height. As her arm lifted, she clenched her fist as a swish of light appeared under her hand, leaving behind a lantern with a ball of light glowing inside, which she now held up to cancel out the shadows.

The glow from the magic inside this lantern shone brighter than any regular flame that might otherwise have created the glow, creating enough light for Alexandra to see well around her. She turned slowly as she looked around the room, and as she faced towards the large archway leading into the next living space, she saw one of the vampire children stood staring back at her.

"Hello," she said, lowering the lantern slightly and dimming the light out of courtesy, "I've come to see the count and countess. Are they here?"

The child, a male, was one of the count and countess' older and more experienced children (meaning he had drunk more fresh blood than others), therefore he was stronger than most of his vampire siblings and often stayed behind as a guard for the count and countess.

He was dressed in tight black trousers which tucked into knee-length, black leather boots. Around his waist wrapped a piece of ashy, grey cloth, from under which hung two light grey pieces of material, one on the front side and one on the back; which reached halfway down his muscular thighs. He wore black leather gloves and a long-sleeved, tight, grey top, which had arched, pointed black shoulder pads reaching from shoulder to shoulder, forming a high collar around his neck in the middle.

He was surprised and also confused to have seen Alexandra use magic, as he hadn't been able to sense her witch scent at all through her cloak... nor had any of them seen magic used by a human in quite some time.

"What's your business with the count and countess?" he asked in a rough, low voice.
"I'd rather discuss that with them," she replied. There was a moment of silence between the two before the vampire asked her to wait, and then proceeded to head up the stairs before disappearing off into another part of the manor. Alexandra waited patiently, stood centred in the entrance hall holding her lantern high, keeping her eyes fixed on the top of the stairs.

About five minutes passed whilst she waited, before she witnessed a small flame soar around the room with flair, setting alight every single candle as it passed it. She let go of her lantern which disappeared in another swish of light as it fell, and kept her focus fixed on the top of the staircase.

As she watched the landing, count Raul appeared from down the corridor which the vampire before had disappeared along, and stood strong at the top of the staircase.

"Count Raul, I presume?" said Alexandra.
"Correct," he replied in a strong, masculine voice.
"I'm Alexa..." she began to introduce herself, though was interrupted by the booming sound of the count's voice.

"I know exactly who you are, witch. What I don't know is why you feel it acceptable to enter my house uninvited and demand my presence," said the count as he looked down upon her from the top of the long, cold staircase.

"Relax, I'm not here to try to cause harm to you, the countess, nor any of your children," replied Alexandra, "However, it's come to my attention that you may have something that belongs to me. Or more, three somethings to be precise. Three witches?"
"Nothing here belongs to you. I suggest you leave, now."
"I'm afraid I'm not leaving here until you tell me what you know of these three new witches…" Alexandra demanded as she stood confidently, alone at the bottom of the stairs.
"You have no control over us, you know the law," threatened Raul as he stepped forward, trying to intimidate her.
"I think you're forgetting, that now I AM the law!" she responded firmly, pushing fear of her strength and powers onto Raul.

As Alexandra spoke, the vampire who'd gone to fetch Raul, and another who was dressed exactly the same, appeared from down the corridor where Raul had entered from and stood solidly at either side of him. Raul stepped forward again slightly, to which Alexandra responded by opening her cloak to reveal her satchel, with her hand ready to reach into it.

The atmosphere in the room grew strong and tense, until it was softly broken by the presence of Vulp as he stepped between Raul and his men with elegance and ease. They all took their focus from each other and gave it to Vulp, as he sauntered out from between them and sat down in front of Raul, then looked up at him. They each wondered what he was doing, when the silence was broken by the sound of Veshnica's honeyed voice coming from down the corridor.

"Now, now everyone, let's not come to battle over a simple misunderstanding," she said calmly as she emerged. "Won't you join us in the Red Room, Alexandra? and perhaps we can put this matter to rest." Veshnica then motioned to Alexandra to come up the stairs and follow them. "Oh, and Paza," (one of the vampires standing by Raul) "Fetch us something to drink, will you?" she said smiling, to which he responded with a simple, short nod.

Alexandra held the banister lightly as she walked up the stairs and followed them through the manor to the Red Room. This was a sort of upstairs, lounge area, with a bar in one corner and a large fireplace along the main wall of the room. There were comfortable chairs and sofas in here, placed facing each other in front of the fire, creating a cosy circular setting to sit and talk. It was called the Red Room due to the tainted red colour of the stone which the walls were built from, and the large, deep-scarlet rug, upon which sat the chairs and sofas in front of the fireplace.

The room was lit before they entered as the others had been, by the small, enslaved, fire-bodied elementame which followed the count and countess around the manor. Veshnica was the first to enter, and she invited Alexandra to take a seat as she sat down on the stiff sofa, joined by Raul.

Alexandra chose a chair at an angle from their seat, so she was on the outside of the circle facing both the vampires and the fireplace; with Tuca perched on her shoulder listening out behind her.

"So, you're looking for three witches I heard you say. Is this true?" Veshnica asked, coyly.
"That's right, countess, and my sources tell me that they've been here to your manor."
"What sources would they be?" she asked.
"I don't think that's any concern of yours. Now have you seen the three witches or not? Because if you have, and

you're hiding them from me, well, we both know that wasn't part of the deal, don't we?"

Raul's anger towards Alexandra grew with her threatening behaviour, he would never be made to feel lesser by someone who was once human, or a decedent of; a species he saw to be beneath him.

"Are you threatening me in my house!" he shouted at her as he stood up from the sofa.
"Rue-Rue please, sit down. Alexandra is just trying to scare us to get what she wants," said Veshnica as she gently touched Raul's arm and sat him back down. "I can assure you, Alexandra, the only witch we have seen in the last two hundred years, is you."

Alexandra assumed Veshnica was lying and insisted that they be honest with her before she takes it upon herself to force the truth from them, one way or another. By this point, Raul had had enough. He'd been threatened in his own home by Alexandra for the last time and suddenly burst up from his seat and stepped aggressively towards her.

"This is the LAST time you, or any of your kind, threaten me or my family in this house! Get out!" he yelled at her.
"No," she said, trying hard not to react to his outburst and remain composed, "I refuse to go anywhere until you tell me where the witches are."

He then snapped his fingers and in ran another twelve or so powerful vampires, who surrounded Alexandra entirely. "Get her out of here!" he ordered as he pointed towards the door.

Two of them went to grab her, however as they touched her cloak it burnt their skin, shocking the vampires surrounding her into each falling a few steps back. Alexandra then stood up sternly from her chair and walked towards Raul and Veshnica, as the other vampires flinched out of her path.

"All witches in this land MUST be brought forward to ME. If I should find that you two have been hiding any, I'll return here to make sure that you won't EVER be doing so again."

As she finished speaking, she looked at each of them directly into their eyes, conveying just how serious she was. She wanted to scare them, to make them think twice about going up against her. Raul made sure he stood firmly between Veshnica and Alexandra, protecting his love from the witch whom he despised. Then, as she'd got the full rooms attention, she concentrated hard on her powers whilst trying to appear to the rest of them that what she was about to do was nothing compared to what she was fully capable of.

Without warning, she emitted a great flash of light, filling the whole room with an intense, white, brightness which burned the skin of each vampire it touched. With it came a thunderous boom, which shattered all the glass in the room, knocked over the furniture and forced the door right off its hinges. The whole thing happened as if they were all trapped in a storm cloud as the lightning struck, and as quickly as it came, the light in the room was back to normal, and Tuca and Alexandra had vanished.

Each vampire had been knocked back by the attack. Raul helped Veshnica up on to her feet as she screamed with pain and anger. Keeping as calm as he could through the pain, he instructed the others to help the countess to her room, where she would find a supply of healing potion stashed away and reserved only for the count and countess.

Potions and magic which were vampire friendly were extremely rare here, as the light of magic gained from the spring burnt their skin. However, luckily for them, there was once a time when vampires and few witches worked together. The witches who befriended the vampires worked hard to create magic that the vampires were able to use. Unfortunately though, there was a law against this. A law stopping humans who possessed magical powers from tampering with the already supernatural beings, in fear of creating creatures far stronger than themselves.

Though some witches had managed to create what they called 'the night light', they had only managed to test it through a few potion recipes before it was discovered by the lawmakers, who then imprisoned the sorcerers who created it. Luckily for the count and countess, their status had granted them access to a small amount of the exclusive night light creations, which had been well hidden and preserved.

Though the vampires would heal within a few hours, the count couldn't bear to see the love of his life suffer. So as instructed, their guards helped the countess to her room, where hidden in her dressing table she found a small glass vial containing a dark red liquid, which she consumed entirely.

Within a few seconds her skin began to bubble as it speedily repaired itself. Then, to all who could see her, her body began to fade into complete blackness. She squeezed the hand of one of her children as it was happening and took in a deep breath which she held onto. For a moment she remained in darkness. Then, as she finally exhaled, her body came back from the shadow it had disappeared into, and her burns from the light had been completely healed.

Feeling at her full strength once again, she threw the vial on the floor in anger and then strutted across her room, exiting out onto her balcony which overlooked the gardens and to the forest beyond them. "We have to find them before she does," she said to herself, looking out into the distance. Vulp walked over to her and jumped up onto the thick stone railings enclosing the balcony. He sat by her as she gently stroked the fur on his back, calming her anger.

CHAPTER SEVENTEEN

The Tale of the Unicorn Man

О ut in the woods, Chloé, Chris and Lancelin continued to try and outrun the vampire bats they knew would be chasing them. Darting between the trees, getting hit in the face by branches and stumbling over rocks and mounds, they struggled to see in the dark setting of the late-night forest. Chris attempted to lead the way as fast as he could, shining their torch to light their way, though it was dimming as it began to run low on battery power. He was so focused on heading forwards as fast as he could, that he didn't hear as Lancelin tripped over a tree root and fell to the ground with a thud.

"Wait!" Chloé shouted, "Chris stop! Lancelin's hurt!"

Chris turned and shone the torch behind him, looking for Lancelin on the ground. Chloé went back to help him, but it appeared Lancelin had hurt his ankle so much so that he could hardly walk on it, let alone run. He insisted that he couldn't go on any further, which didn't surprise Chris in the slightest. Chris still refused to wait there out in the open for the vampires to find them, sparking a heated argument once again between the two of them.

"Stop it you two!" cried Chloé, "Chris what's the matter with you? Can't you see he's hurt?"

Chris completely lost his temper. Lancelin had managed to make him look like the bad guy and turned Chloé against him. "Don't you dare take sides with him over me! Can't you see that this is all calculated? He's trying to break us apart. Ever since he almost let me drown in the ocean."

"Is that what this is about? Chris, he saved your life! Not to mention that he saved it for the second time just yesterday in the woods. I'm not leaving him alone to get caught, we'll have to think of something!" she insisted.

Chris turned away in frustration. He wanted to yell at her, to get her to realise what actually happened that night he was thrown overboard in the storm, from how he saw it at least, but he knew it was pointless. Lancelin had broken into their relationship and was succeeding in pushing Chris out.

With the fear of being found by the vampires, Chloé thought that the best thing to do would be to look in the book for guidance. Frantically she opened the rucksack and pulled it out, though it wasn't with ease as she hadn't opened the top of the rucksack fully through her panic. Setting it down upon her knee, she pleaded for help as she ran her shaking thumb across the edges of the closed pages, desperately seeking its guidance.

Unlike the times before though, she felt nothing. No pull, nor desire to open the book on any page. The longer she tried, the more desperate she became. In an attempt to calm herself down she began to take deep breaths, until she was interrupted by Chris.

"Shh! Wait. Can you hear that?" he asked through a whisper. It was the sound of bats screeching in the distance, getting closer and closer by the second. The bats rushed through the trees until they'd inevitably caught the scent of the three humans. In their entirety, they surrounded the three of them completely and small groups of bats flew together; transforming back into single vampires. Gradually they closed in on the humans, until one of them ordered one of her siblings to go and fetch the count and countess.

Elsewhere at that time, in view of the manor and the wall surrounding the gardens, Alexandra lay on the ground, slowly coming into consciousness and covered by her cloak. As she came around, she cautiously sat herself up. Weakened from using so much power all at once, after being asleep for so long, and then having been thrown onto the hard ground as she landed, she reached into her bag for her healing potion.

With her limited strength, she managed to pop the cork from the top of the small glass vial and drank the light, almost glowing, cherry-red liquid inside. After she drank it, her skin began to glow briefly. Then her arms gave way and her upper-body collapsed back to the ground. She rolled her aching body over onto her back and took in a deep breath, before slowly exhaling a faint, greyish-yellow smoke-like matter from within her; which contained a few glittering sparkles. She had now been blissfully restored to her full strength, and as she gazed up at the stars she pondered over the events that had just taken place. Until it struck her - where was Tuca?

She called out in a whisper, searching the dusty moonlit

floor around her for her pet meowl. She heard a cry, thankfully not far from her, that could be described as that of a yowling cat. She immediately got up and scurried along in the direction of the sound, hunching herself to get a clearer view of the floor around her. Sure enough, she found Tuca lying scrumpled on the floor, with one of her wings clearly broken.

Carefully she knelt down beside her and stroked her gently to reassure her that she was safe now. As Tuca was only a small creature, compared to Alexandra, and Alexandra loved her truly, it didn't take much for her to be healed by Alexandra's magic. With a caring kiss from Alexandra to Tuca's injured wing, it began to repair itself.

The bones cracked and clicked as they reformed, and the joints snapped back into place. The broken skin and torn feathers regrew as new, and the once broken wing was healed. She lifted Tuca up and held her close to her in her arms, "I'm so sorry," she whispered.

As they huddled together, the warm embrace was broken when they heard the warning screeching sound of bats in the distance heading their way. Alexandra covered them both with her cloak and peeked out from under it. She saw a small swarm of bats returning to the back entrance of the manor, but without any sign of the three witches. Once they all appeared to be inside, she began running low and quietly back towards the garden walls of the manor; she knew they were up to something.

As she got close, however, she stopped dead in her tracks as the bats burst out once more from the manor, though this time exiting out from the countess' balcony which over-looked the garden. Had she not been so startled she may also have noticed a small glow from a fiery flame who flew with them. Swiftly she crouched down whilst cradling Tuca in her arms, but thankfully the bats flew straight off in the direction of the forest beyond the back garden walls.

Looking around first to make sure there were no others coming, Alexandra lifted Tuca up into the air as Tuca flapped her wings, then took off into flight. "Follow them, my little princess. You shall be my eyes and I shall keep you safe," she whispered, as Tuca flew off following behind the vampire bats. Alexandra kept her eye on them until they'd vanished into the trees, then ran over to the outer wall of the manor where she sat down against it, huddled under her cloak.

As she sat quietly, she reached into her bag and pulled out a feather that had once belonged to Tuca, and she stroked it gently with her thumb and forefinger, as she chanted;

> *Share with me your eyes,*
> *Show me what you see.*
> *As my power flows to you,*
> *No harm shall come to thee.*

This incantation she chanted over and over, until finally her own eyes faded to completely white and she saw only that which Tuca could see.

Tuca followed the bats through the trees until she saw them reform into their more human-like forms. Hiding in the darkness, upon a high branch with a view of the scene, she watched over the three humans and the vampires completely undetected.

Chloé, Chris and Lancelin were speechless. Caught and trapped by the vampires they'd just escaped from. Chloé slipped the book back into the rucksack, and Chris stood still with fear whilst Lancelin remained helpless on the floor. Veshnica had now joined them as she stood out from amongst her children alone, without Raul by her side. She had come here to bring them all home, though she wished for them to follow her by choice of their own free will, and not through force and fear.

The scene was now lit by Veshnicas elementame slave, who could be seen now to be a male form as he had grown to the size of the average adult male. He stood there blazing away as he cast his light like a bonfire, his eyes burning too brightly to look at directly by the humans. His light was necessary for Veshnica to look right into the eyes of each of the humans, as she was the first among them all to speak.

"You break into my house, yet I offer you food and shelter. Then, in return, you scold my children's faces, break my window and run. I suppose we must seem quite threatening to you?" she said accusingly.

"Oh please," said Lancelin, "We just, did not know, perhaps, what you were going to do with us."
Veshnica glared at Lancelin as a puzzled expression took over her face, after which she continued to address them all.

"Normally, like any mother, I'd want justice brought to those who injure my children. However, there's a greater evil than you three running around here at the moment, one which your very presence has awoken, and I need you three to help me put an end to it once and for all."

"Us? But, we have no powers. What can we do?" asked Chloé. Veshnica walked calmly up to Chloé as she began to answer her, speaking to her as an equal, a friend, and not as prey.

"I feel the answer lies in that very book you carry with you," she said with a hint of eagerness and excitement, "But come, we mustn't speak any more of it out here in the open. This, evil, that you've awoken, has the power to enchant even the earth itself to be her spy."

"Her?" asked Chris.

"Yes, her. An awful witch. One so spiteful that she managed to wipe out all other witches from existence, and trapped all magical creatures here with her to rule over them, forever imprisoned on Île Merveille. Now come, please, we must get back to the manor where it's safe."

Chloé, Chris and Lancelin didn't feel they had much of a choice but to follow Veshnica, though they did so somewhat more willingly knowing she hadn't tried to simply kill them right there and then. Under the protection and guidance of the vampires, they left the scene in the forest and returned to the manor, whilst Tuca waited until they were well out of sight before she returned to Alexandra.

Back inside the vampire's manor, Chloé, Chris and Lancelin were each given a room and a change of clothes to wear whilst theirs were taken away to be washed – another suggestion of kindness from Veshnica, though they were nothing more than old clothes once worn by her children. She then asked them to meet both Raul and herself in the debating room in the centre of the manor once they were changed; this was a room without windows through which anyone could peek in. She'd asked them to meet there to discuss a plan of how they would help each other to put an end to this evil, and insisted that Chloé bring the book along with her.

The rooms they were given were each as grand as the rest of the manor, complete with black-marble fireplaces and dark-mahogany four-poster beds. Chloé and Chris' rooms were connected via a door between them, yet Lancelin's room seemed to be further down the corridor. Once left alone, Chloé and Chris wasted no time in re-joining each other before changing and heading back downstairs.

"I'm scared, Chris," said Chloé, looking into Chris' eyes as hers began to glisten with a hint of tears. Chris held her close in his arms then kissed her on the forehead.

"I know, me too. But right now we don't have much of a choice. Veshnica wants our help, your help, and as long as you're the only one who can read this book, I think we'll be ok." Though what he truly believed was that only *she'd* be ok, he, on the other hand, could easily be spared.

"But what if she's lying? If they just want to use me for access to this book, what will they do when they don't need it anymore?"

"We'll just have to worry about that later, once we know what they're up to. But listen, as long as you are the only one who can read this book, that alone will keep you safe. For whatever reason, the book is guiding you. Remember the visions it's given you? Well until you see that cave for real, I think everything's gonna be alright. In the meantime, let just play along and we'll think of something, I promise." After Chris had calmed her down and they'd built their strength up for more vampire time, they headed hand in hand down to the room where they were to greet Veshnica and Raul.

Chloé held the book tightly against her as they entered the room together. Upon stepping inside, they were greeted by Raul, Veshnica, Lancelin and several of the count and countess' children. They were all sat around a circular wooden table, lit from above by a huge four-tiered chandelier holding countless candles within it. Raul and Veshnica both stood as they greeted Chloé and Chris into the room, introducing them to Raul and then offering up two seats at the table.

The pair smiled and walked over to take their seats, sticking closely side by side for support. Chris stared at Lancelin, wondering what they'd discussed in their absence. Chloé placed the book down on the table and kept her eyes fixated on it, whilst Raul gazed upon the grimoire and examined the cover.

"So, it's true? This is one of his books?" he asked as he reached out his hand to touch it.

"Who's books?" asked Chloé?

"Who's books? You don't even know?" said Raul temperedly.

"Rue-Rue dear, our history slate has been wiped clean in their world, remember? By that wicked, spiteful witch," said Veshnica, keeping her husband's forceful nature at rest.

"Please, could you tell us," said Chris, speaking up, "Who did it belong to?"

"The only worthy sorcerer who ever lived," said Raul, "The great Malicorne."

Raul went on to explain to them about who Malicorne was, and how Alexandra had destroyed him when she took control of Île Merveille, little over two hundred years ago. He told them the story of how he came to be. The story of a once lonely witch back in France, who reared unicorns for the royal family at the time, bred from ones that had been brought over from Île Merveille.

After dedicating her life to working with and understanding unicorns, she'd longed to raise one as her own. So, when the next foal was born, she stole him for herself. Unfortunately for the witch however, hiding a unicorn was far from an easy task, and inevitably the king soon found out.

Straight away he ordered the witch's home to be searched for the missing unicorn which was rightfully his, and upon finding it the witch was to be burned alive for her crime. Afraid to lose her baby and her life, the wealthy witch sought out an illegal magic market, selling potions and incantations that had been forbidden by the kings and queens throughout Europe at the time; and also by the Île Merveille lawmakers. There, she found exactly what she needed, something that would turn her unicorn human, hiding him in plain sight from the king's army.

Her home was later searched and completely trashed by the king's men, who were unsuccessful in finding the missing unicorn. With no proof of her crime, the witch was banished on suspicion of treachery to the king. So, the witch left with as much as she could carry and met up with her new child at a secret location, deep within the woods, in the valley at the edge of the kingdom.

She named her new son Omlicorn, which was later changed to Malicorne by those who grew to fear him. Only that fear is what gave him the strength to become the leader he did.

"But, why did people fear him?" asked Chloé.
"Because he was different. An abomination, as they used to refer to him," stated Raul, "And more importantly, because he was stronger and more powerful than the rest."
"So, how did she kill him?" asked Chris.
"She cast a curse over the entire world, erasing magic from the blood of every single human who possessed it. And the ones who had settled or were even born here, vanished, just disappeared into thin air." Raul paused to take a sip of his thick, dark red drink, which he sipped from a decorated, old bronze-looking chalice, before he continued. "All magic, and evidence of, had been taken from your world, to exist again only here, away from any other human. Except her."

For a minute no one spoke. Chloé tried to make sense of this bizarre story she'd just heard. "Well, that explains why the other books we found were blank I suppose, but I still don't understand why I'm able to read this one. How did this book survive the curse?" she puzzled.

"Malicorne was a very powerful being. I have no doubt that even when he saw the end was coming, he still had a few tricks up his sleeve," said Veshnica, sat confidently in her overly decorated chair, adorned with stunning diamonds and carvings; most unlike the rest which were a matching set of simple wooden chairs.

"Well, if he preserved it somehow, what's my connection to it? Why am I the only one who can read it?" Chloé continued to ask, hoping to get some clarity.

"Well, perhaps you can find that out," said Raul, "By paying a visit to the spring of power."

Raul then went into the details of their plan. The countess and some of her children had agreed to escort Chloé in secret, to as close as they could get to the spring of power. They couldn't take her right to it however, as the burn from its light on their skin would soon kill them with its intensity. Though they couldn't accomplish this journey purely by themselves. So, they'd planned on seeking out help from other residents of Île Merveille along the way, as alone they knew that they'd be no match for Alexandra; who they were sure would be onto them sooner or later.

"The spring of power," said Chloé, "That's the place I've been seeing in my visions. That's where we were heading when we came across this place. But, why do you want to help *me* to get there?"

"Wait," said Chris as he looked to Veshnica, "If Chloé goes, I go too."

"Fine," said Veshnica with a smile, not wanting to come across as controlling or manipulative, "We'll take both of you, though I warn you that it'll add more risk. Anyway, as we were saying..." she continued.

As it turned out, the count and countess were willing to escort them to the spring of power, on the condition that Chloé used the book to find a way to end Alexandra's reign over Île Merveille once and for all. After hearing this, Chris instantly refused to let them drag Chloé and himself into a hundreds of years old fight that wasn't theirs to meddle in.

Unfortunately, Veshnica soon pointed out that they didn't really have a choice, for since the moment they'd set foot on the island, it was only a matter of time before they'd have to face Alexandra; with or without the vampires help. Chris sank back into his chair, with the daunting thought of this situation they'd managed to land themselves into hanging over him. Raul then asked Chloé to have a look in the book whilst they were sat there with her, to see if there was anything that Malicorne had written that would help them put an end to this problem.

Chloé hesitated, she'd only just found out that she was going to have to survive against a God knows how many hundred-year-old witch who wanted her gone, she couldn't even bring herself to imagine how. Chris saw how nervous she was, so he reached out and held her hand in an effort to support her in front of the others, as she gently caressed the front cover of the book with her other one.

"Maybe it won't be as bad as you think," he said to her, trying to sound calm. Chloé then looked at Chris for a moment, before looking back at the book and drawing in a deep breath.

Firmly she ran her fingers down the edge of the pages, as she closed her eyes and thought about what she needed to learn from the book. Then, feeling the guidance from it, she stopped and opened the book onto the page she needed to see.

She opened her eyes again and glanced down at the pages. The booked had opened on a page she'd seen before. The page she saw for the first time the night before they left Antibes, the page which convinced her she needed to agree to sail to Île Merveille, to find out if it was all possible. This was the page she'd been looking at one night on the boat, when she'd lied to Chris about what she was actually reading; for fear he wouldn't share the same views on it as she did.

"Well? What does it say?" asked Lancelin, who'd been

quiet up until now.

"Nothing," replied Chloé, "It's blank."

"Blank?! What do you mean it's blank? I thought you said she could read it?" snapped Raul as he turned to Veshnica.

"She can, I saw her read from it when they were first here," she snapped back, "Why is it blank?"

Chris quickly backed up Chloé, explaining how they'd tried to use it in the woods to help them escape but Chloé hadn't been able to get any guidance from it then either. He insisted that she was just tired and overwhelmed and that they should get back to their rooms so she could rest; then perhaps she could try again tomorrow before they left.

So, with that, Chloé and Chris were excused, as they got up to head upstairs back to their rooms for some much-needed sleep. They agreed to meet up back here later that day, once the sun had risen and set once again. Though as they headed towards the door, Chris stopped and turned back to those who were still sat at the table. "Aren't you tired, Lancelin?" he asked, thinking it odd that he seemed more comfortable in the company of the vampires than they did. This turned all eyes on Lancelin, waiting for his response.

"Bahh, yes, for sure. I am coming too,' he said as he got up and joined the other two to walk back to their rooms. Even though Chris was glad he'd stopped to question Lancelin about him not sticking with them, he was pleased when they'd got back to their rooms and he and Chloé were finally alone again.

The pair of them stayed together in the room that had been given to Chloé. As they sat with each other on the bed, with the fire roaring in the fireplace, Chris began to question Chloé about what she'd really seen in the book.

"I know you lied to the others. I know your face when you see something on those pages, but what was it you saw?" he asked. Chloé needed to tell him, at least what the page was of, she still didn't want to talk about what it meant to her though. "I can't do it," she said, sounding defeated.

"Can't do what? What did it say?"

"Resurrect that sorcerer."

"What?!" shouted Chris, leaping up from the bed.

Chloé quickly shushed him. She was afraid that once the vampires knew what the book had suggested, that they'd force her to follow through with it.

"Is that what it said?" asked Chris in a loud whisper, "That you could resurrect him?" She explained to Chris that all she knew was that she'd asked the book how they could stop Alexandra and that that was the page the book had guided her to.

"So, you're supposed to resurrect an old sorcerer, who used to be a unicorn, and has been dead for over two-hundred years? This cannot be happening right now," he put his hand on his forehead to ease the pain of a headache which was beginning to take over him.

He began pacing across the room desperately trying to think of a way out of their situation. Hearing the commotion coming from the bedroom, Veshnica knocked on the door and asked if she may enter. She did so accompanied by Vulp, who jumped straight up onto the bed and curled up.

"Is everything alright?" she asked. Neither of them knew what to say, they'd been caught off guard in the midst of Chris' panic. "This wouldn't have anything to do with the fact that you lied to us all downstairs earlier, about not seeing anything in the book?" Chloé stuttered as she tried to respond quickly.

"What do you mean, I…"

"You'll find it very difficult to lie to a vampire, especially one as ol… well, as experienced me," she smiled. "It's alright. I realise it's a lot for you humans to take in right now," she said whilst walking over to the bed and sitting beside Vulp, "But please, why don't you share it with me, whilst it's just the tree of us? We need your help as much as you need ours," She stroked Vulp gently as she spoke to them.

Chloé decided to come clean about what she'd seen on the page and with her concerns towards it. Veshnica then got up, walked around the bed and placed her hand on Chloé's shoulder, a touch which sent a chill down her back as the countess' stone cold skin touched her.

"Chloé, if you could do that, if you could bring back our saviour, we'd all be forever grateful," she said with the sound of wonderment in her voice.

"But, what if I can't do it?" she asked nervously.

"But what if you can?" replied Veshnica. "Do you remember when you first came here, and I knew exactly what food to get for each of you? I know the things which you desire, and I know your motivation for wanting to come here Chloé," she said confidently. "I'm sure that if you help bring Malicorne back, he will help you too."

"What desire? What's she talking about Chlo?" asked Chris, he had become agitated by being the only one who didn't know what was going on. However, Chloé remained silent.

"Think about it," said Veshnica as she opened the door to exit the bedroom. As she opened it, Vulp jumped down off the bed and headed back out of the room. She looked back at them both and smiled, "I'll see you after sunset," she said as she left the room.

Chris pestered Chloé to tell him what she meant by her motivation to come here, but Chloé insisted that she didn't know. He knew she was lying to him, but he had no idea why. After a while the pestering had become heated, though Chris managed to rein himself in before he pushed her too far. He had no idea why she wanted to lie to him, but he knew it wasn't worth testing their relationship with it at this time.

In the end they called it a night and got into bed, though they slept for the first time facing away from each other. As their argument fell silent and they lay down apart under the heavy quilt, they weren't to know that Lancelin was stood in Chris' room just on the other side of the door and had been listening in on their conversation ever since they'd got back to the bedroom; pleased with what he'd heard.

CHAPTER EIGHTEEN

Makin' More Magic

Between the time when Chloé, Chris and Lancelin had gone to bed, and the time when the sun would rise again for a new day, Raul and Veshnica called some of their children together. They needed to gather help from other creatures of Merveille, ones who, unlike themselves, could survive in the day as well as night, to assist them on their long journey.

The vampires alone were indeed strong, but should they not reach their first stopover by sunrise, they'd be completely defenceless whilst sleeping outside as bats through the daytime - the only way they're able to survive in the sunlight. They also had no doubt that Alexandra would be doing all in her power to put an end to their journey, and if she was to find out that the three new people were merely humans, she'd soon figure out exactly what they were up to.

So, with still a few hours remaining before the next sunrise, Raul led the search out into the night, whilst Veshnica stayed at home to keep an eye on their guests.

Later that day, at around three o'clock in the afternoon, Chloé and Chris had both awoken after a sleep filled with turmoil. Though they were both exhausted, their minds just wouldn't rest. Chris's frustration towards Chloé refused to die down, whilst her fear of what their future held in store for them plagued her mind through the night. Neither of them had any idea what time of day it was. The only light in the room was that of the now dying flames in the fireplace, with all outdoor light blocked due to the windows being both bricked and boarded up completely.

Chris was the first to get out of bed, as he rummaged around to find the torch in their rucksack, which aroused a whisper from Chloé, alerting him that she too was awake. Speaking quietly to each other, they decided to sneak around to see if anyone else up at this time, all the while hoping that they might have the place to themselves for a short while.

They creped quietly out through the bedroom door into the hallway and headed in the direction of the main entrance hall, with Chris leading the way and Chloé following closely behind carrying the rucksack with their possessions in. As the torch batteries were on their way out, they were pleased to find the corridors of the manor already lit; though somewhat dimly with sporadically placed, heavy, white candles sat in arched alcoves.

As they cautiously retraced their steps from when they were shown to their room, the manor was eerily silent. They followed a thin, red-wine coloured carpet which ran the length of the corridor, back past odd-looking pieces of furniture which they'd noted the night before. Along their way, they bumped into one of the vampires who was patrolling the corridors during the daytime, and who was under strict instructions not to let the humans leave.

"Are you going somewhere?" he asked in a low monotone.
"Erm, we just wanted to know what time it was," said Chris innocently.
"At the moment it continues to be daylight hours, the countess is still sleeping."
"Well, as we're not vampires like yourself, we wouldn't mind seeing some daylight. If that's alright?" asked Chloé.

"I'm afraid the count has instructed that you're not to leave the manor unaccompanied, as Alexandra may be watching. I am to keep you indoors until the time after the sun has set once again." Neither Chris or Chloé knew quite what to say to that. They felt like the vampires' prisoners, however they knew that he made a valid point. "Although, if you really would like to see some daylight" continued the vampire, "There's always the countess' winter garden. It's over-grown enough that you should be safe from outside prying eyes. Though I'd warn you not to touch any of the plants, no matter how enticing and interesting they may appear to you."

They were both relieved at not having to sit in the darkness all day and promised they would keep their hands off the countess' plants. So, the vampire escorted them down to the winter garden, leading on with a gas (or what they thought was gas) lantern lighting way around the ground floor of the mansion, and he assured them he would be standing guard in the dark corridor leading up to it, in case any trouble should arise.

As they squeezed through a small gap in the double-doored entrance, whilst the vampire hid in the direct shadow of it using the door as his shield against the room beyond, Chris and Chloé were relieved to find themselves in a haven of life, hidden at the far end of the otherwise deadly, slumbering vampire manor.

The winter garden was a marvellous greenhouse. It's rippled, domed roof which flowed up to a point in the middle, almost two stories high above the very earthy, ground-floor, reflected down clear daylight from the blue sky high above. Trapping almost all the light from the windowed walls, were all kind of strange, colourful plants, trees and vines, all intertwined, creating a similar scene to what they'd witnessed back in the Tonga jungle.

From where they entered, they stepped down a set of long, creaky, wooden steps from the raised height of the ground-floor within the mansion and followed a winding path through the abundance of green life, to an area they could just about spot from the doorway. They tread with much caution though, as some of the flowers and vines around them appeared to sense their every move, and they seemed equally as fascinated by them and they were with these alluring magical flowers.

They followed the trodden path to an area they could just about make out from the doorway, which was a circular space in the heart of the garden, with a set of brown, rusty and delicately spindly table and three chairs. The air in here was warm and humid, which came as a refreshing change from the dry coolness from the man body of the manor. They sat down on the garden chairs and pulled out the grimoire and the magic goblet from the rucksack, setting them down on the table.

Chris picked the goblet up straight away and hurried back took a deep, wide sink, with a tall, curved, bronze coloured tap, which he'd spotted against the stone walls of the house back at the top of the wooden steps. To his delight, the tap over the sink was working, and he managed to fill the goblet right up with water. Just in case the water here wasn't drinkable, he used the goblets magic and created cold, fresh drinking water inside of it.

As he rapidly guzzled it down, water spilt over the sides and dribbled onto his chin, before dripping off and splashing on his collar. He instantly filled it up again, only this time he took it along to Chloé so she might also quench her beckoning thirst. She used it to create cool, fresh orange juice, something she would normally have every morning, then the moment she'd finished she took herself over to the sink to refill; only this time she had in mind the most perfect cup of tea.

As she was stood over by the sink, Chris reached into the rucksack to see what else they had in there which he may have forgotten about or may be of use to them. Within it he found the magnifying glass, and the two pieces or torn paper, which he'd taken from the black castle along with the goblet and the wand which Chloé picked up.

"Hey Chlo-Chlo," Chris called out, a sound which was dampened as it was absorbed by the soft foliage filling the space between them both, "We still don't know what these do." Chloé, gently sipping her tea, walked back over to the space in the centre and looked inquisitively upon the objects Chris had lifted from their bag.
"Oh yeah, I'd almost forgotten about these."

First, she picked up the magnifying glass and looked through it, wondering what on earth it could be used for. Then she placed it back down and picked up the two pieces of paper, putting together the ripped edges to reveal the words 'Encore Ensemble' written across them. "Together again," she said quietly to herself.
"Maybe you should try the book. It told you how to use the goblet, maybe it can tell you what these do too," suggested Chris.

Chloé agreed and sat herself down in front of the book, carefully placing her hot tea on the table beside it. She took in a deep breath as she attempted to relax her mind and focus on the magic of the book. She actually had no idea if this made any difference to whether the book would speak to her or not, but by doing so it made her feel more in control of it's magic; even if that was just all in her head.

With one of the pieces of paper in one hand, she closed her eyes and gently stroked the edges of the book's pages with the other, until she felt the overpowering urge to stop. Straight away she opened her eyes and then the book, being mindful not to knock over her tea. She was so used to this by now, yet the reality of just how normal this magic stuff had become to appear to them, hadn't even dawned on her.

The page she looked upon was titled 'Two halves of a whole', and she began to read aloud what she saw on the page:

'Bestowing this enchantment upon a single object, creates a bond which knows no bounds; should the object be broken in two. To reunite them once more, hold tightly the half which you possess, whilst with closed eyes you wish strongly for the other.'

"Shall we try it?" Chris hastily suggested. After hearing what Chloé had read out, he wasted no time as he grabbed the other piece of paper left out on the table and hurried over to the wooden steps, away from where they were sat. Chloé stayed where she was and kept her eyes on the piece she held, as she placed it on the table in front of her.

"Ready?" he called, to make sure she was watching the other piece of paper and not distracted by something else.

"Ready…" replied Chloé with a hint of doubt, unsure

how, or even if this would work.

Chris turned to face the doorway and looked down at his hand, clenching the paper tightly between his thumb and fingers. He had no idea what was going to happen, as he held out his left hand as a place for the other piece of paper to reappear, before closing his eyes and concentrating.

He stood silently, whilst wishing deep in his mind for the other piece of paper to appear in his hand before him. But as he started to think nothing was happening, he suddenly became aware that his senses appeared to be failing him.

No longer could he feel the heavy humidity in the air, or the lingering scent of new, strange pollen which wafted around the garden; he couldn't even feel the floor beneath him. He decided to open his eyes to check and see if anything strange had happened around him, when suddenly they were forced closed again by a bright white light. Swiftly he shielded his eyes with his empty hand and faced down in an attempt to look away, but it scarcely made a difference. Then, as suddenly as it had happened, the light began to fade away and soon returned to the familiar brightness of the conservatory.

He stood still for a moment, to listen and to feel. To his delight he could sense the pollen again, at least it seemed like the kind of smell he'd smelt earlier, though he couldn't really be certain it wasn't just in his head. He called out Chloé's name, to which she didn't answer, and with that, he decided to carefully attempt to open his eyes once again.

Starting with just one eye he peeked out carefully, hoping to make sense of his surroundings. The light around him seemed different to when he had closed them whilst facing the wooden steps, slightly shaded to one side as it had been when sat at the table, with several large, heavy green leaves hanging close above them. As his eye opened more, he realised that he was no longer stood by the door.

As he became aware of where he now stood, he opened both eyes wide open, and the first thing he noticed was the piece of paper he'd wished for sitting in front of him on the garden table. He couldn't believe his eyes as he reached down and picked it up, before turning to Chloé who was sat staring at him with her mouth wide open.

"How did I..." he began, "What happened?" he asked Chloé, who continued to stare at him, completely gobsmacked by what she'd seen. Then she lifted her hand and pointed at him and then towards the door. She remained silent for a moment, too in shock to speak at first, and trying to find the right words to answer him.

"You teleported."

Through her excitement Chloé began to explain to Chris what she'd seen, whilst simultaneously he was telling her how it'd felt. Their amazement was getting the better of them as they loudly discussed this phenomenon they'd just witnessed; they couldn't believe they were actually able to teleport themselves right through thin air.

Chloé jumped up out of her chair and grabbed one of

the pieces of paper, then hurried over to another corner of the conservatory to try this for herself. Sure enough, just as had happened to Chris happened to her, and this time Chris got to witness it first hand, right before his very eyes; they were both completely overjoyed and giddy with laughter.

"Okay, okay, so what about this then?" asked Chris, trying to calm himself as he picked up the magnifying glass.
"Oh yeah. Alright, let's see." Chloé took it from him and held it in her hand as she grabbed the book again, with such confidence now.

She calmed herself and controlled her breathing, as she focused once more on the book with the intention of finding out the secret to the magnifying glass. This time, the page which she opened the book on was titled 'To help one see the truth', and there was a list of ingredients along with an enchantment and a set of instructions.

"This page is about some kind of truth spell, I think, but it doesn't say what it has to do with this," she said, holding up the magnifying glass. She began to read out loud the list of ingredients on the page:

'One breath of truth,
The first fallen petal of a Flurverity rose,
Three drops of a Rocklands snagon's venom,
One thimble of blood from a broken heart,
A scripture disclosing one of your deepest secrets,
written by a friend who hadn't already known.'

"What's a snagon?" asked Chris, still slightly giddy. Chloé blurted out a quick laugh with Chris, then continued to read the words on the page, moving on to the incantation.

"Oh wait!" she said, "listen to this – Through this glass of improved sight, the lies I'm told are clear as light. Through this glass. Maybe you can see the lie through the glass."
"But, how do you *see* a lie? What does a lie look like?" asked Chris.

Chloé then held up the magnifying glass and looked through it for an answer, turning her body around as she saw the room through it, just as you would looking through normal glass. Then as she turned to her other side, she stopped as she saw Chris through it; then it dawned on her.

"Quick, tell me a lie" she urged him.
"Like what?"
"Anything, just say something that's not true."
"Okay, how about… This house isn't the creepiest place I've ever been."

As he spoke these words, Chloé watched him through the magnifying glass. As she observed him speak, a glowing, green mist filled the air which he exhaled whilst telling the lie.

"Oh my god, I don't believe it. I can see it! I can see the lie!" she exclaimed.

"What? What do you mean you can *see* the lie?" Chloé passed the magnifying glass to Chris and told him to look at her through it. As he did she spoke a lie, and he saw exactly what she'd seen when he had lied to her.

After all that excitement, Chris and Chloé continued to sit there in the winter garden for the rest of the afternoon and into the evening hours, looking through the book at what else was possible in this new land. Chris was certain that some way of teleportation would be there ticket home, which they could work out once they'd paid a visit to the spring of power. Chloé made out like she wanted nothing more than to return home safely with him, and to escape this conflict they'd landed themselves in the middle of; however, Chris could sense in her voice that there was something else she longed for.

He was worried that the lure of power was drawing her in, and it scared him to know that there was still something she wasn't sharing with him regarding her reason for wanting to come here in the first place, after originally being the only one against the idea. He watched her, wondering as she flicked through the pages of the book, what there might be in there that she wasn't telling him about. Taking advantage of being alone together, he grabbed the magnifying glass and looked at her through it, as he built up the courage and asked her straight out – what was her reason was for wanting to come to this island.

Chris suddenly putting her on the spot like that had stunned her, which she used to buy her some time to think about what she might say. At first she refused to answer, unsure of how he would feel about her motives, but it was getting harder for her to speak the truth whilst also avoiding the question. As she fumbled over her words, neither of them had realised how low the light was now, and to Chloé's relief they were interrupted by the vampire who'd been standing – or more accurately, sitting - guard in the hallway.

"Excuse me for interrupting," he bellowed, "but the countess has awoken early and wishes to meet you in the discussion room." Chloé felt a wave of relief wash over her. This was her chance to ignore Chris' inquest with good reason, and she abruptly closed the book, trapping one of the 'Encore Ensemble' pieces of paper inside, and shoved it into the rucksack along with the magnifying glass and the goblet.

"We'll talk about this later," she said to Chris, making sure not to make eye contact as she stood up from her chair and headed for the door. She'd hurried off so suddenly that she'd left the other piece of torn paper out on the table, though fortunately Chris saw it and grabbed it before he hurried after her. They were then led by the guard to the discussion room where Veshnica waited for them, already with Lancelin, so she could ready them all for their next event.

CHAPTER NINETEEN

Introductions

All four of them sat closely at the table, Veshnica in her ornate chair with Vulp sat on the table just slightly to her side, and a handful of other vampires stood about the room watching over them. Veshnica informed the three humans calmly that they were to await the return of Raul, along with some of their children, who would be arriving promptly and hopefully with the support of some other Île Merveille natives.

Once they'd all gathered, she went on to explain, they were to travel together to the old human settlement of Dragignaan, where the vampires could sleep safely through the next day's sunshine in one of the old houses. It had been agreed that Raul would escort the three humans, along with some of his children, whilst Veshnica stayed behind at the manor ready to gather extra support should they send for it.

Chloé would've preferred to be travelling with Veshnica though, as the idea of travelling with Raul unnerved her; he didn't seem to have the gentler touch when dealing with things. That said, Veshnica assured them that he would take very good care of them and protect them as if they were his own children.

Their plan was to journey on each night along the quickest route they knew, which would lead them north into the hills of the four seasons. It turned out, however, that the vampires didn't actually know the exact whereabouts of the spring, as they'd never ventured to it themselves. Also, the other creatures only knew roughly where it was, for not being human the spring held very little value to them. So, the vampires had planned to search each settlement they came to for a map of some kind, that may have been left behind by the previous magical human inhabitants of the island.

With that suggestion Chloé decided to speak up, reminding Veshnica how she'd been guided earlier along a river, and that trying to find the river again was what had brought them to the vampire's manor to begin with; perhaps she could find that guidance once more upon reaching the hills, she pondered.

A few hours went by as they discussed their future in the dim fire-light of the discussion room, before they heard the main entrance to the manor burst open as Raul arrived home. He'd returned with help for the journey and strode straight into the discussion room where he burst in to announce that they were all waiting outside, ready to leave. With that, Veshnica sent the three humans back to the bedrooms to get changed into their original clothes (which had been washed, dried and returned to their rooms), and then they were to meet up again outside the main entrance.

They each hurried back up the stairs and through the corridors of the manor, so eager to meet these other creatures who were to help them travel across Île Merveille.

"What creatures do you think they'll be?" asked Chris.
"Useful ones I hope," said Lancelin, very unenthusiastically.
"I'm sure whatever they are that they'll be just amazing to see," added Chloé, "maybe some kind of imps or elves perhaps."
"With that witch after us, I'd hope they're something strong at least, like a strong beast or something," said Chris with a touch of excitement in his voice, possibly for the first time since they arrived on the island.

After changing, they met up again in the hallway before heading to the staircase in the entrance hall. Chris decided to try and engage with Lancelin, curious as to what he'd been up to since they'd gone to bed the night before; surely he'd have been awake for quite some time already just as they had. Lancelin insisted that he'd simply stayed put in his bedroom, too nervous to venture out on his own into the dark hallways of the manor.

He accusingly pointed out the fact that they'd left him alone all that time, with no light or anyone to speak to, managing to extract an apology from Chloé. Chris couldn't argue that it wouldn't have been a lonely time for him either, so he used the defence that the two of them just needed a bit of alone time, so they could reconnect with each other after all they'd been through; to which Lancelin bluntly responded with a, "humph."

As they carried on down the staircase, they followed the sound of things going on just outside the front entrance. As they cautiously pushed open the door and stepped through the doorway, the three of them halted on the top step, stunned and mesmerized by the scene they were witnessing.

A crowd had formed around a stunningly lavish, closed, dark-wooden carriage. There was a door on either side and windows with dull, moss coloured drapes fitted perfectly to them, matching perfectly with the interior of the carriage. Both outside and in the carriage hung lanterns, inside of which burned not a flame from a wick, but more downsized, fire-embodied elementames; whom the countess introduced later as allies and support for their journey.

Although this looked to be a normal, horse-drawn carriage fit for aristocracy, albeit colour-wise more suited to a creature of the night, there didn't appear to be any horses around to pull it; in their place lay many empty reins across the ground. The count and countess both stood by the carriage speaking to one another, with Vulp sat down by the countess' feet. To the three humans, this appeared the most ordinary out of everything they could see.

Littered about the place under the fresh night sky, stood a crowd of cerfaurs. Much like a centaur, these creatures were half human looking, though instead of having the body of a horse they had a body more like a deer. The females' bodies were slightly smaller than the males, and their tails were long and slim with just a tuft of dark brown fur at the end. The rest of their fur was a light brown, with blond on their underside, and some even had white spots speckled on their back.

The males were each like a great stag, strong and muscular with just a short tail. Their fur was a darker brown than the females' fur, and their colouring was the same all over. The males also had antlers like a stag, solid and grand, reaching back behind their head, some long enough to even scratch their own back. Both males and females had pale white skin on their human half, and the purest, long blond hair.

They all wore shoulder pads made from a leather-like material, structured with sharp wooden sticks underneath, reaching out slightly beyond the shoulder to form small spikes. Across the chests of the males, these pads were attached together via a chain of wooden links, with a triangular piece pointing down the centre of their torso.

The females had something similar, yet the wooden links were smaller, and they attached to a piece of leathery material they wore strapped around them to cover their chests (something designed for them since they'd once been domesticated by humans). They also carried round, metal shields, made for their kind many years ago from the metal plufort, by a determined sorceress who once used cerfaurs as her army, when she tried to take control of many woodland areas on Île Merveille.

Chloé also spotted, down by the count and countess' feet, three ugly little creatures, stood no taller than the height of the countess' knees. These were corne-trolls, named so due to their skinny, troll-like appearance, and their two short, curved horns sticking out from their heads. Their bodies were covered with a thin, scratty layer of light brown fur, and they each had different coloured eyes. Their appearance would be off-putting at first if you didn't know them, especially their long, thick fingers which merged into black, pointed claws half way along them.

Their faces were a bit less intimidating however, slightly more human-like, and focusing on that was one of the few ways you could grow to like them. Though if you were to see beyond their appearance, they in fact make a very useful friend to a traveller. They are each born with the power to turn anything into food, which is how they survive in the wild, but they are also willing to do this for others; though only those who show them care, loyalty and most of all friendship. Should you begin to treat your pet corne-troll as anything other than a valued companion, you'd be in a lot of trouble.

And, finally, standing out above all the rest, stood an immense, half bird - half human creature, referred to as a sirins. Her head stuck up above the crowd, and she was built much broader than a normal sized human; making her presence amongst them well established.

From the waist down her body was formed like the lower half of an eagle, though on a much larger scale. Feathers covered most of her body from her chest downwards, including tail feathers which she fanned out behind her. Here enormous wings grew attached to her arms as far as her elbow, where the wing and forearm bent away from each other, and her feet were the claws of a great bird of prey.

The colouring of her feathers started as a light-mauve colour on the back of her wing, fading to a deeper plum before ending in brown along the edge of her wings. Underneath her wing the feathers near her arm were a frosty blue colour and changed to blonde halfway down; the rest of her feathers covering her body were a simple, dark-walnut shade of brown.

She had long, thick dark hair that she wore in a loose plait over one shoulder, and she'd decorated her head with a small golden tiara encrusted with blue and purple jewels, earrings like amethyst crystals, and a necklace matching the tiara hung around her neck.

"Ahh, you're here," Veshnica called over to the three humans as she noticed them. "Please, come, I'd like you to meet everyone." Chris, Chloé and Lancelin walked over sheepishly, sticking closely together as they approached the strange, new creatures.

"Orel!" Veshnica cried out into the crowd, prompting the sirins to walk over to them. "I'd like you all to meet Orelzenshina, who will be flying overhead during your travels, keeping an eye out for problems along the way. She might also offer great protection, as her magnificent feathers are perfectly designed to absorb any magic they come into contact with, should Alexandra attempt an attack." The three humans stood silently gawking up at her, intimidated by both her size and ability.

"It's a pleasure to meet you all," said Orel, first to break the silence (and awkwardness). She spoke so confidently to them, coming across as very sure of her strength and leadership, taking it upon herself to lead the conversation the second it fell flat and completely ignoring their shocked expressions.
"Nice to meet you," said Chris, managing to string together just a few words, hoping he'd covered up the sound of nervousness in his voice, "I'm Chris."
"Hello, Chris."
"And this is my girlfriend, Chloé," Chris placed his hand on her lower back as he introduced her, which didn't go unnoticed by Orel.

"Nice to meet you Chloé. Tell me, do you hold any other qualities other than being this man's female companion?" Neither Chris nor Chloé knew how to respond to such a direct question from someone of her stature, and as Chloé began to speak, she merely mumbled whilst trying to get a sentence out.
"I'm Lancelin, by the way," he said as he stuck out his hand to shake Orel's, which was met by a confused glance from Orel. "Chloé is our magical link, she's the one who the sorcerer's book reveals itself to."
"Oh really," said Orel, "Well, it seems you're the most valuable one among us then, good to know. Oh, and please, call me Orel."

Whilst they'd been getting acquainted, Raul had walked off to fetch over the head cerfaur stag, commander of the cerfaurs who were there, along with his son who was second in rank.

"Ah, here comes my Rue-Rue now with the cerfaurs."
"Humans," announced Raul, "I introduce to you, Elkor, chief of the cerfaurs here tonight, and his son, Lousta."
"If you are the ones who wish to bring back Malicorne, then it is an honour to meet you," said Elkor as he bowed his head to them.

"Truly it is," seconded Lousta as he bowed his head a second after his father. As he lifted his head back up, he caught Chloé's eyes gazing at him, in awe of his perfect structure. His torso was perfectly proportioned. He stood strong and upright all the way through to his broad shoulders, which acted as the perfect mount for his head to rest upon, displaying his ever so handsomely chiselled, good looks. As he caught her eye, he winked back at her and gave her a quick glimpse of his utterly charming smile.

Not so quick that it went unnoticed by Chris however, as he saw Chloé smiling back at him too. Great, he thought, someone else to get in their way. Though could he really be worried that someone who was half deer might try to steal her from him, he wondered, bizarrely. "Well, we'll give it our best try," said Chloé, blushing.

Veshnica was suddenly disturbed, she too had been leering towards Lousta's luring presence, until she felt a tug on her dress. "Oh of course!" she exclaimed, "And these are the corne-trolls who'll join you. Try to think of them as your new pets." One by one she picked them up and handed them to the humans, leaving them with one each.

"Pets?" questioned Chris, "Why do we need pets?" As they took them, Chloé's expression had gone from dreamland to disgust.
"What are we supposed to do with them?" she asked.
"Well, now, you must not be rude to them, or they may not serve you so well. Corne-trolls are masters of turning anything into food, and they will do so for each of you should you treat them with kindness and loyalty. Now, you can name them whatever you like, Chris and Chloé yours are both female, Lancelin, yours is male."

They each looked into the eyes of their new pets, wondering what to name them; but what name would be fit for a creature like this, they wondered.

"Er.. how about, Lucy?" said Chris, as a completely random suggestion. As he suggested it, his corne-troll smiled at him, which Veshnica stated was a sign that she liked it. "Alright then, Lucy it is."

"Well if you're going with Lucy, I guess I could call mine…" Chloé paused for a moment whilst she tried to think of a name as normal as Lucy, yet would somehow suit her troll, "Meg?" she guessed, which seemed to be accepted.
"I'll call mine Miteux," added Lancelin after some silent thought.

Now they'd all been introduced, the time had come for them to set off on their way. Chris, Chloé, Lancelin and

Raul all climbed into the carriage and sat comfortably, two facing backwards and the other two facing forwards. The three humans each had their corne-troll sat on their knee, though Chloé held hers more like she was cradling a baby.

Chris and Chloé sat next to each other and kept their rucksack on the floor, trapped firmly behind their legs. Other cases of luggage were loaded onto the back of the carriage, one filled with blood fruit should the travelling vampires get hungry along the way; they certainly didn't want to frighten the humans off with the more traditional vampire feeding habits.

Elkor ordered the other cerfaurs to fan out, scattering six of them, including himself, at the front, two each on either side of the carriage and four at the back, plus his son. As a leader, he carried a horn with him, a slim, carved trumpet, which he blew on to signal the beginning of the journey. He knew the route to Dragignaan well and had agreed to lead them all there. Veshnica said her last goodbye as she peered in through the window of the carriage, then went, followed by Vulp, to stand in the doorway of the manor where she would wave them off.

Whilst all the introductions had been going on, three of the count and countess' children had joined the group and stood over the loose reins from the carriage which lay on the floor. As Elkor blew on his horn and the cerfaurs at the front began to move forward, the three vampires began to transform into a swarm of bats. Seven or so bats made up a single vampire, which each swooped down and grabbed onto the reins, lifting them up before pulling them forwards and so beginning to tow the carriage. The bats flapped frantically as they tugged on this heavy weight with wheels, until eventually they had a momentum going and the carriage commenced travelling swiftly towards a nearby road.

Once the whole group had begun to move forwards onto the dirt road, leading north into the nearby pine forest (nicknamed 'the umbrella forest' due to the shape of the trees which grew there), Orel said goodbye to Veshnica before taking off. Steadily she walked out into the now empty space where the carriage had been parked, and she looked up into the sky as she leapt off the ground and gave a mighty flap of her wings.

As her feet left the floor she flapped her great wings harder and harder, causing a gust of turbulent air beneath her, lifting the dry dirt and swirling it about behind her as she took off up into the sky. Alone, she followed the road ahead, zigzagging and constantly searching for anything that may be out to get them along the way.

As they all pushed on, scouting out the journey ahead, they hadn't thought that they ought to be more concerned about where they'd started. Vampires had always relied instinctively on their sense of smell to detect what, or who was around them. Yet, neither the count nor the countess had noticed that they'd struggled to detect Alexandra's magic the night before, since they already knew she was there as they spoke to her. So, as they stood out in the open late that warm, August evening, surrounded by the mixed scent from the cerfaurs, Orel, the corne-trolls and the humans, they'd been under a deluded sense of security. Whilst they'd been stood around introducing themselves, no one had noticed anyone else who'd been there, right under their noses.

The countess headed back inside the manor after waving goodbye, where she was to remain alone with her children until she heard news from Raul. Once she was back inside she requested a meal to be served for her in the dining hall, after she'd been back to her room to get changed. As she set off up the stairs, she happened to notice that Vulp was no longer following her, so she called out his name into the shadowy room beyond the entrance hall, wondering where he could be.

At first there was no response, though she was sure she could hear him in there, growling.
"Vulp?" she called again. Just as she stepped back down to go and see what was going on, out of the shadows he came running towards her. "What was all that about?" she asked playfully as he greeted her.

She sent her elementame into the room to light it up, before going in there herself to check it out. She noticed nothing out of the ordinary however, and so exited the room and headed on up to her bedroom, as always, closely followed by Vulp. Perhaps had she not sent her elementame into light up the room so soon, she might have noticed the warm, dim, short glow of light come from behind one of the long, wooden benches.

CHAPTER TWENTY

Mr. Stone's Potions

Back in the hills of the four seasons, Alexandra had just returned to her home after learning of the vampires' plan. She hurried straight down into her underground hideout, followed closely by Tuca who delicately trotted along behind her, and headed to a door far down the corridor, hidden within a deep shadow. As it began to get difficult to see where she was going, her body softly emitted a warm, dim glow, just enough for her to be sure when she would reach the door. Tuca caught small glimpses of this light as Alexandra's cape wafted around in the breeze whirling behind her as the rushed on.

She spoke out loud to Tuca as they went, "So, they have cerfaurs with plufort shields and a bird woman who'll absorb my magic. Well, Tuca, that just shows that they're only used to dealing with brawns and not brains. Not to worry, we've got plenty of both," she smirked as they finally reached the door.

Alexandra stopped and stood to face the basic, wooden door, which didn't even have a handle or a keyhole, though it was solidly locked with a bulky, rusty key hanging to the side of it. As she stood still, all the light which was lazily lifting from her body began to drain from her feet upwards and her head downwards, pouring down her right arm and into her hand. As the light collected there, it continued to concentrate into her index finger until the only light remained beaming from the tip of it.

Then, using the light like the nib of a pen, she swiftly signed her name across the wooden panels of the door as the writing burnt its mark onto them. Her glowing scribble remained bright for a moment, all the light from her finger had been used to write with, until the glistening, golden glow began to drain down through the wood towards where a door handle should be. As the magic collected here, it spun and swirled as it lifted from the door to create a round doorknob, with a keyhole perfectly placed under it. Before it had finished, Alexandra had already lifted the key from the hook it hung from, and she was already waiting to unlock the door.

Through here was a wide, open, stone room, like something from a medieval castle. The moment she entered, the room lit up with light shining from small glass lanterns hanging about the place, containing essence of her own magic light. Every step she took in here echoed about the place, the sounds were trapped within the stone walls just as everything else beyond this locked, hidden entrance was.

The door had brought her into the room at the height of a second story floor, and straight away there were steps leading down to the ground. At the other side of the floor from the bottom of the steps, there was an exquisite double-doored entrance, with the words 'Potions, Lotions and Incantotions' written across it in solid gold letters which shone in the low light. Alexandra didn't walk over to this entrance however, instead, she turned right and walked over to stand in front of the wall which held the steps she'd just walked down.

As she stood looking at the chunky grey bricks in the wall, there was one in particular which she placed her hand on and then managed to pull out as if it were stuck to her skin. The whole brick came out of the wall, revealing a narrow tunnel behind it which she reached into with her other hand. Almost her whole arm went inside the space behind it, until she grabbed hold of a handle hanging from the end of a chain. She pulled on it as best she could, which was difficult as the space her arm was in was quite narrow, but it hadn't worked.

She pulled again, and this time she heard a loud clunking noise followed by creaking cogs as they began to turn; which led to unlocking the heavy bolts attached across the large doors. Quickly she pulled her arm out and replaced the brick, then hurried over to the doors as she watched the final latches spring open. Grabbing both handles she pushed against them as the doors eased forwards, prompting the room on the other side light up before her.

This room was an extensive storeroom, the walls were almost completely covered in shelves. Upon them sat labelled wooden boxes, each containing a potion of some sort. The room was curved to form a semicircle, and all the shelves faced towards the entrance of the room.

It was lit from above by a beautifully designed light fitting, like a huge nest of twigs with lights glowing from within and small cuts of different coloured crystals dangling down from it, reflecting tinted specks of light about the tall room. As Alexandra walked towards the centre, the central point in the floor began to swirl into a blur, before dropping down to form something like a small vortex extending into the ground.

She continued to walk towards it as spouts of dim light, the same colour as the beige, stone floor, began gracefully towering up and out from it. The more that came out, they began to remain there and form a shape, looking like a crooked, wooden book stand. The stand began to solidify from the ground up as the vortex beneath it dwindled with the rising stand.

The stone floor now merged into the wooden structure, yet above it, some soft light still remained unformed. Only once the stand was complete did the remaining glow begin to reform into an oversized, bulky book, covered in a dark cherry coloured cloth, held in place by golden clasps around the edge of the cover. Written on the front in gold letters, the title read 'Mr Stone's book of Potions, Lotions and Incantotions'.

Alexandra walked right up to the book, still followed by Tuca who flew up onto a special perch made for her which sat next to where the book was being held up. She flung the old manuscript open and flicked through the pages to the back, where she found a list of the book's contents which she fingered over, searching for ideas.

"Here's a question for you Tuca," Tuca's head tilted to one side as Alexandra began speaking to her, "How do you stop a force that's too big for you to handle?" Tuca stared back at her before attempting an answer.
"Miauoo?"
"That right. Break it up into smaller pieces, and deal with them, one, by, one." Her voice grew to a more serious tone as she finished the sentence, then she glanced up towards the shelves.

As she'd looked through the contents of the book, which listed each and every potion contained on the shelves in that room, she saw titles which sparked some inspiration in her. They offered ways, little tricks, as to how she could put an end to this troupe heading north towards the spring. When she'd found ones she wanted, she called out their names and the potions lifted gently out from their boxes, then proceeded to float down to her and went into her satchel which she held open for them. Each potion had its own page in the book and came with instructions on how to use it, along with an incantation if required - this type of potion had been nicknamed an 'incantotion' by the man who'd created them.

After collecting all the potions she needed, she scribbled down copies on how to use them and any incantations they required, using paper and a quill which she'd seemed to pull simply out of thin air. Once finished, she flung the book closed prompting Tuca to fly down from her perch and onto Alexandra's shoulder. She had collected everything she needed to take with her, now it was time for her to get back out there and stop the others.

As she turned and walked back towards the doors, the book and it's stand disappeared just as it had appeared, vanishing back into the vortex beneath it. Upon exiting the room, she made sure the doors locked fully behind her before she left, protecting the precious contents within the room.

She scurried back up the steps as her cape fluttered behind her, then passed through the long corridor as the magic entrance to the stone room returned to the state she'd found it in, left alone once again in the deep shadow consuming the far reaches of the corridor. Together they exited out through the heavy, plufort door at the end, locking it behind her by miming the action of turning a key as she heard all the bolts within it locking it shut.

Once it was secured in place, with Tuca clung to her shoulder still, she exited up the spiral stairs and back into the quaint, little cottage, closing the secret door and moving the rug to shut off the connection to her secret layer beneath. She held up her hands to Tuca, who stepped down from her shoulder and allowed Alexandra to hold her in her arms, as she stepped out through the deceivingly simple front door of the innocently quiet cottage. As she stood still under the wonky porch roof, she held on to Tuca in her left arm and reached into her satchel with the other, pulling out a small glass vial filled with an earthy-green liquid, which wasn't glowing as some of the other potions had.

Swiftly she tossed back the potion, which tasted like she imagined fresh soil would taste, to which she pulled a quick face of pure disgust accompanied by a shudder of discontent. A glow of light then emitted from the centre of her body and grew until it shone over her entirely. Then the light dimmed, leaving behind an empty space where both she and Tuca had been stood.

They reappeared again via a tree, though not one that had already existed but one which sprouted abruptly up from the ground. It grew instantly to full size, just inside the forest where the road from the vampire manor entered into it. The tree was in fact hollow, and once it had grown tall and matched the others around it a slit appeared in the lower trunk. As it widened, both Alexandra and Tuca stepped out.

Orel, of course, had spotted the movement amongst the canopy, even though the others had ventured deeper into the woods by now, so she flew back down to investigate more closely. As she reached the area she glanced around and noticed this odd-looking tree, unnaturally squished in amongst the others. She flew over to it to check it out, and as she stared at it once stood on the ground, she could think of no animal which could have caused such a thing – nor had she even known a tree to grow so hollow without falling over.

Alexandra's plan had been put into action. She'd managed to distract Orel with the tree, whilst she shape-shifted into an owl and began darting through the trees alongside the road completely unnoticed, followed closely by Tuca. Shapeshifting was something Alexandra had studied as a child and so managed with ease, though it was by far a pretty sight to watch as her bones cracked, broke and reformed, whilst feathers pierced through her skin. They flew on a short distance past the others travelling, before Alexandra landed on the ground away from the road and transformed back into herself again, trying to hold back her magic from glowing too brightly within the twilight forest.

She found a spot to crouch down where she could hide amongst the bushes yet still get a clear view of the road, whilst Tuca sat on a branch high up, ready to alert her as the others approached. From inside her satchel she grabbed a potion vial with a blueish grey liquid inside, and she smashed it on the ground just in front of her. She forced her hand down onto the ground, covering the potion and broken glass which cut the skin on her palm, causing her to bleed out slightly and mixed the potion with her blood.

With her hand still on the floor, she looked ahead out onto the road and pushed it down harder into the ground. This caused her quite a bit of pain in her hand, with the cut glass pushing up in, but it was worth it, the potion was working. As she pushed into the ground a crack shattered across in the earth ahead of her, which grew until it reached across the road and deep into the forest on the other side. It was only a faint split, but it was there all the same, and she waited quietly with her hand held to the floor for Tucas signal.

Tuca kept a lookout as the others approached quickly, they weren't so far behind, and as they got close enough Tuca fluttered her wings. That was the signal. Alexandra knew they were near and she was ready.

As they came charging down the road they were all well-spaced out, and she watched as Elkor and his other cerfaurs crossed over the crack in the ground. Then, just as the bats pulling the carriage flew near it, she pushed down with as much strength as she could muster, causing the ground to split along the crack sounded by an explosion, as the earth around them shook.

The carriage scarcely made it across as the floor beneath it split in two, but three of the cerfaurs either side of the carriage fell down into the gap. Thankfully for them, they'd managed to land on narrow ledges on either side, for below them disappeared into darkness. The rest of the group rushed over to help one of the cerfaurs out onto the north side of the gap, but the others had landed too far down to reach. As they tried to think of a way to help them, Orel came swooping down the road to see what was going on.

"What happened?" she cried as she saw the earth had split and the others trying to help those who were stuck. "It's got to be her," Raul shouted from the other side, stepping out of the carriage, "Can you lift them out and the others across?"
"I'm not sure I'm strong enough, but I'll give it a try." Orel went for Lousta first, who she was able to help up as he did his best to scramble up the jagged rock face.

Alexandra had used the distraction from the commotion as her chance to sneak further along the road just slightly ahead of them, before she stepped out onto it and into the open. Then, she took out yet another potion from her satchel and walked back along the road towards them, until they were just about in view through the darkness within the trees.

Chris, Chloé and Lancelin had stepped out of the carriage after with Raul to offer their help, so Alexandra took this as the perfect opportunity. She took in a deep breath then lifted the potion bottle up to her mouth and popped off the cork. This released a dull, sandy-grey coloured mist, with flickering tiny brown sparks floating within. She then exhaled completely into the mist, causing it to grow immensely in size and take on a life of its own, heading in the direction she'd blown in; towards the commotion on the road.

Orel was just helping the last cerfaur out from inside the gap in the earth, before she would begin to aid the remaining cerfaurs over from the south side of it to join the rest, when she saw the mist coming. Suddenly she gasped and cried out, "dort flies!" Everyone jolted and turned to look in the same direction, only to see the mist rapidly approaching them. Orel left the cerfaur and flew towards them, then flipped over onto her back and attempted to push them away with the gust from her wings, but it failed to help them. These flies had been designed to grow in numbers the more wind that pushed them around, so with Orel's attempt the swarm simply grew and resumed their course.

"Run!" shouted Elkor, "Grab the humans!" Elkor helped

Chris onto his back, then Lousta grabbed Chloé and another cerfaur pulled up Lancelin. They each held on tight, both to the cerfaur and to their corne-trolls. Thankfully Chris had put the rucksack on as he'd stepped out of the carriage, leaving no one with the chance to try and run off with it. The vampires all transformed into bats and flew back in the direction of the manor, whilst Orel flew out of the forest and far into the distance. The cerfaurs all dispersed into the depths of the forest, though as the gap Alexandra had made was so vast, they were unable to leap over the crossing to take the humans south back to the manor.

The swarm of dort flies split. Some followed the vampires whilst others followed the cerfaurs in the different directions which they ran. Tuca flew down to join Alexandra on the road, where she stood pleased with herself; her plan to separate them all had been successful.

CHAPTER TWENTY-ONE

Alluring Confusion

The next morning brought with it the return of daylight to the forest, dissolving the darkness between the trees where the group had dispersed the night before. True to the nature of the dort flies which attacked them, in their wake they left an unconscious collection of creatures. Every being who had been caught by the swarm had been sent into a deep, deep slumber, as the blood from their bodies had been drained to almost deadly low levels.

Thankfully for the three humans, one of a cerfaurs magical abilities is to be able to dart amongst the trees at great speeds; even in the densest of forests. As they'd scattered off into the night, those of the cerfaurs running without a human on their back had selflessly given themselves to the swarm in an attempt to slow them down. Once each fly had either found something to drain blood from or run out of energy trying, their bodies fell to the ground and buried themselves into the earth; eventually leaving behind only their eggs.

As the sun rose in the sky, painting the land gold with its fresh morning rays, it began to shine down upon Lousta as he watched over Chloé who slept up against him, cradling her corne troll as if it was an old teddy bear. They were resting in a quiet little spot far from anywhere, alone and sheltered above by the canopy of the umbrella pines.

They were enclosed within a circle of ash, another circle of protection Chloé had created before she could rest peacefully outside, though the campfire had since burnt out. Lousta had slept on and off, unsure how safe the fire circle actually was – especially in a dry forest – but now the sun was up he found it hard to sleep any more.

On this morning, after the attack of the dort flies, the forest around them was tainted with an eerie stillness, with the only sounds of life sung way in the distance, as birds and other creatures who hadn't been attacked were beginning to wake up. Lousta lay his deer-like body on the floor as motionless as he could, admiring the design of Chloé's human form propped up against him.

He felt so privileged to behold her and to be of comfort to her. As he was caught up in a dreaming gaze, the sunbeams slowly began to angle further down, creeping from his body and onto her face. Through his eyes she appeared so delicate, so unique and definitely something worth saving.

As the rays of sunshine lingered over Chloé's sleeping eyes, bringing warmth to everything they touched, the light gently pulled her from her dream-world and back into reality (though these days the two seemed to have switched around), as she began to wriggle slowly and wake up. Blinded at first, she instinctively lifted her hand to shield her eyes from the sunlight as she blinked them open, so she might look around and make sense of her new surroundings.

"Morning," said Lousta, breaking the silence, unashamed of the way he had been admiring her as she slept.

Chloé, seeing his furry, deer-like body either side of her head, bolted upright and turned to him. "Oh! Lousta, morning," she blurted out. Then she looked down at what she held in her arms, "And Meg! you haven't run off. I hope that means she likes me," she nervously joked to Lousta. "What happened to us all last night?"

"It must have been Alexandra, presumably forcing us all to split up to make it easier for her to catch you."
"What was it exactly that we ran away from?"
"They were dort flies. They're only supposed to be found in the desert lands of eastern Merveille, where the dry, hot winds break open their eggs, but I guess

she found a way to create her own. When they bite you, they drain almost all of your blood and send you into a deep sleep, which would have made it all too easy for her to capture you."
Chloé gasped at the thought, "She sounds awful!"

Lousta stood himself up, as he scanned around to check for anything suspicious or threatening. He knew it wouldn't be a good idea to stay out in the open and alone for too long, and thought they ought to get moving on to Dragignaan. Chloé remained sat on the floor and looked up at him, just as her stomach began to rumble.

Instantly, Meg picked up on that sound and scurried off, disturbing the circle of ash before Chloé had the chance to realise what was happening. "Meg!" she cried after her, "Where are you going?" She stood up and began to walk after her, only to be stopped by Lousta's hand gripping her shoulder.

"Wait, it's not safe for you alone," Lousta warned. Chloé looked out into the direction where Meg had run off, with a sigh of disappointment thinking that she'd lost her new little pet; strange as she was.
"I was supposed to look after her in return for her making sure I wouldn't go hungry. I don't suppose there're any fruit trees around here?"
"I'm not sure," said Lousta, as he looked around and up into the branches above them, "But there's plenty of grass and leaves, and probably even some nuts." Chloé's expression hid no secret in how she felt about that idea.

Lousta took Chloé by the hand and lead her away from where they'd slept, assuring her that'd he'd find her something to satisfy her hunger. She politely followed.

The heroic act of saving her the night before and his caring nature in the light of the new morning had more than earnt her respect. The last thing she wanted to do was wound his pride as he attempted to look after her, which is why she was overwhelmingly relieved by what happened next.

As they'd began to wander away from their sleeping place, and as Lousta was examining the fauna around them, out popped Meg from beside a bush close by. She hurried up to Chloé whilst making a quiet, yet excitable sound. In her hands she carried a stone as if it were a food tray, though with only one flat-ish side which she held face up, and upon the stone were two slices of toast with strawberry jam and a banana.

"Oh my god, I don't believe it, breakfast!" said Chloé with glee. Meg handed it to her smiling and nodding. She accepted it and thanked Meg for bringing it to her. "But, how did you know?" she asked. Meg looked at her, then began to imitate the rumbling sound she'd heard Chloé's stomach make a few moments ago. Chloé laughed, "Ah I think I know that sound," she said before she stroked the back of Meg's head and thanked her again.

Whilst Chloé sat back down and ate her breakfast, Lousta foraged around for some things to eat for himself. He would've preferred to have been the one to satisfy Chloé's needs that morning, but he tried not to let it show.

After they'd eaten it was time for them to move on, and they set off walking side by side through the trees. Lousta couldn't be sure exactly where they were, but he did remember roughly in which direction they'd run from the road. He hadn't a doubt in his mind that his father would've escaped too with Chris, and that he would head on to Dragignaan as was the original plan. Though even there, none of them would be safe staying still for too long, so it was vital that they moved quickly.

"Hey Chloé, would you like to ride me?"
"Would I what?!" replied Chloé, a little taken aback. They both stopped.
"On my back like last night, I just think it'd be safer for us to get there faster."
"Oh, right, yea of course, if that's alright with you? And I'm not too heavy," she blushed.

Lousta laughed off Chloé's last comment, assuring her that to carry her would be no difficulty for a cerfaur as strong as he. He then lowered himself down to the ground, aiding her as she climbed onto him and somewhat awkwardly straddled his body. She placed one hand down onto his fury back to steady herself and held Meg tightly to her body with her free arm.

Though as Lousta jolted back up she wobbled slightly, prompting her to instinctively reach forward and grab hold of the human part of his body in front of her. Feeling a little awkward to be touching another man's bare skin around his waist, she loosened her grip and kept a distance between the two bodies.

"You're going to have to hold on a bit tighter than that if you're only using one arm," said Lousta. As he said it, he grabbed her hand which was holding him and pulled on it, wrapping her arm around his taught, naked, muscular abdomen, and bringing their two bodies closer together, "And just make sure you don't let go." Chloé gulped as her heart fluttered.

As he spoke to her whilst holding her arm around him, he had twisted his chest and head around so that he could just about face her behind him. For a moment he paused as they both looked into each other's eyes, waiting for recognition that she'd got the instruction. Chloé nervously nodded and agreed to hold on tight; nervously because she was afraid to show how much she was actually enjoying the closeness with this handsome stranger.

As they began racing through the forest searching for a route to Dragignaan, the same was true for Lancelin and the cerfaur who'd rescued him. She was a female cerfaur named Hinder, and unfortunately, they weren't experiencing the same enjoyment of being stuck together as Lousta and Chloé were.

Lancelin acted as if he were her superior, after all, she wasn't the head of the cerfaurs, and they were only there to aid and protect the humans on their quest to reach the spring. As it was, he showed an ungrateful attitude towards her, and it was he who insisted he ride on her back as she raced on in search of Dragignaan.

Both teams thought well to head straight there as it turned out, as Orel, Elkor and Chris, sat patiently hidden inside an old house, once belonging to one of the many humans who'd emigrated there around five hundred years ago.

The town of Dragignaan was cosily nestled in amongst rugged, rocky hills, partially covered in dry, shrubby forest. Dotted about amongst the hills were steep cliffs, most of which came complete with small cave entrances, safely placed away from the ground at the top and bottom; housing the local species of thorn dragons native to the area.

They were named thorn dragons not because they had thorn-like spikes on their body, but for their ability to eat wood and throw it back out as flaming thorns. This didn't put the new human inhabitants off from building their town in such a spot however, since the dragons were herbivores and grew to about the size of a medium-sized dog. In fact, the interest in these creatures was part of the reason people settled here; that and the natural hot spring rivers that flowed up from the surrounding hills right into the town.

The settlement had a rural, central European feel to it, only with one major significant difference - there was no church, nor any kind of religious building or shrine to be seen here. There was, however, a large town hall in the centre, with a grand fountain drawing focus in the square in front, which once flowed with the warm waters of the Dragignaan river.

To the eastern side, sitting slightly higher at the foot of a hill, was the area which clearly housed the more powerful people who settled here, as they looked down upon the town and stole the best views of the surrounding landscape. The lower, poorer, western side was where the road which the group had intended to travel along entered the town. The houses at this end had not all lasted quite as well as the bigger homes in the east, and they were all packed in closely together, trying to be as close to the centre as they could.

The house which Orel, Elkor and Chris were waiting inside of, didn't seem such a wise choice from the outside, which is why Elkor had chosen it. One side of the house had crumbled, leaving parts of its wooden skeleton standing bare in the open. This once humble home had been built right next to the Dragignaan river, and the cobbled road which ran in front of the house leapt right across it in the form of a ramshackle, old stone bridge.

From the side of the stone-built house that was still standing, Elkor stood hidden behind the wooden shutters of a downstairs window, watching for any sign of the others, whilst Orel slept on the floor; conserving her energy in case she had to fly Chris away to safety. They'd left Chris asleep on the stone floor at the back of the room, which was heated just enough by the passing warm air above the river, to keep it from getting too cold during the night.

As the day grew, Elkor barely left his lookout post, constantly sure that the others would come leaping into the town along this road at any moment. Another of the cerfaurs magical abilities was their ability to camouflage, though this became slightly more difficult whilst they were travelling with others. Nevertheless, Elkor knew he'd be able to spot them coming whilst Alexandra would find it far more difficult.

Chris managed to sleep through most of the day, by this point his body clock was all over the place, and whilst he rested on the warm floor of a room merely speckled with a few hints of daylight, his senses were completely at ease. At least they were for some time, until around mid-afternoon when his ears picked up a sound calling to him, just loud enough to bring him gently out of his sleep.

Or had it? For a while after he still could not be sure. The sound he heard was soft and caring, filling his mind with wonder and erasing any pain he may have had – physical and emotional.

He stood up and looked around, for a moment he wasn't even so sure where *he* was, let alone what the sound was or where it was coming from. Perhaps he was having a vision, he thought, like one of the ones Chloé had received from the book. Perhaps his body was actually lying asleep somewhere after escaping whatever it was that attacked them, and he was holding the book just as Chloé had been.

Though what he saw around him didn't look anything like what Chloé had described, and he seemed to remember coming into a house with Elkor the night before. It was merely the feeling of abstract curiosity and the unnatural loss of his fear, that led him to believe that this couldn't be real. With that in mind, he decided to go forth and find the source of this alluring melody, coming from somewhere outside the house, where he felt the world was living in peace and harmony.

As he walked over and opened a door at the back of the room, leading on to another room with a gap in the back, broken wall of the house, wide enough for him to fit through, Elkor didn't pick up any sound of his movement. To see Chris now, anyone would assume he was simply sleepwalking, though every sound he made or could hear, existed only in his reality and was muted to those around him. He followed the sound through the next room and out the back of the house, where it seemed to float towards him on the gentle breeze on this hazy summer afternoon.

As he looked around to gauge which direction the pleasing, lullaby tune was coming from, he was met by a world where everything seemed to emit an aura of its own soothing light. Nothing was harsh or precise, all he saw was pleasing and welcoming. Whereas in true reality, he stood amongst overgrowth of the old gardens behind the row of houses, filled with odd dead trees, shrivelled bushes and overgrown grassy areas.

Unaware of his true surroundings, he'd sensed the noise was coming from back inside the forest and began making his way in that direction. The song in the air guided him towards it, directing him along an old footpath between the gardens, which lead to the trees beyond the town away from the road.

Chris entered the forest in awe of its fruits and peaceful offerings. He began to feel a more direct pull within him, coming from something that, although he didn't know what it was, his heart was drawn to undoubtedly. As he walked on, he noted a small babbling brook filtering through the forest floor, which seemed to play a tune as it trickled across the stones and broken twigs in its path.

He followed the brook upstream, still in pursuit of the music he could hear in the air, when at last, a voice joined it. Someone was singing softly to the tune of the sunlight, the brook and the trees around him, though to Chris this tune sounded more like pianos, harps and violins, all harmonizing together. The voice didn't sing any words but merely hummed and 'ahhh'ed, beautifully complimenting the music.

He walked on, pulled by the force he felt tugging on his emotions. He thought to himself how he'd never seen such an enchanting forest before, or ever heard a sound quite so mesmerizing. He headed slightly uphill as the water babbled down next to him, and as he reached the brow of the hill, he saw a mysterious group of trees gathered together ahead of him; from within which came the babbling brook he'd been following.

The trees were different to the other trees in the forest, they were shorter than the rest and looked like a type of birch tree, only their bark was a dull-fern colour whilst their leaves reflected a pale mint green. They were stood in a circular formation, though staggered and dense enough to make it difficult to see anything beyond them. Soft light of different colours oozed out from within, with golden sparks twinkling amongst them, drifting on the wind like sunlight fire embers escaping a bonfire. The ones that landed on the water flowed down towards him as he walked fearlessly up towards the trees, eager to find out who, or what was dwelling within.

He entered into the circle from where the water exited, and as he peered inside his eyes widened whilst his heart pounded. The small brook snaked two-thirds of the way across a space of about forty square meters, concealed within the cluster of trees; though there was the odd rogue tree scatted about within. The cool, fresh water escaped from a deep, crystal clear pool, which rippled smoothly across from the other side where the source flowed from.

Around the pool there were a few rocks of odd shapes and sizes, but it was one of the rocks, just on the edge of the pool to the right, where his attention was drawn to. It was a small, wide, boulder, upon which sat the most beautiful woman he believed he'd ever seen; it was Alexandra.

She sat there alone, without her cloak or even Tuca anywhere to be seen. Her left side faced Chris as she peacefully watched the ripples on the water, and continued to sing effortlessly whilst playfully dipping her toes in the fresh spring. Her long, wild, crimson-red hair flowed freely from her head, curling and waving its way down – although, as if she was underwater, it seemed almost weightless somehow.

As Chris lusted after her she innocently raised her left leg, lifting her toes from the pool and holding it straight in front of her with them pointed, sitting herself up straight. This allowed the gap in her red, rag skirt to fall open, as she enjoyed the sensation of the cool drops of water running freely along her leg, all the way to where her thigh sat upon the rock.

She then crossed her leg over the other, as she swished her hair over her left shoulder and turned to face him, "Hello Chris," she said in a kind, welcoming voice now that she'd stopped signing.

As Chris leered at her, her beauty seemed to spread to everything around her. She appeared to him like Aphrodite, beaming down her light of love upon him. "Hi," he said with wonderment.

"You can come closer if you like, Chris. There's no reason for you to be afraid here," she smiled. Chris started heading straight towards her, fumbling over the running water and rocks as he stepped in and out of the brook, not looking where he was placing his feet. Alexandra spun herself around upon her rock so that her whole body was facing his direction, keeping her legs crossed with the exposed left leg on top. Then, in an attempt to further seduce him, she raised her arms above her head and began lifting up and pulling back her glossy hair away from her face.

"Stop!" she cried out suddenly, letting some hair fall down over her face, shoulders and breasts as it suddenly began to obey the laws of gravity once more when she thrust out her palm towards him. "Oh Chris, before I can let you come any closer, I need you to do something for me. Would you do something for me?"

"For you, I'd do anything. Just tell me and I'll do it, so I can be near you."
"I need you to, please, oh, how do I ask such a thing? Chris, I need give up your magic. Release it from your blood and into this water, where it may return to the earth. Then, we can be together."
"But," Chris began, slightly confused, which tugged at him as if the thought of anything other than her would bring him racing back down to earth. "I don't have any magic." Assuming that would please her, he lost all feeling of confusion and continued to walk towards her with a look of pure content over his face.

"Stop!" she cried again, this time with both her palms faced towards him and with more of a confused look on her face, other than an angelic, sad one as before. "What do you mean, you have no magic?"
"I mean, I have no magic. I am mortal, just as you desire."

The shock on Alexandra's face was reflected in the sudden dulling of their surroundings, as the suggestion that she'd been wasting her time and potions was thrust upon her. "What about your two friends who you arrived here with, they have the magic light, don't they?"
"It is not my desire to contradict you, most beautiful creature, but no, they possess no such magic light within them either."

Alexandra paused for a moment, trying to make sense of the situation and not let it get out of her control. "So, what brought you three to this place? *How* did you get here? Why do some believe you to possess the light from the spring?"

"It all started when, my girlfriend, Chloé…my girlfriend…" he stumbled over his words. Something inside him was beginning to feel strange, feelings of uncertainty and fear began to creep back to him as he remembered his true feelings for Chloé, which distorted his magically created ones towards Alexandra.
"Yes? What did she do?" she urged him, trying to get him to focus on what she did rather than Chloé herself.

For a moment, he still hesitated to finish his sentence and instead stood still in thought, thought that worried Alexandra. Seductively she raised her hand to her mouth and blew a kiss in his direction, a kiss that was carried to him in a cloud of pink smoke, which surrounded him until he inhaled it. After that he slipped back into his trance and looked back towards Alexandra.

"She found a book, in an old castle, that only she can read. It lead us here. The vampires say it belongs to a man who was once a unicorn, a man who'll soon save us from... from you."

Alexandra's biggest fear had just been presented to her, the chance was real that Malicorne would come back and steal control of magic and the whole island away from her. "And how will this unicorn man save you from me, if he does not still exist?" she questioned, trying to keep control of her fear.

"A resurrection spell, I believe, one Chloé has seen in his book. Soon she'll bathe in the spring as perceived in her vision, and then she'll have the strength and guidance to perform the ritual. Oh please, dearest, enchanted being I see before me, you make it so painful to keep me held back so. Might I come close to you now?" Chris' desperation to be near her was growing stronger the longer she held him at a distance, and she risked it sparking a fiery rage within him, like that of a jealous or betrayed lover.

"Yes, you may come close, up to the rock here where I sit before you. I will give the word when you may touch me." Alexandra was anxious not to let Chris touch her, for if she let him through his blinded will, the spell he was currently trapped within would take a more permanent hold, making him act like a puppy for her love and attention until the day she would be able to severely break his heart in some way. "Before we go further, my love, I must warn you of the truth. You must listen to me."

Chris walked over to Alexandra, feeling as if he was floating upon soft clouds, though in reality he was merely shuffling his feet through the dead leaves and crumbled rocks on the ground. "My dearest creature who holds my heart in her very hands, what is it you must warn me about? Please hurry, for then I may be able to present my true love's kiss upon thy lips."

Alexandra tried hard not to roll her eyes in front of him and to keep acting within the moment, for fear of sparking that rage of passion so close within – a downside to the incantotion she'd used to lure him away from the protection of the others.

"Listen to my words, Chris," she said more hastily, "Malicorne is not the leader you have been promised. He is an all-powerful Métis, a crossbreed, the worst that could possibly have been created. Though he is half human, he uses this strength against our kind and wishes for nothing but to dominate both worlds. Upon seizing control over humans, his wish is to make us nothing more than his slaves, using our knowledge and unique use of magic solely for creating a new race of Métis', who will rule over all of mankind."

Chris stood frozen, his dreamy expression now a bewildered stare. His eyesight ran down her body as his head began to drop, whilst he processed this chilling revelation. His neck muscles loosened with the weight of the information he'd just taken in, whilst still in his lustful trance.

Alexandra's body passed before his eyes, her face, neck, breasts, waist and then onto her crossed legs as she sat on the rock. The sight of her perfect beauty snapped him back into full dream state, though he didn't show this switch through any action from his body. He then reached out to touch her slowly with his right hand, "Will you save me?" he asked, about to touch her bare knee. She flinched quickly, forbidding the meeting of their flesh. Chris held back his hand and paused for a moment, before throwing his glace back up to her face, casting a hateful stare towards her.

"You hate me! Why do you hate me!? I give you my body and my soul and you throw it back at me and laugh! You're nothing but a filthy…" Alexandra stopped him suddenly by holding up her hand in front of him and squeezing the air, as if gripping tightly on to an invisible apple, causing his body to lock tight.
"Chris, please I beg you! The time for us is not in this moment."

Alexandra, keeping her hand as level as she could and without taking her eyes off him, slid down from the rock she was sat on and stood with it between them. "I will save you, but first you must bring me the book. I, your love, fear that if I fight the ones who protect it, I may kill them. You wouldn't want that, would you?" Alexandra gently eased off her grip holding Chris, making sure he had calmed down before letting go completely. Thankfully he had, but just as he began to ask how he might get it to her, their intimate meeting was broken with a cry from above.

"Chris!" cried Orel, having spotted him amongst the trees from a distance. Chris then, curious about the muffled sound he heard coming from the sky above him, dragged his focus away from Alexandra and looked up wearily. Thanks to the sound of Orel's call managing to break through into Chris' semi-conscious state of being, his mind came racing back to full consciousness.

He searched the sky that he could see through the sparse canopy as he heard the cry come again, though much clearer now, and he spotted Orel's hefty, half human, half bird-like body swooping over across the treetops. He wasn't sure if he was worried for Alexandra, for himself, or just nervous of the consequences of the two meeting with only himself in the middle; but something made him turn hastily back to Alexandra. He felt compelled to urge her to hide from Orel, yet to his shocking surprise she had already gone. All he saw was the rock where she'd been sat, in a now seemingly empty, dusty setting.

The pond, the babbling brook, the circle of strange trees and Alexandra had all since vanished, revealing a rather ordinary part of the dry, rocky umbrella-pine forest. Chris reached forward and touched the stone where Alexandra had been sat, wondering if any of it had been real - though then he began to question the differences between what was real and what was simply an illusion in this new place.

Even if what he saw had all been inside his head, if she'd planted it there for him to see, was it not then just as real as if she'd actually been there? For now, it was stored away with all his other memories. Just because his reality, for a moment, had been different to anyone else's, was it not still a reality, he pondered. Where she'd been sat on the rock was warm to his touch.

As for the words that had passed between their mouths, he only vaguely remembered what had been said during this lustful encounter. He remembered it like a dream he'd had just before waking up, where most of the unimportant detail began to slip from his consciousness the longer he had his eyes open. The passion he'd felt for her whilst under the spell lingered inside him too, though faint now, he felt it merely as a treasured memory; the feeling he remembered more than what had actually happened.

CHAPTER TWENTY-TWO

The Tale of the Scorned Witch

"Chris," said Orel as she landed close to him, "Are you alright? Don't you realise the danger you're putting yourself in, being out here all by yourself?"

"I'm sorry. I think… I suppose I just needed some space, that's all. Everything has just been so crazy lately. For us, non-magic people I mean."

"I'm just glad she hasn't found you out here, alone and vulnerable. Come on, I'll take you back to the house. Lousta and Chloé have arrived and we're just waiting on

Lancelin and whoever managed to save him, if anyone managed to save him."
"Oh don't worry about him, he'll be fine I'm sure. He always seems to keep coming back," muttered Chris.

He and Orel walked cautiously back to the house were the others were waiting, Orel shielding Chris under her wings as they stepped out from the shelter of the trees and into the broad daylight; attempting to absorb any of Alexandra's magic that might be out seeking him. As they entered through the front door of the derelict townhouse, Chloé greeted Chris with a tight embrace and a lover's kiss, born slightly out of guilt for having enjoyed Lousta's company as much as she did. Chris responded as any partner should to such acts of affection from their other-half, though inside he couldn't shake the feeling of discomfort, something within telling him that this public display did not mimic how he now felt towards her.

"I'm so glad you're alright! I was so frightened when we all split up last night. I didn't know when or if I'd see you again. What were you doing outside alone?" pestered Chloé.
"I just, needed some space that's all,' began Chris, trying to avoid eye contact as he lied to her. "We were outside alone only a few days ago before all this shuffling around in secret began, we seemed to be alright then."
"Yes, but we still had each other, and I had the book to guide us which kept us all safe."

Chris had mixed feelings about their current protectors since his encounter in the forest, which he knew he needed to discuss with Chloé. Though, whilst in the company of the others, it was neither the time nor the place to let on that he had conflicting thoughts. "You're right, sorry," he said as he shook his head, "I'll be more careful in future," he smiled.

Now that most of them were there, they decided to begin planning their next move whilst waiting for Lancelin, should he turn up. They knew they couldn't hide out in the house for long, and that the sooner they reached the spring the better, now that Alexandra was on their trail. The all sat together on the hard stone floor, shuffling every now and then to get comfortable.

"From where we stand now, there are two passes up into the Hills of the Four Seasons…" Elkor began. "The closest one is about a four-day journey from here, though unfortunately, I'm not aware of any herds of our kind living close by, should we need to rest. Orel?"
"Are you talking about Open Gates Pass?"
"That's it."
"I could fly ahead and scout out anyone who's able to house us in the area?"

"What about the other pass?" asked Chris, curious as to why it didn't seem to be an option.
"That one is at least nine days journey from here, though I do know many who live close by."
"Would it not be best to take a longer, safer route?" Chris asked again, trying to be part of the leaders' decision making.

"There's always Eppon Creek Pass?" suggested Lousta, in a mysteriously subdued manner. Elkor and Orel looked at him, Orel confused and Elkor displeased.
"Out of the question," insisted Elkor.

"What's wrong with Eppon Creek Pass?" asked Chloé curiously, "Is it dangerous?"
"The *path* isn't exactly," answered Elkor, "It's what lies beyond it that is."
"What lies beyond it?" asked Chris.

"The Weeping Woods," replied Lousta.
"Exactly. Which is why we cannot pass through there."
"What's wrong with the Weeping Woods?" Chris asked, innocently.
"It's a dangerous place for anyone human. Even Malicorne himself, being half human, might not pass through those woods alone without trouble. And the fact that we ourselves function much like humans, may make it uneasy for us, too," warned Elkor.

"But no one has had any trouble there for years now, some even believe the spirit has finally moved on, which Alexandra probably won't know about since she's been in hiding all this time," suggested Lousta.
"What spirit? What exactly is the problem with these woods?" Chris asked again, getting frustrated from the lack of a simple answer to his question. Lousta looked at Elkor and they shared a glance, one that seemed to give Lousta permission to fill them in on the details of the Weeping Woods.

"It was many years ago now, so tells the legend, when humans inhabited Île Merveille and possessed the light from the spring. Whilst some lived here to support a thriving new magical community, others preferred to take their newly enlightened blood back to where they came from, returning as a superior being among 'mortals', as they called you. One lady who journeyed back was a witch named Klara, who used her new status to get close to one of your royal families at the time, and she ended up falling in love with a prince who loved her in return; but unfortunately for Klara, his devotion to his kingdom was stronger than his love for her…"

"How so?" asked an intrigued Chloé, completely drawn in by the story.
"The word that reached back here, was that although these humans who now had this new power inside of them were respected and often sought after back where you came from, they were no longer seen as pure in the eyes of your religious leaders. Therefore, there was absolutely no way that a prince could ever marry a witch, no matter how much he loved her."

"So, now she haunts those woods?" Chloé interrupted again.
"No, not Klara. The prince was betrothed to a princess from somewhere else, so the story goes, though he had promised Klara that the week before his wedding the two of them would escape together and live somewhere far away, forever, just the two of them. Unfortunately for us all, the prince broke this promise and left Klara waiting on her own where the two had planned to meet. When she later confronted him, he told her that he could never choose a witch over his kingdom and that it was best for both of them if she returned here, to Île Merveille, alone."

"Oh, poor Klara," sighed Chloé, "So, what did she do? It's not the prince's spirit in the woods, is it?" she guessed, eager to find out the end to this tale.
"No, it's not the prince. Klara was devastated, she took to her home and barricaded herself inside, though it's told that people could hear her cries of pain for miles

around. She spiralled into an uncontrollable depression from the heartache, so far that she almost took her own life just to end the pain and suffering that consumed her. Until, at some point before the wedding day, an idea for a remedy to her pain came to her..."

"...In her eyes, she was not the one who should be in pain. She was a witch, she had the power to take whatever she wanted. So, on the morning of the prince and princess' wedding, Klara stole the princess away in secret and locked her up, hidden somewhere within her house. With the princess trapped, Klara cast a spell to transfer her pain onto the princess, to rid herself of the agony she felt after the prince had chosen his duty, and this princess, over her. Then, she transformed herself to look identical to the princess on her wedding day and went on to marry the prince of her dreams, without ever revealing to him what she had done, or who she really was."

"But then, who's is the spirit in the woods?" asked Chis.
"Oh, right. So, the princess was locked away in Klara's old house, tormented by Klara's heartache. Unfortunately for Klara, the princess' cries could also be heard far and wide just as hers had been, and the prince's guilt – believing it was still Klara who yearned for him - urged him to go and speak with her. After he left for the witches house, Klara hurried back there to greet the prince as her true self, then tells the prince she shall return to Île Merveille to end her suffering..."

"...However, she, in fact, brought the princess back here, then bound and cursed her to an area of the woods, now known as the Weeping Woods. Klara's curse made it impossible for the princess to speak of what had happened, so instead, the princess sang songs of woe and sorrow to ease her pain, unknowingly spreading it to all who heard. The princess' grief grew with her loneliness, and the songs she sang were too much for passers-by not to be moved by. People who heard her songs quickly became suicidal, tormented by any inner turmoil they had bottled up and stored away."

"Wait, if the princess couldn't speak of what happened to her, how do you know all this?" asked Chris sceptically, trying to make sense of it all.

"Humans who visit the spring are able to learn all kinds of magic, though children born of two magical parents, were often born with a gift. A magical ability which may take some many years to learn and most may never master. One local girl who was born with the rare gift of seeing into the past, known as a Bygone, had her sense of hearing removed and preserved in the Merville Academy of Wonder…"

"What's the Merveille Academy of Wonder?" asked Chloé with a hint of awe in her voice.
"A place where humans would go to learn how to use, and to experiment with their magic."
"So, like a magic school?"
"I guess," shrugged Lousta. Chloé's face lit up with excitement as she turned to Chris, who was actually more interested in hearing the end to the story.

"You were saying, this… Bygone girl, did she see what had happened then?" asked Chris.
"Yes. She went to the woods and found the princess, held her hand and saw her past. Once everyone

knew what had happened, unable to undo the curse, they killed her, hoping to finally set her free. But unfortunately, her spirit still remained trapped. So, saddened even more that they had simply killed her instead of trying to track down Klara, which they hadn't done for fear of causing a larger rift between magic and non-magic folk, her spirit now preys on any scent of a human it can, with its deeply depressing song."

Chris and Chloé sat back and looked at each other, realising that although this land was new to them, so much lost history had happened here which connected with their own, and the land itself had been scarred by the act of human invasion. Chloé wondered if it would it be right for them to bring all that back to reality. Should they resurrected Malicorne, there was no telling what he would be able to restore of this lost and forgotten world. After all, it had apparently only taken a single sorceress to end it all.

Perhaps this time it could be done right, thought Chloé, for history teaches us how we learn from our mistakes and are able to evolve, so surely magical humans deserved another chance to exist as they had. Even more so, she concluded, they might even be able to find cures to the current world's problems; things like hunger, cancer and even climate change.

"Of course, this was all over two hundred years ago, before Alexandra ended it all for the humans here. She might not even know about the Weeping Woods. In fact, she wasn't known to be from this land, just, suddenly arrived as the others were expelled. So, if she does follow us in there, and the princess' spirit still haunts the area, she might just get rid of Alexandra for us,"

Lousta suggested.

"What makes you think we'll make it out any more alive?" Chris snapped, feeling completely against the idea since hearing the tale.
"You'll have us to look out for you. If the spirit wanted Merville creatures we'd have heard about it, don't you think so, father?"
"That doesn't mean to say we won't be affected by the song," warned Elkor.

Chloé turned to Chris and asked him for the book, as he'd had the rucksack last, so that she might seek some kind of guidance or protection from it that might help them make it through the woods alive. He fetched her the rucksack and she slid the book out carefully from inside, as the other items in there slid about into the large empty space it left behind. She sat with it upon her lap, closed her eyes and focused. Laying her hand on the book she thought hard about the answers she sought after, questioning it about the Weeping Woods; but there was no response.

Minutes of silence passed as they all watched Chloé in anticipation, as she was desperately trying to ask the book for help, until Elkor spoke up, "This is Malicorne's book, correct?"
"So we've been told," replied Chris.
"Malicorne was not from here either, he grew up in your world. There are a few stories of his visits here and we all heard of his great power, but mainly he would send his followers back and forth to carry out his tasks for him. Even he may not have heard of the Weeping Woods either."

"Nothing," exclaimed Chloé, sounding defeated, "What should we do?"

"I reckon we can make it," said Lousta confidently, "I've heard of others passing through without hearing a single note sung. Even more so recently."

"How recently?" asked Elkor.

"Well, I didn't want to worry you before, but, I've travelled through many times with a few others to make it up into the hills," Lousta admitted, then turned to Chris as he continued, "There're some good-looking centaurs who pass through the plains just beyond." Chris nervously smiled and laughed back, not really sure how to respond to such a comment.

"You risked your life to see a centaur?" snapped Elkor.

"Not really, that's the point, none of us ever heard her singing. She might even have moved on."

They continued to discuss the pros and cons of the three different passes, until eventually they agreed to risk heading up via Eppon Creek as it would save them much time; with the idea that Orel would fly ahead and find the shortest route through. Elkor convincingly announced that it would be much wiser to head on without help from the vampires, as this time of year they had more hours of daylight than they did of the night.

As Lancelin and Hinder still hadn't shown up, they decided to keep together for that evening and spend another night in the house; should Lancelin not arrive by the next dawn, they would have no choice but to leave without him.

Chris was desperate to have a private talk with Chloé about what had happened earlier that day, to discuss his concerns about their current situation. The fact was, he didn't know who to trust now. All he knew was that they would need some kind of magic soon, if only to send them home.

CHAPTER TWENTY-THREE

The Old Millhouse

Lancelin never returned to them that night, though he hadn't been captured by Alexandra as Chloé feared. He and Hinder had, in fact, arrived close to the house where they all waited when they stumbled across a clearly possessed Chris talking to himself in the woods. Hidden by Hinder's power of camouflage, they watched and listened to Chris' side of the conversation, becoming certain that he was talking to Alexandra. They heard him reveal their plans to her and watched as he pleaded with her to save him; there were no doubts in their minds that he was under some kind of spell of hers.

Hinder, loyal to her own kind, wanted to carry on ahead to warn Elkor, but Lancelin argued against it. He insisted they needed to warn the vampires of Chris' possible betrayal before rejoining the others, their ability to read others' inner desires may help them discover what Alexandra had persuaded him to do for her. So with that, they raced back through the forest to the vampire manor where they patiently awaited the sunset, then spent the night discussing a new plan of action with the Raul and Veshnica.

About half an hour before sunrise the following morning, Chris awoke to find Orel standing watch at the window whilst the others slept. There was no way he could sneak in a conversation with Chloé without Orel hearing, they were not to be out of her sight as long as she stood guard. Unable to sleep, he got up and walked over to her. "Any sign of them?" he asked.

"Not a single creature has passed this way on my watch," she said solemnly, "And it's almost dawn," she added with a hint of concern.

Chris peered out of the window to take a look around for himself, when he spotted something completely unexpected coming down the street. Surprised and greatly impressed by what he saw, he held his breath so as not to make any unnecessary loud noise and nudged Orel, "What are they?" he whispered to her through his tensed mouth.

What he saw were beings made up of shining coloured light. They had no physical body of their own, but took on a vague form of skinny little people, who stood between 50 centimetres to a meter in height. They flew and danced gracefully through the air, each emitting a light of a different colour which hung around their tiny forms like an aura, trailing off behind them. There were seven of them that Chris could see, and although he was unsure what they were, he was dazzled by their magnificent display of light and movement.

"Oh, they're just light nymphs. They've been playing in the warm water from the river. I guess they'll be gone soon, poor little things."
"What are light nymphs? And where are they going?"
"They're born from Lumen flowers, which only grow on trees which have at least one root touching a source of magic light underground. You get them a lot closer to the spring of course, and every now and then you'll find the odd tree that just happens to stretch its roots in the right direction. The light from the moon on a clear night, when it's over half full, causes the flowers to open, then out comes the nymph."

"Wow, that's quite cool. But, why do you say poor little things?"
"They can only survive in the darkness whilst their light glows, as soon as the sun's light overpowers theirs, they disappear."
"Oh, that's kind of sad, especially as it's almost dawn and they still seem so happy. Could they not hide in the dark somewhere?"
"They could, but then they wouldn't be free I suppose. Some creatures have tried to help by hiding them in caves, but they don't seem to have any sense of danger and eventually they all dance away into the light."

Chris watched the light nymphs as they effortlessly twirled and moved about, like tiny, little, floating ballerinas, heading down the street back towards the woods, where they would continue to dance in the shadow of the trees until the sun rose high enough to break through.

Just after dawn, everyone had awoken and there was still no sign of Lancelin or Hinder. They all stood together to discuss their plan, as Elkor announced that during the night he had changed his mind on Eppon Creek Pass. He didn't feel confident enough to lead everyone through what was beyond it, as he'd had no experience of the Weeping Woods himself. Lancelin argued that he was just being over cautious, and he insisted that he trust his son's experienced judgement. Still, Elkor thought that it posed more risk than an extra two to three days of travelling to the next pass, so it was to be discussed no more.

Their journey that day was to an old mill house, that'd been built years ago by humans who'd experimented there, making potions from the magical plants and rocks in the area. The house was situated at the foot of a small range of baron, rainbow rock hills (named so by the tints of different colours seen when its rock is lit by the sun, and also from the geodes found within containing multicolored crystals), and sat in an open area of grassland, bordered on one side by dry pine forest, and humid tropical jungle on the other.

The jungle was downhill from the pine forest, and often its moist, humid air would venture up towards the mill, making it a warm, though often wet place to live. To get there, Elkor planned for them to follow the edge of the jungle/pine forest border until they reached the open grassland where the house was situated. Once at the foot of the hills, they would simply follow the lower ground until they reached a mountain pass which they were comfortable to pass through.

In the light of the warm, fresh morning, after Chris and Chloé's corne trolls had both kindly brought them each some breakfast, the group set off heading through Dragignaan and exited from the south-east side; closest to where the pine forest met the jungle. Chloé rode upon Lousta again and Chris upon Elkor, whilst both carrying their corne trolls and sharing the load of their heavy rucksack. Orel flew on ahead, scouting for signs of trouble or perhaps some helpful allies.

They headed on through the forest along a well-trodden path, which separated the two different regions like a border to a new realm. The trees from either side arched over them, imitating a tunnel which they could safely pass through, hidden from the outside. The cerfaurs moved forwards at a much quicker pace than they could if the humans were to walk with them, though still, it took until just after sunset that evening before they reached the gradual separation of the two forests and the grassland between.

Whilst hurrying in the direction of the mill house out in the open, the blanket of darkness gradually grew thicker as it hid them well beneath it. The two forests parted further and further from each other until neither could be seen by the group, who now relied solely on Elkor to lead them in the right direction. Chloé and Chris both held on tightly as the cerfaurs raced on, occasionally checking the world around them, spotting only glowing, golden-pink clouds far on the horizon and the first few twinkling stars above.

The cerfaurs seemed to keep running long after sunset, until daylight was but a faint blue glow in the west, before they eventually began to slow down."Do you hear that?" asked Elkor, holding his arm out to slow Lousta down.
"Hear what?" replied Lousta.
"The river. It'll be the one that powers the mill. We're almost there, this way!"

Again they ran. Chris squinted his eyes as he tried to spot anything that could be a house out ahead, though he was surprised to discover that what he thought was just a cloudy night sky, was, in fact, a silhouette of hills rising before them. The sound of the river grew louder as they approached it, it's shallow water gushing over all the rocks and stones. They ran on heading up river for a little while, until eventually the sound of creaking wood and turning cogs could be heard – it was the water wheel attached to the mill, still turning after all those years.

Once Chris and Chloé knew the house was there, they saw it quite vividly in the silver light of the waning moon. The house had been built into a slight rise in the ground, where the river would've come tumbling over. Instead, whoever had built the house had managed to capture most of the water and flow it out through a spout, pouring it over a large wooden water wheel attached to the side of the house, causing it to turn steadily. The water then landed in a huge pond which surrounded the front and both sides of the wooden building, before flowing out to continue its original course.

The house was at least two stories high, with more windows randomly poking out of the roof. The back of the house seemed to start from the first floor, where a small veranda stood out over the higher ground on that side of the building. It appeared a questionable structure, as the first floor expanded further than the foundation of the ground floor, held up by bent and twisted wooden pillars rising out of the water beneath.

The wheel was connected to the first floor of the house on the left-hand side, which was a section of the house very square in structure, unlike the right-hand side which appeared to have much more character to its design. A crooked brick chimney stuck out of the back-right hand side, towering slightly above the slated roof. To get to the main, ground floor entrance of the house, one had to first cross an old, wooden jetty-like bridge, that was roughly sixty meters long and sat just inches above the surface of the water.

"Would the other door not be a bit safer?" asked Chris as they arrived close by the bridge.
"With less risk of getting wet?" added Chloé.
"It's bolted shut, I've tried it before," admitted Elkor, "Thankfully though, the downstairs door was left unlocked."

"Don't worry, I'll make sure you don't get wet," Lousta said to Chloé softly, as he reached around and touched her arm reassuringly; which didn't go unnoticed by Chris as he saw the two of them smile at one another.

"Shall we not go in single file? To distribute our weight?" Chris suggested, intentionally interrupting Chloé and Lousta's gaze. Elkor agreed, and so decided to go first after letting Chris down from his back.

Behind Elkor went Chris, keeping spaced well apart and making sure not to put too much weight on any one section of the old, possibly rotting bridge. After Elkor was almost all the way across, Chloé stepped out to follow Chris, her nerves causing her legs to tremble as she tested out each plank of wood before her.

Chris turned back once he'd reached the other side and assured her that it would be alright, saying how secure the bridge had felt to him. After he'd mentioned it, however, the next step she took just happened to be onto a broken panel, and as her weight moved forward the wood under her foot gave way and snapped across the centre. Her leg rapidly plunged straight into the cool, still water, setting off a reaction which none could've predicted.

They all cried out as she fell and caught herself on either side of the broken plank, with Meg (who'd jumped from Chloé's arms as she fell) stood upon the bridge jumping around in a panic. "Argh!" Chloé screamed.
"Chlo! Are you alright?" yelled Chris.
"I'm fine, I think, I just have a wet..." Chloé paused.

She noticed the space below her under the water begin to light up with twinkling pale green lights, calming her urge to lift herself out. More and more appeared rapidly, as the water began smoothly swirling around her. Feeling a gradual pull from under the water, which only grew stronger as the speed of the swirling water increased rapidly, she tried again in fear to scramble back out.

The next wooden board broke away just as the one before it, causing the rest of her body to sink below the surface. She only just managed to grab ahold of the next board along as she desperately reached for something to stop her from being completely pulled under.

She screamed out for help. The swirling water was pulling her under while the depth of the pond seemed to spiral further and further away, as the once twinkling lights spun past her with the rushing of the water. Chris hesitated, trying to think of the best way they could reach her, but before he could act he saw that Lousta already had.

He'd wasted no time in leaping out onto the bridge towards her, then straddled the gap where she'd fallen. Reaching down he grabbed hold of Chloé and pulled with all his strength to lift her from the suction of the swirling pool. As he lifted her she clambered onto his back, clutching at clumps of skin and fur to drag herself up as Meg jumped and clung to her clothes. The swirling water still gurgled and rushed beneath them, whilst Lousta instructed Chloé to hold tight as he leapt from board to board, dashing across the bridge as fast as he could.

"Shit, Chloé! Are you alright?" Asked Chris, high on adrenaline from the panic.
"I think so," she slid down from Lousta's back, "Thanks to Lousta," she said, with her hand still touching him.

"What the hell!? Why would you bring us over water

like that?" Chris yelled at Elkor.
"I didn't know it did that, I swear. I've never seen anyone fall in before. Chloé, I'm so sorry, really."
"It's alright now," she said to calm the situation, whilst her body was still shaking from the fear, "Let's just get inside before we draw any more attention to ourselves."

They entered inside the house, where a dark, motionless atmosphere contrasted with that of the swirling pool of water outside. Chloé, soaking wet and cold, hoped she might find an old blanket or something to wrap around her.

The ground floor was set out like a small shop, with tables and shelves displaying oddly shaped bottles filled with different coloured liquids, a variety of rocks and withered, dried up old flowers. At the opposite end of the room was the counter, where an old and dusty register sat. Behind that, there was an open door leading to a staircase.

"Is this a shop?" asked Chris, wondering if it was still in use or not.
"I assume so," said Elkor, "Unlike the vampires, I wasn't alive when humans were around, but from what I've heard, that's what this was."
"Why does it smell burnt?" asked Chloé, sniffing the air and trying to follow the direction of the scent of old ash.
"That'll be the fire a friend and I started here once," Elkor continued, pointing to a corner of the room where everything was covered in scorch marks, "By accident I mean."

Chris, who'd thankfully been carrying the rucksack since before the bridge, took out the torch to get a better look around, though he didn't recognise anything that the shop was selling. "I wonder if these are potions?" he said, as he shone the light through the coloured liquids. "Most likely," warned Lousta, "So be careful."

Chris stared at some that were close by to him, wondering what incredible things just a single drop of some of these liquids could do to them, or potentially awful things they could do too. Elkor picked up a handful of something that looked like gravel from a wide bowl, sat on a table close by the area of scorch marks. "Come on, we'll go upstairs where there's more space," he said.

They all followed him up the stairway behind the counter, which was difficult for the cerfaurs to fit through (especially with their antlers), into a large, open room where it was clear that the water wheel was connected; though in the darkness they could only assume this due to how clear the noise from its cogs sounded. The ceiling height went way up into the eaves, with a wide, wooden, circular structure hanging down in the middle, that had little lanterns hanging from it, which they noticed as the glass casing reflected Chris' torch's light.

Elkor led on through another door into the next room, which they found to be a spacious living area with chairs and an impressive, corner fireplace. There was space in the room enough to fit them all in there comfortably. "Wait here," said Elkor, "And turn that light off!" demanded Elkor, as he left them by the door and felt his way across the room.

First he went over to each window and closed the

shutters, blocking out all the moonlight that had been dusting the furniture with a slight hint of silver. "Alright Chris, could you now shine that light of yours over into this corner?" he asked. Chris did as instructed, and saw that he was shining his torch on the fireplace. Elkor stood to one side of it, then suddenly threw the gravel like stuff that he'd picked up from downstairs into the fire pit. Instantly upon impact of the tiny stones, a blazing fire roared into action, simultaneously lighting and heating up the room.

"Amazing!" exclaimed Chloé as she ran over to it in her wet clothes.
"Wow," exhaled Chris.

Chloé was conscious that she needed to get out of her wet clothes soon but felt far too embarrassed in such company, especially in front of Lousta. "I don't suppose there's anywhere I can change out of these clothes is there? Or even, anything else I can change into for that matter?" she asked. Chris offered his loose, dull-sand coloured t-shirt to her, along with his mid-wash denim shorts, leaving him in only his navy-blue boxer briefs. He didn't mind though, he was more than happy to help Chloé out in a way which Lousta couldn't.

To change, the two of them headed through into the next room and closed the door behind them. Using the torch to look around, they appeared to be in some sort of kitchen, which wasn't half as spacious as the living area.

"I'm so glad we're alone," whispered Chris once the door was closed, "I need to talk to you about something."

"What?" asked Chloé as she started taking off her wet clothes.

"Yesterday afternoon, when Orel found me outside by myself, I think... That I was lured out there by that witch."

"You mean the one we're hiding from?"

"Yea, it was almost like I was dreaming, but yet, I was having a conversation with her."

"What do you mean a conversation?" blurted out Chloé, both shocked and concerned whilst trying to keep her voice as a whisper. "Why didn't you tell the others? She could've killed or captured you!"

"Yea, but she didn't," he said as he started taking his clothes off to hand to her.

"It was weird, I couldn't control myself properly, but, it was still me talking, I think. Then it all stopped when I heard Orel calling out my name."

"Speaking of Orel, where is she?"

"Exactly, I don't know either, just like I don't know anything that's going on anymore. I don't remember exactly everything that was said, but weirdly, I do remember feeling safe, like she was going to make everything alright. What I definitely remember though, was that she told me that *Malicorne* is who we should fear, not her."

"Well of course she's going to say something like that, she's evil, evil people lie," insisted Chloé.

"But so might evil vampires and weird half deer people," urged Chris as he gestured to the other room.

The two were abruptly interrupted by Elkor as he knocked on the door, "Are you two alright in there? You haven't disappeared again have you, Chris?"

"Hah, no!" Chris said through a fake laugh, trying to disguise the fact that the knock on the door had sent a shock right through his body.

"These wet clothes were difficult to get off," said Chloé, "Almost done." She then turned back to Chris to carry on whispering, as she began to dress herself in his shorts and t-shirt. "Look, I don't know for sure what's going on here, but what I do know is that whilst these guys are helping us to reach the spring, that witch has already tried to kill us. So as long as we're with the people helping us to get magic of our own, I'm going along with them."

Chris knew he wasn't going to convince her in this dark, whispering moment. In fact, it was dawning on him that they hadn't been agreeing on many things lately, and that his role in the group was being completely overshadowed by her ability to read the book and the obvious attraction between her and Lousta. Also, Chloé still hadn't been honest with him about what she'd seen in the book that had made her want to come here, though after what Veshnica had said about the resurrection spell, he was sure it had to have something do to with her father. He then remembered the feeling of love in his heart that had pulled him towards Alexandra, during their moment in the woods, which gave him a warm and comforting feeling within, telling him he needn't feel so alone.

The pair of them exited the room and lay Chloé's clothes out by the fire, then sat themselves within close reach of its heat. Lousta and Elkor both sat down on the floor a bit further away, before laying down to go to sleep.

"Will Orel not be joining us?" asked Chris, now suspicious of everything they were up to.

"No, but she'll be alright. It's too risky for her to be the lookout and then join us at the end of the day, but don't worry, she can take care of herself," Elkor assured them.

The two cerfaurs fell asleep first, quite exhausted from the day's travelling, though Chris knew that if he were to make the slightest sound, one of them would be up and alert. The corne trolls spread themselves out on the chairs to sleep after fetching their new friends something to eat.

Once they'd eaten, Chris and Chloé used the rucksack as a pillow and lay down together by the fire, though as Chloé's mind drifted off to sleep, Chris couldn't get his meeting with Alexandra out of his head; wondering how he might get the book to her as she'd asked, without Chloé knowing.

CHAPTER TWENTY-FOUR

Flowering Fog

The next morning, the two humans awoke to the sound of Lousta opening the shutters on one of the windows. The latch had made an abrupt clunking sound, as it unhooked at both the top and the bottom of the window frame. He carefully pushed the left side open to peer out of the window, which let in a dull, grey light. The sun was but fifteen minutes from rising, and the weather that morning brought about a low mist on the ground, with lingering, hazy clouds sitting well below the tops of the rainbow hills.

"Looks like a grey start today," Lousta announced in a low voice.
"Ah, you get them here too?" joked Chris.
"Yes, it's not uncommon for this area," replied Lousta, oblivious to Chris' reference to the world-renowned dull English weather which he was used to. "It'll clear by late morning, but it's probably best that we take advantage of its cover and get moving."

Chloé checked her clothes, thankfully they'd dried overnight, even though the fire had since burnt out. She picked them up and took them to the other room to change into, followed by Chris.

"How did you sleep?" he asked.
"I was thinking," began Chloé suddenly, "Say we can't trust anyone here, the witch, these guys, anyone, all we need to do is get to the spring, right?"
"I guess," shrugged Chris.
"So, let's say we do what they want whilst they're helping us, then once we reach the spring we'll have magic of our own, plus all the knowledge in that book, so we won't need to any others to help us. Then *we* can decide what we do with our magic. We don't *have* to bring Malicorne back from the dead, or wherever he is."

"Do you think it'll be that easy? To use magic?"
"We've done alright so far haven't we? Using the information in the book. Besides, if the witch is right and Malicorne is dangerous, we'd be caught up in trying to get rid of him again; when all I want is to just start enjoying all this."
"Me too," said Chris as he reached out and held Chloé's

hand. Their eyes locked for a moment in a peaceful, familiar gaze. Right before they re-joined the others, they shared a loving kiss with each other, which strengthened once more their weakened bond as a couple; though inside, Chris felt it more like the last attempt to save a failing relationship.

Instead of them all exiting out through the downstairs door and going back across the pond, the cerfaurs went that way alone before making their way round to the back of the house. There, Chris, Chloé and their corne trolls, all waited by one of the living room windows which faced out that way.

When Lousta and Elkor both arrived safely under the window, Chris first passed out the cerfaurs' plufort shields, followed by both of the corne trolls. After that, Chris helped Chloé out of the window and held on to her as she lowered herself down into Lousta's arms, before finally lowering himself down, wearing the rucksack, to be caught below by Elkor.

Due to the slope of the ground they stood on, Elkor, though he couldn't see far through the mist, was able to lead them in the right direction towards the mountain passes. Their route for that day would lead them to a herd of cerfaurs, with whom they could safely spend the night.

By nature, cerfaurs made their homes deep in the woods out of branches, moss, stones and pretty much anything they could find to create a wide, sheltered den to sleep in. Elkor hoped that the mist would hang around just long enough for them to reach the pine forest once again, where it sat at the base of a greater mountain range - the Southern Alps of Merveille.

As they hurried on, however, the mist only grew thicker, eventually turning into a dense fog. Elkor struggled to lead in this increasingly poor visibility, therefore he decided to lead the group uphill slightly, hoping to climb above it. Unfortunately, this didn't help them as he'd hoped, and soon he brought them all to a halt to reassess their surroundings.

Nothing at all could be seen except dull, grey fog. They felt completely alone in a world which seemed to consist of nothing but cloud. Worried for their safety, he called to Lousta to stay close and to yell if he was losing sight of him before he began to hurry on almost aimlessly into the dull abyss.

He ran and ran, feeling the tilt of the ground under his feet as he tried his best to keep the hills on their right, pleading that he would soon see signs of the pine forest. The grassy ground became rockier, but that didn't slow him down as he continued to push on. As more time passed he was beginning to fear that they'd stumbled into another of Alexandra's traps, until eventually, thankfully, he came across a tree; a natural sign of life which washed a wave of relief over them all.

Then another and another as they spotted more of them randomly appearing around them, at first appearing like lingering shadows which grew into something real as they stepped nearer. This must be the edge of the forest, he thought to himself. Chris turned to check Lousta and Chloé were still with them as Elkor began to slow down. The fog seemed to thin slightly as more trees appeared around them, though navigation was still exceedingly difficult.

"What was that?" jerked Chris as he suddenly flinched his head upwards, scouring the space above them.
"What was what?" asked Elkor.
"I swear I just heard something, like, flying over us."
"Could it be Orel?" asked Chloé optimistically.
"I hope so," said Chris, "But how could she have followed us through all this fog?"

They carried on cautiously through the sparsely spaced trees, assumingly entering the forest. Lousta was next to hear something fly past them, thinking he saw its dark shadow swooping through the fog alongside them. His pace slowed down as he tried to keep watch all around, which sparked huge concerns in Chloé.

"What? What do you think it is? Please, tell me you think its Orel," she begged.
"I'm afraid I can't tell you that, but there's definitely something…"
"Look! There!" shouted Chris, pointing towards the face of something wolf-like appearing through the fog ahead of them.
"What is it?!" cried Chloé.

As it slowly crept closer it's body became visible, though what they saw was not at all what the humans expected after having seen its face.

What they were looking at was indeed a type of wolf, though scruffy and scrawnier than your average wolf found in the wild, with tattered, thin fur. Like many creatures in this land, however, it had something uniquely different about it.

This wolf had a pair of huge wings identical to those of a bat, which stuck out from its back just below its shoulders. Each wing had three points to it, with a sharp claw at the tip of each one. Their eyes were a light grey/white colour, seemingly glowing against their tree-bark brown fur. These creatures were known in this land as batwolves, and they'd zoned in on this specific group of travellers.

Elkor turned to run away from the one he saw ahead of them, only to be met by another four appearing through the mist coming at them in pairs from both directions. He reared his two front legs in the air in an attempt to intimidate them, prompting Chris to grip onto Elkor tightly as his corne troll clung to his clothes. As they landed back down with a heavy thud, he saw that Lousta had already spotted another approaching from behind. They were now completely surrounded.

"Hold on," Elkor said quietly to Chris, "Lousta, prepare your shield!" He shouted. After hearing this instruction, Chloé gripped hold of Lousta as tight as she could, whilst her corne troll hid between their two bodies. Elkor then let out a frightening war cry as he charged at the batwolf stood directly ahead of him. His shield was up, his muscular arm fixed firmly behind it and his antlers pointing out and upward above it. The batwolf stood its ground as Chris prepared himself for impact, only to be caught by complete shock when he felt a sudden blow from the side that threw him to the floor. "CHRIS!" screamed Chloé.

Chris quickly opened his eyes after landing on the ground, only to find that Elkor had been knocked over too. He saw one of the batwolves charging straight for him until it was halted by Lousta as he grabbed its wing pulling it away from him. Chris' corne troll, Lucy, scurried off into the forest as Chris picked himself up from the ground.

The other wolves then came in closer as Elkor and Losta began to fight them off, using their antlers as weapons. Chloé hung on tight to Lousta, realising she had no escape from the fight, whilst Chris backed up against a tree, fearing that this would be the end for them all. He pleaded for it to be over as he watched the fight savagely play out in front of him. Outnumbered, Chris frantically wished that the cerfaurs size and strength would be enough to save them all.

Two of the batwolves had been severely injured by Elkor's antlers, as the two cerfaurs continued to fight the other four, not noticing that one of the injured ones had locked onto Chris' scent – a lone, powerless being with no protection. It pulled itself up off the floor and began to limp over to him, though luckily Chris managed to spot it in time. Whilst both slow and injured, the batwolf would still be able to overpower Chris should it get a hold of him, and Chris was determined not to let this happen.

As he backed away whilst trying not to make any sudden movements, the batwolf picked up its pace and began gaining on Chris, causing him to panic and run for his life. He ran off into the fog until he was out of sight of the others, all except the lone batwolf who was chasing his scent. He ran faster and faster with the heavy rucksack on his back, heading aimlessly through the woods. The ground was uneven and rocky, and with the weight of the rucksack bouncing around on his back his foot coordination was all over the place. As his feet landed on the ground with different twists and turns to his ankles, he continued to run through the strain in his legs; scared for his life, he managed to find the strength to just keep going.

Despite all his effort, finally, he was struck down as he thrust his right foot upon a small rock, twisting his ankle. He tumbled instantly to the ground and did so again as he tried to pick himself back up without first checking the severity of his injury. In a final, frightened attempt to save himself, he scurried over to the closest tree he could see and hid behind it, waiting to find out his fate.

He could hear the batwolf sniffing the air somewhere not too far away, a sound which only seemed to get closer. It could sense that he'd stopped moving as his scent suddenly began to grow stronger with every step forward the batwolf took. It slowed down its pace and began to stalk its victim. Chris huddled himself against the thick trunk of the tree he hid behind, squeezing his eyes shut as he pleaded to be saved.

Even with the magic he'd witnessed so far, he could hardly believe it when his prayers were answered as he was interrupted by a shrieking batwolf cry, as something stopped it dead in its tracks. Without taking a moment to consider what might be happening, Chris assumed it must be one of the cerfaurs attacking the batwolf who'd followed him. With that in mind, he looked out from behind the tree to see which one it had been who'd saved him.

Before he had the chance to see anything though, his eyes were forced closed by a blinding light, seemingly between him and the batwolf. As his eyes recovered under the protection of his eyelids and his hands, he began to see an afterimage that the intense light had burnt on his retinas; he saw the brightness emulating from within a tall figure. Cautiously, he reopened his eyes with his hand ready to shield them, as he attempted to peer in its direction once more. Again there was a bright light, but with the source shielded from his vision, he was able to see more clearly that from within which it shone.

He made out the shape of a cloaked person or being, with their hood up over their head and facing away from him, stood out in the open. To the side of them he saw the defeated batwolf laying lifeless on the ground. The light emitting from them dimmed, and so he took a chance and slowly moved his hand away from his eyes, hoping to get a better look at what was happening.

The cloaked figure was slightly see-through, like how you'd imagine a ghost to be, and its colours seemed like different tones of shadow. The small ball of light, now harmless to the naked eye, appeared to be on the other side of the shadows.

The figure then turned and moved towards Chris. He attempted a shuffle backwards, but he was too engulfed by its presence and heroic act of saving him to move too far. Slowly it approached him. Now that the being faced him he could see hints of its unthreatening body under the cloak, with the ball of light being held out in front, hovering above the palm of their right hand.

They crouched down in front of him, at first facing downwards shielding their identity, until the mysterious entity looked up at him and their facial features became clearer. He knew he'd seen them before – it was Alexandra. Why she wasn't there in her full form he didn't know, but he was overwhelmed with relief to see her again. She looked at him as she held the light out towards him. Around it began to form a lantern of smoke, or at least something of that colour and consistency, allowing the light to be transported within.

"Take my lantern," she whispered, "Its light will help you find your way back." Chris was feeling the trance-like state wash over him again, knowing it was her who had come to save him.
"Please, may I not come with you?"
"We may not touch until you deliver to me your book of magic, shall you do this for me? For us?" To which Chris merely nodded. Alexandra then held the lantern out in front of him as he sceptically reached to pick it up by the handle. To his disbelief, he was able to hold it unaided by her, and it felt so real in his hand.

No sooner had he taken the lantern did the ghostly embodiment of Alexandra disappear in a swirl of smoky clouds, leaving him alone and lost on the floor in the forest. As her swirling clouds were disappearing, some tailed off and wrapped around his ankle, which then seemingly soaked into his skin.

At once his injury and the pain vanished, so easily that he couldn't quite believe it. Though he didn't hurry off at first, he carefully stood himself upright and give it a little test to check it had truly healed. With his health restored and Alexandra's light to shine the way, he headed off back in the direction he felt he came.

Whilst he walked back he held the lantern out in front of him. As the light from within broke through the haze of the fog, he was able to see further than he had been able to without it. A minute or so after he'd set off, however, his blissfully safe state was banished by a piercing screech shredding through the forest. The screech was so unbearable that he instantly dropped the lantern in favour of covering his ears with his hands. As the hellish noise came to an end Chris held on to the sides of his head, fearing it would come tearing through him once again.

The noise didn't sound a second time however, so eventually Chris lowered his hands away from his ears; though as he did he noticed a small drop of blood had rubbed off onto each of his palms. Without hesitating he reached down to the floor to pick up the lantern, wondering if somehow it could heal him as he'd been healed before. Much to his horror his protective light had vanished upon hitting the ground. Worried that the noise had caused some serious damage, and fearing walking alone without the light, he began to whisper a plea for help from Alexandra; which was ultimately muted by the sound of Chloé crying out his name.

"Chris! Can you hear me?"
"Chlo? I'm here, I'm alright!"
"Chris! Follow the sound of my voice!"
"Ok, keep shouting!" Chris wiped the blood off onto his shorts then followed the sound of Chloé's voice right back to where the fight had begun.

As he approached them and they became visible through the fog, he was surprised to see a few others had since joined them.

"Lancelin? Is that you?"
"Hello, Chris. Is everything ok, with you?"
"I think so, but, what are you doing here?"
"After Alexandra's last attack, Hinder and I headed back to the vampire manor for help. Paza (Lancelin motioned to a vampire stood next to him) was sent to escort us back to you, and it seems we were lucky that he was."
"Why's that? Hello, Paza," Chris said awkwardly with a small gesture of a wave.
"He warned off those awful things by screeching at them," said Chloé.
"By the scent of your blood I see it hurt you too, I am sorry for that," admitted Paza.

As Chris came to terms with the frustration of seeing Lancelin with them once again, he suddenly noticed Elkor lying on the floor, his human body cradled by Lousta who was on the floor next to him.
"Oh my god, Elkor! Is he alright?" asked Chris as he hurried over to them.
"He'll be alright, I hope," said an emotional Lousta, "But he is no longer able to travel with us." Elkor had bite marks all over his legs and a deep wound on this side of the deer-like part of his body.

"But we can't just leave him here, can we?" said Chloé as she stood by them, clutching her corne troll, Meg, like a small pet.
"The other vampires can stay and watch over him until sundown, then they will help him reach the herd of

cerfaurs where he can rest and be healed," said Paza.
"What other vampires?" asked Chris.
"They're here, in the trees."
"They were part of the escort," added Lancelin.
"They cannot be in their human form right now, even with the fog as shelter, for it could thin at any moment and allow the sun to burn them."
"But, what about you? Won't it burn you too?"
"I'm alright, at least for a few days. The count and countess kindly gave me their las…. Well, one of their light living potions they have saved away, it will enable me to be unharmed by the sun's harsh light whilst I aid you in your passage to the spring."

Hinder, who felt guilty for not having returned straight to Elkor after the dort fly attack, insisted she stay with him and the other vampires and promised Lousta that she'd make sure he stayed safe.

"But, I just don't understand," said Lousta, "What were the batwolves doing here? I thought they never left Broulyard Woods?"
"We found these whilst tracking your scent early this morning," said Paza, as he held out his hand revealing a hand full of small, white flowers, similar to snowdrops. A steady, though weak stream of mist was flowing out from within their petals like a fog fountain.
"A broulyard flower, so someone created the fog," continued Lousta.
"It has to be Alexandra, another attempt at splitting us up," said a weary Elkor, "No doubt she summoned the batwolves like she did those awful flies."

Chris kept quiet about his encounter with her. They all seemed so convinced that she was out to get them, yet she was the one who'd saved him and aided his return to the others. He was struggling to make sense of it all. Paza then reminded everyone that his time with them was already ticking away, and that they had no time to waste in getting the humans to the spring. It seemed only a matter of time before one of Alexandra's attacks could see the end of the three humans and the hope of Malicorne's return.

So, all who were to continue on set off together deeper into the fog-laden forest, ever hopeful that they'd soon begin to see clearly through it. Elkor had advised Lousta to keep the slope of the mountain base rising to his right-hand side, as they headed blindly onwards through the pine forest, which appeared to grow thicker as the fog slowly began to fade into a misty haze.

"Look!" shouted Lousta, "There's light coming into the forest over this way, the fog must be thinner there which means we might be able to get an idea of where we are. Follow me!" He'd taken it upon himself to lead in his father's absence, though they moved forward at a much slower pace now without the humans each having someone to ride upon.

As they headed towards the light, the ground below them began to get steeper as they climbed further up the base of the mountain. Though his father had advised him to keep the sloping ground rising to his right, Lousta couldn't miss out on the opportunity to escape the fog and get a clearer view from above.

They climbed higher and higher until eventually they were out of both the fog *and* the forest. The view over the ground below was a huge breath of fresh air to them all, after being lost for so long in the cloud below. They all stopped on a ridge sticking out above the trees, and they looked back over the hidden land they'd trekked across. Treetops stuck out over the thick silver fog like green pipe-cleaners sticking up through a mass of cotton wool. The fresh blue of the sky lightened their spirits whilst the sun warmed their bodies – which was welcomed by all but Paza.

"Do you know where we are?" Chloé asked Lousta. He looked out ahead before he turned and looked at the mountains behind them, spotting the entrance to a narrow valley about two hundred meters along from where they stood.

"Yes," he said, "We're at Eppon Creek."

CHAPTER TWENTY-FIVE

The Weeping Woods

"What?!" blurted out Chris, "Wasn't that where we were trying to avoid?"

"It's either that or we descend back into the fog..." suggested Lousta.

"Where no doubt *she'll* be waiting," added Lancelin, "But, I don't understand. Why we would avoid this route?"

"Elkor decided it was too dangerous, due to the spirit who haunts the woods at the other end," said Chloé nervously.

"Ghosts don't frighten me," responded Paza in a gruff voice. Chris sheepishly glanced sideways towards him and stepped slightly back away from him.
"This one has been known to kill witches, back in the day," said Lousta.
"Well, we are no witches here," Lancelin pointed out.
"I suppose, if you think about the story, she has no reason to be mad with *ordinary* humans," suggested Chloé.
"That's right, only humans who possess magic. Which means if Alexandra tries to follow us there's a good chance she won't make it through the woods alive," added Lousta.

"But we are three humans, to two, umm, natives. What if she does try to attack us?" Chris asked, concerned for his life.
"That's a good point, does anyone have an idea where Orel is?" asked Chloé.
"She'll be about somewhere, hopefully watching out for us from a distance. When we get to the woods we'll just have to keep together and get through as quickly as possible," Lousta instructed.

"*When*? So, it's decided?" asked Chris.
"Feel free to head back into the fog if you like, then you can find your own way and meet us on the other side, if you make it," said Lancelin, undermining Chris' concerns.
"Chris, we have to, if we want to reach the spring," said Chloé as she reached down and squeezed his hand, whilst holding Meg in her other arm.

Ironically now, it seemed to each of them to be their safest route at this point. Lousta, being the route leader now Elkor had gone, insisted they all follow behind him, minding each step as they went. He led the way along an uneven rocky path, marked onto the side of the tall mountain they stood below, towards Eppon Creek.

Scrambling along the side of the hill, the path was only wide enough for them to walk in single file. They kept close together for safety, whilst out of the cover of the trees they were all as vulnerable as ever to Alexandra. Though the longer they trudged on along the narrow path, the more it seemed strange to Chloé that they should be in any immediate danger at all, as the weather and her surroundings at that moment were so captivatingly beautiful.

Looking out over the misty woods below them and onto the lower jungle hills far off on the horizon, she thought about the places they'd journeyed through so far. The warm blue sea with water as clear as glass where they had been shipwrecked, the lush tropical jungle where they'd spent their first full day in this new land, and the dry, dusty pine forests between them and Dragignaan; what landscape would they venture into next, she wondered silently to herself.

Colourful birds, or at least what Chloé assumed were birds, could be spotted occasionally swooping across the treetops and going about their daily life. The soothing warmth of the sun caressed their skin, as cool, fresh air tumbled down over them periodically as it dropped from the high ground above. She wondered to herself which kind of magical creature they might come across next - perhaps a fairy or a beautiful wood nymph she hoped, or at least something friendly. The more she thought about how incredible this place was, the more eager she was to get to the spring and absorb its power, forgetting about the dangers that lay out ahead of them. That was until her daydream was suddenly interrupted.

"Here we are," announced Lousta, stopping where the path came to a corner. They were overlooking the gap in the hills where Eppon Creek ran, splitting the earth apart with a gradual uphill climb to the higher ground where the water sourced. This time of year was perfect for passing through along the creek, due to the dry August months providing very little rain to feed it. "We'll follow this path until I can find us a safe route down to the water, then we can follow the dry part of the river basin up to the other side of these hills."

Chris, looking at just how high the hills either side of the creek rose, became very aware of how tired and hungry he had already become.b"How high will we be climbing to exactly? And, do we have a plan for lunch at all?" he asked.

"Oh no! Where're your corne trolls?" asked Chloé suddenly, realising that she was the only one who was still looking after hers.
"Mine ran off during the batwolf attack," explained Chris.
"And mine at the first attack, just as we all left the vampires' mansion," said Lancelin.

"Could we not discuss this down by the water and under the shade of the trees?" interrupted Paza, "This potion may allow me to walk in the sun without dying, but it doesn't stop me from feeling just how exhaustingly hot that thing is!"

"Alright, let's get on then," said Lousta as he began walking, heading into the pass.

"Perhaps Meg might be able to get food for all us," Chloé suggested as they all began moving on, still in single file, whilst cradling Meg gently to make her feel appreciated.

A little bit further into the pass, Lousta broke off from the rough path they were following (which was more or less just a flatter section of the hill that was easier to walk on) and he began scrambling down towards the wooded, lower basin where the creek ran. Some parts of the track down were quite tricky to manoeuvre, and there were some sections where the rock scree slid down as they stepped upon it, resulting with the humans slipping and falling a number of times. After a tricky start though, they reached the wooded area close to the creek, where their descent became easier as the ground began to level off; that, and also, whilst out of the sun's light Paza's aggravated presence began to mellow.

They stopped at the edge of the trees where Lousta pointed out the dry riverbed, which stretched about thirty meters across and had a thin stream running roughly down the centre. From this point the route was clear and straightforward, walking just within the shelter of the trees running alongside the river, they followed it upstream gradually climbing higher through the pass.

Chris, Chloe and Lancelin were beginning to lag behind, their clothes weren't exactly suited to trekking in the

mountains, and after quite an early and eventful start to the day their stomachs were being to rumble. "I don't suppose we could have that lunch break now, could we?" asked Chris.
"I wouldn't mind a break too actually," added Chloé.
"Okay, I suppose we can stop here for a moment," said Lousta, "I'll just go and rummage through the trees and bushes to gather some bits to eat."

Chloé put Meg down on the ground and held her tiny, scrawny hand between her thumb and forefinger. Meg looked up and Chloé and locked eyes with her for a moment, before pulling away and scurrying off into the trees and bushes nearby.

"Is she coming back?" asked Lancelin.
"Oh, yea. At least, I hope so. This is what she normally does when she brings me food. But, umm, what will you eat, Paza?" Chloé asked politely.
"I'll feed at night, whilst you sleep," he replied. Chris' head suddenly flinched and turned to him as he said it, with a started expression clearly present on his face. "On some small creature I'll find in the woods, not on you three, of course."
"Of course," laughed Chris nervously.

A few minutes passed before Meg came rushing back empty handed, then she began tugging at Chloé. "What is it?" she asked. She then proceeded to followed Meg back in the direction she'd come from, worried that it was to face some more bad news. However, much to her delight, she found a gluttonous picnic had been laid out for them across the dry, earthy ground.

There were sandwiches, cakes, biscuits, fruit, chopped

and prepared vegetables, chocolates and even some dips cupped in little bowls made from leaves. The food was kept off the floor by clean stones and pieces of dry wood, and there were beautifully coloured flowers arranged around the picnic area. The sight of all this delicious food was an extremely welcomed relief for their hungry stomachs.

"Oh Meg, this is absolutely amazing!" exclaimed Chloé, as she picked her up and hugged her tightly.
"Wow, she must really like you!" said Lancelin. Chloé's love and care had indeed been the cause of Meg's generosity, but the inclusion of her in their group is why Meg had put out enough food to share amongst everyone.

Lousta arrived back around ten minutes or so later, with his hands full of berries and seeds, only to find them all stuffing their faces with Meg's delicious food. He didn't know exactly what some of what they were eating was and so stuck to his own, foraged food at first, until Chloé urged him to try a piece of baguette with some goats' cheese, honey and pine nuts. After just one bite of the delicious, creamy cheese mixed with the sweet honey, he was hooked. After finishing off the whole sandwich, he wasted no time in grabbing some of the other food on offer at Meg's picnic feast.

They each ate exceptionally well and thanked Meg for her gift, as they lay back on the floor exhausted from gauging on all the food. Chris had taken the magic goblet from the bag and passed it round to be used with water from the creek. He even taught Paza to use it for turning the water into blood, hoping that it would then be less likely that he'd be feasting on him during the night; though even with the potion, he could feel the light from the magic tingling against his skin.

After an hour or so of napping, they agreed that they ought to be getting on, should they not want to be halfway through the weeping woods when night fell. The walk up Eppon Creek would take them at least another two hours, assuming they had no more uninvited interruptions. So they set off once again, Chris insisting on carrying the rucksack still so that Chloé may focus on looking after Meg, as she did so well – her magical ability wasn't one he felt like losing anytime soon.

Onward they marched up the creek, almost joyfully on this warm summers day, freshly fuelled up from the indulgent picnic. Up and around the corner of the narrow valley they went, as the fauna around them began to change once again, away from the dry, coarse, Mediterranean looking pines, to more recognisable trees and plants, native to regions of the world they were much more used to; places that get ample amounts of rain throughout the year.

The forests of the hills of the four seasons were much like pictures from a fairy tale book. A medley of different trees and plants growing harmoniously together, with colourful flowers and berries breaking up the lush green surroundings. Damp moss grew around rocks and tree trunks, and patches of grass were scattered about amongst the fallen leaves and twigs on the floor. Sunlight beamed in through the gaps in the treetops, lighting up the floating seeds in the air with golden sparkles. The smells from the abundant life here during this time of year were released through the moist air rising from the damp, dewy floor. If there was anywhere where they might find fairies, thought Chloé, this was it.

The end of the riverbed path they were following began to appear ahead of them, as the river narrowed and deepened up to a point where Eppon Creek dribbled down from a floor a bit higher above them. Lousta crossed over the lazy stream and broke left, then began zigzagging a route uphill leading to where the water flowed from.

"Early in the year, and again later in the year, this part of the creek is a nice little waterfall," Lousta pointed out as they headed up the steep path to the top. Once up higher and level with where the water fell from, they were out of the trees they had previously been walking through and faced an open grassy meadow, where the creek flowed through. To either side of them stood steep, tall, rocky slopes. The only way forward was across the meadow, to where the Weeping Woods awaited them.

As they crossed and began to approach the other side, a drop in temperature became apparent as an icy chill in the air brought goosebumps to their skin, as if stepping into a cold cellar from the heated living space above. The charming meadow had come to an end, as the grass died and withered away to reveal a hard, dry, dusty ground as they passed the first weeping willow tree at the edge of the woods.

These woods were not like the other fairy tale type forests of this region, for here, the weeping willow tree was the dominant species. Some were even forever dead but still stood strong and tall without their leaves. They grew scattered amongst few other odd-looking varieties of trees, some even sheltering small ponds, connected by discreet streams which spread throughout the woods like veins. There were a series of trodden paths leading in every direction, constantly splitting off into new ones and connecting to others; should one not know which paths to follow, they could easily be lead in circles forever trying to reach the other side.

Walking through the woods was every bit as eerie as the name implied. Haunting sounds of living beings in pain and discomfort came from deep within the trees, and confusing reflections shone back at them from the surface of its dark, lifeless ponds. Chloé held on tight to Chris' hand as they focused on following closely next to Lousta, who seemed to know the way through. Lancelin didn't appear to be worried, as he walked silently on the other side of Lousta from Chris and Chloé, and Paza kept his eyes on them all as he walked as a guard behind them.

The light inside the Weeping Woods was not as if they were walking on such a bright sunny day as they had been, but more as though it was cloudy and about to rain at any moment. This caused them to lose all sense of time and direction that would normally be given by the bright, beaming sun somewhere above them.

No one spoke as they all focused on getting through the woods as swiftly as possible, though that did make it easier for the humans to become distracted now and then, by the curious sounds attempting to lure them away from each other; deeper into the woods.

"We're almost there," said Lousta, breaking the silence after about forty-five minutes of silent walking.
"Oh phew," exclaimed Chloé, "Because this place is really creeping me out. Wait a minute…" she stopped them all.
"What is it?" asked Lousta, keeping his eyes out ahead.

"Chris, get the book out of the bag for me."
"What? Why?"
"Can it not wait?" asked Lousta as he turned to her, breaking up their walking formation and now creating more of a group circle.
"I don't know, but I have this sudden urge that the book is calling to me, telling me I need…wait, did you hear that?"
"Hear what?" asked Chris frustratedly.

As they began to listen, all except Chloé heard the distant, eerie voice of the singing, trapped princess, as she sung out her heart aching balled of misery and sorrow. The sound seemed to float to them on a cold, lingering breeze, distracting Chris at first before he shut off his ears to it; but to Chloé, the voice was much different.

"That! Did you not hear it that time? It's my dad!"
"That's your dad singing?" asked Paza, confused by it all.
"Chloé, it's not your dad. C'mon we better get moving, now!" insisted Lousta.

Chloé was so sure in herself that that was who she'd heard, and she soon forgot about the feeling from the book urging her to take it.

"Chlo, look at me, your dad's not here. We need to get

out of these woods, come on," said Chris as he reached his hand out to take hers. Chloé didn't agree though, and she instead passed Meg to Chris who took hold of her straight away without thinking.
"Yes he is, I can hear him calling me. He's here!"
"Chloé," said Chris sternly, "Your dad's gone, remember? That's the spirit you can hear, we have to keep moving!" he urged as he reached out for her hand again.

"But what if he didn't die? What if he was brought here? I have to help him!" Before any of them could react she ran away in the direction she heard the voice coming from, and as Lousta launched himself in her direction to grab hold of her and pull her back, he and the others were swept aside by a white, gusting cloud of thick, misty, icy cold haze and toppled to the floor. They each instantly tried to get back up again, only to find they were helpless against this unseen entity they were being held down by.

Chloé soon disappeared off into the woods alone, crying out for her father as she ran, darting about between the trees following the sound of her his's voice. The rest of them were pinned down until she was nowhere to be seen or heard, when all at once they were released from the ground and each able to stand upright again. Chris' first instinct was to run after her, but he was halted by Lousta.

"You don't know these woods, you're too vulnerable."
"But I have to help her! Just let go of me!" Chris struggled against him.

"Paza, can you smell Papillon Petals?" asked Lousta. Paza took a moment to seek out all the scents lingering in the air around him.

"Faintly, why?"

"Good. Follow that scent. Take these two and don't let go of them until you're out of the woods and in the meadow of Papillon Petals on the other side, where they'll be safe. I'll rescue Chloé."

"But…" began Chris.

"C'mon you two, as much as I love the dark and coldness in here, we better get you out," said Paza, as he grabbed Lancelin and Chris by the arms.

At first Chris struggled against him, as the site where he'd last seen Chloé begin to disappear from his view, but Paza's vampire strength was far too great to even be phased by his pulling. Once Chris had given up pleading to search for her, the three walked together side by side - Paza in the middle with his tight grip around both their wrists.

The path they were following was wide at this point, it seemed the trees were thinning and a sense of relief began to creep up on them. That was, of course, until Chris happened to stumble over an unseen rock or tree root, disguised by the drab, lifeless floor under the shadow of the treetops looming over them.

As he tripped, the grip from Paza was released and he only just managed to catch himself from falling over. He stopped and glanced back to see what he had tripped over, before he reached out for the security of Paza's grip again, only to find it missing. He looked ahead and saw Lancelin and Paza walking together, though Lancelin had switched sides and taken Chris' place.

"Hey! What about me!" he yelled at them, though they

didn't respond. Instead, he saw them mutter something to each other, before Lancelin glanced back and smiled at Chris. "It was you!" Chris yelled again, "You're still trying to get rid of me!" This realisation instantly tapped into Chris' inner rage for Lancelin and his sinister behaviour.

He ran up behind Lancelin and tackled him to the ground, not for a second finding it odd that he managed to pull him away from Paza's impressive grip. They rolled about on the floor fighting against one another, throwing punches, kicking, and Chris was even trying to grab hold of Lancelin's neck. He shouted at him over and over, swearing angrily and yelling, "Why do you keep trying kill me!?" but Lancelin wouldn't respond.

Chris then threw a punch at him knocking him almost unconscious, before he dragged his weak, beaten body over to one of the small, murky ponds. Holding Lancelin's head and shoulders face up above the water, he yelled at him once more, demanding that he tell him who he really was. But when Lancelin still didn't answer, he plunged his head fully under the water and held it there to watch him struggle for his own life.

CHAPTER TWENTY-SIX

U.P

In reality, Chris tripping up was no accident. As he did, the initial tap on his foot had split him into two entities. The Lancelin he saw was, in fact, himself, and both Paza and Lancelin had continued to walk on with Chris until he was suddenly thrown down to the ground by an unknown force, hurtling itself on to him from behind. The force had been great enough even to overpower Paza and release Chris from his secure grip, forcing poor Meg to jump down and scurry away from him. Lancelin and Paza were then each held back, completely helpless, whilst Chris continued to unknowingly try and kill himself.

Several times Chris shoved what he thought was Lancelin's head under the water, as Lancelin and Paza had to watch him struggle for air. Each time he was released he would ask his questions over again, until inevitably thrusting his head back under the water once more. Finally, Chris asked one last time before he insisted this would be the last chance for survival, then proceeded to gather his enraged anger ready to thrust his own head back under the water until death would put an end to their fight. Yet still, there was no reply. So, Chris' weak body was forced to use its last strain of energy to struggle for his life as he held himself under the surface of this disturbed little pond.

The real Lancelin and Paza, who had no choice but to stand by as the scene played out in front of them, shouted and bellowed out cries for help to anyone in the woods or nearby who may be able to stop him. Luckily for Chris, just as his life was beginning to slip away, an array of different coloured brightly lit orbs came floating along in their direction. Following amongst them came two white unicorns pulling along a pale-wooden, open-top carriage – which had been crafted with no seat for a coachman.

"Oh my word, what on earth is going on??! Stop this at once!" demanded an unknown, slightly shrill voice.

Instantly the unicorns' horns began to glow a warm, golden colour, and the spirit's hold on everyone around was broken. Paza immediately rushed over and pulled Chris' weakened body from the pond, then turned him onto his side as he coughed up the water he'd inhaled. As he came around, he was weak, unstable and confused.

The being who had found them at first glance appeared human, like a royal fairytale princess who sat high upon her unicorn-drawn carriage. She wore a long, strapless, blossom pink gown, fastened up like a corset around her body, with a darker pink ribbon tied together and hanging between her breasts.

The dress' skirt was made from a soft, thick and heavy material. It had decorative lace patters around the hem and small bows tied and placed scattered about over the rest of it. She wore her hair, which started off a pale brown and faded to a light, sandy blonde, wavy and long, tumbling down past her shoulders to her waist. On her head, she wore a golden tiara encrusted with different coloured gemstones and the symbol of the unicorn's horn in the centre. To look at her she would seem to be of Native, North American decent, though she was not actually human at all.

In her carriage, she sat upon a mixture of white, pink and purple, pastel coloured cushions, and the outside of the carriage was adorned with rainbow coloured ribbons and clusters of beautifully coloured flowers. Following behind them were three more unicorns – one sky blue coloured, one pink like her dress and one as green as fresh grass. Their manes and tails hung from each of them more like human hair than horse hair, in fact, they wore it long and wavy just as she did, as if they were all set for a magazine photoshoot, and their mane colours matched their bodies, though a few shades lighter.

Then there were the different coloured orbs surrounding them all, assumingly forming some kind of protection, the others thought, if not merely lighting their way through this dull, woodland area.

"Would someone care to tell me what all this chaos was about? Who are you people?" said the woman in the carriage, "And why was he drowning himself? Is he sick?"
"He was attacked by the spirit," replied Lancelin.
"What spirit? Is there someone else here?" she began to look around her.
"It seems you've scared them off," said Paza, whilst feeling threatened by her light and scent. "But as long as you're here, we could do with a hand getting him out of these woods."

"Is that so? Well, here, put him in my carriage. We were on our way out of this dreadful place any... Oh, my! Are you a vampire?" No sooner had the lady realised what Paza was did the unicorns horns begin to glow again, with their light steadily getting brighter and brighter.
"Yes, but you can tell your unicorns to calm down, I'm not out here hunting. Do you think you could you get him out of here?"
"He's not a vampire too, is he?"
"No, he's human," stated Lancelin.
"Oh my heavenly days, really? A human? Well, quick, quick get him up here and I'll lead the way... Erm, that is, if you don't mind, walking behind?"

Paza helped Chris into the carriage where he sat slouched amongst the cushions, whilst Lancelin picked up Meg and also the rucksack - which Chris had struggled out of during the attack. Then he and Paza followed closely behind the other three unicorns.

Soon, at last, they were all out of the woods and in the meadow of Papillon Petals that had been promised on the other side.

"How is he?" asked Paza.
"Weary," replied the lady in the carriage, "He's definitely human, you say?"
"Yes," said Lancelin.
"Well then, there's no reason my unicorns and I can't help him out a bit. Right then..." said the lady, confidently.

She took in a deep breath, held Chris' hand and looked upon him with sympathy, feeling his pain through the empathy inside her for the state he was in. Within a few moments, the three coloured unicorns had gathered by the side of the wooden carriage where Chris sat, right before their horns began to glow.

Each horn glowed with the colour of the unicorns' body, and then the light began to flow out from them and onto Chris. It seemed to sink into his skin whilst his cuts and bruises began to heal, right before their eyes. Just as the last wound was closing, his strength returned to him and he attempted to sit up as he noticed what was going on.

"What's happening to me?" he blurted out in a slight panic.
"Shhhhh, don't worry, my new human friend, U.P is here to look after you," she said as she stroked his hair with her free hand.

"Youpie?" he asked with a confused expression. The unicorns' light stopped once Chris was fit and well again.
"Yes, U.P. It stands for Unicorn Princess."

"Oohh, U.P."
"Yes, that's what I said."
"Sorry, I thought you said your name was Youpie, not the letters U and P."
"Oh, yes, I suppose that's different," she said as she quickly glanced away from him with a confused look on her face, "Anyway, are you alright now? My unicorn friends were just healing you."

"I think so," he said as he rubbed his head.
"Good. Now, would someone please tell me what was going on back there? Who was trying to kill whom?"
"The spirit of the weeping woods, I hear she targets and kills humans," said Paza.
"But not vampires and, whatever he is," said U.P, gesturing at Lancelin by wafting her hand out in his direction.
"Whatever and whoever," added Chris in an accusing tone.

"I'm human too. I guess I was going to be next, had you not come along in time."
"Oooo, I sense a bit of tension. What exactly brings this quirky threesome together?"
"We're on our way to the spring of power."

"Wait, where's Chloé?" asked Chris as he suddenly became alert, panicking as he looked around for her, "Has she come out yet?"
"Who's Chloé?"

"My girlfriend."
"And the only one who can read the book," said Lancelin.

"What book?"
"The magic book they found in Malicorne's castle."
"*Malicorne*?" she responded, rather surprised, "Why, that's a name I haven't heard in a long time. Wait, so there is *still* magic outside of this land?"
"It seems there was, but only Chloé can see what's written in the book," said Chris.
"So, she's a witch?"
"No."

"Wait, wait, wait, I'm lost... So, your girlfriend can read a magic book, but she's not a witch."
"Correct. I think," said Chris.
"And he's human but wasn't attacked by the murderous woodland spirit who kills humans."
"Right," said Lancelin.
"And he's a vampire, even though I've just realised he's stood out in the sun and not dying."
"I drank a potion," replied Paza.

They then proceeded to fill U.P in on how the humans had made it to Île Mervielle, before Chris began to grow agitated again by the fact that they were still missing both Chloé and Lousta. He tried to head back into the woods himself, only to be stopped by Paza. He pleaded with them for someone to help him go back in to look for Chloé, but U.P refused to let either of the humans put themselves at risk again.

"I'll make you a deal," she said as she began to elegantly step down from her carriage, "I'll go back in on one of

my unicorns and search for Chloé and the cerfaur."
"If…?" asked Paza as she paused during her speech.
"If, when you humans possess the powers from the spring, you bring back my long-lost love who was ripped away from me, by that wretched witch Alexandra."

Chris was shocked and in a way, offended, by this seemingly unjust remark U.P and branded his saviour with. He couldn't for the life of him, understand why Alexandra would have reason to take someone from such a kind, unthreatening person. Unless this was all just a front, he thought.

He often wondered if anyone he'd met here was who they really appeared to be on the outside, or if everyone had some ulterior motive and some long-awaited vengeance for each other, that he, Chloé, and Lancelin had been caught up in the middle of; or perhaps even just he and Chloé. His urgency for finding Chloé and getting her out safe at this moment, took precedence over these thoughts, however, and he agreed with certainty that they would do whatever they could in return for her safety.

"Then I shall do my best," announced U.P once it had been agreed.

She turned to face her white unicorns and the carriage, and as she looked at them, the carriage began to disappear in swirls of different coloured light, forming into the coloured orbs like those that had surrounded them in the woods. The orbs then began to encircle one of the white unicorn's bodies and the light began to reform, creating an elegant, ornate saddle, once more adorned with the same rainbow ribbons and flowers to match the carriage that the light had once been.

Of course, U.P then proceeded to mount the unicorn in the most dignified manner. As she approached, she began to step up through the air as her bare feet touched upon rays of light that appeared out of nowhere. She had reached just the right height by the point that she was stood just next to the unicorn, so that she was able to sit down with ease in a side saddle position, without the unicorn having to move at all.

"Keep an eye on Makawee's horn," she said as she pointed to the other white unicorn, "If her horn lights up, it means we've found her and we're on our way back."
"How will you know it's her?" asked Chris, desperate for a reason to go with them.
"How many human girls to you suspect to be lost and wandering through these woods searching for their father?"

Chris stared back at her with his sad, hopeless eyes. "Look, I'll do everything I can to get her back to you, I promise. Let's go Helaku," she said to the unicorn she rode upon, as they set off back into the dark, haunted woods.

Back inside, since they'd last seen Lousta, he'd been darting through the trees trying desperately to catch any sign of Chloé, whilst keeping camouflaged with the grim surroundings hoping that it'd make it harder for the spirit to stop him. He ran in all directions, though it was so difficult for him to track his position in his head as he ran, since every tree in the woods looked equally as sad and gloomy as the next.

He decided to rest for a moment, his legs and body were covered in cuts and scrapes from running so quickly through the woods for so long. As he stopped to catch his breath, he leaned wearily against a lifeless, yet sturdy corpse of a once flourishing sycamore tree.

Whilst he rested, convincing himself not to give up hope, the sound of his heartbeat pounding by his eardrums began to calm, and the sounds from within the woods began to creep through. He heard a slight breeze push around dead leaves scattered about on the floor, a weary bird squawking way off in the distance, and then he heard something else, something seemingly more human.

It was a voice he could hear, but he couldn't be sure if it was Chloé's or the spirits. It was a cry way in the distance, repeating itself over and over, though he couldn't quite work out what was being said.

"CHLOE!?" he yelled, to which there was no reply. Yet the voice carried on crying out. Surely it had to be her, he thought to himself. The spirit, after all, had only ever sounded to them as a sad songstress roaming the woods. Without giving it any more thought, he called out again to Chloé, "I'm coming for you Chloé! Just don't listen to the spirit!"

He ran, galloping again through the woods, stopping periodically to listen out for her voice, checking he was still heading in its direction. Sure enough, the voice became louder and clearer, it was most definitely Chloé's -

"DAD! I'm coming! Hold on Dad!" she cried out wearily.

Lousta's heart began to beat faster and faster as he neared her, he pleaded with his own strength not to fail him until he'd saved her from the spirit of the Weeping Woods. He stopped again, allowing him to home in on the exact direction the sound of her voice was coming from. It had become so clear now that he knew he was merely a few moments away from spotting her, and that if it were not for the dim light in the woods he would surely have found her already.

Another cry from Chloé caused him to turn his head slightly to his left, where he looked towards a clearing in the trees far ahead of him and spotted, just for a second, a vague figure of a human body walking away.
"CHLOE!" he cried, "WAIT!" He began running towards her as fast as he could, seeing her more clearly as he neared her, and the light coming through the clearing in the woods was able to shine down on the open space.

As the scene became clearer still, he noticed that this wasn't just a clearing, but the edge of the woods where they met the top of a cliff, towering hundreds of meters above a forest below. Panicked, he kept calling out to her as the trees that stood between them seemed to become more dense and tricky for him to hurry through.

"CHLO..." he began, before his speech was broken as a sudden, unseen dip in the ground threw him off balance and he fell to the floor, bashing his head against a tree trunk as he tumbled. Dizzy and in shock, he slowly pushed his human half upright and held one hand to the side of his head where he'd hit it. Pulling his hand away again he looked upon it and saw blood smeared across he palm, but before he had any time to worry about that, he heard Chloé's voice again.

"Dad, I'm here, it's me, Chloé!" He looked up as she spoke and saw her clearly, not too far ahead of him. It all happened so suddenly. As he came around, recalling the circumstances he was in as he fell, hearing Chloé call out to something that wasn't there, he remembered the trance state she was in as she stepped forward once more; right up to the edge of the cliff.

He yelled out her name again, though the strength it took made the pain in his head feel like someone was stabbing a knife into it. For a moment his vision blurred, yet he pulled himself up and began to run as well as he could, though it was all for nothing; he was too late. She'd already taken her final step forward, over the edge of the cliff. His body, readjusting and pumping with adrenalin, managed to refocus his vision and save him from ending up over the edge too.

He halted himself there, knocking over some loose rocks and debris which plummeted straight down in a long silence, before emitting a clattering sound upon hitting the floor below. The sound echoing back up assured Lousta of just how far down the drop was. He shouted her name again as tears were forced through his eyes, then he glanced down over the edge for any sign of her body, though all he saw was rock and trees.

He dropped to the floor, there at the top of the cliff, as he tried to grasp the reality of what had just happened. Tears ran down his face as he looked helplessly at the ground below. He couldn't bear to take his eyes off of where she had fallen, scared that if he did, it would be like admitting that all hope was actually gone for good.

As he sat staring down, an ice-cold breeze blew over him, coming up from below the cliff and heading back towards the forest. This icy chill that swept past him caused his eyes to follow in its direction without him even thinking about it. He looked back towards the woods, wondering if it might be Chloé's spirit.

As the breeze left him for the trees, it began to turn white, like a smoky mist travelling through the air. The mist stopped just at the edge of the woods and began swirling before forming a new shape. Lousta watched in anticipation, not knowing how to feel if this should turn out to be Chloé. Would he be pleased to get to see her again? Or broken knowing that she had died there that day, whilst in his care.

It turned out however, the mysterious mist was not Chloé at all, but the spirit of the princess bride who'd haunted them. She stood tall in her ripped wedding gown and dishevelled hair, looking directly at Lousta with her blank, soulless eyes, before slowly shaking her head.

His body filled with rage towards her and he pulled himself up from the ground, "She was just a human!" he yelled. Then he charged directly at her, forgetting that she was merely a spirit and hoping to tackle her to the ground. Instead, however, she tilted her head back and let out a screeching cry which echoed it's piercing sound throughout gloomy woodland. Upon Lousta's impact of her willow-the-wisp like form, her body split into escaping tendrils, slithering through the air and back into the deepest parts of her woods.

Lousta carried on running, shouting out to the spirit and asking why, why she had to take Chloé's life from her, and from him. His cries carried through the woods and caught the ears of U.P, who had stopped still after hearing the spirits shrieking cry only moments earlier.

She urged her unicorn, Helaku, to gallop in Lousta's direction, as reins formed around his head for her to hold on to, and a pair of gloves appeared on her hands which matched her dress perfectly. It didn't take long until their paths came close and she spotted him.

"STOP!" shouted U.P as she saw him running aimlessly through the trees. As she shouted, a burst of golden sparkles dazzled Lousta, slowing him to a halt as he watched them settle and disappear on the floor around him. "Lousta, is it?"

"Yes," he sniffed, "Who the hell are you?" he asked as he wiped the tears from his face with the back of his hand. "I'm U.P. I promised your friends I'd come into these dreadful woods to escort both you and Chloé out of here." Lousta didn't respond but instead stared at her for a moment with a blank expression as his heart sank, completely speechless.

He turned his head towards the floor, ashamed to reveal his emotions. "Oh no, don't tell me she's already..." Lousta glanced back up at U.P, she didn't need to finish the question. "Ahh, I see," she paused for a moment. "Well, look, we're not doing anyone any good standing about in this awful place. Come, Helaku will find us the quickest way out of here and back to your friends."

The blast of sparkles had helped to calm Lousta down,

and in doing so had progressed his emotions from anger to sadness. After taking a look back into the woods where Chloé had been lost to him, Lousta walked over to U.P as they began their dismal walk through to woods to re-join the others.

In silence they walked side by side, U.P occasionally turning to Lousta to check that he was holding up okay, and also glancing about the woods now and then just in case there was any sign of hope left. Around them, the woods remained still and cold, with the eerie presence of the dead princess' spirit lurking amongst the trees. The route back probably would've continued all the way in this morbid silence if, to each of their surprise, Helaku's horn hadn't suddenly begun to glow; the very glow that U.P had told the others to look out for, on Makawee's horn.

CHAPTER TWENTY-SEVEN

(Short-Version)

The unmissable glow from the unicorn horn lit up the woods around them. Lousta stared at it, dazed by it's warm, glistening light, unaware of why it was happening. U.P gazed at the horn curiously, confused by the conflicting reports she was now faced with. "Didn't you say that... that Chloé was dead?" she asked Lousta.

"What?" he replied, shaking his head as he was brought out of his mesmerised state.

"The girl you were looking for, you saw her die, didn't you?"

"What do you mean? Of course I did. I wouldn't just stop looking for her if she was still here, would I?!" he snapped back at her.

Lousta felt insulted and instantly became defensive, feeling accused whilst still plagued with guilt for perhaps not doing enough to save Chloé's life whilst he had the chance.

"All right, all right, no need to get all riled up. I guess she really was a popular one."

"What's that supposed to mean?" Lousta said with a hint of aggression in his voice.

"Oh, never mind. The thing is, you see I told my other unicorn, Makawee, to shine her horn just like Helaku is doing right now, should she sense from him that we'd found Chloé. So, that fact that Helaku's horn is glowing, suggests to me that…"

"Where's your other unicorn?" demanded Lousta.

"They are in the field of Papillon Petals, with your friends."

Lousta wasted no time and took off instantly, darting through the trees desperate to find the edge of the woods where the others waited. U.P and Hekalu set off again gracefully, trotting through the woods calmly and without any such urgency, knowingly aiming straight towards the others.

Eventually, Lousta ran into her again whilst searching for his way out, flustered and panicked from feeling trapped within the woods. "Slow and steady will win the race you know," she subtly hinted as he stopped next to her.

"Which way is out?" he demanded.
"To be honest I have no idea... But Helaku however, does. So, if you'd like to follow us, then please, be our guest."

Feeling a little smug over taming Lousta's heart throbbing rush to get back to see if Chloé was alive or not, U.P lead on elegantly through the woods, closely followed by an anxious Lousta. He constantly pestered her, asking how much further it would be and if they could go any faster. U.P however, would only ever ride side saddle, so going any faster would risk her falling off and quite probably getting trampled on – a risk she refused to take.

After about twenty minutes or so of travelling, the edge of the woods was finally in sight and Lousta rushed ahead of U.P. Sure enough, Helaku's homing instinct to his family's collected magic had led them all straight back to the others. As he exited the woods, Lousta stopped for a moment as he caught his first sight of them all, stood huddled together in a circle.

"Lousta, you're back," said Paza, who was the first to notice him. He'd caught his scent first before anyone had noticed he was there. Everyone turned to face him as Paza spoke, revealing Chloé who was lying on the floor between them all, with Meg stood by her side placing a caring hand on her shoulder.

"Lousta, it's you! Are you alright?" asked Chloé as she sat upright, concerned that he'd put himself in danger to save her.

"Chloé? Is that really you? I… I don't understand."
"Yes, it's me," she replied.

As Chloé spoke, a confused Lousta looked around at everyone else who was there, which is when he spotted that Orel had re-joined them too. "Orel saved me. Like you said, she was always somewhere watching over us, and I'm so glad she was."

Orel began to explain how she'd seen that not everyone had exited the woods at first, and so she'd flown back overhead to find out why. With the low cloud covering the trees of the Weeping Woods, it had made it impossible for her to spot anyone, though thanks to Lousta crying out for Chloé, she was able to follow the sound of his voice.

With her advantage of having a bird's eye view over the area, her attention was drawn almost instantly to Chloé's movement once she was out of the woods near the cliff; though she was still quite a distance away. As she flew over to her she saw Chloé reaching the edge, right before it dawned on her what was just about to happen, merely a second before Chloé stepped out above the steep drop below. Then, as fast as she could, she raced over and dived out of the sky, hurtling herself towards the ground at racing speed in an effort to catch her before she hit the rocky floor below.

Chloé was lucky, for just as she was nearing the treetops and solid rock at the base of the cliff, Orel grabbed her legs with her clawed feet and squeezed onto them tightly, whilst spreading her wings in a desperate attempt to pull them both away from the floor. Orel's effort wasn't quite enough to stop them both being dragged down, but thankfully she managed to slow the fall sufficiently for them both to survive it.

After crashing through the trees, they both landed on the dry, sloped ground and rolled downhill until their path was blocked by the rotting carcass of a fallen tree. It had taken them a little while to come around after the shock of the fall, and Chloé couldn't recall anything since she'd left the others back in the woods.

Orel had suffered a few injuries whilst falling through the trees, though determined to get Chloé back to the others, she pulled herself up and began to stretch out her wings, ready to fly again. She helped Chloé up onto her back and told her to hold on as tight as she could, whilst she focused all her energy on getting them both airborne.

It proved difficult for her with the extra weight on her back and the trees blocking their exit above, so getting beyond the treetops required a mixture of both flying and scrambling through the branches. However, Orel persisted on with all her energy and eventually they broke free of the canopy, where Orel launched off from the top of one of the trees and soared out over the forest as it dropped with the slope of the ground below them.

It was clear to everyone who was there that they could go no further until both Chloé and Orel had been healed of their injuries. Chloé was covered in cuts and bruises, unable to move her right arm and her legs bled from the grasp of Orel's fearsome claws, as she'd gripped them tight to catch her. Orel was bleeding from a cut on her thigh where she'd hit a branch on the way down and felt weak from exhorting herself by carrying Chloé so far through the air.

"U.P, you're back!" cried Chris as he saw her emerge from the woods beside Lousta, "Please, we need your unicorns to heal Chloé and Orel, just like they healed me," he pleaded.

"Yes, of course. Though I'll need everyone to stand back and give us some room," she said as she wafted her hands out in front of her, motioning everyone to move aside as she strode towards them upon Helaku.

"Who's this?" asked Chloé, somewhat rudely.
"This is U.P, she saved my life," said Chris.
"Youpie?" questioned Chloé.
"Yes, it stands for Unicorn Princess," said U.P.
"Ooh, so U, P, not Youpie?"
"Just, whatever's easiest," replied U.P, tired of explaining herself.

U.P asked again for everyone to move back as she stepped down from Helaku. She walked over and knelt down beside Chloé and Orel, who'd both collapsed on the floor. Then, she asked Chloé to close her eyes as she began to look upon her, absorbing the feeling of her pain from the injuries.

Carefully she held Chloé's hand between both of hers and realised the full extent of her pain, including the longing she had to see her father again (which U.P had not anticipated). She squeezed her eyes shut as tears began leaking out from them, and with that her family of unicorns came over and began to heal Chloé just as they had Chris; though her emotional pain from losing her father once again, could not be masked through magic.

Once healed, both U.P and Chloé opened their eyes and U.P placed her hand on Chloé's shoulder. "I'm sorry, but your pain inside we are unable to heal," she began, "Though, hopefully, if we help each other, we will soon be able to put both our heartaches to rest." Chloé looked back at U.P but didn't say anything, as they sat in silence for a moment, both feeling the aching in Chloé's heart.

U.P then moved on to Orel as she let go of Chloé's hand and reached out for hers, however, Orel flinchingly pulled away. "It's no use," she said, "A Sirins' feathers absorb and deflect all magic used on them, good or bad. I'll just have to heal myself the slow way. I'll be fine after I've rested for a while."
"Can't she at least try?" asked Chloé, "I feel awful leaving you injured like this whilst I'm healed."

Orel allowed U.P to take hold of her hand as she sought out her physical pain, but just as Orel had said, U.P and the unicorn's magic was useless against her, and they sensed nothing but her touch. "Like I said, it's no use."

"Wait a moment, I'm sure we have some first aid things in the side pocket of the rucksack, I'll see if there's anything we can use to at least clean the wound up," said Chris. As he rummaged around, everyone came closer together and sat on the floor around Chloé, Orel and U.P.

"So, U.P, you said 'if we help each other'..." began Chloé, "how exactly can we help you? And, if you don't mind me asking, who, or what exactly are you?"
"Oh, well, would you like the long version or the short version?" she asked, pulling a sort of dissatisfied

expression as she mentioned the words - 'short version'. "I guess we have time for the long version, if you'd like…"

"Wonderful! Well, you see I wasn't always known as the Unicorn Princess. Actually, I began life as a regular sized fairy, and my real name is actually Ahote. Then, one day, a man named…" U.P stopped as she was interrupted by Chris, who'd found a compact first aid box with a small rolled up bandage and some antiseptic wipes; he hadn't really been paying attention to the conversation since he began looking for it.

He walked over to Orel and asked her permission to clean up her wound before applying the bandage, to which she agreed though soon regretted as her wound stung as he cleaned it. "It's alright, that's perfectly normal," he said, secretly worried that this substance from his world might have an opposite, horrific effect on a being from this world, "Right, well, I guess that's clean enough now… I'll just wrap it up."

"So, U.P, you were saying… what was his name?" asked Chloé.
"Ah yes, his name," she began, "His name was Rex Bookale, he was one of those humans with magical powers, and he'd managed to shrink himself down and mask himself as one of us fairies in order to learn more about our little world. Most fairy colonies didn't warm too well to the invasion of you humans into our world you see. Which was fair enough I suppose, as some fairy habitats were destroyed to make way for the new human settlements. You know, there was one colony whose leader was even captured by a witch, in an attempt to…"

"Umm, Is this a necessary part of your story?" asked Paza, who was already growing bored of her tale.
"Well it might have been, but I guess you'll never know now, will you," she responded, "Anyway, to cut a long story short I suppose, we fell in love and decided to live together as humans. Now, my fairy power was able to make me human-sized, but it was only ever an illusion, and by doing so for long periods of time would eventually exhaust me…"

"… So, he began to search for a way to transform me for good. Not into a half human, half fairy of course, that was against the new laws of the land, but into a full human, so that we could spend the rest of our lives together. Well you see, the thing is that he only managed to transform my *body* to a more human size. For, as he was preparing the next stage of the spell… he… well, he…" U.P found it hard to speak. Her lip began to quiver, her eyes twinkled as tears started to form as her voice broke.

"Oh U.P," said Chloé as she reached out and gently grasped her hand.
"The Curse. He disappeared, didn't he?" said Lancelin. U.P nodded as a tear ran down her cheek.

"Everything went so quiet, the room felt so still and empty, and I never saw him again," she said as she squeezed her face tight before hiding behind one of her hands. Chloé leaned in and hugged U.P in an attempt to console her.
"Of course we'll help you to get him back."
U.P sniffed and dried her eyes as she sat back slightly, releasing herself from Chloé's gentle embrace, "Thank

you."

"So," Chris cleared his throat, "How did you end up being known as the Unicorn Princess?" he asked, feeling rather uncomfortable around a crying stranger.

"Oh, well, as I couldn't reverse his magic I could no longer go back to live with the other fairies, though, to be honest, I didn't really want to, it felt like it would be admitting to myself that Rex had gone forever. So I began searching for a way to find him, to bring him back to me, and along the way, I made friends with Helaku and Makawee, the two white unicorns. Later, they went on to give birth to their three children, Pavati, Ashkii and Abeytu, and we became a little family."

"I had no idea at first, that to give a unicorn your unconditional love and to receive theirs in return, creates a bond between your powers and theirs. Since we became a family through our love for each other, my power of imagination can create more than just an illusion. Though, unfortunately, it seems it takes more than just power to change one's being, or to bring someone back from, well, wherever he is."

They all sat silently for a moment, reflecting on U.P's loss and the loss of the whole magical human world that had once existed here. Not being one to get emotional, Lancelin was first to mention the fact that the sun would soon be setting, and they were quite without shelter.

Orel took that moment to say goodbye to them all before flying off, she had no choice but to head back to her family nesting ground to rest, whilst her wounds healed and she gained her strength back. As for the rest of them, the only place Lousta knew of, an old human town, was too far for them to reach before sundown. Plus, everyone was terribly exhausted from the day's events and the thought of moving on much further didn't exactly appeal to most.

"So, what are we going to do? We can't just sleep out here," said Chris.
"Well, we could stay at my house?" U.P offered kindly.

CHAPTER TWENTY-EIGHT

The Man in the Window

As U.P made the suggestion, she stood up and stepped away from everyone as they watched her in anticipation, facing outwards towards the huge field of Papillon Petals which stretched away from the Weeping Woods. Papillon petals were a type of flower which grew here in abundance, their petals mimicking a group of butterflies huddled together – because that's exactly what they were. Each flower bloomed butterflies with a unique pattern, and all throughout the long, warm summer days, the butterflies would flutter about to mate with each other, before laying their eggs in the ground to eventually bloom into fresh new Papillon Petal flowers.

U.P stepped away from the group about ten paces, and as the unicorns began walking over to her she closed her eyes to look inside herself. Then, before they'd reached her, streams of different coloured light began to radiate from her chest in a soft, lose form. The others watched by in awe of what was happening, as they saw the light from her body begin to swirl and dance in the open space before her, beginning to take on a new form. More and more light continued to flow, as it created the home she'd once shared with Rex, right before their eyes.

Beginning from the ground up, her magic created an old Victorian style home, put together with a wooden frame and creamy-white brick walls. Starting with the steps up to the veranda which led around to the left of the house, after that appeared a central doorway and the living room protruding out to the right of it.

On the first floor, there was a small balcony which sat above the main entrance, facing slightly to the left, leading into the master bedroom above the living room. To the left of the balcony and sat slightly back from it, there stood a turret reaching an extra story higher than the upstairs rooms (meeting with the attic space at the top of the house) with a high, pointed roof; claiming the highest point of the building.

Not a single detail had been missed in designing this home. It was more like a piece of artwork than an actual house. The outside had been painted a mixture of cream, daffodil and pear colours, and vines of different coloured flowers grew up the walls. Ribbons woven of different colours adorned the railings of both the veranda and the balcony.

Then finally, behind the house to the right, her light gathered again to create large stables where the unicorns would rest, which matched all the characteristics of the main house. Just as it seemed the light that was flowing out of her seemed to dim, it suddenly grew brighter again as the house grew in size, widening the hallways and lifting the ceilings.

"I thought I better make it a bit roomier inside, so hunky deer-man over there doesn't have to sleep in the stables, too," she said, referring to Lousta, prompting a laugh from Chloé and causing him to blush.
"That's definitely your house," said Chris as he gazed at it.
"I admit, I have added a few new colours and flowers to it since Rex left, but inside it's still the same little home we once shared." U.P gave each of the unicorns a kiss as they left for the stables, before inviting everyone inside.

The interior of the house seemed, to the humans at least, like an antique shop or the set of a T.V period drama. Crisscross parquet flooring in different toned wood covered the floor, except for in the kitchen and bathrooms which were tiled. Wood panelling reached halfway up the walls, leaving the rest to be covered by decorative wallpaper and framed pressed flowers. There was a vase or pot on almost every unused surface, filled with colourful, sweet-scented and odd looking flora from all over Île Merveille.

As well as those, U.P had placed in each room a small ceramic bowl, filled with seashells. Each one was filled with shells of many shades of the same colour, which she'd collected on her visits to different shores around the island. To light the place, instead of gas lamps she had clear-glass balls, hung from what appeared to be the ends of branches which had been mounted on the walls, from within which a magic ball of light glowed.

It was a visually stunning home, littered with different kinds of gadgets and magical tools which Rex had been working with before his disappearance. Heavy drapes hung by the windows, made from luxuriously soft fabric interwoven with magical thread, which offered silence from any noise seeking to enter through the windows and disturb the current residents.

At the far end of the hallway entrance, a curved staircase elegantly swooped to the left, leading up to the first-floor landing and shading a small stained-glass window beneath it at the end of the corridor; which depicted a man sat under a tree by a clear, blue pond. The window was not merely a work of art, but blessed with magic. The tree itself would change with the seasons and ofttimes move as if blowing in the wind, and the man, one way or another, may give you a hint to something lying in your not too distant future.

"Will we be safe in here?" asked Chloé as she held Meg close to her.
"From what? The woods?" asked U.P as she led them all into the dining room at the back of the house.
"No, I mean from... Alexandra."
"Alexandra? Isn't she supposed to be sleeping? or dead,

or whatever?"

"She's after these guys and their book, probably to either kill them or lock them away so they don't bring any other humans back here," said Paza. Lancelin nodded.

"She has already tried to kill us," he added, "More than once."

"We don't know it was she who attacked us though, that's just been assumed," said Chris, finding it hard not to snap back in Alexandra's defence.

"You mean you don't know if the ground suddenly split on its own? And desert Dort flies just felt like rampaging through the woods one night? No, that was definitely some kind of human magic manipulation," argued Lousta.

"And what about that weird creature I saved you two from back in the jungle on our first day here?" said Lancelin, "As soon as I'd captured it with that chain of flowers, it just disappeared, into thin air!"

"Ah yes, that incident," began Chris, "Well that raises many questions doesn't it."

"Alright, enough squabbling now, please boys…wait, you mean to say she's back and she's actually out to get you?"

"She is," replied Paza, "She even threatened my mother and father, the count and countess, warning them not to disobey her orders by helping the humans. Though, she believes them to be witches."

"Does she now," said U.P, looking rather lost for a moment as she realised that the person who she'd felt so much anger towards for so many years, could soon be finally there for her to face.

She shook her head, pulling her attention back to the room, "Well, as you're all my invited guests, that nasty witch will have to get past the unicorns before she can get to any of you lot, now that's protection worth having!" she said as she led on through to the dining room.

Whilst about to offer them each a seat at her gorgeous dining table, it dawned on her that Lousta couldn't quite manage a chair as the others could, so she stopped for a moment and transformed the table and chairs into a delightful indoor picnic area, with plush pillows scattered about to help make everyone comfortable. "I guess we better get used to eating on the floor, whilst travelling around with someone who's half Bambi," Chris muttered to Chloé.

As everyone began to dig in to the food laid out for them (including Meg, who felt so blessed to have someone serve food to her for once, and Paza who was given a plate of assorted blood fruits) U.P began to inquire further into their plans for the journey ahead, and to each of their motives for seeking out the spring.

"Well, personally, when we found this magic book in a hidden room, in an old abandoned castle, which only Chloé could read and had a map to a magic island inside it, it just seemed like an adventure too good to miss," said Chris.

"I was sceptical at first," began Chloé, "But after reading some of the things that could be possible with magic, I just had to try. I'd do anything to see my dad again."
"And some of us just love the idea of humans being

around again," said Lousta as he smiled over at Chloé, "The stories I've heard of their magical abilities are incredible, not to mention what I've seen of their settlements."

"What about you Lancelin, how did you end up with these two? The three of you don't exactly... I mean... well... are you related, perhaps?"

"No, I live in the small village near the abandoned castle. I'd heard the stories of magic once existing there, the old folk tales, but I'd never been able to find anything in the castle to prove it or to show me how to find it. So, when I saw these two enter the castle one day, I watched them to see if they could find what I couldn't, which they did."

"I see. And mister vampire, what about you? To be in the presence of the spring's light would surely kill you, would it not?"

"It would, but the humans and the vampires have a deal... we aid their journey to the spring and they'll help us bring back Malicorne, who will put an end to Alexandra's claim over this land."

"Fair enough, though, whilst she was sleeping, did she really have all that much control over you?" asked U.P.

"Well, let's just say there were a few disagreements we had that remain unsettled."

"I thought as much."

It seemed to the humans that their ancestors' involvement with the island, and with its magic, had left such a mess that it couldn't simply be put right by suddenly abandoning it all. Both Chris and Chloé felt they were in way over their heads, however, Lancelin continued to seem as eager as ever to get to the spring of power.

"So, how exactly are you planning to reach it?" asked U.P as she took a sip of tea from her china teacup, decorated with delicately hand-painted butterflies.
"On foot," answered Lousta, causing U.P to spit her tea back out.
"On foot?! Well, that'll take you, what, another two to three days? No, no, we'll fly."
"Umm, but we can't fly though," mentioned Chris.
"Well, of course *you* can't, my little human friend, but it's no problem, you may ride in my carriage with me," U.P said, smiling.

Once relaxed in her home, she felt a wave of tiredness wash over her as she began to yawn. It had been a long day for her and the unicorns. They'd travelled far in search of the field of Papillon Petals, though this new venture had easily won over her attention. She assured everyone that all would be explained in the morning regarding her plan for getting them all in flight together, and wished them all goodnight before heading off to bed.

She offered the two spare bedrooms upstairs to Chris, Chloé and Lancelin, and the living room to Lousta. As she wasn't too sure whether Paza would sleep or not, she simply allowed him to make himself comfortable anywhere else that was free during the night. She also hinted to them that there was a main bathroom upstairs with fresh water and that they were all welcome to use it. In fact, she more or less insisted that they were to be clean and fresh before they travel any further together.

As she exited the dining room and began up the stairs in the hallway, the stained-glass window caught her eye. The tree was swaying as if blowing in a light breeze, but there was something else to be spotted in the way the man was holding his hand behind his back. Quietly she crept back down the first few steps, hoping not to draw anyone's attention from the other room so that she might decide herself if this information should be shared or not. As she got up close to the window, she saw clearly the gesture he was using. He stood facing away from her, looking out across the pond, through the window and towards the outside wall of the dining room. The hand he held behind him, he held with his fingers crossed.

A lie, she thought, but the window holds clues to the future, not to what has just happened. Betrayal, that's what the window was warning her of, she would soon be betrayed by someone currently in the house. He gave no clue as to who it would be, though the only one who had promised her anything in return for her help, was Chloé. It was even quite possible that the person who was to betray her may not even know it yet, which gave U.P every reason to keep her guard up around them from now on, sharing with them only what was necessary to get Rex back. It wasn't in U.P's nature to be closed and untrusting, so keeping this secret wasn't going to be easy.

As she stood looking at the window, she heard someone get up from the floor and begin to walk across the dining room. She didn't want anyone to be aware that she hadn't gone straight up to bed, and so instantly transformed herself back into her tiny fairy form and hid under the staircase.

She was of a different race of fairies than those found in the southern, tropical regions of Île Merveille, and her wings were the main difference. Unlike their colourful, butterfly-esque wings, U.P's people had wings more like those of a fly or wasp, with clear skin that shimmered hues of yellow and orange when touched by the light just right.

It was Paza who came out of the dining room, he was heading back outside to enjoy the dimming light and to relax in the darkness of the night which was coming. U.P watched him walk down the hallway towards the front door, then held her breath as he stopped and began to smell her lingering scent in the air. Of course, to him, the whole house wreaked of fairy magic, but for some reason, it seemed slightly stronger at that moment in the hallway. However, he merely shrugged the scent off and continued to exit the house. U.P let out a sigh of relief and waited for a moment to listen out for signs of anyone else coming her way, before buzzing up the stairs and straight into her bedroom; locking the door behind her once she'd transformed back into her human form.

She sat down on her cream quilted chaise longue, which was draped with a soft, lilac blanket and positioned in the corner of her room, with a clear view out through the windowed door which led to her balcony. She sat in the low, dusk light, gazing out at the mountains surrounding them beyond the field, going over and over in her mind about the image she'd seen in the window, and wondered what she could do about it.

Downstairs, the others had decided to disperse after they'd finished eating, to call it a night. Lousta made himself as comfortable as he could, sleeping on a large rug on the living room floor, laid out in front of an unlit fireplace, whilst the other three headed upstairs with Meg.

The two spare rooms consisted of one double and one single room. The double room was part of the turret on the front of the house, and the single sat at the back above the dining room. There was also a wooden spiral staircase on the landing, leading up to the attic space above them.

Chris and Chloe took turns using the bathroom to wash up before bed, and to their delight, they found soap and warm running water, which poured out from a metal spout in the wall just above the freestanding bathtub. After eating well and feeling clean for the first time since arriving, they both fell asleep as soon as their heads hit the thick, soft pillows on U.P's cosy, wooden guest bed, with Meg curled up by their feet like a pet dog.

They both slept peacefully through the night, until the early hours of the next morning when Chris awoke feeling dehydrated. He fumbled around for the goblet inside rucksack as quietly as he could (whilst in complete darkness) and grabbed the torch too as he felt it, then tiptoed across the creaky, wooden floors to the bathroom. After using the goblet to make sure what he was drinking was pure water, he exited the bathroom to go back to bed. However, whilst he was getting his drink, the batteries in the torch had run out and so he was forced to head back in the dark.

As he carefully stepped out on to the landing, he heard a slight murmuring sound coming from the attic. He stopped to listen as he began to feel sick in his stomach, his nerves getting the better of him, whilst he thought about what could possibly be going on up there. He decided to creep up the spiral stairs as quietly as he possibly could, to see if he could hear what was going on a bit more clearly.

As he reached the small landing at the top of the stairs, he noticed a shimmering light escaping out from under the locked door he found there. Chris paused for a moment, scared to let himself be known to whoever was in the attic, but he was so close that he could almost make out what was being said.

Bravely he decided to continue all the way up to the doorway, hoping that the sound of the voices would cover up any sound he might make. Carefully he crouched down and peered through the keyhole, tightly closing one eye so that he might focus as well as he could on whatever he could see on the other side of the door.

He couldn't quite make out who it was. There was a shimmering light which had turned them into a blurred silhouette, seemingly sat in an armchair facing away from the door. In their hand, they held a glowing conch shell in front of them, emitting the shimmering white light like sun rays flickering on a clear ocean floor. Chris turned his head and put his ear to the keyhole, and to his relief, he was able to make out roughly what was being said, and who was speaking.

"I'll tell the others that you've gone back to the vampire manor, due to the power from the potion running out," said a voice which sounded undoubtedly like Lancelin's. "Are you sure she'll be able to resurrect him?" asked another voice, most definitely Paza's thought Chris. "The book is all she needs. As long as she continues to trust us and the book, there shouldn't be a problem."

"And what about that over-sized fairy?" asked Paza. Immediately after that Chris heard a female voice gasp from within the attic, much clearer than the other voices. He looked back through the keyhole, it was most sure to be U.P, he thought. She was somehow listening to the other two having a conversation via this conch shell she held. Then it struck him. The bowls of seashells in each room, they were probably enchanted somehow so that U.P could eavesdrop on any conversation being had around her home.

"...the reason we're able to keep going," Chris heard Lancelin say, catching only the end of the sentence, "All she wants in return is to have her man back. We'd be best to just keep on her good side and let Chloé deal with her later. Besides, once Malicorne is back none of that will matter, there'll be no human around strong enough to get in his way again." There was a brief silence in their conversation, before Lancelin continued, "Now fly off back to your family, let them know we won't be long."

Chris's heart was pounding in his chest, he knew Lancelin had some hidden agenda, and now he was sure he had to find a way to put a stop to it. He waited there by the door, wondering if there was anything else worth sticking around to listen to, until he heard the front door open from downstairs. As Lancelin began to creep along the corridor towards the stairs, Chris crept down the spiral-stairs and swiftly moved back to his bedroom.

U.P spent the night up in the attic, resting comfortably by the conch shell which she'd placed on a round, wooden end table next to the armchair. She sat up waiting for it to glow again, a sign of a conversation being had that she ought to be listening to. However, eventually, she too fell asleep.

Chris sat up in bed next to Chloé, eager to share with her what he'd heard through the keyhole, though he knew their conversation would surely be overheard as well. For the rest of the night he barely slept, wondering who Lancelin was including when he said, 'we won't be long', and why someone would need to 'get in his way again'.

He wished he could speak to Alexandra for help, but perhaps even she wouldn't be much use. After all, through her efforts she hadn't been able to stop them getting this far, but still, he was desperate to speak to her; for the lust which she had planted within him still burned strong.

CHAPTER TWENTY-NINE

Up, Up and Away

In the comfort of U.P's sumptuous home, that night they each had a well-earned rest, which continued on well into the late hours of the morning. Chris awoke next to Chloé, unaware of the time and still itching to speak to her about what he'd heard during the night. He knew he had to keep his mouth shut about it though, whilst in the house at least, and he had a growing concern over how his false reaction to Paza's absence would be received by the others.

He heard footsteps coming down the stairs from the attic, which he assumed to be U.P, followed by one of the bedroom doors opening then closing. Knowing that someone else was up and about, he decided to make it known that he too was awake, by exiting the bedroom and heading over to the bathroom with heavy footsteps, over the ever-creaky floorboards.

Upon his exit from the bathroom, U.P appeared from the master bedroom as if for the first time since she went to bed, yawning and stretching her arms out. She'd come out wearing a floor-length, silk, midnight blue nightgown and robe, tied tight around her waist.
"Morning," said Chris.
"Good morning, or well… no I think it is still morning, isn't it?" she laughed, "Breakfast?"
"That'd be great," he replied politely, "I'll just see if Chloé's up."
"Wonderful, I'll meet you all downstairs."

Chris went back into the bedroom to find Chloé beginning to sit up in bed, "Morning," he said, greeting her as he closed the door behind him.
"Morning."
"Did you sleep alright?"
"I think I had the best night sleep I've ever had. Seriously, if I get magical powers, I'm gonna have to conjure me a bed like this." Chris smiled and let out a small laugh as if everything was fine.

"How about you?" she asked him.
"Oh fine, like you said, that bed is really comfortable. Anyway, I just saw U.P and she's waiting for us downstairs with some breakfast."

Chloé sighed a joyful sigh, "I wish all of our nights here had been like this. Then again, if we reach the spring today, perhaps they might be!" she said, ever hopeful that magic will come ever so easily to her and that it'll provide a fix for all of life's problems. The pair then neatened themselves up, as much as they could whilst still in their worn, dirty clothes, and they headed downstairs for breakfast, closely followed by Meg as she jumped down each step behind them.

U.P had created a picnic in the dining room again, where she sat with both Lousta and Lancelin as they all tucked into the delicious food that was on offer.

"Good morning Chloé. Please, you two, help yourselves, we've got an exciting day ahead of us."
"Is Paza still sleeping?" Chris blurted out, too eager to get his faked surprise over and done with to think about how odd it was that that should be his first concern.
"He left," replied Lancelin, "He came up to my room during the night and told me how he could feel the potion wearing off, and that he'd felt weakened from the daylight yesterday."

"Why your room?" asked Chris, trying hard not to blurt out what he knew in front of everyone.
"I don't know. Perhaps he could sense that I wasn't sleeping so well."
"How could you not? Our bed was amazing," claimed Chloé, "U.P, I'm going to have to find out how you created them so well." And with that, the subject of Paza's departure was buried for the time being.

After they'd overindulged at breakfast, they were all

anxious to find out U.P's plan for flying to the spring. She suggested that they all meet in front of the house in around 10 minutes, insisting that they used their time to wash up and gather all their belongings.

Unfortunately, washing themselves didn't do much for the smell of their clothes, but having nothing else to wear, Chris and Chloé each begrudgingly put their dirty clothes back on to their cleansed bodies. Chris offered to carry the rucksack again, suggesting that Chloé does a far better job at looking after her Corne Troll than he did with his. Once they were ready they headed back downstairs and out of the front entrance, where Lancelin and Lousta were already stood waiting.

U.P had hung around in her room until she could see that everyone was outside waiting for her before descending to meet them, mainly because she wanted them all to take note of the exquisite ensemble she had created for herself that day. She made sure to make a noise whilst turning the doorknob of the main entrance, alerting the others that she was about to exit.

She stepped out of the front door with her head held high and, as ever, with an air of grace about her. Her dress today had a touch of far eastern style to it, with a waist clinching, Persian blue corset which just about covered her breasts and reached down to her hips. Out from the top of that came four strips a light, pale green, floaty material, covering her chest and back and attached over her shoulders, with the remaining material left trailing almost all the way down to the floor; fading in colour as it neared the end.

From beneath the corset, a shimmery pearl coloured

silk skirt hugged her curved thighs all the way to her knees, where the skirt split and hung down to the floor; with excess material purposefully trailing on the floor behind her. Her shoes were high stilettos and pearl coloured, like her skirt, which glistened even when not in the light

To accessorise, she had a piece of thin, decorated cloth (matching her corset) tightly fitted to her left arm from her wrist until about an inch before her elbow, a glistening pale pink diamond ring on her right ring-finger, and of course, she held a fan in her right hand, which she flung open and used whether she was hot or not. For her hair, she wore it loosely plaited, hung over her left shoulder and had small bunches of cherry blossoms randomly placed throughout it.

"Oh U.P, you definitely live up to the princess part of your name. You look incredible," exclaimed Chloé.
"How sweet of you to say, Chloé. I do, don't I?" she said smiling, as she whipped open the fan and proceeded to fan herself as she sauntered over to them. "So, do you have all your things?"
"I think so," said Chris.
"Everything's in the bag," said Chloé as she gestured to it with her head, whilst holding Meg in her arms like a toddler.
"Great. Then let's get on."

As she said that, U.P's house began to break up into different coloured light behind her as she walked away from it, which danced and swirled around in the space where the home once stood, before fading and disappearing to leave the field of Papillon petals as it had been the day before. Once it had all vanished, the unicorns began walking over to stand with them, well rested from their night in the stables.

"So, how exactly are we all going to fly to the spring?" asked Lancelin.
"We'll take my carriage."
"A carriage?" questioned Lousta, wondering how she intended for him to ride in such a thing.
"Well, not you, you'll have to be upfront with the unicorns. You don't mind, do you?" Lousta remained silent, puzzled as to how she imagined this all working.

As the unicorns reached them they stood together in double file, with the two white ones (Helaku and Makawee) at the front, the blue and green unicorns (Pavati and Abeytu) in the middle, leaving the pink one (Ashkii) alone at the back. U.P then instructed Lousta to stand next to Ashkii and asked them all the space themselves much wider apart.

She stood herself so she faced them sideways on at a slight distance away, then asked Chris, Chloé and Lancelin to get behind her. As she looked upon the unicorns and the empty space behind them, in the same way that she'd created her house the night before, streams of coloured light began to escape from her chest. It was another unmissable, spectacular sight for the humans to witness, as they stood by watching with their mouths wide open, mesmerised by the incredible display of both the unicorn's and U.P's magic.

As the light danced through the air, it swirled around the unicorns and Lousta, forming into reins which linked them together; resembling those normally used for horses to pull a carriage. Then, behind them, the light gathered and grew to create a spectacular, closed carriage that was fit for French royalty. Once that was all done, the final part of U.P's creation began to take shape, on each of the unicorns and also Lousta. The light swirled around their bodies, spinning faster and faster until suddenly it penetrated their skin and disappeared inside them, leaving Lousta rather concerned about what he was allowing her to do to him. Then, one by one through a series of quick bursts, rays of light came shooting out from their sides forming into great wings, which they were able to control as if they'd had them all their lives.

Lousta proceeded to flap his about in a nervous panic, fearful of his new ability and what U.P was asking of him. Flapping as he did, however, caused him to lift off the floor slightly and stumble about the place, whilst linked to the other unicorns.

"Please, please, stay calm," said U.P, "It'll be alright, just follow the lead of the unicorns, they know what to do."
"But... I've never flown before. How am I supposed to do it? What If I fall and pull us all down?"
"Nonsense. You'll be a natural, trust me," said U.P as she dismissed his concerns, turning her attention back to the humans.

"Now then, as for your clothes, let's see if we can do somethi..." U.P was interrupted by Helaku as he let out a loud neigh. "Oh, surely we can spare a little more magic?" Helaku responded by lifting and then slamming his front, right hoof on the ground. "Alright, alright, let's leave it then."

"You have a limit on your magic?" asked Chloé.

"Well, sort of. For fairies, it's like the energy you have each day when you wake up. You only have so much you can use before you become exhausted and need to sleep. And, as most of this is created through my power of imagination, with just a touch of help from the unicorns to strengthen it, I guess it's best I don't become exhausted mid-flight."
"Yea, perhaps that would be best," said Chris.

As she was warned from spending her magic frivolously that day and so was unable to clean them up, she suggested that Lancelin ride up-front as the coachman, to eliminate at least one set of old clothes from being in a tight, enclosed space with her; and that way he could keep Lousta company too.

"Shouldn't he at least have some goggles or something?" asked Chloé.
"Some what?" replied U.P. She had no idea what goggles were, but with a simple description from Chloé, she was able to conjure up a creation from her own imagination, which Lancelin would soon be grateful for. She was also glad of the excuse to get Chris and Chloé alone with her, so she might warn them of Lancelin's secret late-night talks with Paza – she was desperate for a quick gossip about them.

Chris and Chloé then entered inside the carriage with both the rucksack and Meg and sat side by side, leaving U.P her own, personal seat which faced forwards. Once they were all in, U.P opened the little window next to her seat and called out to check if everyone was ready to leave. She didn't receive a very confident response, but still she proceeded to give the order for the unicorns to begin take off, instructing them to carry them all through the skies towards the great cave, where the spring of power awaited them inside.

The unicorns began to run through the field, pulling along Lousta who was trying his best to keep up with what they were doing. As they ran they disturbed hundreds of sleeping butterflies from the Papillon Petal flowers, which created quite a remarkable display all on its own as they all scattered and fluttered away.

They began to flap their wings in a slow, strong motion, which again Lousta attempted to imitate. As they got faster and with each forceful, persistent push from the wings, they all began to take off, as sparks of golden light lit up beneath their feet as they galloped up into the air.

The light tailed off behind them and under the wheels of the carriage, steadying it as it was pulled further and further away from the ground. Once they were all airborne and high above the treetops, the unicorns and Lousta stopped running, pulled their feet in towards their bodies and continued to glide effortlessly through the soft, warm summer air.

The mountainous terrain of the hills of the four seasons stood proudly around them, as they soared along the steep, green valleys and high above the deep, pristine lakes. The weather on this particular August day was delightfully warm and calm, barely a breath of wind and not a cloud in the sky above them. Of course, however, with each day growing hotter, the hazy clouds on the horizon were beginning to grow into thick, heavy storm clouds, which lingered in the distance as a warning that change was on its way.

"This place is so beautiful," began Chloé as she looked out of the window in awe at the landscape, "Everything about it is as if it's be…"
"Right you two, I'll be honest, I'm glad it's just the three of us in here," interrupted U.P, "Now, how much do you actually know about your friend Lancelin?"

"Lancelin?" asked Chloé, unsure what U.P was getting at, "Well, he's just a human like us, we met him in France."
"Alright, but does that explain to you why he's been having…"
"Late night talks with Paza?" interjected Chris, finishing off U.P's sentence as a way to let her know that he too had heard the conversation last night.

"What?" Chloé asked, a little befuddled.
"How do you know?" U.P asked Chris.
"I heard it through the keyhole in your attic door as you were listening to them last night."

"Oh, you did, did you? And did you stumble upon any other secrets as you rummaged around my home during the night?" U.P snapped, irrationally fearing that her control over their situation was slipping from her.
"No, no, it wasn't anything like that. I just, went to the bathroom in the night and then I heard voices coming from the attic. I would never have been able to sleep had I not gone to find out who they were coming from. Though, finding out didn't actually help me sleep either."
"Nor me."

"Wait, please, will someone just tell me what's going on?" demanded Chloé. U.P sat back and stared at Chris, gesturing to him to carry on his story, though she was clearly unhappy that he'd taken it from her. He remained silent and sunk back slightly into his seat.

"Well anyway, Chloé, last night, I, or rather, *we*, overheard a conversation between Lancelin and Paza which they were having outside on the veranda whilst they assumed we were all sleeping..." U.P continued to fill Chloé in on the details of their conversation.

"So...I guess it seems like Malicorne *is* the bad guy, just like you said that Alexandra said to you," Chloé pointed out as she glanced over at Chris, "But what about her? Do you think she'd keep trying to stop us if she knew we had no intention of bringing him back?"

"I think her main objective is to make sure nobody comes back, bad or good. Which means stopping you two from gaining powers from the spring will continue to be her main objective, and that makes her bad in my book. She took my Rex away from me, my whole world, and nice people just don't do that." U.P sniffed and turned her head dramatically to face out of the window as she opened her fan again, proceeding to fan herself though with a rather limp wrist.

"As for Malicorne, well, I never met him, but whilst he was alive, rumour on the island was that his magic was the strongest ever to exist, which is why so many other sorcerers, witches, humans or whatever, were searching for a way to stop him."

"He was stronger because he wasn't human?" asked

Chris.

"I guess they would've feared him," said Chloé.

"Exactly. So, for Alexandra to have been able to stop him…"

"She must be pretty powerful too," Chloé said disheartened, as she slouched back into her seat and turned to look out of the window just as U.P had.

The atmosphere in the carriage had switched from courageous to glum, the feeling of defeat hit both Chloé and Chris hard when they'd realised they were on their own, sided in both scenarios by far superior contenders.

"Well, let's not give up now!" said U.P once she'd realised how low everyone's mood had sunk, "Don't forget, Malicorne is still dead, and for whatever reason Alexandra hasn't managed to stop you yet. So, here's my proposition. We use Lancelin and the vampires for as long as we can, to do whatever it is they're doing that seems to be keeping Alexandra away, whilst you two get your magical powers from the spring and learn how to use them; with the help of that book and whatever else has been left behind from the study and teachings of magic years ago…"

"…Then, we'll work out how to bring an end to Alexandra's rule over this place, bring back our loved ones and be free to live out the rest of our lives however we want; with me and my unicorns by your side every step of the way. What do you say?"

This offer brought some hope back to Chris and Chloé. With U.P's convincing proposal, it all seemed potentially possible once more with the help of their new friend. They had no idea quite how much use both the unicorns and U.P's combined magic would be in their hours of need, for they were still yet to experience the full strength of magic harnessed by a human, but right now this was by far their best option; and so it was agreed.

Neither Chloé nor Chris would attempt to bring Malicorne back from the afterlife (wherever that was) for the risk that what Alexandra told Chris that day in the woods was true. Until now, neither of them had been sure whether to trust what she'd said to Chris, but feeling like they were being used by Malicorne's followers simply to bring him back to life, scared them into imagining how they might be disposed of once they had fulfilled their wishes. As for Alexandra, it was their loyalty to U.P who so far had been nothing other than loyal to them, which kept her as an untrustworthy, suspected enemy to their plan to bring their lost loved ones back to life.

The three of them sat in the carriage and discussed their next plan of action after both Chris and Chloé had visited the spring. U.P was sure that Lancelin wasn't as human as he appeared to be, and that that would become much clearer when the time came for any humans to step foot into the flowing light of the spring, nestled within the great cave.

Chris tried to seem in agreement with them, but he couldn't silence Alexandra's sweet, lovely voice inside his head. The image of her alluring beauty he had witnessed that day he'd been drawn out into the woods alone, had been burnt into his mind. The longer that time went by, and he still hadn't done as she'd asked of him and delivered the book unto her, made him increasingly anxious and agitated. Still, he managed to keep quiet about it, knowing that they'd only disagree and do what they could to stop him. As far as he was concerned, it was all down to him to do the right thing, to save them all.

CHAPTER THIRTY

The Great Cave

As they raced on high above the ground, the three of them had just begun to discuss team codewords with each other when, all of a sudden, they were silenced by a deep feeling of sickness in their stomachs as the carriage felt as if it was dropping out of the sky. At once it lifted again, then dropped a second time before it began to jerk from side to side and bump around like an aeroplane experiencing dramatic turbulence.

"Oh my God! What's happening?" cried Chloé as she clutched onto Chris' arm and the side of her seat. The four of them tumbled about, alternating between being lifted from their seats and then being dragged back down into them.

U.P managed to fling open one of the windows and held on to the opening to steady herself slightly. "Lancelin! What's…" the carriage tumbled and turned over, spinning those inside as if they were going around in a tumble dryer.

"U.P! HELP US!" screamed Chloé. She and Chris grabbed hold of each other as he tried to keep them fixed into one corner of the carriage.
"I'M THINKING!" screamed U.P. Meg squealed as she was tossed around, before Chloé managed the grab hold of her and held her tightly with one arm.

Chris caught sight of U.P's face as her expression abruptly changed from panicked to shocked, "What? What's happening?" he asked through all the commotion.
"TAKE US DOWN!" she yelled out to the unicorns.

They flapped with all their might to fight the force against them whilst attempting for a safe landing, though it meant they were unable to slow themselves as they tried to descend. What's more, the ground below was completely covered with forest.

"There's nowhere to land!" shouted Lancelin as he clung on to Lousta for his life. He'd been thrown up and out of his seat in the first instance, though fortunately for him he had been holding tightly onto the reins. It was at this point that U.P became genuinely worried and feared for their lives.

Thankfully for all of them, Helaku and Makawee were able to sense U.P's fear through their loving bond which tied them all together as a family. In order to protect each other, the magic within each unicorn would be subconsciously activated during a time of great panic.

It began to act as if it were its own entity, doing what it must to save its host unicorn and the hearts of those who they held closest to their own. Each of the leading, white unicorns' horns began to glow and sparkle with warm, white light.

The rays of light shone down far out ahead of them, focusing on one area of ground even as the unicorns were still battling against the forces determined to sabotage their voyage. The white light penetrated the forest and cut into the trees, causing them to fade away and leave behind a sparse, open field. This made a perfect place for them to land, and with all their strength behind them, they flew the carriage towards the grassy floor and attempted to bring them all down in one piece.

Everyone inside, and also those outside who could speak, yelled out to each other in an attempt to communicate what was going on. Lancelin yelled to them to hold on as they speedily raced towards the floor, but no one anticipated what was to happen next.

The carriage was severely bashed from above, provoking the unicorns to counteract the force and try to pull them all upwards to avoid hitting the ground too soon, but with the harsh jolt of the carriage U.P's head flung against the wall behind her. Bashing her head as she did, triggered her to lose focus of the magic she was using to create the wings, the reins and the carriage, which all disappeared in a sudden mass explosion of different coloured light; even U.P's outfit disappeared with it, leaving her wearing nothing but a drab, scruffy pair of trousers, made from a bulky, itchy, natural fibre, loosely stitched together down the sides of her legs.

Abandoned by what had once been keeping them all in flight, they were thrown to the ground and scattered about across the grass like a handful of pebbles thrown over a green lawn. In her panic, Chloé threw Meg away from her in fear that she might crush her when they landed, as Meg continued to squeal in a cry that sounded like a pig being tormented.

Silence fell once they'd all landed. The unicorns magic proceeded to heal them and also U.P, though now that the field was no longer necessary for their safe landing, glittering light began to twinkle in the air all around them as the forest faded back into existence. Cut off from each other, the healed unicorns stood themselves back up, re-joined as a group and awaited U.P who, alone, sat herself up and looked around; trying to make sense of their situation after the fall.

The first one to make themselves known was Chris, as he called out Chloé's name. She called back to him, alerting him to her whereabouts amongst the trees, which was not all that far from where Chris had found himself.

"Is anyone hurt?" U.P shouted out, before gasping as she realised what she was now wearing. Quickly, hoping no one had yet noticed, she recreated her outfit as it had been earlier, then pushed herself up and set off looking for the others.

She spotted Lousta and Lancelin first who had landed close to each other, it seemed Lancelin had thrown himself from Lousta just seconds before they hit the ground. They helped each other up as they confirmed to her that they appeared to be ok, bar a few cuts, sprains and possible bruises. Chris and Chloé maintained their communication between one another as U.P headed towards the sound of their voices.

She struggled along across the forest floor in her glittering high-heels, rolling up her skirt and holding the excess fabric, along with her fan, in her right hand. Of course, it would have been quite possible for her to simply change her outfit to suit the activity, but she refused to let any situation force her to look any less fabulous than she cared to be.

She spotted Chloé first. "Oh wait there, I'm coming over," she said as she hobbled across the uneven floor, "Are you alright?"
"I think so," replied Chloé, "just a bit woozy and sore. What happened to the carriage?"
"I hit my head and lost control of my magic, I'm ever so sorry," she said as she approached her, holding her hand out for Chloé to grab hold of.

"Any idea where all these trees came from?" asked Chris as he emerged onto the scene where U.P was helping Chloé onto her feet.
"They were already here. It was the unicorns who turned the area into a field for us to land in," said Lousta through an achy voice. He and Lancelin had followed

U.P over to where she'd found Chloé.

"Oh no, Meg," said Chloé worriedly as she remembered that she'd thrown her. "Meg!?" she cried out. The sound of her voice was followed by a faint rustling noise far to the left of them. Lousta was the one who spotted her emerge from amongst some dead leaves and twigs on the ground. She looked at him with fear in her eyes, shook her head, then darted off into the forest.

"I'm not sure if we'll be seeing her again anytime soon," said Lousta.
"What? Why? Is she alright?" pestered Chloé.
"I think so, though I think this trip just became way too much for her little mind to handle."
"Poor Meg, I hope she'll be alright."

U.P proceeded to call over the unicorns as Chris asked her, "What on earth happened to us up there?"
"Elementames, at least three of them," stated U.P.
"Ele-whats?" asked Chris.
"I counted four. Two male and two female," added Lousta. Chris asked again in regard to what they were, urging U.P to fill them in on what they were up against.

"They're like a soul without a physical body, and they can switch between earth, wind, fire and air to embody themselves. What I don't get, is why four of them would want to attack us and pull us out of the sky like that though," she added.
"Well it seems obvious to me," said Lancelin, "They must be working for that witch, another one of her attacks."

"If you're so certain it's she who keeps attacking us, then

why doesn't she just come and see us off in person and get it over and done with?" snapped Chris

"Listen," interrupted U.P, "Whoever it was, failed, the unicorns are as fit and healthy as ever and the spring is not so far away. We shall ride for the rest of the journey. Of course, that is, if you're able to continue on your own feet?" she said as she looked at Lousta.

"I'm sure I can manage," he replied, never letting himself appear defeated.

"Wait," blurted out Chloé, "Where's the rucksack?!"

"Oh!" replied Chris instantly, "I think it landed somewhere near me, I managed to hold onto it until I hit the ground. I'll go and find it." With that, he shuffled off out of sight from the others, back to where he had landed in search of the rucksack.

During Chris's absence the unicorns re-joined the others and, aided by U.P, healed those that needed it, then U.P helped Chloé and Lancelin onto two of the coloured unicorns to ride. After that she used her own magic to aid herself up onto Makawee, leaving Helaku free to lead and one unicorn left for Chris to ride on.

It was another few minutes before Chris returned, though it seemed much longer to everyone who'd been stood waiting. To their relief, he returned with the rucksack secured on his shoulders. With a slight waft of her hand, U.P created some steps to aid Chris up onto his unicorn. Then, as they were all ready, they continued through the forest, being mindful to keep close together in case of any more attacks.

After a few hours of walking, the ground under them began to rise and became too steep for them to walk in a straight line towards the great cave. Helaku had no choice but to guide them up the slope in a wide, zigzag pattern through the trees, now and then reaching small gaps in the forest where they could appreciate just how high they were climbing.

Onwards they went until the ground began to level out again, and as they continued further, through the tops of the trees a great, huge, sandy brown coloured rockface could be seen towering high into the sky. The more of it they saw, they noticed it glittered slightly in the sunlight, and it became clear that they were heading to the base of it.

The number of trees ahead of them began to diminish as they neared the base of the immense rockface. The ground became grassier, with rocks and boulders of different shapes and sizes scattered about. They walked over the gentle brow of this part of the hill, to where the ground lay flat across a sparse clearing in the forest, sided by the slope carrying on up the mountain and covered in forest, as if this section had been purposefully scooped out. At the base of the rocky peak, standing before them across the opening in the forest, they were met by the breath-taking entrance to the great cave.

The unicorns carried the others halfway across the space between them and the cave, then stopped to let the humans down so that they might proceed of their own accord. Chloé, Chris and Lancelin slowly walked over, with Chloé slightly out ahead of the rest.

"This is it," she said, "This is the cave I saw in my vision." As she got closer, she could see the immense space inside and caught a glimpse of the glistening magic light of the spring as it flowed from the wall at the back of the cave. She noticed the pile of rubble beginning just inside the entrance, which she remembered from her vision as she'd stood at the bottom of the pile, down on the cave's solid floor. Though uncommunicated, they'd all subconsciously allowed Chloé to be the first to enter, as they stood slightly back from her when she stopped on the grass, right before it met the rock just inside the cave.

She lifted her foot to take the first step inside, quivering with anticipation, but, as she attempted to cross the threshold they were all startled by an ear-shattering BANG, accompanied by a crackling sound as she was launched back into the air and thrown beyond even where the unicorns stood waiting. She screamed as she was flung away from the entrance and was hurtled towards the ground for the second time that day.

"CHLOE!" the majority of them shouted once the sudden explosion was over.
"Chloé! My dear, are you alright?" asked U.P as she jumped down from Makawee and ran over to her. She crouched down by her side and lifted her head up, as Chloé blinked opened her eyes. Lancelin and Lousta headed over to her too, but Chris looked on from the side with the look of fear and guilt in his eyes.
"I hope so," said Chloé as she rubbed her head.

Before anyone could ask about what had just happened, the air began to blow around them, swooshing by in a sudden surge of wind. The wind commenced in a swirling motion around them as it grew stronger, picking up twigs and dead leaves from the ground as it raced by.

"More of those things?" shouted Lancelin above the noise.
"I can't tell. Normally you can make out their faces and bodies," shouted U.P, as she worryingly looked about for an explanation whilst holding Chloé tightly in her embrace.

The swirling wind moved away from them and gathered to one side of the cave entrance, where flashes of light began to appear amongst the debris it had picked up, like lighting in an angry storm cloud swept up in a whirlwind. One of the flashes was so bright that it caused everyone to shield their eyes from it, and when they looked back they saw something else had appeared there.

A tall dark figure stood with their cloak wafting amongst the swirling wind, as the flashes of light grew duller and less intimidating. The wind then began to die down and the area around them became still once more, with a hooded figure wearing a long, charcoal coloured cloak which reached down to touch the floor, stood by the cave. The figure stood with their back to them all and there was a moment of still silence brought on by fear.

Breaking the silence, a cry was heard coming from the nearby forest behind them, a cry which was unmistakably the sound of a meowl, letting out a long, sharp "Miauoooo". The meowl swooped down over their heads and flew over to the dark figure, landing neatly on their shoulder.

If any of them had seen her when she'd visited the vampire's manor, they'd know for sure that this was Alexandra and Tuca. Though she wasn't really one for such dramatic entrances, she had no time for messing around at this point and needed them to fear her in order for them to follow her instructions. She lowered her hood before turning around to face them.

CHAPTER THIRTY-ONE

Together Again

"Is that who I think it is?" whispered a terrified Chloé.

"I'm afraid it might be," replied U.P as she held on tightly to Chloé. Chris stood alone between Alexandra and everyone else, trembling with guilt knowing everyone was to learn what he'd done.

"I'm afraid this is to be the end of your little journey," said Alexandra as she turned around, trying to sound big and superior, "The era of humans and magic has been and gone, and I'm afraid I cannot allow you, nor anyone else to bring it back."

"That's not for you to decide," shouted U.P with a trembling voice as she attempted to stand up to her. Using her fairy magic, she created a snagon around Alexandra's feet which grew and grew as it coiled around her legs. The snagon slithered it's slithery, serpent body around and around her and began to spit out small blasts of fire. For a brief moment, Alexandra looked scared, as she tried to pull herself together and quickly find a way out of the snagon's constricting grasp.

Chloé used this opportunity to scurry over to Chris, but just as she was about to reach him, she was startled when U.P let out a loud scream as she realised that she too was being encased by a snagon. As that snagon grew, five or six warrior fairies or a race again different both the Tawhio fairies and U.P, began to appear from within the woods closest to Alexandra.

"I'm afraid you're nothing more than an oversized fairy," said Alexandra as the two snagons were halted at equal points on both U.P and herself - just below their hips, "Though you have the love of these unicorns, you know as well as I, that their powers may never be used in your weapons."

The fairies that appeared from within the forest flew over and landed on small ledges in the rock, close to where Alexandra was trapped by the snagon. They were mimicking U.P's fighting magic in an attempt to warn her from going any further.

"Unfortunately for you, you're pretty out-numbered today when it comes to whether fairies would like to welcome humans back here or not. Do you not recall the decision that was made years ago amongst all the high-fairies?" Alexandra questioned her.

Whilst the two fought, Chloé began to rummage in the rucksack as it hung from Chris's back, "Where is it?" she said rather hysterically. Chris said nothing and continued to look away to conceal his emotions, he had no idea how to tell her. "Chris! Where the hell's the book?!"
"I'm sorry Chloé, I thought it was for the best..." he mumbled as he began to quiver.

"Looking for your book?" Alexandra interrupted, causing Chloé to stop what she was doing and look fearfully over to her. "I'm afraid killing me now will only make matters worse for you. I don't know how you managed to read what is written on those pages, or how the magic you received from that book was able to escape my spell, but it's now sealed away in that cave along with the spring, which from this moment neither I nor any other human has the power to enter. Even if you kill me, the magic used to create the forcefield around this cave is not of my own, but from a potion created by the most skilled of all potion masters many years ago, therefore the forcefield shall still remain and you'll be stuck here, completely powerless..."

"...However, if you put an end to this attack and your whole mission, I will offer to you a safe passage back to your homeland."

Chloé couldn't quite believe what she was hearing, "Did you...You gave her the book?" she asked in disbelief.

"He did the right thing," said Alexandra, "Magic is an incredible phenomenon, until it falls into the wrong hands."

"I witnessed the world I knew get torn apart by fear and power. The reason I am here now, is ultimately to stop it from ever happening again."

"How can we trust you? You ripped away good people from this land who didn't deserve it, you never even gave them a chance to say goodbye," accused U.P.

"Please, can you just send us home?" asked a tired and emotional Chris.

"What? What about my dad? And Rex? Don't you care about them?"

"Of course I do, but can't you see? It's not all that simple. We've been used and lied to, since day one," he said as he glared at Lancelin, "All because you had a gift, in that you were able to read the book. That's how life would be if we get ourselves any further into this mess. I think Alexandra is right, it all needs to end here."

No one spoke as Chloé and Chris looked at one another, tears building in Chloé's eyes as the realisation of defeat was hitting her. "But Chris, if she is really good, then why doesn't she bring back the people we love before sending us home?"

"And then what? How would we explain that to your family? How would we explain to your mum and to Théo that your dad has been brought back to life?" Chloé stared into Chris's eyes, she hadn't yet thought that far ahead and just assumed everyone would be happy to see him.

"Well, we'd work something out," she sniffed.

"Trust me Chloé," began Alexandra, "Magic creates far more problems than it can ever solve. It feeds greed in some people that you could never imagine existing, even in people you would never expect would be capable of it."

Whilst they'd been talking, Alexandra had managed to slip her hand inside her satchel, which were both hidden under her cloak. She'd picked out a potion bottle which she'd rushed back to collect once she learned that they had teamed up with a fairy, a being that, unlike a vampire, would not flee from her power of imitating sunlight.

After the sound from popping out the cork drew everyone's attention to the fact she was up to something, she quickly swallowed what was in the potion and began blowing out ice cold air from her mouth directly onto the snagon around her.

The snagon's body froze instantly, both inside and out as if it'd been buried for years under deep snow, and she was able to shatter it into a thousand pieces which faded away as U.P's creation had been destroyed. U.P was still trapped in the snagon created by the other fairies. "And there's plenty of ice left if you fancy trying anything else," Alexandra warned them.

They all looked at Alexandra feeling helpless. U.P had been their best bet at fending her off, but they had not anticipated the unicorns magic being so helpless in a fight. "This is ridiculous," shouted Lancelin, "U.P, get behind your unicorns and let's charge at her!" He shouted it more like an order, which no one listened to. He stood there frustrated and desperately searching for a way to fight back at her, when he, unfortunately, spotted something he would soon regret.

Orel had heard about them falling out of the sky, many creatures on the island had been following their journey, wondering how it was going to turn out. Feeling like they needed her help, she'd gathered her strength that afternoon and had flown to the spring, where she saw them all head to head with Alexandra. She'd skillfully flown around them whilst keeping out of Alexandra's radar and was now hurtling herself towards her from behind.

Unfortunately, as Lancelin had drawn attention to himself, Alexandra noticed the change in his expression as he spotted her in the sky, prompting her to quickly turn and look for herself.

With the surprise attack hurtling towards her, she instinctively blew out the icy air onto Orel in an attempt to save herself, so quickly that Orel was unable to shield the bare skin on her face with the protection of her magical feathers covering her wings. They all witnessed her body rapidly turn to ice and come crashing down to the ground, where she shattered into a thousand pieces just as the snagon had done.

"NO!" screamed Chloé as she ran over to where the shattered, frozen pieces lay scattered across the floor. The ice was red with her blood and glistened slightly from the natural magic within her body, though it soon faded.

Chloé threw herself to the ground and burst into tears by Orel's remains, "She was just trying to save us!" she yelled at Alexandra. "She was trying to help," sobbed Chloé through her tears in a broken voice, looking grievously at the remains. Alexandra was just as in shock, she'd never actually killed anyone before and just assumed that this has been another fairy illusion.

"Bring her back," demanded Chloé as she stood and turned to Alexandra, "You're a witch, bring her back!"

Alexandra thought for a moment. She actually had no idea how to bring someone back to life, or if it was even possible after the way Orel had died, but an idea came into her mind of a way she could use this to her advantage for the greater good.

"Alright," Alexandra paused, "But only if you leave."
"What?" asked Chloé.
"If you promise to leave this place, I give you my word that will restore this creature's life before I return to my rest."

Chloé thought for a moment, realising that she was completely out of options. If she should stay and fight, they could all end up like Orel, however, if she took Alexandra's offer, only her hope of seeing her father again will have been lost.

"Alright," she said quietly.
"Sorry?"
"ALRIGHT!" she yelled, "You win."

Chris walked over and offered Chloé his hand, which

she refused. "Orel could still be here if you hadn't betrayed us," she said accusingly, "When we get back, I never want to see you again." She proceeded to walk over to the others who all stood together.

"Well then, if you humans could follow me, I'll find a good spot to send you home." They didn't really understand what Alexandra meant by that, but their spirits were too broken to even care about how she was planning to do it.

"So that's it? We're just going back? Giving up completely?" Said Lancelin, standing his ground and refusing at first to step any further away from the spring now that they were so close to it.
"Forget it Lancelin, it's over," said Chloé solemnly.

Alexandra led the way back towards the woods, whilst all but Lancelin followed in silence. "But, the vampires! Wait until nightfall and they can help us!"
"How?" asked Chloé, "they can't even come near the spring, let alone break into it. Just face it, it's over."

Lancelin looked back at the cave entrance and ran towards it, desperate to get through, but Just as Chloé had been he was repelled away by the forcefield and thrown through the air away from the cave. Aching, he pushed himself back up, "This isn't over! The vampires *will* help us!" he claimed before running off into the woods alone.

Alexandra allowed him to run, he was no threat to her and nor were the vampires, as long as the cave was secure she knew she would simply deal with him later. Continuing on into the woods she began concentrating on looking for a place to create her portal; anything that could be used as a frame for a doorway. She examined the branches of trees stood closely together, looking for a pair that touched to create a kind of archway between two trunks.

The group shuffled along glumly, like broken down prisoners following the warden to their fate. Chloé's mind began to wander as she thought about what had and what could have been. Going back to the first day they arrived on the island, her mind wandered over her memories of the places they'd been.

Until suddenly, an idea caught her attention when she'd reached back to a time in the vampire's manor when she and Chris had been playing about with the things they'd found back in the black castle; an idea that was about to turn the tables on Alexandra's power over them.

She discreetly moved herself whilst they all walked forwards through the trees, so that she was right behind Chris. Then gently, she put her hands on to his hips and whispered to him, "please, don't say anything." Chris stayed silent, wondering why she was suddenly willing to speak to him again and to be so close. He hoped that in her sadness, she might have wanted to be close to him for a moment, to find comfort in a familiar sense of something that had once meant so much to her. He enjoyed feeling her close to him again after what they'd been through, and so he decided to simply enjoy the moment, as they stopped together and he lifted his right hand up and placed it on her left arm as it rested on his waist.

He hadn't noticed her slip her hands into his pockets,

until suddenly she yanked them back out again and tore herself away from him. He turned around and asked, "What are you doing?" then he noticed. She had one-half of the two pieces of paper, which together had the words 'Encore Ensemble' written across them. She held it to her chest and closed her eyes, wishing to be with the other half. Everyone was drawn to the bright light that surrounded her, before it consumed her entirely and left behind nothing but empty space.

"What! Where did she go? Somebody tell me! Where did she go!?" demanded Alexandra.
"To the other half," said Chris in disbelief.
"What other-half? Where is she?!"
"It's in the book."

Malicorne's magic had truly been the strongest, as it managed to penetrate the forcefield and transported Chloé back to the other piece of paper, which she had tucked into the back of the book. Slowly she opened her eyes and looked down at the book which she now held in her hand, open on the back page.

A feeling of déjà vu dazzled her, but it wasn't just a feeling, she had in fact seen this all before. She was stood in the centre of the cave just as she had been in her vision, with no one around her to stop her and the spring flowing so magnificently out from the wall ahead of her.

Alexandra rushed back out of the forest and up towards the cave, unable to go inside. She stopped at the entrance and yelled at Chloé to stop, but she was completely powerless – and Chloé knew that.

By the time Alexandra had reached the entrance of the cave, Chloé had cautiously walked over to where the light gathered like a pool of water on the floor at the back of the cave. The sunlight beamed down through the entrance and lit up the floor, causing it to glisten as she'd walked across it. She inhaled a deep, steadying breath and took her first step into the pool of light.

She continued walking into it, just as she had in her vision, until she completely submerged herself and the book. She then lifted her head back out and remained motionless in the light, focusing inside herself to see if she could sense if anything had changed. Feeling no different, she slowly exited the pool and walked back into the centre of the cave, feeling slightly underwhelmed, but never the less continuing to do as she had foreseen in her vision.

Everyone was watching now from the cave entrance (all except Lancelin) and saw her standing there looking down at the book. They all waited in anticipation, wondering if she had absorbed its power or not. When, just as she was about to open the book to see if it would give her any guidance on what to do next, it began to glow.

The light grew brighter and brighter, everyone except Alexandra looked away and shielded their eyes, even Chloé was forced to drop the book on the floor to free her hands as she shielded hers. Golden light then began to rush around both her and the book, picking up speed as she stood still in the centre of it all. Some of the rays of light flickeringly began changing colour into different shades of blue, as she was completely surrounded and hidden from the other's view.

They watched as best they could. It became slightly easier on their eyes once most of the light had changed from the bright, golden light into the softer hues of blue, until finally the light began to disappear. What they saw frightened them though, there was someone stood in the centre of it all, but it was definitely not Chloé.

As the light had almost completely faded, Chris and U.P noticed Chloé's body lying motionless on the floor to one side of the figure who stood before them.
"CHLOE!" shouted Chris.
"Malicorne," whispered Alexandra.

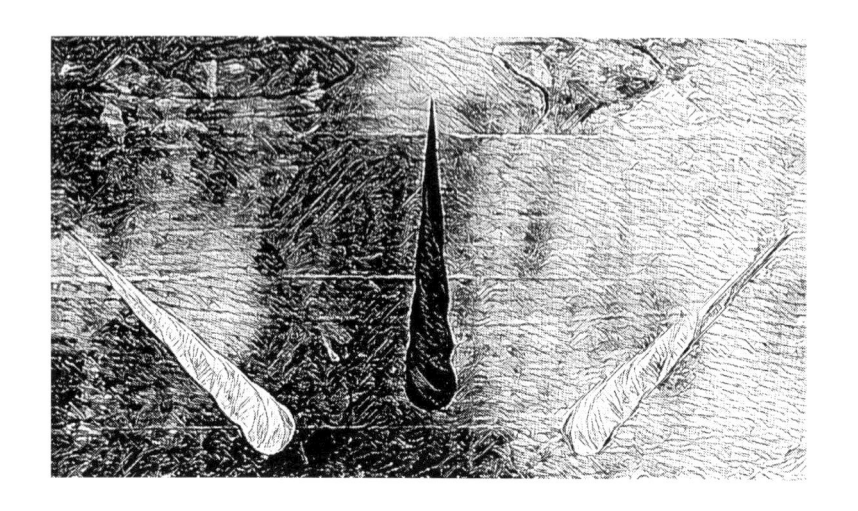

EPILOGUE

Alexandra's body trembled at the sight of Malicorne's return. "We need to run," she insisted to the others, "Now! Follow me!" Tuca took off from her shoulders and flew into the forest, followed by Alexandra whose cloak fanned-out behind her as she ran.

Chris was unsure what to do, unable to turn his eyes away from Chloé's body lying motionless on the floor of the cave, afraid that he might never see her again if he did. U.P backed away slowly as Helaku came up behind her. As she hurried up onto his back, she admitted to Chris that she may not be able to protect him from whatever happens next, but he was welcome to run with her if he wished. Yet he said nothing, and only continued to stare at Chloé whilst U.P left with her unicorns without him.

He watched as Malicorne looked around himself, noticing his own body and the glistening cave in which he stood. Chris recognised him from the tapestry both he and Chloé had seen, hanging in the dining room back in the black castle. The distinct three horns pointing up and back from just within his hairline, the centre horn being the biggest and most prominent.

He wore his chest length, dark brown hair straight and with the front section tied back neatly. Standing there, he was dressed in a floor-length, sapphire blue gown, clinched in around his hips by dull, brassy coloured cloth, which was tied on his left side leaving the rest of the material to hang down almost to the floor. Above the belt the gown parted like an open robe, though fitted to his body, and revealed a plain, indigo coloured item of clothing covering his torso underneath, reaching up to his collar. The sleeves were wide and open, resting bunched-up at his elbows revealing his bare forearms.

On his hands, he wore two dark-gold rings, one on his left index finger and one on his right ring finger. The one on his right hand was a simple band with some sort of inscription carved into it, and the one on his left hand had a sapphire diamond fitted onto it, with tiny, lilac jewels surrounding the base. His nails were long, thick and pointed, growing darker in colour towards the tip.

Chris saw him look down at his right hand and begin to clench it slightly, as if holding an imaginary ball. As

Malicorne stared at his palm, sparks began to appear in the space above it, before an intense ball of bright, white light began to form. It continued to grow in size until it was just slightly smaller than a football, when Malicorne stopped looking at it and looked up at Chris, held in a trance at the cave's entrance.

He pulled his arm back then abruptly launched the ball of electrified light straight at Chris. The light exploded upon impact as it hit the forcefield blocking the cave entrance, though the shock of it sent Chris tumbling backwards onto the ground. Thankfully for Chris, Malicorne had underestimated the strength of Alexandra's potion and so he was saved for now, but he hesitated no more and scurried off to find Alexandra.

Hearing the commotion, Lancelin had turned back towards the cave and arrived just as Chris was disappearing into the trees. He walked over to the entrance and looked down to see Malicorne standing by the spring, "Master, you have returned!" he cried with relief.

"Ah, Mosh, it's good to be able to speak to you again. I trust you have it?"

"Of course, sire." Lancelin, or Mosh as he was originally named by Malicorne, tore off his shirt to reveal his naked, upper body, to which he had strapped a wand made from a unicorn's horn. Around the wand, Lancelin's skin was covered in sores, cuts and bruises, where the wand had been digging into him all along the journey.

Malicorne instructed him to stand back from the entrance and to hold out the wand, pointing it towards the centre of the forcefield. He then stood facing it from the cave floor, holding his arms out with his palms facing up towards the entrance. With his eyes closed, he summoned the magic from within his body and from within the wand to meet.

Light electrically began shooting out from both like bolts of lightning, meeting on either side of the forcefield and spreading out over it like a plasma globe. The energy from the magic became increasingly intense, until ultimately the forcefield was destroyed and shattered into millions of glittering sparkles of light, as the magic that had made up the forcefield flickered out of existence.

Lancelin dropped the wand as the magic had erupted, due to the skin on his hand being severely burnt in the process. Still, he contained his agony and picked up the wand with his other hand now that the magic had been done, then scurried inside the cave to present it to Malicorne.

He knelt down before him, offering to him his wand which he'd carried with him ever since the day they'd parted. Malicorne picked it up gently in his right hand, then offered his left hand as an aid for Lancelin to stand up again. It was Lancelin's right hand which had been burnt, but still, he used it to hold on to Malicorne as he stood up, when to his delight his loyalty was rewarded as Malicorne's touch healed him.

He then followed Malicorne back out of the cave as they worked their way back up the pile of rubble and across the wide, open space in front of it. As they reached the edge of the forest, Malicorne stopped and turned back to face the cave entrance whilst Lancelin made sure to always be stood slightly behind him. As he looked upon the cave he held out his hands, clutching the wand as they stood in silence for a moment. Then Lancelin felt the earth begin to tremble.

Before their eyes, the ground rose up in front of them as Malicorne effortlessly recreated his once magnificent castle, claiming the spring of power and Chloé now concealed deep within it. The castle towers rose well above the treetops and became an awesomely intimidating feature on the side of the mountain. Malicorne took a moment to admire his work, with a smile on his face to see his beautiful home again.

The thunderclouds which had been so distant earlier that day, had now rolled in over the hills and were beginning to rumble and flicker with energy.

"Come, Mosh," said Malicorne in a serious tone, "We'd best get settled in. We have a lot of work ahead of us."

◆ ◆ ◆

In the forest, Alexandra had waited for Chris as she knew her spell on him still persuaded his thinking. Just as she knew he would, he followed after her as best he could and she caught him as he came dashing helplessly into the trees.

"Chris, are you alright?'
"Please," He said through his panting, trying to catch his breath, "You have to help Chlo…" Alexandra slapped him

fiercely across his face. "...OW! What th..."
"I'm sorry!" She exclaimed quickly with her hands up in the air, "I'm sorry, I had to do that, to break the spell."
"What spell? Oh, no, are you going to kill me?" he asked, feeling exhausted and defeated.
"Of course not, but I'm afraid that if we hang around here for too long then we both might be killed."

Chris clasped his hands on either side of his head and squeezed his eyes shut. "Please, let me just wake up from this," he whined, "I just want to go home."
"Good, and so you will!" Alexandra said as she grabbed him by his left wrist. "And so will the girl."
"Chloé? She is alive, isn't she?" Chris begged her to put him out of his misery.

"I think so, for now. There's a reason he could connect to her through the book, or himself, assuming he was the book. Perhaps that's how he escaped the curse?" Alexandra thought out loud. "Whatever that reason was, I'm sure it'll be worth him keeping her around. But, I can't think out here with the stress of him being so close to us plaguing my mind, we'll be safer back at my house."

"Your house? Is it far?" Chris asked, longing for this all to be over as soon as possible.
"It is, by foot, but I still have the portal potion I was going to use to send you three home, but I guess that plan will just have to wait."
"Do you know how you can stop him? You did it before, didn't you?"
"Before was different, he was in your world when the curse stripped all magic away from it, which was supposed to include him too. That won't work here,

but hopefully my father's potion collection will offer us some new options, which is why we need to get back right away."

Alexandra had been scoping out a good archway to use the potion on whilst Chris had been questioning her, but as the ground they stood on began to tremble, the conversation came to a halt brought on by fear. Alexandra uncorked the potion bottle in her hand and splashed the pale-yellow liquid inside it over each part of two trees which she had found creating a makeshift archway. Chris watched in anticipation whilst the ground continued to rumble. The archway had been sufficient enough for the portal to take shape, though it was too low for them to walk through whilst stood upright.

The entrance to the portal was visible only as a glittering sheen over what could be seen of the forest beyond it, until Alexandra spoke a short enchantment under her breath then blew forcefully onto it. The image of her quaint little cottage then rippled into view under the branched archway. The ground continued to tremble beneath them.

"Quickly, you first," she insisted.
"Will, will it hurt?" Asked Chris, as he tried to comprehend the fact that he could see two completely separate parts of the island at once.
"It shouldn't do. My father created this specifically for use by both people with or without magic inside them."
"Your father? Is he here too?"
"No. Now quickly, go!"

Chris crouched down and scurried under the low arch

almost on his hands and knees, with his eyes tightly shut. Tuca then swooped in after him followed by Alexandra, who turned and ripped the image of the woods where they'd just escaped from out of the air behind them; shattering it into tiny pieces of glittering light which soon faded into nothing.

◆ ◆ ◆

The dawn of a new era had risen this day on Île Merveille, an era quite possibly out of Alexandra's control. A powerful being of mixed abilities had risen as a new leader, seemingly set on undoing the witch's curse. Whether that was a good thing or a bad thing, Chris couldn't quite be sure, though he had a sickening feeling it wouldn't be long until he found out.

Next?

I hope you enjoyed the beginning of Chloé and Chris' adventure on Île Merveille, the island of wonder and magic. Soon their journey will continue in book two, but for now, happy dreaming..

Printed in Great Britain
by Amazon